CW01646417

DIRTY PADRAIG

THE OUTLAW CHESS SERIES

HARLEY DIAMOND

Copyright © 2023 by Harley Diamond

All rights reserved.

No part of this book may be reproduced in any form or by any electronic or mechanical means, including information storage and retrieval systems, without written permission from the author, except for the use of brief quotations in a book review.

This book is a work of fiction. Unless otherwise indicated, all names, characters, businesses, places, events, and incidents are either the product of the author's imagination or are used in a fictitious manner. Any resemblance to actual persons, living or dead, or actual events is purely coincidental.

Published by House of Books Press

www.harleydiamond.com

Edited by Karen Sanders Editing

https://www.karensandersediting.com/

PA Services by Arcane and Reverie

contact@arcaneandreverie.com

Cover Design by Vicious Desires Design

https://www.instagram.com/viciousdesires/

Cover Model is Janis Danner via Daniel Jaems

https://www.instagram.com/janis_danner/

https://www.instagram.com/danieljaems/

❀ Created with Vellum

Blurb

FOR NEVER WAS A STORY OF MORE WOE

Fate chose her for me, but I was forced to accept another.

My Disney princess then wed my own brother.

Does she love me? Does she not?

Does she love him? Does she not?

What a tangled web we weave, but the truth will out.

It always does.

The domino of deceit toppled, bringing down the house of cards used to gameplay.

Blood spilled. Secrets spilled.

Sentences served. Penances paid.

And what of her?

The keeper of the biggest secret?

Will she be my end game?

Or are we to be nothing more than star-crossed lovers?

Playlist

Kiss Me by Ed Sheeran

Trigger Warning

This book contains mature content, violence, swearing, and other potentially triggering situations that some readers may find offensive.

Please do not read this story if you are uncomfortable with any of the above.

Thank you.

Author's Note

PADRAIG'S story starts from where EOIN's ends.

DIRTY PADRAIG is NOT standalone.
DIRTY PADRAIG is BOOK 6 of a SERIES, which contains an INTERCONNECTED STORYLINE.

These books contain MULTIPLE POVs from characters across the entire series.

Due to the nature of the CONTINUING STORYLINE, these books MUST be
READ IN ORDER.

ACE
DIRTY CILLIAN
RAZR
DIRTY DYLAN
DIRTY EOIN
DIRTY PADRAIG

CHAPTER ONE

PADRAIG

The Ruocco Home, Agrigento, Sicily

I think about the day I died at least a million times a day.

I know that may sound like a lot, but I reckon it's a step in the right direction. I was thinking about it way more when I first arrived here.

Maybe I should change that wording to something a little less melodramatic like *I think about the day my life ended at least a million times a day.*

That sounds far less theatrical, even if the former is way more fitting, but then I'm told I've always been the kind of fella who likes to over-dramatize things.

My life ended almost a year ago now. The day I gained Sophia. The day I lost Jaine.

Not that the latter was ever mine to lose. I realize that now.

My wedding day was meant to be the happiest day of my life. A day when I should have taken the vows with my Disney princess, and we then went on to live the happily ever after together.

My soul mate. My fated other. My one and only.

My Jaine Jones.

It should have been the girl of my dreams. Instead, it was the one from my nightmares.

I think back to the complete carnage that took place. When Jaine personally hand-delivered permanent cease-and-desist notices to two of her sniper comrades.

That was the last thing I clearly remember from the day my life ended before I packed up the full one I was living in New York and headed off to start existing in a life of limbo in another country.

It was all about survival, you see. It was easier to stop living. It was easier to start existing with my eyes closed.

All this time, I've stayed away. I willingly took my finger off the pulse and instead stuck them firmly in my ears, refusing to listen to anything that wasn't business-related.

Why?

Because I don't want to hear about what it's like living in the real world when I have to exist in a pretend one.

It may seem a bit extreme. It might also seem a bit selfish. But I needed to at least attempt to heal. To try to piece back together the shards of my broken heart.

A heart that was shattered by the realization that my cliché blonde, my Holy Grail of women, and the girl I've been in love with since I was nineteen doesn't love me back.

Never has. Never will.

Not that it matters. I'm married.

And here's me once again thinking about the day that my life ended. Make that a million and one times a day.

Have I healed? Don't be daft.

Take it from me. Adopting the burying your head in the sand approach doesn't work. All it does is make the single biggest regret you have to live with echo even more loudly around your lonely skull.

You can pin your wishful thinking and foolish hopes on whatever makes you feel better, but in my experience, dreams don't come true, and prayers remain unanswered.

At least for me.

All the time spent away has achieved is to make me more accepting of what is now my existence. A day to day that I can't change, and one I've got no option but to continue on with because there's no alternative.

I stare at the email on the screen for the second time.

Through choice, email is the only real form of communication I have with the outside world these days. Dylan and I have traded places. He's now the outgoing one. I'm the hermit.

It's from Fletch, one of my old classmates from Yale, who moved to the UK not long after graduating.

Hey, Paddy,

Long time, no speak. I hope life's treating you well. I'm heading back to New York on a fleeting visit and was trying to coordinate a reunion. I'm asking some of the old crowd to come along. It would be great if you could make it.

I've dug out some photographs. Those were the days.

The date and venue are attached. I hope to see you there.

Take care, bud,

Fletch, aka Cody Fletcher.

I'm not sure how he got my email address. The Duster office, perhaps? Then again, I probably emailed him in the past. Back when I was the outgoing me and not the shadow of my former self that I am now.

Not that it matters. I can't go.

For one, because I live in Sicily now. For two, I know if I've been sent the email, then Jaine will have been sent it too.

Sorry, *bud.* No can do.

Not when I'm still trying to heal from something I won't ever be able to heal from.

I move the mouse and let the cursor hover over the attachment.

Photographs.

I frown at the tempting file.

There can't be any images of Jaine and me, surely. Not back at a time when three months passed in the blink of an eye under a haze of parties, alcohol, and sex.

We barely remembered to study most days, let alone take pictures.

I have to force myself to open the attachment. In the end, I'm glad I did.

A smile covers my face for the first time in I don't know how long as I flick through memories of the antics of a group of nineteen-year-old students who were living the life of Riley and who still had their endless futures stretching out ahead of them.

It feels like a lifetime ago. In many ways, it was. I see Sasha, and then I spot Cherry's bright red bob. Please let there be one of Jaine and me.

Click. Click. Click.

Tears prick my eyes to complement the sad smile that I'm now wearing.

Her arms are snaked around my neck while my hands span her tiny waist. She's wearing her standard tank and combats combo and gazing up at me with an adoring smile plastered across her face, her blonde hair a messy bun atop her head as it always was back then, and her glasses perched on the end of her nose.

I'm wearing jeans and a band t-shirt, with my hair pretty much as it is now, but it's my expression that I can't stop staring at. I'm looking down at her with all the love in the world shining from my eyes.

There's no disputing how I've always felt about Jaine Jones.

Fletch is right. Those were the days. Days I wish I could do over before I made one silly mistake.

A mistake I'd live to regret for the rest of my life. A mistake that's seen me living in limbo with the wrong woman when my soul will forever be intertwined with the soul of the right one.

12 Years Earlier (Age Nineteen)
Yale University, Connecticut

I glance around the cream-colored administration office with its array of lopsided notices all blue-tacked to the badly finger-marked wall surface. I'm sitting on a chair, waiting for an amended class schedule to be printed off.

There's a group of us taking additional lessons so we can graduate quicker. My da wants me to step up and do my Duster duty, and I can't be doing that while I'm lazing around a fancy pants college, according to him, so I've been given no choice but to enroll.

It smells of lavender in here. The secretary, who's as wide as she is tall, obviously has a thing for purple as she's wearing it head to toe. She smiles at me from behind her desk and waits for me to approach.

"Thank you, Miss Houser. Efficient as always." I shoot her my winning smile. The one that typically gets me away with everything and also gets me anything I want, especially when it comes to the female of the species. Despite being middle-aged, she blushes like a schoolgirl in response.

Works every time.

Shoving the piece of paper into the back pocket of my jeans, I turn to leave, colliding with a girl as I do.

My eyes trail over her tall, slim shape, dressed in blue jean shorts and a white tank top, and finished off with a beat-up pair of high tops.

She's the most beautiful thing I have ever fucking seen.

"Sorry, darlin'." I step back with my hands raised before shooting her the same winning smile. For the first time, it doesn't garner a reaction. She doesn't even make eye contact. She mouths a silent apology, then walks straight past.

Indifference is not a reaction I'm used to getting from the opposite sex, and they don't typically keep on walking when I pay them any attention, either.

I shrug and start to walk away.

"I'm here for my new class schedule, Miss Houser."

I stop in my tracks when I hear her speak. She's not from around here. She has a west coast accent.

It's the most beautiful thing I've ever fucking heard.

"Here you are, Jaine."

I turn to look at her, grinning as I watch her try to balance her backpack on one knee while pushing her glasses further up her nose at the same time. She's trying to file away the same piece of paper I've just been given.

My smile widens when I realize we'll be in the same classes.

My eyes drift over her tanned skin and the golden hair tied in a messy bun on top of her head.

It's then, I know.

That my future wife is called Jaine.

"I DIDN'T KNOW YOU WERE INTO THE LIBRARIAN LOOK, PADDY."

Fletch smirks as he elbows me in the ribs when he catches me staring across the auditorium at Jaine. I've seen her a few times around campus now, and I still don't think she knows I exist.

The opposite of me, she seems to be the quiet sort. She keeps to herself and gets on with her studies, only ever conversing with the two girls she hangs around with unless someone asks her a direct question.

"Me neither, Fletch." I grin as I reply to my friend, my eyes remaining fixed on Jaine the entire time.

Professor Young enters the room, dragging his feet. You can tell he's the type that signed up for lecturing because he thought it would be an easy life with its countless holidays and its well-behaved almost-adult students. That is until he was handed the endless list he needed to checkmark every day and for the rest of his teaching career. Before he realized that how well we perform reflects personally on him.

Given that most of his class comprises reluctant students with zero interest in the subject matter at hand and who are only in attendance at the insistence of their wealthy parents, he now realizes he has his work cut out for him.

At the realization that he may well have bitten off more than he can chew and going by his rosacea-covered cheeks and a nose that would give Rudolph a run for his money, he's clearly started drowning his sorrows in drink.

I turn my attention back to Jaine as soon as the lecture begins, a smile crossing my face as her little red-haired friend notices my overt attention, whispers in her ear, elbows her in the ribs, and nods in my direction.

Jaine shakes her head at her friend.

In disinterest? Jesus Christ, it's not like me to have confidence issues.

Jaine mumbles something back to her before glancing at me, and our eyes meet for the first time.

And there goes my heart.

I smile as her friend elbows her once more, this time causing her to lose her grip on her pen. In her attempt to grab it before it drops to the floor, she knocks over her pink fluffy pencil case. The pen drops and the pencil case follows suit, its entire contents rolling down to the front of the auditorium.

I can almost feel the heat radiate from her cheeks as everyone turns to look at the girl who's disrupting lessons.

I instantly feel possessive. I don't want them looking at her. She's mine to look at.

"Have you been hit by the clumsy stick today, Miss Jones?"

Jaine Jones.

Have you ever heard anything so perfect in all your life?

I instantly feel guilty. This is my fault. She's obviously not used to being so blatantly admired, and it's landed her in hot water with Mr. I-hate-my-fucking-job.

He peers at her over the top of his glasses, which are attached to a multi-colored lanyard, his face getting redder by the minute as he impatiently waits for her to respond, his ill-fitting hairpiece now wobbling in sympathy.

"No, sir."

That. Fucking. Accent.

He stares at her for a moment longer. Too long. I suddenly have the urge to gouge out his eyeballs.

Stop. Fucking. Looking. At. Her.

"Pick them up at the end of class, Miss Jones."

"Yes, sir. Sorry, sir."

Lesson over, I walk across to where Jaine is on all fours picking up the contents of her pencil case.

I run my hand through my hair.

For the first time in my life, I feel nervous around a girl. For the first time in my life, a girl's shown no interest in me whatsoever.

What do I say? Usually, they'd be all over me by now.

My nervousness is quickly superseded when, at the sight of her perfect backside in the air, my nineteen-year-old lust-addled brain connects with my dick, causing him to twitch.

"You need some help?" I laugh.

I watch as she spins around so quickly that she bangs her head on a chair.

"Oww." She sits on the filth-covered floor and rubs her hand over the sore bit on her head.

And then she looks up at me.

A heart-shaped face, pouty lips, and eyes as green as emeralds.

My mouth suddenly feels dry, and I'm even more lost for words as I see the perfection that God's crafted.

Just for me.

Because I know I'm going to fall head over heels in love with Jaine Jones. I really need to make sure she falls in love with me too.

"I'm Padraig, by the way. Padraig O'Connell." I smile as I hold out my hand, silently praying to The Almighty that it's not all hot and sweaty. She grabs hold of it, and I pull her to her feet. I then watch as she wipes the dirt off the back of her blue jeans using the other.

She stares up at me. I can tell she likes what she sees when her cheeks slowly flush. I'm relieved. I'm usually a cocky fecker, but I feel out of my depth around her for some reason.

"I'm Jaine. Jaine Jones."

She glances down, her cheeks reddening further, when she realizes we're still handholding.

"It's a pleasure to meet you, Jaine Jones. Can I buy you a coffee? Or a tea? Even better, can I kiss you?" My grin widens.

"I'll take the first offer, thank you." She laughs.

Its sound? It's as perfect as the rest of her.

CHAPTER TWO

JAINE

Rising Cemetery, Rising, California

I TAKE IN THE UNINTERRUPTED VIEWS OVER RISING AND BREATHE IN the familiar scent of petrichor and wildflowers being carried on the gentle breeze.

No matter where I was born or where I live, Rising will always be home for me.

So many memories. So many regrets.

But life must go on. And it has. For everyone else, even if not for Ace.

It's been one whole year since my beautiful boy was taken. Each day I wake, and for the first few precious seconds, I still think he's alive until reality hits home like a goddamn sucker punch.

That he's not. That he's here. Alone and buried in the cold, hard ground.

Husband. Father. Son. Friend. Biker.

He was only thirty-one years old. The age I am now.

I'm sitting cross-legged at his final resting place. Six feet of unforgiving earth separate us, the soil once unsettled now firm and unyielding. It's letting me know that this is final. That there's no way back for him.

The guilt has started to ease now, but I know I'll never find peace. Not until I end the lives of those behind his killing. Not until I know why they wanted him dead so much.

I appreciate that we all have enemies, but his attack was planned. It wasn't just in passing. It wasn't just random.

It was personal.

The shooters went out of their way to carry out the hit. They came up close to make sure they had the right person, but also to make sure that they didn't fucking miss.

I felt no sense of justice when I ended Abel's life for the part he played in Ace's death, and I'm sure if I ever catch up with the second guilty party, the trigger puller himself, ending his unworthy life will still see me left with an itch I can't quite scratch. Because I need the organ grinder, and right now, he's nowhere to be found.

Was he also behind the drive-by shooting that saw my son the target and Eoin almost killed? My gut is telling me he was. I hope it's fucking right because if there's more than one faction involved, we'll be looking over our shoulders for the rest of our days.

With a shaky sigh, I lift my hand and trace the scrolled letter A behind my left ear. I don't need to see it to know its exact outline. I'd give anything to see my initial behind Ace's ear right now or the PJ inked over that big heart of his.

At times, we take so much for granted. We blindly believe we'll live to see another sunrise, and when one of you doesn't make it, the one left behind has to dig deep and somehow find the strength to make it to the end of every day that follows.

It's all about survival, you see. Because when there are children involved, you're left with no other choice but to keep on going.

My phone vibrates, and I glance at it.

A plethora of missed calls from Eoin and a still-to-be-opened email from Cody Fletcher.

I ignore both.

Because, right now, it's all about me and Ace.

The Angels of Hellfire Clubhouse, Rising, California

More tractor tires fill the compound these days, and even though each is filled with an array of vibrantly colored flowers, their addition still does nothing to disguise the overall unattractive appearance of the bland, black clubhouse.

A building I grew up in.

A building filled with treasured memories.

A building filled with regrets.

I've been trying not to take a step backward on the treadmill of healing that I'll forever be on, but I'm struggling to place one foot in front of the other right now when I'm drowning in everything Ace.

I'm Jason, and I'm eight. I'm Jaine, and I'm seven.

He surrounds me here. So much so that if I close my eyes and reopen them, I'm sure I'll see him standing right in front of me. The boy who was born to be stared at with hair as black as the midnight sky and eyes as blue as the bluest thing ever.

I'm told his room remains untouched and that no one is allowed to enter. They'll be waiting for me, I'm sure, but I can't venture in there. Not yet. I'm not ready. Twelve months may have passed, but it's still too soon.

Aside from his last two years, he spent his whole life living out of that room waiting for me to come home. I left him behind without a backward glance and didn't look back for ten goddamn years.

He reached out, and I ignored him.

What I'd give to replay things. To sit my selfish ass down and listen to the words he so desperately wanted me to hear. To read his messages.

You'll always be my creep and my weirdo, same as you'll always be my plain Jaine Jones.

His soul is engraved on the very walls of that space. How can I pack it up? How can I let go of everything Ace?

When he passed, he took part of me with him. Every day since I've tried to plug up the gaping hole he left behind, but nothing will ever fill it. It will forever remain echoingly empty. A constant reminder of the beautiful boy I lost way too soon.

I'll be waiting right here, sweetheart.

I pull up his hog and dismount. In some ways, it feels wrong to be riding it, but I can't let it go to waste. He loved his classic. It was his pride and joy after his two boys.

I key in the code that Clay messaged me in advance, and the heavy metal gates give out their familiar reluctant groan as I swing them open. Riding into the compound, I park up, then walk back to pull them closed before giving them a thorough shake just to be sure.

When I turn, I make eye contact with the biker who's stepped outside to greet me before slowly walking toward him.

"Lucifer."

We agreed to meet here. I can't be in Rising for longer than an overnight stay because of the safety risks. Given that my husband was killed and my son was targeted, there's every reason to suspect that I'm currently in the number three spot on this other sniper's hitlist, so I definitely can't extend my trip to take in the sights of Nevada.

I stare at Jessie and Bailey's daddy. At Delaney and Dylan's father-in-law.

My gaze drifts over him. He's a brute of a man with pale blue eyes, long light blonde hair which is starting to grey, and a well-kept beard. He's not traditionally handsome. He's more angular features and sharp lines, which makes him striking to look at.

I can't help but compare him to Jessie and Bailey. I figure Jessie looks more like her mom because, when I look at the man in front of me, it's Bailey that I see.

"Jaine." I take in the Irish accent. His voice, while menacing, holds the undercurrent of something else.

Uncertainty.

He's unsure of himself. He's nervous about what he's about to say.

I immediately feel my nose tingle and my eyes fill as I stare at the prez of the Sons of Satan, the man who willingly stepped in front of a bullet with Ace's name on. I can't seem to stop the tears as they start to fall.

"Thank you for what you did…. for trying…" I can't even get the words out as the familiar lump appears in my throat.

It's all too much. Being here is just a stark reminder that Ace is never coming back.

He steps forward and pulls me into his arms, and the warm scent of his cologne immediately envelops me. He feels familiar somehow.

Eventually, he places his hands on my upper arms and pulls me back, his eyes grazing over every inch of my face. "Is there somewhere we can talk in private?"

I nod with a watery sigh. "I was just about to head to the river."

"Mind if I join you?"

I nod again. We've been putting off this chat for long enough.

It's time.

We both turn our heads as Duke steps out of the clubhouse. He's wearing a frown as he looks between us, and I nod at him in reassurance.

Then I take Lucifer to the spot where Ace first showed me how to skim stones.

Jaine's House, Rising, California

I lean my head back against the old familiar cream sofa, my distracted brain still reeling from today's events and findings.

"You can't just disappear without a word, Jaine!"

I knew Eoin wouldn't be pleased that I set off for Rising without telling him, but I never expected him to be this furious.

"I told Roisin where I was going, and it's only an overnight stay."

It's a lame excuse; we both know it. I only told Roisin as I needed her to look after Fin and JJ, because Duke was coming with me. Even then, she was sworn to secrecy. I wanted to let Eoin know at a time when it would be pointless him trying to follow.

"You should have told me, not her!" he hisses, his voice noticeably more Irish, which means his dark side has come out to play.

"If I told you where I was going, you would have insisted on coming with me." In contrast, I keep my own voice calm. There's no point in antagonizing him further.

"And would it have been a problem if I had? You're my fiancée. Perhaps I might have welcomed the opportunity to meet the people you grew up with and to see your hometown for myself."

Guilt flows through me.

Under normal circumstances, I would have told him, but since we started pretty much living together a few months back, he never lets me out of his sight, and when he does, it's on the strict basis that I have his right-hand man, Declan, in tow. I appreciate that it's partly because we have invisible targets on our backs and that he almost died when he willingly intercepted a bullet with Finian's name on, but it's too much.

I'm quickly realizing that loving Eoin O'Connell and living with him don't necessarily go hand in hand.

He's set in his ways. I am too. And his controlling behavior on top is starting to make me feel hemmed in. It's like he wants me to lose my own identity and become part of his. He wants to own me, mind, body, and soul.

And I refuse to be owned.

The reason I didn't tell him where I was going was that I needed to spend some quality time with Ace. I also needed to speak privately with Lucifer.

Had Eoin insisted on coming with me, it's unlikely he would have allowed me to do either on my own.

Until today, I had no idea what the conversation with Lucifer would contain. In the end, I'm only glad it was just him and me, as I'm still struggling to take it all in.

"I'm sorry. I'll be back tomorrow. I need to visit the clubhouse in the morn…." I realize I'm talking to myself, and he's already disconnected the call.

Eoin never hangs up. It's always vice versa. My guilt magnifies tenfold. I was hiding one thing from him, and today I've just added another.

Running my hand down my face, I stare up at the ceiling.

I get that we shouldn't have secrets if we want this relationship to work, but take-two of me and him is still brand new, and I'm already having doubts.

Of course, I love him. I will always love him. But I know now that loving someone doesn't mean jack shit. It doesn't mean you'll be together forever.

Look at me and Ace.

Look at me and Irish.

From my experience, happily-ever-afters seldom happen in this life, Disney fucking princess or not.

And even if they do, they're short-lived. At least for me.

Eoin is possessive. He's also protective.

I don't like being wrapped in cotton wool. I realize if I told him my sniping secret, he'd be less likely to behave that way because he'd then know that I'm more than capable of looking after myself. But that's not guaranteed. It could have the opposite effect.

I stare at my handset, sighing loudly as my finger hovers over the email from Cody Fletcher.

Why haven't I opened it?

Fletch was from another life, that's why. A life that was filled with nineteen-year-old students, back-to-back classes, and wall-to-wall study.

A life that included Irish.

Closing the door on the chapter that contained him was one of the hardest things I've ever had to do. More so because, unlike Ace, he's still alive.

I'm not sure I want to reopen it until I have no choice, and that will be if and when he ever decides to return to New York.

Not now.

Not when I'm still trying to heal from something I won't ever be able to heal from.

CHAPTER THREE

PADRAIG

The Ruocco Home, Agrigento, Sicily

Since moving here, I've had an entire suite made available for my own personal use. It means I can keep to myself, which is something I choose to do more often than not.

It's clear that no expense was spared when fitting out this luxurious neutral-colored space, but then money will be no object. Much like my own, this family will use every available opportunity to flaunt their vast wealth.

I stare out the window of the room I use as my office. The Ruoccos own everything for as far as the eye can see and beyond, or so I'm told.

Olive groves. Vineyards. Orchards. Properties.

They're a big name around these parts. Also, a feared name, much like the O'Connells are in New York.

I'm sure the family does extremely well for themselves off the back of their legitimate business enterprises. They have no real need to get involved in any illegal wrongdoings to top up their already amassed fortune.

But the same could be said for the Dusters.

Then again, you can never have enough money or power, or at least that's what my da and my eldest brother think. Doing wrong is also what we do right.

In this life, we're each born with the mobster equivalent of neonatal abstinence syndrome. It's easier to embrace our addictive birthright rather than try to outrun the hellish withdrawal symptoms we'd be faced with if we didn't.

I open the window and inhale air that carries hints of both sweet and salty, of fruit trees laced with the scent of the ocean.

I left New York in order to survive, and I've missed the smell of trash, the sound of honking horns, and the wail of sirens ever since.

The only sound here is that of the camaraderie of the small army of workers as they carry out their daily duties on this massive manor-house estate. Many are young children, no doubt used illegally by the Ruoccos as cheap or even free labor.

Taking a seat at my desk, I open up the photographs from Fletch once more and stare at the image of me and Jaine.

12 Years Earlier (Age Nineteen)
Yale University, Connecticut

This is date number three.

Toward the end of date one, Jaine finally relented and let me hold her hand. On date two, she let me snake my arm around her shoulder even though she clearly wasn't receptive to the tactile gesture. My public display of affection made her as stiff as a board.

I'm a fella who likes to push my luck, what can I say?

Normally, even a little effort on my part instantly produces the required results from the fairer sex, but not with Jaine Jones.

Is today going to be the day that she finally caves in and lets me kiss her? Because I can't think about anything else. Even my studies are starting to suffer.

By now, I'd usually have fucked my latest conquest and sent them on their way before moving on to the next in a very long line. You're only nineteen once, after all. Life is for sampling, tasting, and living at this age.

I thought maybe it was the coffee shop. That with it being on campus, it was just too public for her. That she didn't like the idea of being overly familiar with me while surrounded by a load of other students, many of whom we both know.

It's hard to pinpoint things with Jaine. She's not introverted or withdrawn or anything like that. She's a girl who tends to speak her mind when she has something of note to say and not just to fill an awkward silence. It means that she never gives much away. There's definitely something holding her back.

I need to find out what it is.

She is my future wife, after all.

It's a pleasant day, so we've decided to meet at a local park off campus for a change. I've chosen a bench that affords us a bit of privacy while not being too discrete that Jaine starts to think my intentions are anything less than honorable. I frown at the realization that, for once, they really are. That if Jaine needs me to take things at a snail's pace, then that's what I'll do.

Raising my face to the sun, I close my eyes, appreciating the warmth as I listen to birdsong and inhale the smell of freshly cut grass.

For some reason, I know she's close by.

Lowering my head, I open my eyes to blatantly admire her, a

smile crossing my face when I'm rewarded with her cheeks flushing pink in response.

My gaze drifts over her.

Ma would describe Jaine's figure as being straight up and down. I've decided that the straight-up-and-down look is now my favorite on any girl.

In the time we've spent together, what I've come to realize about Jaine is that there are no heirs nor graces with her. What you see is what you get. She doesn't give two flying fucks what anyone thinks, me included.

It's one of the things I respect most about her when typically, I'm surrounded by yes-people and everything fake. She's like a welcome breath of fresh air.

She's wearing white jean shorts and a tank top today, her beat-up high-tops finishing off her typical student look.

Most girls would come dressed to impress if asked to go on a date with me, even if it was only to the local park. I know I'm popular with the ladies. It's in part because I checkmark a lot of boxes.

Good looks. Winning personality. Influential family. Loaded.

I'm what many would call a good catch.

But what impresses the other girls doesn't seem to work with Jaine. Then again, she may not even be aware of the last two boxes since she's not from around these parts. Maybe I should tell her? So she knows exactly who she's getting involved with and about the mobster family she's going to be marrying in to.

I smirk at that thought as I close my eyes and lift my face back up to the sun. I can tell she's now blatantly admiring me, even if I can't see her doing so.

I catch her staring a lot when she thinks I'm not looking, so I already know she likes what she sees. That's not what's holding her back.

The seat shifts as she sits down.

"Penny for them."

That. Accent. I could listen to her talking all day, every day.

"Will you tell me about that tattoo behind your ear, darlin'?"

Silence. I realize it's because I've asked a question she doesn't want to answer, but we both know I can't take it back now that it's out there.

With my eyes remaining closed, I reach out, take her hand in mine, and give it a gentle squeeze of encouragement.

For the first time in my life, I want to know everything there is to know about a girl. I want to know all about Jaine Jones.

I don't rush her. I just wait.

There's no expectation for her to answer the question at all. She could change the subject to something far safer if she wanted to, and it would be left at that. For now, at least.

"It's the initial of a boy."

Envy flows through me—another first. I can actually taste its bitterness on the tip of my tongue.

I'm jealous that some other fella meant enough to her that she had his initial permanently inked on that perfect skin of hers. I don't say anything. I just let her continue in her own time.

"He was my first." Her voice is hesitant like it pains her to talk about it. About him. "I loved him. That's why I got the tattoo. He slept with me, then immediately slept with someone else. I guess, in the end, he didn't feel the same way… and that I was a disappointment when it came to…."

"Is that why you left home?" I interject to save her from any further embarrassment.

"No." There's a pause. "My pop studied law at Yale. I wanted to follow in his footsteps. That's the reason I left my hometown." Another pause. "The boy is the reason I'll never go back."

Unrequited love.

I turn to look at her. I see it now—the sadness behind those big green eyes. I now know why she's been so reluctant to move forward with me. He broke her trust and filled her with a mass of insecurities.

I turn to face her, then reaching out my other hand, I gently cup the side of her face, my gaze dropping to her lips. She knows what I'm going to do. Her tongue flicks out to lick their fullness and to give me all the permission I need.

I lean toward her until she's breathing me in, and I'm breathing her in. I know even before my mouth touches hers that she's it for me.

My end game.

I slowly press my lips to hers. I never want to forget this life-changing moment.

Soft. Warm. Hesitant. So fucking perfect.

That's what her mouth feels like under mine. I move my lips gently, and she does the same. Her mouth is unsure yet inquisitive at the same time.

Her hand reaches up to tangle with the back of my hair, and taking that as a sign of encouragement, I dip my tongue into her mouth.

I need to know if she tastes as good as she does in my dreams.

The moment my tongue touches hers, she pulls back.

"I…I need to go."

I simply nod at her stuttered words. I don't ask her to stay, and I don't go after her as she quickly stands and walks off.

I've achieved enough for today. I've made a breakthrough. Anything else is too much, too soon, when she's clearly still nurturing a broken heart.

All she needs is time.

And I have all the time in the world to give her.

CHAPTER FOUR

JAINE

JFK Airport, New York

I KNOW THE MINUTE I STEP OUT OF THE AIRCRAFT THAT I'M IN serious trouble.

Two SUVs are waiting on the tarmac, so one of us isn't going straight to Chez O'Connell. It's my guess the unlucky person who pulled the short straw is me.

I stare up at the rain-laden sky, suddenly apprehensive. I haven't spoken to Eoin since he disconnected the call yesterday, even though I tried several times to make contact. He was beyond pissed. He likely didn't want to say anything he'd regret. He'll also want to make sure that what he does have to say is said face to face.

Privately. With no witnesses.

Duke looks concerned on my behalf but says nothing. I nod at him reassuringly, then make brief eye contact with Dec. His deadpan expression gives nothing away as he silently loads my luggage while I get into the back of the vehicle.

I'm probably heading straight to the docks. I don't know that for sure, and I'm not going to waste my breath by asking. Dec won't tell me. He reports to Eoin, not to me, and I'm pretty sure my next destination will have been hand-chosen by my ex-husband.

I'll just have to let Dec take me on a mystery tour. I pull my phone from my pocket as soon as we've set off.

Jaine: *Should I be worried?*
Dylan: *I can't believe you didn't tell him where you were going, Jaine.*
Jaine: *I had my reasons. What's his mood like?*
Dylan: *Ma says he's not been home since he spoke to you yesterday.*
Jaine: *Is that common?*
Dylan: *Only when he's so wound up, he's not safe to be around other people.*
Jaine: *Jesus Christ.*
Dylan: *Praying might not be such a bad idea.*
Jaine: *I can look after myself.*
Dylan: *I know that, but he doesn't. You need to tell him.*
Jaine: *I will.*
Dylan: *He has a right to know. You're meant to be in a committed relationship.*
Jaine: *I am committed.*
Dylan: *Then act like it. No lies. No deceit. In this life, it's the only way. You know that. Don't underestimate how much he loves you. He's never had to deal with these sorts of emotions before. This is all new to him. He's struggling, Jaine. You're his kryptonite.*
Jaine: *Should I change my name to Lois?*

Dylan: *It's not funny. Ask yourself this. How would you have felt if he had disappeared without a trace and without bothering to tell you?*

I shouldn't have made a joke of it. It was wrong of me. Dylan has a point, I'm well aware of that, but I do have my reasons, and they are valid.

I'm concerned that the Mr. Smug. Selfish. Pompous side of Eoin O'Connell will view me as some sort of prize trophy once I tell him, and that, even though he won't be able to share my secret with anyone, he'll put me under even more pressure to get married for a second time. And I'm in no rush to retake the vows, not after everything that's already gone wrong between us.

The past may be water under the bridge, but a calm surface can easily betray the raging currents still lurking below.

And with my secret laid bare, will he then allow me to live my life as I see fit? Because I'm not so sure that he will. My concern is that it may cause him to tighten the reins of control even further.

If his dominating behavior doesn't stop, it will see us forever butting heads because I refuse to spend the rest of my days seeking permission from someone else to live my own life.

I'm a grown woman. I'm still standing, having stared death in the face more times than I can count. I'm more than capable of looking after myself.

I also want us to work for the right reasons. I don't want any life decisions to be influenced by the knowledge that I carry out serial-killing atrocities in my spare time. I definitely don't want any decision to be affected by the fact that I saved his life.

Twice.

Which he will know the moment all is revealed. I don't want the reason we stay together to be because he feels beholden to me. My feelings for him won't ever change, but that doesn't mean his won't for me.

I don't want him to wake up one day only to realize that he loves my alter-ego more than me.

We've only just got back together. We should be in the honeymoon period of our relationship. Yet, here I am, being driven to the docks because my actions over the past forty-eight hours have resulted in him being so pissed off, he's not safe to be around other people.

Physical. Volatile. Intense.

Our relationship is all of the above. Eoin and I can bring out the best in each other. We can also bring out the worst. The trouble is there's no in-between. It's all or nothing. Black or white.

I'm clearly a Molotov Cocktail to his extremely short fuse. Is that reality going to be sustainable long-term?

Back and forth. Push and pull. Can any relationship survive what we put each other through at times? Because I don't see ours changing any time soon, if ever.

The Docks, Hudson Yards

My thoughts are disrupted when the SUV comes to a standstill. As I suspected, we're at the docks, the stacked containers appearing tall and colorless against the heavy, overcast sky, their looming presence resembling an array of giant headstones.

I hope my name's not on the list of the deceased.

Eoin comes here to kill. Does he also come here when his darkness overwhelms him? Like he should have done when he punched the wall repeatedly at his apartment until he made his knuckles bleed?

Dec opens the door, and I step out. A shiver runs through me, and I run my hands up and down my upper arms. I'm only wearing blue jeans and a tank top, having just left the much warmer climate of California.

He doesn't ask me to follow him; I do so automatically. There's no point in saying I already know the way, as he won't let me out of his sight until I'm safely handed over to his boss, at least not if he values his own life.

The container he stops at isn't the same as before. Does each hold a different house of horrors? That depending on what mood Mr. Dominating. Dangerous. Deadly is in, he selects the one with the most fitting playroom?

Dec knocks on the door once. He doesn't speak, and there's no audible response. It remains eerily quiet like even the breeze crossing the river is scared to make a whisper in case it riles the occupant of this freezer-like metal box.

Opening the door, he motions his head for me to step inside. I do as he asks, he closes it behind me, and I immediately get swallowed up by pitch black. Eoin's in here. I know he is.

Awareness.

I shiver as the tendrils of his darkness seductively wrap around me. I'm sure he can hear my heart thudding in my chest and sense my skin prickling.

I don't speak. I'm not stupid enough to anger him further by making lame excuses. I'm sure the punishment he's selected for me will more than fit the crime. I stand and wait.

Expectation.

I know he's approaching. Our bodies are so in tune mine starts to silently scream out for his now that it realizes he's close. It's then I feel the sharp point of a blade at the base of my spine.

Is he going to pierce my skin? Is he going to run me through?

I shouldn't feel aroused, but I do, and the soft groan that escapes me lets him know just that.

Fear. Arousal. Addiction.

The latter will be my downfall. I'm addicted to him, and he knows it. Like a junkie, I'm forever craving the unique high only he can give me. I'm fucked. Because even if I could convince my brain to let him go, my body never will. It would betray me every goddamn time.

The blade moves slowly upwards, cutting through the material of my tank top, which then drops to the floor. My nipples instantly pebble. Still no words.

Anticipation.

A hot breath against my ear as two calloused hands come from behind to cup my tits, causing the nipples to tighten further, sending a message straight to my clit. Another groan, this time answered by a low growl.

He strokes the peaked tips until they ache, and I reactively press my ass backward until it collides with his groin.

He's hard.

I hold my breath as one hand slowly circles my throat and the other fists my hair. Yanking my head back, his mouth connects with my neck, and he bites down.

Pain.

I arch my back, pressing harder against his impressive length. Now I want the pleasure part.

"Do you want my cock, Miss Jones?" Dark. Dangerous. So fucking Irish, and all fucking mine.

"Yes."

"Strip."

He releases me, and I quickly discard my shoes and other clothes. The frigid air kisses my exposed skin, causing me to shiver.

"Walk."

I move forward until my knees collide with something. I reach down—a sofa or similar.

"Kneel."

I do as he asks, my hands using the back of the furniture to brace myself because I know what's coming next. He's holding back right now, but he won't be for much longer.

I'm light-headed at the thought of him losing control. I need him to as much as I need my next fucking breath.

The head of his cock wets the skin of my ass, and it instantly cools in the cold air. Spreading my legs, he tilts my hips, then lubricating his dick with my slickness, he pushes into me with one punishing thrust.

"Fuck." I hiss at the perfect intrusion as he pauses momentarily to let me adjust to his impressive size, then he punctuates every word with a single thrust.

"Never. Deceive. Me. Again." His breath is hot against my ear. "Am I making myself clear, Miss Jones?" His voice is low, threatening, and laced with anger.

"Yes."

My walls clench around his cock, and he grunts his approval. Moving his hands to grip my hips, he pulls back, then slams back into me.

Possession. Authority. Dominance. He's exerting all three.

"Fuck me, Eoin." The whine falls from my lips, and he responds by pistoning into me with ruthless, determined, selfish thrusts. Gripping the back of the furniture, I meet each one.

Demanding more. Needing more. Needing him.

Everything hurts. Everything burns.

"God," I whine.

"God has nothing to do with it. He can't save you from me, and it's not his cock you're about to come on," he hisses.

I shatter at his words, and he fucks me harder as he brutally claims what he views as his. Me.

Pushing back against him, I silently beg for more, the sounds of our mutual growls of appreciation and flesh slapping hard against flesh, painting the empty space.

"Say, please."

"Eoin."

"Say please, or I'll stop."

"Please."

Fisting my hair, he yanks my head back. "How can I refuse when you beg so fucking prettily, Miss Jones." His smug voice is hot against my ear as he turns it up another notch.

I deliberately clench as hard as I can, earning myself a cussed slap on the ass, his movements quickly turning erratic as I break his perfect stride.

The animalistic sound of his low growl, as he finds his own pleasure, causes me to shatter once more, my gripping walls demanding that he spill his seed deep inside me, his twitching dick obliging as he empties himself in steady thrusts. We stay where we are.

Panting. Hot. Sweaty. Sated, for now.

I lean back until I'm pressed against his torso, welcoming his strong arms as they snake around to pull me close. We stay there until the sweat sheening our bodies starts to cool.

He moves one arm, and soft lights suddenly surround us. I glance around. This container has furniture in it. I can't see it all, but it's my guess it's fitted out like a small apartment.

No words are spoken. He's still too angry.

He pushes my hair away from the back of my neck before placing a soft kiss against my skin. He then pauses. I know why.

Because regardless of whether we stand the test of time or not, nothing will ever change the fact that I love Eoin O'Connell.

And I'm guessing he's just seen my visible declaration of that as he takes in the scrolled letter E that I had Gusto ink on the back of my neck this morning.

CHAPTER FIVE

PADRAIG

The Ruocco Home, Agrigento, Sicily

"When?"

My wife looks smug as she studies my adverse reaction to the breaking news that we'll be returning to New York imminently.

"Within the next few weeks. Luc has insisted that it's time and that we must return together and display a united front as a family."

I nod slowly from where I'm standing at the window of my office.

This unlikeable pair need all the extended family members they can garner, given that any immediate ones have been killed in one retaliation attack or another due to the Ruocco's untrustworthy ways.

They have a plethora of enemies, which means not only do I have the Duster ones to contend with these days, I also have theirs.

Is our return unwelcome news? I'm not sure. Even though I've shut myself away from everything I've ever known for almost a year, it still feels too soon.

Rightly or wrongly, I've gotten used to solitude.

Regardless of what my family may think, it was my decision to relocate to Sicily, not Sophia's. I did what was expected of me. I took the vows with her. I refused to be backed into a corner over anything else, however, including the consummation of our marriage.

I may have fucked her once before we wed, but it will never happen again.

She knows if she's not happy with that reality, then we can have the marriage annulled. She just has to say the word, and I'll handle the matter both personally and discretely. That I'll also gladly throw in every cent of my personal fortune to buy my freedom.

Don't get me wrong; I would have attempted to give it a go. She deserved me to at least try to make a concerted effort. But while Sophia is attractive enough with her long dark hair and olive skin, her beauty is only skin deep. It doesn't extend below the surface. Sophia has a nasty streak that makes her quite the unpleasant girl to be around.

From the moment I arrived, I've witnessed her treating people like shite. Adults and children alike. The more I pulled her up on it, the more she deliberately went out of her way to be a bitch toward them. I then realized that it's a family trait. That her brother, Luc, is exactly the same.

In the end, I had to learn to bite my tongue because my well-intentioned interference made life even more unbearable for the unfortunates she targeted with her acerbic mouth. The unwarranted verbal attacks sometimes became physical, especially when other females were involved.

Her treatment of people was alien to me, more so when I come from a life where ours are treated like an extension of our own family.

Sophia and I aren't compatible. We will never be compatible.

I made it clear to her then that our marriage would only ever be in name only. That she could take it or leave it.

Undeterred, she has attempted to woo me with her feminine charms on several occasions, but, frustratingly for her, her efforts remain unfruitful. I steer clear of whiskey. I steer clear of her.

History will never be repeated.

I wrongly assumed that her brother would put a gun to my head to make me perform my husbandly duties, but our lack of intimacy is of no interest to him.

On the rare occasions he and I have spoken, it quickly became apparent that he wanted to add a Duster to his family for political purposes rather than procreational ones, given that any resultant offspring would be an O'Connell and not a Ruocco.

That may all change, of course. This family likes to move the goalposts.

"I'll start packing," I answer dismissively before looking out the window.

She knows our conversation is now at an end. That she can fuck off and do some more shopping on her Duster credit card.

Once she's gone, I sit at my desk.

I know I shouldn't be doing this. I realize it's not helping my healing. That it's only dragging me back into the past and filling me once more with foolish hopes and pipe dreams. With wishful thinking that I could change things.

But I can't change things. There's no do-over to be had.

I cheated on Jaine, and this existence is my deserved comeuppance. Once more, I stare at the image before printing it off and placing the hard copy inside my phone case.

12 Years Earlier (Age Nineteen)
Yale University, Connecticut

We're in her room, lying on her bed, and partaking in my new favorite thing to do.

Kissing Jaine Jones.

Being allowed to put my tongue in her mouth makes it taste all the sweeter. And right now, that appendage wants unrestricted access to that little pussy of hers.

We're being sensible. We've done our work, and now it's playtime.

Fortunately, she doesn't have to share her room with any other students, and she's also chosen me to be her study partner.

Win-win.

With my mouth still on hers, I gently roll her onto her back before prizing her thighs apart with my hips and grinding my hard-on against her. It's met with a soft whimper.

Result.

Pushing her top up, I expose her pink, pebbled nipples. My mouth drops to taste one, and then the other, and my reward is her instinctively raising her hips to silently beg for more.

She's aroused. She wants me as much as I want her. And let me tell you, I have never wanted a girl as much as I want Jaine Jones right now.

My dick is so fucking hard that it hurts.

I grind against her once more, rewarded this time with short fingernails digging into my back. Slowly dropping my hand, I reach for the button of her pants.

If I could reach third base… but just when I think my luck's finally in, she pushes me off and snaps her legs closed—locked out of heaven once more.

Don't get me wrong, I enjoy a bit of heavy petting and dry

humping as an appetizer as much as the next person, but it's been that and only that for the past two months.

I'm a hormonal teenager. I need more. But I don't want to push her. I don't want her to have any regrets when it comes to me. Not when I'm in this for the long haul.

Not when I'm so totally fucking besotted with her.

I roll onto my back, exhaling in frustration, but I don't make a big deal out of it. If she needs me to keep on waiting until she's ready, then that's exactly what I'll do.

We lie side by side, both of us staring at the stark white ceiling, lost in our own thoughts. Resting on her elbow, she looks down at me. I take in her now swollen, pouty lips. I don't want anyone else ever kissing them.

Her hand reaches out to trace the birthmark on my inner wrist. "It's shaped like a horseshoe."

She's trying to distract us from what just happened.

I run my other hand through my hair and force a smile. "All of the males in my family are born with it, darlin'."

"Does it ever bring you luck?"

I don't answer that question, and she knows the reason why. Because, right now, I don't feel very lucky. Rejection is an alien experience for me and one I can't say I enjoy all that much.

There's a silence. I know I'll need to fill it before it becomes an awkward one.

I look up at her as I tuck her hair behind her ear. "Tell me about the logo on your leather jacket."

There's a brief pause. I already know what it is, but I'm curious to see if she'll admit it.

"It's the club patch for the Angels of Hellfire MC in Rising, California. I grew up around their compound. My pop is best friends with their prez, Duke, and he also represents the club legally. I spent most of my time there. Well, at least I did before I left."

I frown. "Surely, that wasn't an ideal place for a young girl to grow up. I mean, you must have witnessed some right horror stories."

She shrugs. "If you're asking if I've ever seen a person killed, then the answer is yes, I have. They're bikers. Everything they do is illegal, and when they're not doing that, they're riding hogs, drinking tequila, and fucking cum sluts."

"Cum sluts?" I raise an eyebrow.

"You know. The women who willingly sign up to be fucked by multiple bikers at any one time."

I snort as I laugh, and she chuckles.

"Girls are typically queueing out the door as soon as there's a vacancy. Most will have just reached the age of consent. They sign up, hoping one of the bikers will fall in love with them and make them their old lady. It's the equivalent of being a wife but without the marriage license.

I guess for the brothers cum sluts are seen as being part of their reward system. Free pussy from the club as a thank you for all the illegal wrongdoings they're expected to commit on behalf of their patch."

"And your da is their lawyer, you say?"

She nods.

"Do you know anything about my family, Jaine?"

She nods again, this time slowly, her cheeks turning red as she admits to having been curious about me beyond our student life here.

"The Hudson Dusters. Your family is the Irish Mob."

I smirk as I gaze once more at the ceiling. "We do most things legally."

"Most." She snorts.

It's my turn to shrug with a smile. "For the stuff we don't, well, I guess that's why my family needs me here, studying the law."

She's silent for a moment. "Have you ever killed anyone?"

I turn to look at her. Tell her the truth, that I'm a bloodthirsty fecker, or lie? She's grown up in the life. She's just admitted to witnessing death, even if she's never taken a life.

"I have, darlin'."

She nods slowly once more.

"Does that frighten you?"

She shakes her head. "Nothing frightens me, Irish."

Could she be any more fucking perfect?

"Irish?" I raise an eyebrow.

Her cheeks turn pink as the corners of her mouth turn up. "You have a slight accent, so in my head, I always think of you as Irish."

I snicker. Is it wrong that I like the fact that she's just given me a nickname? "Irish it is then, Jaine."

There's a pause as she runs her finger over my birthmark once more, a small smile playing on her lips. "I guess I'm the one who's been given all the luck because I never thought I'd have feelings for anyone after him, but I was wrong. I love you, Irish."

Right now? Even though I've got blue balls? I feel like I'm king of the fucking hill.

CHAPTER SIX

JAINE

Jones & Associates Legal, Upper East Side, New York

I'VE JUST BEEN DROPPED OFF.

I've had to promise Eoin I won't go anywhere without Dec taking me and that I'll let him know my precise movements.

My tattoo seems to have made him even more possessive, if that's possible. Now that I've inked his initial on my skin, he seems to think he has an even bigger claim on me. It's like he's viewing it as some sort of fucked-up brand.

I've agreed with what he's asked for today only, but only because my pussy's still paying the price for the last small lapse in communication. I'm also having to wear a scarf to hide the damage his monster inflicted on my neck.

It's seven a.m. The office is already buzzing.

You treat people right and reward them well, and in return, they work hard and go the extra mile when needed. Or at least that's always been my experience.

We pay top dollar, and both the relocation and benefits packages we offer are second to none. There is a hierarchical structure in place simply because there has to be in an organization of this size.

Every employee is aware, however, that I operate an open-door policy. If someone has a problem, they know they can come straight to me, but for that level of investment of both my time and my money, I expect their loyalty and dedication.

Due to the expansion of both JAL and JAA, I've now had to take the entire building off Delaney's hands. A big investment, given that I insisted on paying top dollar as I always do.

I leave all of the number crunching up to Jessie these days. If she says we can afford it, I'm confident we can. As the best accountant in the business, she knows what she's doing. I trust her advice completely.

My thoughts drift to her. We haven't spoken in a few days. With a smile on my face, I dial her number. As I do, I glance around my office with its grey carpets, white walls, and black furniture.

It's too large now that Cherry and Sasha have vacated the premises, but I'm loathe to give it up for a smaller space. These four walls hold way too many memories, and these days, I try to preserve as many of those as I can.

Jessie answers straight away. "What am I in trouble for now, partner?"

"You sat there twiddling your goddamn thumbs, as I'm not even sure it rang," I joke.

"I saw it was you. You never call me, so I figured you've either misdialed or I'm in some sort of trouble. Given that you never make mistakes, I opted for the second."

"I just thought I'd touch base."

"Is that so? So, now you're spying on me?"

"I'm just calling to see how you are." I chuckle.

"Are you, by any chance calling to tell me all about what you and my daddy discussed? I tried to prize that information from him, but he referred me back to you."

I want to tell her, but it's way too soon. I'm still trying to digest it all myself. It's also something that needs doing face to face.

"Soon."

"Soon. What does soon mean? Next week? Next year?"

"Soon means just that. Soon."

"You legal types just like tying the rest of us up in knots. Next, you'll be pleading the fifth amendment." She huffs.

I laugh out loud. "Now, why didn't I think of that? Anyway, I called for a reason."

"So, you didn't call to ask how I was doing?" I can tell she's pouting.

"Well, that too, but there was one other thing."

"And that is?"

I reopen the email from Cody Fletcher.

"I got an invitation from an old school friend from Yale. He's hosting some get-together at the end of the month. I wasn't sure whether I should attend or not."

"Read it out to me."

Hey, Jaine,

Long time, no speak. I hope life's treating you well. I'm heading back to New York on a fleeting visit and was trying to coordinate a reunion. I'm asking some of the old crowd to come along. It would be great if you could make it.

I've dug out some photographs. Those were the days.

The date and venue are attached. I hope to see you there.

Take care,

Fletch, aka Cody Fletcher.

"Do you think he sent the same email to everyone?" she asks.

"I think so."

"Do you want to go?"

"I'm not sure. I know Sasha won't want to, and Cherry can't, as she's still on her sabbatical trying to recover from the ordeal of me putting her in charge of my company for two years."

"Did you enjoy your time at Yale?"

"Yes and no."

"Shit. That's right. You went to school with Paddy."

There's a pause. She's silently adding, 'It was back then that he cheated on you.'

"Do you think he's been invited?"

"I would suspect so. He and Fletch were best friends back then. It's not like he'll be able to attend, though, as he's currently living in Sicily, so it's not like I'll run the risk of bumping into him."

"Do you think Eoin will want to tag along?"

I roll my eyes, even though she can't see me. "I've checked his calendar, and he's out of town that day looking at several real estate properties in Chicago."

There's a pause. I know what she's going to say before she says it, and it's already fucking me off.

"After what's just happened, you really should check in with him first. You don't need him going off on one again, Jaine. None of us do."

I exhale in frustration. "I can't live my life if I'm wrapped in cotton wool, Jessie."

"I understand that, but you won't be able to live your life if you're dead either."

"So, do you think I should go?" I change the subject away from Eoin.

"I don't see why not? Surely it would be nice to see these people and find out what they've been doing with their lives after all this time?"

"I'll think about it." I'm still not sure I want to drag up that part of my past. There are some memories I'd much sooner forget.

"If you do decide to go, just be sure to mention it to big bad Eoin beforehand. Even if he is out of town, he'll still want to know if you're going to be anywhere other than in your office or the safe space, Jaine."

"I will." Another eye roll.

"Anyway, is it soon yet?"

I chuckle. "No, but as soon as soon arrives, you'll be the first to know."

I disconnect the call, then stare at the email attachment.

To open it or not? That really is the question. Trepidation butterflies flit through my stomach at what I may find if I do.

My traitorous fingers ignore the doubts crossing my mind as they move to open it. Neither do they pay me any mind when I ask them to stop clicking through the plethora of images. I'm not sure my heart will be able to take it if there's one of me and Irish among them.

I see Cherry. I see Sasha. I see Irish. And he's with me.

A painful sob escapes me. It shouldn't after all this time, more so after he messaged me those twenty generic words letting me go once and for all, but when you're looking at the carbon copy of your little boy, it's hard not to feel emotional.

I love him. I miss him. I wish things could have been different for us.

I gaze at the photo. At my arms snaked around his neck, and his hands circling my waist. I'm wearing my usual tank and combats combo and staring up at him with all the love in the world shining from my eyes.

Nineteen-year-old me. Back when I was plain Jaine Jones. My

hair's piled on top of my head, and I'm wearing braces and glasses, but Irish didn't care what I looked like.

And if I ever doubted that he loved me at any point back then, I was wrong to because, in this image, he's staring at me like I'm the sun, the moon, and the stars.

Two teenagers madly in love. And then he cheated on me.

I click on further, and that's when I see her. The girl he cheated on me with.

Brittany Mason.

If Emilia had a doppelganger, then I'm looking straight at her.

Hey, Fletch

It's good to hear from you. Thanks so much for reaching out. I'd love to attend and catch up with everyone. I'll see you there.

Take care,

Jaine Jones

I'll worry about Eoin agreeing to it all closer to the time.

Adjusting the size of the image of me and Irish, I press print before placing the hard copy in the case of my burner phone, alongside the image of me and Ace and the one of my two boys.

CHAPTER SEVEN

PADRAIG

The Ruocco Home, Agrigento, Sicily

Is it wrong that I haven't told my family that I'll be returning to New York imminently? The old me was the type who would have welcomed any opportunity to be made a big song and dance over, but I'm not sure that fella even exists anymore.

The only person I've maintained any dialogue with the entire time I've been away is Ma, and that's been under strict instructions that she's not allowed to mention anything about what's going on back in Dusterland.

I don't want to know.

I don't want to hear about how happy everyone else is with their lot when I'm the complete opposite with mine.

I don't want to hear about pregnancies or children when I'm never going to experience being a da.

One of the hardest things I've ever had to do was cut off all contact with our Dylan. Me and him were as thick as thieves. We always had been. But I had no choice. Through no fault of his own, he became the middle person—the go-between between me and Jaine.

It would have been impossible for him never to mention her, given they'd become such close friends, even more so when his wife was her business partner.

I couldn't put him in that position. Not after the countless sacrifices he'd already made on my behalf. I asked so much of him that, in the end, he almost lost out on his own chance at happiness all so I could continue to live out my lie for a little while longer.

But any talk of Jaine needed to be off-limits. I had to let her go. Because she'd already let me go. It was the only way that I could survive.

So, in the end, I had to let him go too.

I'm not sure how the family would react if they knew I was coming back. Would they be glad or not? I'm pretty sure they'll all have gotten on with their lives in my absence, pleased they don't have to listen to mardy arse me continually complaining about how unfairly treated I am.

But I had a reason for moping around—a valid one. I should have had a say in my own future.

I'm aware that many wealthy, influential men were insulted at me indiscreetly sleeping with their wives and significant others right under their noses. That I was steadily creating a long list of very deadly enemies and making a lot of trigger fingers itch.

I didn't have some sort of death wish. I wasn't trying to goad Fate himself every day to see if he'd answer my silent prayers and put me out of my misery by sinking a bullet into my skull.

I was searching for another Jaine.

I found out pretty early on that it was an impossible task, but it didn't stop me from going round and round in a never-ending circle all the same.

I appreciate that I became a liability to the family. The Dusters had to put an end to the problem, or someone else would have. Permanently. So, I understand why they did what they did, but it doesn't mean I will ever accept it.

What does any of it matter anyway when my reason for living decided that I wasn't hers?

12 Years Earlier (Age Nineteen)
Yale University, Connecticut

"You want me to order pizza?"

We're sitting on the floor of her room, surrounded by books, having just halted a marathon study session. I watch as she stands and stretches before sitting on the edge of her bed to reach for her phone.

My eyes graze over her long, tanned limbs in little white shorts. Legs that I want to part so I can access the paradise at the apex.

Fuck food. The only thing I want to be eating is her sweet pussy. I pounce on her, and she giggles as I push her back against the pillows.

"We can eat later, Jaine." I chuckle against her neck, inhaling the smell of wildflowers. It's the most addictive, potent scent that I've ever come across in my whole life.

Then again, everything about Jaine is addictive. I love her so fucking much that my heart throbs with need even more than my dick these days.

My lips find hers, my tongue stroking deep as my hands explore her body. I'm rewarded with a shiver and a soft groan.

Please let my luck be in today. I'll do anything, God.

Any-fucking-thing at all.

Prizing her thighs apart with my hips, I grind against her.

"I want you, Jaine." I'm tempted to beg, but I don't. I don't want a pity fuck. I definitely don't want her to feel under any pressure. I need her to want this as much as I do. I need her to want me as much as I want her.

I lift her top and feast on her nipples. Raising my mouth back to hers, I smirk at her newly found confidence when she parts our lips just long enough to yank my white t-shirt over my head, her small, inquisitive hands exploring every inch of my torso.

Fuck, I never want her to stop touching me. Anywhere. Anytime. I'll take anything I can get from this girl.

Bypassing the button of her shorts, my hand drops straight to her pussy to rub her through the denim material. I can feel how hot she is, and my efforts are rewarded as she instinctively grinds against me.

So near, but still so fucking far. I reach for her zip.

Please, God. Please, God. Please, God.

She freezes.

Game over.

"No, Jaine. Please don't do this to me again." I don't normally react, but this time, I can't stop myself from groaning against her neck in frustration. "We've waited three months, darlin'. I've shown you how committed I am by not pushing you and going at your pace, but I'm a man, Jaine. I need physical interaction as well as mental stimulation. My doc says I have the worst case of blue balls he's ever seen."

Running my hand through my hair, I lift my head and force a smile.

She immediately turns away and starts tracing the outline of my birthmark. "I'm sorry, Padraig. I'm just not ready."

Time passes.

Eventually, she stands, picks up her phone, and orders the pizza.

When it finally arrives, we study in silence for the length of time it takes us to finish eating, and then I make my excuses and leave.

It's not a reaction to the fact that she wouldn't put out. I'll get over it. I have been for the past three months. It's a reaction to the fact that I'm worried her feelings for me aren't what she says they are.

Does she love me? Does she not?

Right now, I honestly think it's the latter.

CHAPTER EIGHT

JAINE

The O'Connell Home, Darling, New York

Lying on his back, he thrusts upward, forcing me to take his massive cock all at once before gripping my waist and pulling me down until our groins collide. Until there's no part of him that isn't sheathed by me.

"Perfect. Fucking. Fit." He presses in further, smirking smugly as he watches me rotate my hips while hissing at the stretch and burn.

God, it hurts, but in the best possible way. I'm so fucking full. I don't know where he ends, and I begin.

He pulls back, then snaps his hips forward again, his dick connecting with every sweet spot. I groan my approval, my nails digging into his abdomen as he starts to fuck me with slow, steady strokes, each one quickly elevating me higher, each one more brutal than the last.

Our sexual chemistry is as insane as the man himself. We crave each other so much that we find ourselves fucking wherever and whenever possible. No matter how often, we're never sated for long.

It's frenzied. It's feral. That side of our relationship is fucking perfect.

"Eoin," I whine. Leaning forward, I place my hands on either side of his head, and I'm immediately overwhelmed by the intoxicating scent of spicy cologne and clean, male sweat.

I can taste possessiveness on his tongue the moment our mouths connect, his green gaze holding mine as I shatter around his cock for the first of many times.

He continues to ram into me, his tongue stroking deep, his hands gripping my ass as he helps himself to what he considers to be his. Every time we fuck, that's exactly what he's doing. He's staking his claim by bruising my flesh with his hands and mouth and coating me with his cum, inside and out.

I clench around him, and I'm rewarded with a hard slap on the ass.

"Disobedient, evil woman. How many times do I have to explain myself? You come when I decide. I come when I decide." His arrogance is so fucking hot that it makes my clit throb with need every time he opens his conceited mouth.

I hate him. I love him more.

Flipping me onto my back with his cock still inside me, he kneels and pushes my legs against my chest before withdrawing and thrusting straight back in. I grimace at how deep he can go in this position.

Too deep. Not deep enough.

More. I need more.

I press my hands against the wall, pushing back to meet every thrust of his hips until his movements become erratic.

"Come with me." A demand.

His cock thickens and hardens, then, with a low, feral growl, his hot release coats my insides, the sensation causing me to tighten around him once more.

He flips us over until I'm lying on top of him, and we lie there, my head tucked under his chin.

Panting, hot, sweaty, and covered in cum.

My mouth connects with his inked skin, my tongue flicking out to taste its salty surface. It's addictive. He's addictive.

None of my senses can ever get enough.

Lifting my head, I stare up at him. He's so fucking good-looking, and doesn't he just know it. Mr. Smug. Selfish. Pompous is fully aware that I'm blatantly admiring him.

"I love you." The words fall so easily from my lips these days.

He smirks as he raises one eyebrow. "Words are all very well and good, Miss Jones." He drags his thumb across my lower lip before pushing it into my mouth. I watch his nostrils flare, and his eyes burn green when I suck on it hard. "I'd far rather you put your cussing little mouth to better use by wrapping those pouty lips around my cock."

I smirk at him, then, making my way down his chiseled torso, I do just that.

We lie there with our legs tangled and the cream sheets twisted around us. My head rests on his chest once more, listening to the steady thrum of his heart. His arm is wrapped around my shoulder, his fingers trailing up and down my upper arm.

Slowly but surely, the trust is beginning to rebuild between us after the shitshow that went down before. Back when I set out to deliberately fuck up his life. Back when I personally delivered him a penance for a sin he didn't even commit.

Eoin lives with us most of the time. He gets on well with Duke. Let's face it, his seal of approval would always have been a deal-breaker, regardless of how well-matched the suitor was. More importantly, the kids adore him, and the feeling's mutual. He'll make a great father one day.

Will that one day be with me? Right now, that's anyone's guess.

I push that thought aside for now. We're not ready to contemplate that bridge, let alone consider crossing it. At least not from the side I'm standing on.

I'm sure he thinks we're more than ready. The problem is that Eoin will expect me to cross over to his side. I'm not prepared to do that.

I've quickly realized that he's a closet misogynist. Pregnant. Barefoot. Tied to the kitchen sink. That's what he expects from me, even though he would deny it.

He wants me to be his good girl, but I'm not a good girl. I'm a bad girl. I'm a very bad girl.

Our almost-living together has revealed a somewhat turbulent relationship. I guess it was to be expected. The signs were all there, given how highly charged things had been between us over the years.

We'd purposely go out of our way to point score. We're both strong-willed and opinionated people. That reality has called for many heated exchanges and resulted in a lot of angry fucking.

I'm not complaining about the hot mobster sex, but is what we have conducive to a long-term relationship?

Eoin is dominating and assertive. I suspect to complement him, he needs someone submissive and compliant. Unfortunately for him, I'm neither of those two things.

We need to find a balance. I won't compromise myself for anyone, even if I do love them.

I didn't with Irish. I didn't with Ace.

Everything is fine until it's not, but there's no gradual. It switches instantly from one extreme to the other. Right now we're not arguing, but we will be imminently.

We'd typically spend the afterglow finding out more about each other. Or at least I'd find out more about him, given he knows pretty much everything there is to know about me. Apart from my secret, that is. It's a time when his guard is down, and I encourage him to dig deep to share a locked-away memory.

I want to know everything there is to know about him. I love that he lets me strip away his layers each time to reveal something deeper and more personal. He's never let his walls down for anyone before now. Each bare admission makes me love him even more.

Today, it's deathly silent, and it's because I'm feeling tense.

I have to broach the subject of Fletch's reunion. I know it will turn into an issue even before I open my mouth.

Ever since the trouble brought itself to New York, Eoin hasn't wanted to let me out of his sight. I don't know how much more of his over-protectiveness I can take. I'm sure most women would be only too happy to wallow in a sea of attention and possessiveness, but I'm not most women. I'm drowning.

Even when we're not physically together, he's trying to control my movements. Pretty soon, I won't be able to visit the restroom without him insisting that either he or Dec go with me.

I get it, in part, at least.

After what happened with Fin, we're all still on high alert. I appreciate and agree that the kids need to remain on lockdown pretty much twenty-four-seven. On a property this extensive, where there's plenty of indoor and outdoor space, that's not such a problem for a child.

But the way things are shaping up, and with our enemy continuing to remain faceless, I know it's not going to be long before Eoin insists I do the same.

And I can't do that. I won't do it. I need to be able to live my life.

I understand that if I'm not under lock and key, and if someone wants me dead, I will be. I'm a sniper. I know how easy it is to dispatch someone from afar. But that's my choice to make.

"One of my old classmates from Yale has been in contact. He's holding a reunion. He's asked if I'll go, and I've said that I will."

The baton of tension passes from me to him as the fingers that were gently stroking my shoulder stop.

"I don't think that's a good idea, Jaine, given the risks we're all currently facing." His response is calm. For now.

"It's at The Meeting Rooms. I'm sure it will be fine."

"Then I must insist on going with you."

"I would be happy for you to do that, but I've already checked your calendar. You're in Chicago that day."

"Then I think it's best that you don't go."

The baton passes straight back to me.

"I've already RSVP'd."

"Jaine...."

I sit upright. "I don't have to take orders from you, Eoin."

"You're my fiancée. My future wife. It's my job to protect you."

"I'm a big girl, Eoin."

"I must insist that you do as I say, Jaine."

"The hell I will!"

He yanks me down, pinning me beneath him, his nostrils flaring in annoyance. His fingers grip my jaw as his mouth captures mine, his tongue thrusting deep.

The taste of adrenaline floods my mouth, along with all the

other addictive flavors that make up the feral side of Eoin O'Connell.

I groan against his lips as he prizes my legs apart with his slim hips before grinding his hard-on against me, rubbing its impressive length up and down my slickness.

Sometimes I hate how much I fucking love him. Our clashing personalities make me want to kill him and fuck him at the same time.

I need him inside me. I try to angle my hips so the head of his dick meets with my entrance, but every time I do, he pulls back.

"Shall we both watch as your greedy little pussy chases my cock, Miss Jones?" He smirks at my frustration with one eyebrow raised.

"Fuck you, asshole." I hiss.

"It's you who'll be getting fucked imminently." He runs the entire length of his dick up my wetness so I know exactly what I'm currently missing out on, then his hand drops to cup my pussy. "This is mine. You're fucking mine."

We both know he's right.

I don't get a chance to respond as his lips cover mine once more, his tongue filling my mouth and stroking deep.

His fingers dip into my slickness before he thrusts two inside. I pant against his lips as I welcome them, my legs parting further as he moves them slowly back and forth.

"Can you hear how wet you are, Jaine?"

I should be embarrassed, but I'm not. "I don't want your goddamn fingers. I want your fucking cock."

I watch as he sucks the glistening digits into his mouth before dropping his hand to line up his dick.

"Then take my cock like a good fucking girl."

He fills me to the hilt in one brutal thrust, and I hiss at the intrusion. His hand fists my hair as he bites down hard on my neck, bruising me for the world to see.

He fucks me hard, every powerful thrust more savage than the last. I'm well aware that each is a punishment for my daring to ask for even one moment of freedom.

Kneeling, he lifts my hips off the bed until they're suspended and level with his before withdrawing and ramming back in. I groan at the feeling of being perfectly fucking full. He pounds into me.

Claiming me. Marking me. Stealing yet another piece of my soul.

My walls clench around him, never wanting to let him go.

"Eoin." I push against him, whining like a bitch in heat as I near the peak. "I need…." He tilts my hips and gives me exactly that. What I need.

"Look at me."

I stare into eyes of burning green as I claim my release, my mewls of pleasure filling the silence. He pulls out, his abs tensing as he uses one strong, veiny hand to stroke his hard cock. His gaze never leaves mine. I watch his face contort when, with a low growl, he claims his own pleasure, covering me in ropes of hot cum. He then watches as I slowly rub his release into my skin.

Eoin's way of changing the subject is to use the strong physical connection we share. Well, if he thinks this conversation is over, then he's wrong. It's far from it because I'll be attending that reunion whether Eoin O'Connell likes it or not.

Asshole.

CHAPTER NINE

PADRAIG

The Ruocco Home, Agrigento, Sicily

I'M PACKED.

I realize I'm way ahead of schedule, as we still have a week to go until we fly out, but I like to be punctual. I don't appreciate other people's tardiness either.

In the end, I decided not to make anyone aware of my return. I want to see genuine reactions when I turn up on the doorstep of the family home unannounced, having been gone for a year. I don't want to see painted-on expressions.

They'll be shocked, I'm sure, but I'm more interested in knowing if they missed me or if they just continued on as normal in a world without me in it.

I'm regressing. I know I am.

I need to get out of here now. I've gone from feeling content at being isolated to feeling like I'm about to self-combust.

I stare out the window, taking in views that won't be mine for much longer. Sights that, although stunning, I won't miss. I know I'll never return to Sicily. I came here to heal, and I'm undoing the little I did by digging through my past with Jaine line by line.

All it took was one email and a bunch of decade-old photographs to pretty much take me back to square one. Proof, not that I needed it, that stealing myself away for the last year was pointless. It achieved nothing.

My brain has been plagued with thoughts of what she's been up to these days. When I had no return date, it was far easier to push those thoughts to the back of my mind because it didn't matter. I didn't have to witness her moving on with a life without me in it and without a backward glance.

Now I'm headed back; it's all I *can* think about.

How is she? How are the kids? Has she met someone new? Does she still not love me? Does she still not miss me? Did she return to New York as she had planned? Is she living there now? I'm not sure how I'd feel about that. Knowing I could bump into her at any given moment just by turning a corner.

That we'd be breathing in the same air.

It would be far easier for me if she were out of sight permanently. She'll never be out of mind, but at least it would be half the battle.

I stare at my phone.

New handset. New number. New start.

I guess now that I'm returning to my old life, I could revert to my old number. Did anyone care enough to call me or message me? Aside from my family, did anyone even notice I was gone?

Good old Paddy. Always game for a laugh. Always the life and soul. Until the day he became soulless, his laugh nothing more than a distant echo.

And here's me once more thinking about the day I died. Make that a million and two times a day.

We fly back in on the day of Fletch's reunion. Maybe I'll drop in unannounced.

12 Years Earlier (Age Nineteen)
Yale University, Connecticut

"Brittany's having a party at her house tonight if you're up for it." Fletch ruffles my hair on his way past, and I bat his hand away.

Annoying fucker.

Unlike Jaine, I share a room on campus. It's not because I can't afford to have one of my own, obviously. It's just that with me being the sociable sort, I much prefer to have a roommate.

The space I share with Fletch consists of four plain white walls, two unmade beds, and a single fridge that's always empty aside from beer. It reeks of feet, sex, and dirty laundry.

Life's too short to worry about the latter. I let my ma arrange to have it collected and dropped off once a week. My excuse is that I need to focus on my studies. And given that I'm her favorite, my wish is her command.

On the other hand, Brittany stays in a five-bedroomed property in New Haven. Her loaded parents insisted they bought it as an investment, but we all know it's to save their precious daughter from having to board on campus and mix with the hoi polloi.

To go or not to go.

Brittany's been after me since we enrolled. She's been quite vocal about the fact that she saw me and her as being the newest celebrity couple on campus.

Don't get me wrong, she's a beautiful girl. There aren't many fellas who wouldn't give their right testicle to fuck her, but I'm not interested in the dark-haired, olive-skinned former cheerleader. I mean I was, but that was before I met Jaine.

I frown as my thoughts drift to her. She's been avoiding me for the past week. Her constant rejection is making things awkward between us, more so when she keeps giving me the green light before switching to red at the last minute.

Obviously, I'm not going to pressure her into doing something she doesn't want to, but it does have me constantly wondering what the real reason is.

Slouching back further on the burger-shaped beanbag, I throw a baseball in the air before catching it in the complementary leather mit.

"Jaine told me she loves me," I mumble like it's not a big deal when, to me, it means everything. I should feel happy, but I don't.

"Aww, how sweet," Fletch smirks before making kissing noises, causing me to launch the baseball at his head. He snickers as he catches it with ease before running his other hand through his shaggy blonde hair.

As a former high school quarterback, he's also extremely popular with the ladies, hence why our room constantly stinks of sex.

He makes full use of the space while I'm at Jaine's and sometimes even when I'm not. Trying to drown out the noise of people fucking while you're trying to sleep is not easy, even with earplugs and a dozen pillows stacked on your head.

Maybe I'm just jealous because I'm not getting any.

As much as Fletch looks and acts like your typical jock, he's actually a pretty decent guy. I know I can tell him this sort of stuff without him taking the piss.

"And did you say it back?" he questions, one eyebrow raised.

I stare at him before realizing that I didn't. I do love her. Of course, I do. I shake my head. "I didn't."

"Any reason for that?" He tosses the ball in the air and catches it.

"I guess because I'm not sure if she really meant it?"

"Why would she say it if she didn't mean it?" He looks confused as he throws the ball back at me, and I catch it in the mit.

I shrug. "I reckon she only said it to appease me."

"Because she still won't put out?"

I nod. "I get that she's been hurt in the past, but surely waiting all this time proves to her that I'm in this for the long haul and that I'm not just chasing one thing?"

"Do you think there's any other reason?"

I shrug again. "Who knows? Maybe she doesn't like me enough. Maybe she's trying to friendzone me."

"Do you think she's still hung up on her ex?"

"I think she's more than hung up on him, Fletch. I reckon she's still in love with the fella. Three months and I've not even seen her pussy, let alone licked it or fucked it," I complain as I toss the ball in the air once again.

"Your next fuck will be like your first time all over again." He snickers.

"Eeejit." I throw the ball at his head and miss a second time.

To party or not to party?

Fuck it.

It's not like I've got anything better to do.

THE PARTY IS ALREADY IN FULL SWING BY THE TIME FLETCH AND I arrive.

It's a neo-Tudor-style property set in its own plot, which is just as well as there are people in various stages of undress outside, some fucking against the walls or on the grass, while others are smoking weed or vomiting up alcohol.

You know. Just the usual shenanigans that go on in the life of most nineteen-year-old students.

Sexy and I Know It is on full blast when we step inside. We're immediately slapped on the back and high-fived by our peers like we deserve recognition just for turning up. It's what comes with being so popular. Everyone wants to be your new best friend.

"Padraig." The voice is coming from behind me, so high-pitched that I'm sure the neighborhood dogs will be arriving soon.

I roll my eyes at Fletch before turning around to take in Brittany. She bats her eyelashes at me as she stands there waiting for me to admire her.

Not that I'm in any way interested, but I do the necessary by dropping my gaze to take in the short black tube dress she's barely wearing, which highlights a worked-hard-for-slim body and long shapely legs. Her tits are clearly plastic, and her dark hair is a result of extensions, or so I'm told.

Suddenly missing Jaine with her unfake everything, I now wish I hadn't bothered coming. I'd much rather be moping around my room alone.

Going by her reaction, Brittany's pleased that I've turned up and finally paid her some attention, no matter how little. She sashays over with her trusted blonde sidekick Skylar.

"I'm off to get my dick sucked," Fletch whispers. He's not even bothered to get changed. He's still wearing his basketball shorts and workout tank. He waggles his eyebrows at Skylar before taking her hand and dragging her outside.

They're not a couple or anything like that. At parties like these, most guys expect to get at least a blow job just for showing up, and most girls are only too willing to oblige.

Fellas like me and Fletch can get pretty much anything we want from any girl we want. Given Brittany's hanging off my arm with her other hand resting on the button of my jeans, it's pretty clear what she's chasing.

"Let's go get a drink." She yanks on my sleeve.

It's my turn to be fake as I force a smile before following her through the crowd of people as we make our way to the kitchen. More high fives. More smiles and nods from people I don't know but who clearly know who I am.

I pour myself a three-fingered whiskey. I wasn't going to drink, but what the hell. In my melancholy mood, drowning my sorrows may not be such a bad idea.

I instantly feel better as the amber liquid burns and then warms my throat. I quickly pour myself another, chasing the next alcoholic buzz.

"So, where's your girlfriend?" Brittany is still hanging possessively from my arm and has now put on her best pout. Apparently, she's still miffed that I chose Jaine over her.

I shrug. "I'm not sure."

I watch her lips curve slowly upward, cursing myself for being such an eejit. She's interpreted my vague response as meaning Jaine and I are having problems. Maybe we are. I pour myself another whiskey.

"Didn't you invite her along?"

"This isn't really Jaine's scene."

"But it's your scene."

I shrug. "It used to be."

"Oh, come on, Padraig. It still is." She rolls her eyes dramatically. "You haven't changed. Your tomboy girlfriend is just trying to turn you into someone as boring as she is."

"She's not boring." I defend Jaine because she's far from being boring. She's the most interesting girl I've ever met.

"You okay, bud?" Fletch slaps me on the back, a broad, shit-eating grin on his face because I'm sure his cock's now sporting Skylar's missing red lipstick.

I nod. But I'm not okay. Because the more I drink, the more convinced I am that Jaine's not interested in me. That she's still in love with the boy from her hometown and always will be.

"You need to slow down, Paddy." Fletch frowns at the new drink that's appeared in my hand courtesy of Brittany. He's not much of a drinker, hence why he's the designated driver most of the time.

Which is perhaps just as well, as I'm already feeling a wee bit worse for wear.

My tongue is stuck to the roof of my mouth, and it feels like someone's holding a pneumatic drill to the side of my head.

"Fuckin eejit," I mutter.

I know it's the after-effects of too much whiskey. It's not the first time, but I need to make sure it's the last.

While I've been with Jaine, I've been teetotal. She doesn't drink, so I've never felt the need to, either. I can take it or leave it. My problem has always been that I don't know when to stop once I get started.

Fletch did try to warn me, but I'd already downed several in the time it had taken him to get a blow job, and by then, I thought I knew best. I didn't.

I try to swallow, but there's no saliva in my mouth. How is it even possible to be dying of thirst and desperate for a piss at the same time?

I try to open my eyes, but it's way too bright. Squeezing them shut, I pull the cover over my head before attempting again. When I do, I take in pink sheets that smell of expensive perfume.

Fuck.

I swallow thickly before glancing down. As I thought, I'm stark-bollock naked. In a blind panic, I throw back the covers before sitting bolt upright and looking to my right. I'm not alone. I hoped it was Jaine. It's not.

Lying beside me in her girly bedroom is a very naked Brittany Mason. If that wasn't bad enough, on the mirrored bedside cabinet beside her is an open box of condoms and one very condemning empty foil wrapper.

What the fuck have I done?

But I know exactly what I've done. In a drunken stupor, I've obviously spilled my guts to Brittany, then, feeling sorry for myself, I used her willing pussy to salve my wounded male pride.

How could I have done that to Jaine? Even drunk, how could I have done such a fucking thing to her? She didn't deserve that. I've gone and fucked everything up.

I run my hand over my face in frustration. Why the fuck did I have to take a drink? Why the fuck couldn't I just stop at one?

Because now we're over before we've even began. Because I know what I've done, and I also know that once Jaine finds out, she will never forgive me. And it serves me right.

I'll never forgive me, either.

Jaine: *It's over.*

I DON'T NEED TO ASK WHY. WE BOTH KNOW THE ANSWER.

I'm not going to ask for a second chance. We both know she won't give me one. I know I don't deserve one.

I'm lying in my room on a bed that's never made and staring at the ceiling. Aside from taking necessary breaks, I've been lying here for a day now.

Waiting.

For something, I knew was coming. It was only ever a matter of time. What was the delay her end, I wonder? Was she lying there staring at the ceiling, too? Was she also thinking of all the stuff we had planned to do together? Stuff that we now never will because I was a fucking fool.

I should have respected her need to wait. She had her reasons. She's been hurt in the past. And here I am, hurting her all over again.

I shouldn't have made everything all about me. But I did. Because I've always been used to getting my own way. Because I've always taken and never given in return.

I wanted to give her everything because she was my everything. Now I have nothing. Because I no longer have her.

I let out a shaky breath as I brush the tears from my eyes with the back of my hand.

Padraig: *Can we still be friends, darlin'?*

Time passes.

She's going to say no. I know she is. She's going to tell me to fuck off and never darken her door again. It's no more than I deserve.

There's only one sliver of hope. I know Jaine's not the vengeful sort.

So, I lie there and pray to The Almighty that she allows me to remain part of her life. That she'd never want to let me go for good.

Because I love her. Because I miss her.

And even though we're over, I hope that in some small way she loves and misses me too, even if, in the end, she loved the other fella most.

Jaine: *Yes.*

It's a strange feeling. I've just been dumped, but I still feel like a winner as I get to keep her. And right now, I'll take anything I can get where Jaine's concerned.

Padraig: *Do you want to hear a joke?*
Jaine: *Do I have to?*
Padraig: *Don't be such a mardy arse, Jaine.*
Jaine: *Go on then.*
Padraig: *What do you call an Irishman with a bad case of chickenpox?*
Jaine: *I don't know.*
Padraig: *A lepper-chaun.*
Jaine: *I'm starting to wish I'd said no to being friends.*
Padraig: *Now, now. Don't be like that, darlin'. As my ma says, if you haven't got anything nice to say, then don't say anything at all.*
Jaine: *I'll bear that in mind. If I don't reply to the majority of your messages, then you'll know the reason why, Irish.*

I chuckle. I can't help myself. Then I lay my head back on my pillow and, with a watery smile, stare once more at the ceiling.

God, how I fucking love her.

Little did I know that, from that moment on, I would start to live for her messages and phone calls because, without her, everything seemed pointless.

Little did I know that, after her, I would ricochet from one woman to the next because none would ever compare to my Jaine Jones.

My cliché blonde. My Disney Princess. My Holy Grail of women.

And my end game that never will.

CHAPTER TEN

JAINE

12 Years Earlier (Age Nineteen)
Yale University, Connecticut

LYING ON MY BED, I WIPE AWAY TEARS BEFORE STARING AGAIN AT our text exchange.

Almost twenty-four hours ago, Sasha was told by Skylar Knox that Irish had hooked up with Brittany Mason and that they were going to be making things official between them. That they would become the new celebrity couple on campus that everyone had expected them to be right from the start.

There was no mention of the fact that he already had a girlfriend. Not that we'd ever put a label on what we were, but still. After three months, I expected more than to hear on the school grapevine that he was sleeping with someone else.

Skylar would never have told me the breaking news personally. She would never lower herself to speak to the likes of me.

I was an anomaly. A biker shit stain on their pristine world that, for one reason or another, had turned the head of the most eligible male student.

Padraig O'Connell.

Plain Jaine Jones didn't fit in with the beautiful people—the unattractive, skinny girl with the glasses and braces that kept to herself.

Most of them probably wondered why Cherry and Sasha befriended me. Most likely thought it was out of sympathy. They've assured me that wasn't the case, but if Ace and Padraig can so easily pull the wool over my eyes, maybe that's what they've been doing all this time too.

I'm not crying because of what people think of me. I'm way too thick-skinned for that. I'm crying because I expected more from him. I told him about my past. About Ace and me. I also told him I loved him.

Because I did. Because I do. Because, like Ace, I always will.

I wipe away more tears, but they're quickly replaced.

The first time in my life my heart got broken was when Ace kissed Emilia after almost kissing me the very same day. The second time was when he started ignoring me because he had started fucking her. I swore I wouldn't let it happen again, but here I am, a fool for a third time.

Third time is meant to be lucky. If this is luck, I'd much rather be unlucky for the rest of my life.

Was this because I wouldn't sleep with him? If it was then I guess it's better to find out now that he's a player and that I meant nothing. He wouldn't have slept with someone else if he truly cared about me.

Maybe it was only ever a game to him. Or maybe it was out of sympathy. Maybe he just wanted to prove to everyone that he could put a smile on the face of the ugly duckling charity case to make her feel better about herself. To convince her that she wasn't such a loser after all. Or maybe the aim was to turn her into the laughing stock on campus that she is right now.

I've been lying here staring at the ceiling, thinking of all the stuff we had planned to do together. Stuff that we now never will.

When he asked to stay friends, I couldn't say no. Because I love him. Because I already miss him. Because despite the fact that we're over, I don't want to let him go.

How pathetic am I?

Little did I know that from that moment on, I would start to look forward to his messages and his phone calls more than anything else. That his lighting up my phone screen a million times a day would light up my life just as much.

Little did I know that, in the end, I would need to speak to Padraig O'Connell every day as much as I needed air to breathe.

That he would become my life raft. My sounding board. My confidant.

Until he wasn't.

The Meeting Rooms, New York

Eoin relented in the end, but it was on the strict basis that Dec be allowed to wait outside the entire time. I wanted to argue that I'm sure Dec had far better things to do with his evening than babysit me, but I knew there was no point.

I'm filled with trepidation.

Not at reacquainting myself with the people from my past. It's because, all day long, my gut has been telling me that something's going to go down tonight, and it's seldom wrong. I allow Dec to escort me to the entrance as agreed before making my way inside.

I spoke to Fletch earlier. He explained that he'd extended the invitation to include some of his other peer groups as several of our crowd couldn't make it, Cherry and Sasha being two.

The positive is that if I do decide to leave sooner rather than later, it's unlikely I'll be missed, which is good given my gut is already telling me to turn around. Irish apparently didn't even bother to RSVP, and he won't just turn up unannounced.

The familiar venue affords the same pomp and circumstance it always does, with everything looking like it's been touched by Midas in advance. I barely get a chance to glance around the ostentatious environment before I hear a familiar laughing voice.

"Well, if it isn't Jaine Jones."

I spin around to take in a smiling Fletch. He looks exactly the same, his shaggy blonde hair tied back at the nape of his neck. To fit in with our over-the-top surroundings, he's wearing a black suit on his tall, lean frame, a crisp white open-necked shirt finishing off his professional image.

I always liked Fletch. Most of the nineteen-year-old boys I knew back then only had one thing on their minds. He was one of the few that could hold an adult conversation that didn't include the words 'fucking' or 'blow job.'

Then again, I was with Irish, so it was most likely out of respect for his friend more than anything else.

"Well, if it isn't Cody Fletcher," I respond, matching his smile.

He gives me the once over as I stand in a black evening gown. It's not in a leering way, so I don't take any offense. My smile widens when he lets out a complimentary low whistle.

"Well, you've certainly changed, Jaine." He pulls me in for a hug, and I return his embrace. "Where's the tank and combats?"

"Where's the tank and shorts?" I quip back. "How have you been?"

He grins broadly at my question. "Taking London by storm, but then you'll have done your homework in advance, so I'm sure you're already aware of what I've been up to in my business life."

I chuckle because he's right. "Senior partner at Crown and Temple and currently vying for the CEO position. You've obviously been dedicated to your craft since leaving school."

"Not as dedicated as you, it would seem. Your name is above the door of one of the most prestigious legal firms stateside, and if that wasn't enough, you've only gone and added an accountancy string to your bow. I think we would all have to agree that you've been the most successful out of all of us who managed to graduate."

I accept a flute of sparking water from one of the passing waiters. "It depends on how you measure success. Most went on to work for family organizations, as you know, and there aren't many who would wish to interact with the majority of my clients, let alone take their chances by agreeing to represent them on a legal playing field."

He waggles his eyebrows at me. "Yes, you managed to keep your background well and truly hidden, didn't you? Paddy the Irish mobster, and Jaine the outlaw biker. It's no wonder you two were so well matched."

I smile politely. "We weren't that well-suited given what happened." I raise my hand to take a sip of water. As I do he glances at the vulgar engagement ring Eoin insists I wear. "But that's a story for another time, perhaps," I cut the conversation short when I notice the girl partially responsible for my heart being broken that third time.

Brittany Mason.

It takes two to tango. She was the female who willingly spread her legs for Irish while he was with me. It's like déjà vu. She hasn't changed. She even has Skylar Knox by her side, and still hanging on her every word.

A plethora of emotions run through me, none of which are positive, but I show nothing outwardly. There's no point. Time has moved on. It was twelve years ago now.

A lifetime.

None of us can change what happened in the past, no matter how much we may wish to.

I observe the pair as they make their way over. Black seems to be the color of the evening. Like me, Brittany and Skylar are also dressed head to toe in black. Brittany in a sequin gown, Skylar in a simple skater-style dress.

Is it a reunion or a funeral?

I guess there's an element of the latter, as I suspect Brittany's about to attempt to bury the hatchet.

When they reach us, Fletch snakes his arm around Skylar's waist. Has the reunion seen them pick up where they left off, or is this something else? It's then I notice the sparkling engagement ring on her finger.

"You remember Skylar, don't you, Jaine?"

I smile warmly at the blonde. Her eyes scan me from head to toe, but not in the bitchy way they did back then.

"It's good to see you again, Skylar." She smiles, and it's sincere. "Are congratulations in order?" I look at the ring and then between them both.

She smiles up at Fletch, her face glowing with happiness.

"Yes." She beams at me. "It's part of the reason we've flown in. So Cody could ask my daddy for my hand."

I'm pleased for her. She was obsessed with Fletch back then, and all he did was use her mouth as a convenient receptacle for his cum in between fucking his way through a long line of other girls.

Not that they were an item back then so I guess Skylar knew what she was signing herself up for. I'm not sure I could have been with someone who treated me like a cum slut, but I guess we're all different.

I finally turn to look at *her*.

"It's good to see you, Brittany." It's a lie, obviously. It's not good to see her. She changed the course of my life when she willingly spread her legs, although the fact remains that Irish is still the one who cheated.

"Is it?"

I frown inwardly at her response, but her face gives nothing away. Up close, it's clear that she hasn't aged quite as well as Skylar, but she's still extremely beautiful. I can see what Padraig saw in her.

She looks so much like Emilia. It's like God was trying to punish me twice over with the same goddamn girl.

"Can I have a word in private, please, Jaine?"

I want to say no and run. Instead, I nod without speaking, my stomach instantly tying itself in knots. She's going to tell me something I don't want to hear. I know because I've been expecting it all day.

We're watched by Fletch and Skylar as we make our way toward the restroom. From their silent perusal, it doesn't take a genius to work out that they already know what news she's going to break.

We make our way inside, allowing the restroom door to close quietly behind us.

Silence. Blinding. Unwelcoming.

We stand side by side at the restroom mirror, each staring at the other's reflection. We're of a similar height, but my build is much slighter, and her olive skin and dark hair contrast my tanned, blonde appearance.

"You look good, Jaine."

"Thank you."

What else is there to say? She can clearly see that I'm no longer the ugly duckling I once was. The braces have gone. The glasses have gone. I've lost weight recently, so I'm slimmer, but given the year I've had, right now, I just feel lucky to be alive.

"You look well, too," I add. Manners cost nothing, and she does look good.

She smiles weakly. "Congratulations on all of your successes since leaving Yale. You've achieved a lot. Way more than the rest of us."

I nod. She's buying time, nothing more. These are delaying tactics for something she wants to say but doesn't. I know she didn't do anything with her qualification, so it's not like we can compare legal resumes. She married a billionaire, became a full-time wife, and moved to Houston.

Is she happy? She doesn't look particularly so, but maybe that's got more to do with what she's about to reveal.

"What is it you want to say, Brittany?" I cut to the chase.

"I'm sorry."

Two words, followed by more silence. We both know what's she apologizing for. She doesn't have to spell it out. It's twelve years overdue, but I guess it's better late than never. I don't respond because, going by the way she's wringing her hands, she hasn't finished getting whatever this is off her chest.

"I'd always liked Padraig, and I know he liked me too until you came along that is." Her tone isn't accusatory in any way. It's just matter of fact. "I was jealous. All the girls were. That he turned all of us down and instead…."

"Settled for a plain Jaine like me," I interject.

She nods sheepishly, then frowns. "Jaine, what I did… I'm not proud of it. I wasn't then, and I'm not now, regardless of what you may think. I had no choice but to keep up the pretense."

The warning bells are now ringing so loud they're deafening.

I'm tempted to ask her to stop. That as much as this may be a salve for her guilt, her spilling her guts isn't going to help me. Her clearing her conscience is just going to cause my life to implode once more.

"What pretense?" My mouth feels dry. Why the fuck am I asking when I know it's going to be something I don't want to hear?

Please, God, don't let it be what I think it is.

"When Padraig and Fletch came to the party that night, Paddy began drinking heavily. He was upset. He didn't drink often, but when he did, he just never knew when to stop. That night, he kept on going. In the end, I took him upstairs….to my bedroom. It wasn't pre-meditated. I was just going to let him sleep it off. He was crying. He kept telling me how much he loved you, but that he thought you didn't love him. That there was a boy from your past you were so hung up on you couldn't or wouldn't commit to him."

She bites her lip nervously as we approach the crux of the admission.

"He passed out not long after. When the party ended and before I went to bed, I removed his clothes, then mine. Then I staged the condoms."

My blood is pounding in my ears as my life since that moment flashes in front of my eyes. A life that could have been very different.

"What exactly are you saying, Brittany?"

"Padraig and I never had sex. I saw an opportunity. I thought if you didn't want him and he thought we'd slept together, that we could become a couple. We didn't. It was quite the opposite. When he looked at me afterward, all I did was remind him of what he'd lost. I couldn't say anything back then. Not without making myself look like a loser."

"But you didn't mind making me look like one," I bite.

"I'm sorry, Jaine. I wish I could take it all back. I've wanted to tell you so many times, but I needed to do it face-to-face so you'd know how truly sorry I am. I didn't want to be cowardly about it."

I stare at her reflection. Her expression is riddled with guilt as she continues to wring her hands.

Does she feel better now? Well, fuck her and fuck her guilty conscience. What about my life?

What about Irish's life?

My nose starts tingling as I struggle to hold back twelve years' worth of tears.

"Did you have any idea how much I loved him?" My whispered voice breaks as the memory of his betrayal hits me like a sucker punch.

A betrayal that never fucking was.

"As much as he loved you, I'd imagine. Drunk or sober, he would never have slept with me, Jaine. I realized that the next morning, but by then, it was too late to turn back."

I swallow lumps of pain, regret, self-pity, and anger. It's all in there, and it all tastes fucking vile.

"All this time, I thought he cheated on me," I sob-whisper.

"He didn't. He would never have cheated on you. He loved you so much. He'd just managed to convince himself that you didn't love him back."

I stare at my reflection. At the blonde girl in the mirror who has silent tears running down her cheeks over what might have been.

Things happen for a reason, I know that better than most. Who's to say things would have worked out for us even if we had stayed together? His head may have always been turned by beautiful girls with olive skin and dark hair.

Like Brittany. Like Emilia.

"All I ask is that you let me tell him," I say as I wipe fresh tears from my cheeks.

She nods in silent agreement.

Leaving the restroom, I take in the frowns that both Skylar and Fletch are wearing.

They knew. They all knew. And yet they said nothing.

They've allowed me to believe the worst of him for twelve years. Worst still, for twelve years, they've allowed Irish to believe the worst of himself.

CHAPTER ELEVEN

PADRAIG

Padraig's Apartment, Hudson Yards, New York

I GLANCE AROUND MY APARTMENT, TAKING IN THE FAMILIAR CREAM and navy décor. Is it good to be back? I'm still undecided.

It feels like I've entered the twilight zone.

Nothing's changed here in my own space, but in the outside world, everything has. What's reality and what isn't? Through choice, reality isn't something I've faced up to in a long time.

There is one apology I do have to make.

Padraig: *Hi, Fletch. It's Paddy. Sorry, I couldn't make your reunion. I've only just got back to New York. I was going to drop in unannounced, but the flight was delayed.*
Fletch: *No worries, bud. Maybe we can catch up before I have to fly back to London? It's a shame you couldn't make*

it. An old acquaintance of yours turned up, although she didn't stay very long.

I wait for him to continue, but he doesn't. Same old Fletch. Annoying fucker.

Padraig: *Don't keep me in suspense.*
Fletch: *Jaine.*

I almost drop my phone. So, she is back in New York. Unless she's just flown in for the reunion, but then why fly all that way not to stay longer?

Padraig: *How was she?*
Fletch: *Her business is doing well, and she looked beautiful —quite the transformation.*
Padraig: *She was always beautiful.*

And she was. It fucks me off that no one could ever see past her braces and glasses.

Fletch: *She was also sporting a rather vulgar engagement ring.*

So she has moved on. I can see he's still typing so I wait.

Fletch: *She and Brittany had a private conversation.*
Padraig: *About?*
Fletch: *There's only one person and one event they would ever be conversing about.*
Padraig: *Mind telling me what was said?*

Fletch: *If you want to know more, you'll need to get it straight from the horse's mouth.*
Padraig: *Brittany?*
Fletch: *Jaine.*
Padraig: *We don't talk these days.*
Fletch: *Sorry, bud, but my lips are sealed. Jaine asked Brittany to keep it to herself, and that command has been passed down to Skylar and me.*
Padraig: *Was it anything important?*
Fletch: *You'll have to ask Jaine. Anyway, let me know what your movements are. I'll be in New York for another week before flying back to the UK.*
Padraig: *Congratulations, by the way. I'm glad you finally decided to make an honest woman of Skylar. It seems only fair, given how many times she sucked you off. Your cock must be permanently imprinted on the inside of her mouth.*
Fletch: *Why do you think I'm marrying her?*

I smile before placing the phone on the table. Did Brittany give Jaine the lowdown on what happened, or did she pull her aside to apologize?

I'll never know the answer. I'll never know what happened that fateful night either since I can't remember a thing. At least, that's something to be thankful for.

No flashbacks.

My smile quickly evaporates. The news of Jaine's engagement now sitting like a dead weight in my chest where my heart used to be.

Was I secretly hoping he'd say something I wanted to hear? Like she missed me or that she loved me still? In the end, all I got was the confirmation I'd known all along. That in three years, she's never looked back once.

Jealousy claws at my gut. I never expected her to move on so soon after Ace.

Who with?

Not that it's any of my business. I just pray to God that it's not someone I know. That really would be rubbing salt in a wound that refuses to heal.

At the end of the day, she's following her path the same as I'm having to follow mine. It's unlikely they'll ever cross in the future, so it doesn't matter who.

Why would they cross? We lived in the same city before and managed to go nine years without bumping into each other. Was that intentional or not? I'm not entirely sure. I never really gave it much thought.

We spoke so often back then, it didn't seem to matter that we didn't physically see each other. I didn't go out of my way to avoid her. Did she try to avoid me?

Probably.

I cheated on her, after all. Why would she have wanted a constant reminder of that in her face?

Anyway, I'm sure she'll let me know through Dylan if her conversation with Brittany contained anything for my ears.

Sitting on the leather sectional, I stare at the crystal decanter across the room. I ignore its temptation these days because I can. Both single biggest mistakes of my life were caused by consuming way too much of that toxic liquid.

It caused me to fuck Brittany. It caused me to fuck Sophia.

I can't undo the past, so my future means having to live with the consequences of both those regrets. If I want to avoid any more mistakes, I have to learn to live without the drink.

I glance around my apartment once more. Now we're back in New York, Sophia and I have agreed to live separately. She wants me to keep our mutual agreement to myself by pretending to the outside world, including my own family, that we're a happily married couple.

I'm not sure why. Everyone is aware that ours was a marriage of convenience. A union forged for political gain and not much else.

Perhaps she'll find herself a fuck buddy. I'm not bothered either way. I know she won't grant me the same leeway, not that I'd be interested.

I'm Sophia's possession and will remain so until the marriage is annulled, although it's unlikely that will ever be agreed to.

It won't be Sophia who'll hold me to ransom. It'll be Luc. The Dusters are a big fish in our world. With me as his brother-in-law, he has an automatic alliance with my family. I can't see him relinquishing that priceless relationship any time soon, if ever.

I stare into space. In Sicily, I had nothing much to do, so one day tended to just bleed into the next, but now I'm back, I feel restless. My mind keeps drifting back to Jaine. I don't want to sit here and wallow in self-pity.

Did Dylan see me enter my apartment? Should I message him? He won't message me. Not when I placed a do not disturb sign on my existence twelve months ago.

I cross the room, access the panel then switch off all the security for the apartment. If I've to keep up the pretense of being a happily married man, I don't need an observant Dylan witnessing that I'm not. If I have any visitors and they notice the lack of Sophia-related items, I'll just say we're living at her place in the main.

I look at the clock—nine p.m.

The hands seem to be turning slower than they would normally. I should make the most of it. I'll be back on the Duster treadmill soon enough. I then realize I don't want to make the most of it. I've been in storage long enough. Should I go to my parents' now or leave it until morning?

I guess there's no time like the present.

The O'Connell Home, Darling, New York

I stand outside the gated entrance, having caught a cab.

It didn't seem right letting one of our drivers know I was back before I'd told any of my immediate family. Had I used one of our own people, I'd also have felt obliged to converse.

About married life. About my wife. About what I've been doing these past twelve months.

Marriage sucks. My wife is on paper only. And I've been doing nothing.

I'm not sure they'd have appreciated that response. It may have made things rather awkward, but then I no longer wish to partake in idle chit-chat. I no longer feel the need to fill silences with the sound of my own voice.

It's a clear night, so the temperature is frigid. Staring up at the array of stars, I consider my current dilemma. How to get past the Fort Knox security.

I have two options. I can either call Ma or I can call our Dylan.

I'm nervous when contemplating talking to my brother after all this time, but I dial his number anyway.

"How's it hanging?" An alien silence follows my opening line of old. I shuffle awkwardly on my feet while waiting for him to respond, watching as my warm breath collides with the cold air.

"Paddy." He sounds shocked.

"Dylan, I'm…."

"Are you back?" I can't miss the underlying worry in his tone. Worry over what exactly?

"I'm standing outside Ma's house. I need the code for the walk-in gates."

"You're outside the house? Right now?" His worry encroaches on disbelief. What the fuck is going on?

"That's what I just said, brother. Now, it's freezing, so I'd appreciate you giving me the code so I can get inside."

"I'll message it to you now."

My phone vibrates, letting me know it's been received, and I key in the digits.

"We weren't expecting you, Paddy. You never mentioned anything."

"I wanted it to be a surprise."

"Well, it's definitely that."

I get the distinct impression that it's not being seen as a good one.

I approach the mansion-like property, striding up the driveway and welcoming the familiar sound of gravel crunching under my feet.

I can't help but feel deflated at the lack of warm reception. I thought Dylan would be full of questions or at least have given me a sign that he was happy about my return.

Instead, his stilted responses are having the opposite effect. They're making me feel like I'm about to rock the boat and disturb the sea of peace and tranquility they've all created for themselves in my absence.

Would they rather I not have returned? Would they rather I turn around, go back to Sicily, and continue to exist on my own?

It's clearly been a case of out of sight and mind, but then what did I expect? I can't cut off communications then expect them to welcome my unexpected return with open arms. It's been a year. Everyone has moved on. It's just me who's been stagnating.

"Paddy, there's something you should know."

I force a laugh. "I'm sure there's plenty I should know, Dyl, but

I'll worry about all that tomorrow. I'm fucked. I just want to let our parents know that I'm back."

That I'm still alive. *That I'm still existing.*

"Anyway, I'm outside the front door. I'll give you a call on the way back. And can you sort out my old cell number? I'd like to switch back now that I've returned to New York."

More hesitation. Why?

"Will do, brother."

As I disconnect the call, I notice the two cars outside. Ma doesn't have her own, as Liam drives her everywhere. Da always has a Duster SUV at home, just in case, which accounts for one of the vehicles. Why are there two parked up? Do they have visitors?

I'm tempted to flee back to my apartment. Unlike the Paddy of old, I'm not in the mood for being the center of attention or being expected to spin a joke at every turn.

I attempt to open the front door, surprised to find it locked. It's never locked unless everyone is already in bed, but they can't be as the lights are still on inside. I press the bell and wait. Not ten seconds later, the door is flung open.

His hair is whiter, and he looks older, but aside from that, he's the same. I smile at my da.

"Padraig." A whispered voice as a myriad of emotions crosses his face, the marred forehead he ends up wearing letting me know that the negatives far outweigh the positives. His look matches Dylan's worried, less than receptive responses.

He's clearly pleased but not pleased that I'm back, the frown he's wearing letting me know that the arrow is swinging more toward the latter.

I guess my turning up unannounced hasn't given them any time to prepare. *Prepare for what?*

He stares at me like he's wondering what to do with me. Like he can't even decide whether or not to invite me into my own family home. I feel my nose tingling as my emotions threaten to get the better of me.

Is it wrong that I expected more? That I needed more? That after twelve months of being a nobody, I wanted to feel like a somebody again? That I wanted to feel important? To someone. To fucking anyone.

I don't want to be alone anymore.

Welcome home, Paddy.

"Well, aren't you going to invite me in?" I suddenly feel awkward, wishing I'd just told them of my plans because, right now, I feel like an outsider in my own family.

They clearly don't want me here. If I don't belong here, then where do I belong?

Nowhere.

"Yes, of course. Come in, son." He steps aside to let me pass, then pulls me in for a hug, causing the sob I've been holding in these past twelve months to escape. His hold around me tightens further, but he says nothing.

I'm surrounded by the familiarity of my childhood home with its flocked wallpaper and smell of home cooking, and I'm being embraced by my da—a man who's meant to love me no matter what. But right now, I don't feel loved. Right now, I feel unwanted.

Like an inconvenience.

He releases me. I don't look at him. Instead, my eyes immediately scan the shrine of photos to see if any new ones have been added. Something that could perhaps give me a visual indication of what's changed in my absence, as something clearly has given my own family appears to no longer wish to have me around.

My gaze stops on the image of a little boy.

His hair is as black as coal, and it's contrasted by the pale skin of the Irish. Blue eyes sparkle on his little face, and he's holding a soft toy in his hand, his exposed chubby arm clearly displaying the O'Connell horseshoe birthmark.

I stare at the image, my brain trying to connect the dots. He can't have been born in my absence as he's maybe two years old. Is he the son of one of my cousins? The other wall is usually for images of our Irish kin. This spot reserved for our immediate family. Maybe it's an old pic of one of us. That'll be it.

"Who's at the door, Fergal?" Ma shouts.

Da smiles at me for the first time, but it's little salve to the feeling of rejection that now threatens to overwhelm me. I follow him into the kitchen. I can hear her muttering away to herself as we approach. I'm finally greeted by the familiar sight of her in her twinset and pearls, finished off with sheepskin slippers.

"Fergal." She spins around, no doubt to have a go at him for not answering her straight away. The plate she was holding slips through her fingers and drops to the floor the moment she takes me in.

Old age has shrunk her further, and she has fewer stubborn auburn streaks in her hair these days, but Ma still looks the same apart from that.

"Padraig." A whisper as she lifts her hand to her mouth in shock before exhaling. It's the sound of acceptance. Acceptance of what? I don't get a chance to dwell on it.

I hear the footsteps before I see the person. It'll be the owner of the other SUV parked up outside, but then why is Ma wearing slippers if she has a guest?

"Roisin, I heard a smash. Is everything okay?"

A west coast accent. It's still the most beautiful thing I've ever fucking heard. It can't be. Not here. Not now. Surely to God, I'm hearing things.

I turn around, my eyes taking in her straight up and down frame before coming to rest on her heart-shaped face with its pouty lips and eyes as green as emeralds. The perfection that The Almighty crafted just for me. Or so I'd once hoped, prayed, dreamed.

"Jaine." I'm not sure it's even audible, which is just as well as it would have collided with the single word she uttered. A word I thought I'd never hear again.

The best fucking word in the world.

"Irish."

CHAPTER TWELVE

JAINE

The O'Connell Home, Darling, New York

"Irish."

My name for him slips from my mouth, then time stands still as I take in my eldest son's daddy. The boy I fell in love with when I was nineteen years old. The boy I'm still in love with even now. The boy who broke my heart that third time, but, in the end, he didn't because earlier today, I found out that he never even cheated.

How do I feel about that reveal? I'm not sure. It's only been a few hours. I'm still trying to process it.

And now here he is.

I'm not sure where I find the strength to remain upright as I take in the boy with the inky black hair and eyes the exact shade of sparkling blue as his son's. My love for him is threatening to overwhelm me right now.

He stares at me. I stare at him.

I've waited so long to see him, and yet I'm so fucking unprepared. We all are.

I was grateful Eoin was away today so I could have time to reflect on my life. On what might have been. One thing I do know is that me being in possession of that knowledge back then would have changed everything.

My Irish.

Me and him. Him and me.

Marriage. Children. The Disney princess could have had her happily ever after with her prince after all.

Then again, maybe not.

Fate played the cards he did for a reason, I'm sure. And time decides who you meet in your life and in which order.

I love Ace. I love Eoin.

But all paths were always going to lead to this moment of truth. Because the truth will always out, even if it takes twelve years.

"Our souls have always been intertwined. You feel that too, darlin'?"

I feel our connection like a second heartbeat. A bond so strong that it's stood the test of time, no matter the distance. Fragile and stretched to almost breaking point at times, but it's still there, or at least, for me, it is.

He's married to Sophia. He can't feel it any longer.

You and Eoin have my blessing to move on with your lives together, darlin'. I wish you all the best.

Twenty generic words.

He allowed me to move on with his brother. Surely that's proof that he doesn't need or want me anymore. If that wasn't the final nail in the coffin that contained him and me, then I'm not sure what was.

I love him. Always have. Always will. But he doesn't love me.

We've moved on. This is simply a crossroads, but neither of us can deviate from the path we're already on. Our ship has sailed.

Fin.

What to say? How to say it? When to say it? Because it must be said.

He's showed up unannounced, that much is clear going by the shock still registered on the faces of Roisin and Fergal.

No one's taken the time to plan, even though we've had twelve months to prepare for this day.

The ducks are not in a row, and right now, everyone is afraid to open their mouths. No one is singing from the same hymn sheet because no one knows the words. No one knows which song it is we should all have been rehearsing.

"What's going on?" A voice that's deep and sensual with just the perfect hint of Irish lilt. A voice I never thought I'd hear again any time soon.

"There was a drive-by shooting. We believe Fin was the target. It was suggested I stay in the safe space underneath the property with the kids until the person responsible is found." I'm surprised by how composed my voice sounds when I feel so fucking overwhelmed.

He searches my face. Is he looking for signs that I'm lying to him? I'm not. At least, not about that.

"I guess there's a lot I'm not aware of." He sounds almost defeated.

"You've been gone for twelve months, son," Fergal speaks quietly. "A lot's changed since then."

We all turn toward the front door as it opens and then closes. Three of us know exactly who it is.

Eoin strides into the kitchen, his face remaining impressively impassive as he takes in his youngest sibling, even though he must be as surprised as the rest of us.

"It's good to see you, Paddy."

"Is it?" Irish mumbles his response as he glances at his brother before turning and leaving the room. We all stare at each other as the front door opens and closes once more, signaling the fact that he's gone.

He clearly didn't feel welcome by his own family in his own home, and I can't help but feel responsible for that.

I CAN'T DEAL.

I didn't want to listen to the guaranteed fallout after Irish left. I knew all eyes would be firmly fixed on me, waiting to gauge my reaction to his unexpected return, so I excused myself by pretending I was going to the restroom, then I left too.

I walked to the rear of the property, got on my hog, and drove out the gates. Once I'd driven around the corner, I pulled up before sending a message to both Roisin and Duke.

> **Jaine:** *I've gone for a ride to get some air. The kids are tucked up in bed. I've left the monitor in the kitchen.*

I then head out of town. I know exactly where I'm going.

Thirty minutes later, I turn off the highway, driving over the same uneven terrain as before until I pull up in front of the small boating lake.

Dismounting my hog, I stare across the water, watching as the moonlight kisses the surface, resulting in its silvery reflection being bestowed back on itself. A lone owl hoots.

Is it the same one? Can he remember me being here from the first time around?

It's peaceful. Tranquil. Still. Everything is the same as it was before. There's only one thing missing.

Irish.

It's been three years since I was last here, having just shot Lebedev in the head. We then waited in the vehicle, not knowing whether the pedo fucker was alive or dead.

Three fucking years.

It feels like the blink of an eye, but so much has happened since.

I'd never been here before that night, and I've never been back since, so I guess this is our place.

Little did I know, I was already pregnant with Fin when we were here last. Our son. A child he still knows nothing about.

I sink to my knees as the day finally takes its toll, my tears turning cold as they run down my face. I don't even know why I'm crying.

I'm happy. He's happy. Surely, it's enough?

Maybe I'm just grieving what we had. What we will never have again. There's no escaping reality now that he's back. A past with him. A future without. My present is right here, right now.

Is it the gift everyone claims it is?

My phone vibrates in my pocket. I don't want to look at it. I don't want to answer any questions.

Where are you? Don't you understand the risks we're all facing?

Fuck it. None of that matters right now.

"What do I do, Ace!" I raise my face and yell at the star-laden sky. My question is met with another lonely hoot from the owl, followed by blinding silence.

Words spoken. Words unheard.

Time passes. My tears dry.

Do I tell Irish about my conversation with Brittany? What's the point when what happened in the past won't impact the future?

When do I tell him about our son? Fin's parentage can't be kept a secret forever. In fact, his being targeted is likely because someone already knows.

What a fucking mess.

I pull out my phone before removing it from the case and staring at the photo of me and Irish.

Back then, everything was so easy until it wasn't. A past of lies and deceit resulting in a present of tears and regrets.

I stare at the screen.

Half a dozen missed calls from Eoin and three messages from Dylan.

Dylan: *Jaine.*
Dylan: *Jaine!*
Dylan: *Jaine, Eoin is going nuts.*

Staring up at the night sky once more, I curse quietly. I'm sick of hearing how everything I do adversely affects Eoin. What about the effects all his restrictions are having on me? Why is it okay for him to live his life as normal but not for me to do the same?

Misogynistic bastard.

Jaine: *I needed space.*
Dylan: *Jaine, you can't go off without letting anyone know.*
Jaine: *I let Duke and Roisin know.*
Dylan: *After you'd ridden off into the night on your hog.*

Breathe in. Breathe out.

I'm reaching breaking point. I try to compose myself before dialing his number, and he answers immediately.

"Listen, Dyl. After the day I've had, I refuse to ask permission to take a ride on my hog so I can clear my own goddamn head. You and

I both know that even if I asked nicely, Eoin wouldn't have allowed me to venture out into the big bad world on my own. Right now, I've had it with being smothered and told what I can and can't do!"

"But you know the reasons, Jaine."

"I'm a grown woman. I've stared death in the face more times than I can count and lived to tell the tale. I can look after myself. I don't need your big brother's protection twenty-four-seven. As far as I'm concerned, if my number's up, it's up."

"You need to tell him, Jaine."

I snort at the same repetitive bullshit. "If you can swear that my telling him will see him tone his possessiveness down, then I'll call him right now and spill my guts."

His silence speaks volumes. He knows as well as I do that rather than grant me access to the freedom I need to live my own life, my reveal could have quite the opposite effect.

"Can I at least tell him you've made contact and where you are?"

"You can tell him I've made contact but not where I am."

"Can you at least tell *me* where you are? I promise I won't breathe a word."

"A boating lake."

"Does it have a name?"

"I'm not sure what it's called. Irish brought me here once. It was after I carried out the hit on Lebedev."

"I think I know the one. Our parents used to take us there when we were kids." He pauses. "Why did you go there, Jaine?"

He lets out a sigh when I don't reply. I'm not sure why he's even asking. He knows exactly why I came here. Because of the memories it holds. Memories I had boxed away as I had no one else to share them with. Until now.

"No one knew he was coming back. We're all just as shocked as you are." He continues when I don't respond. "Anyway, how did the reunion go."

I snort. "Today really was a day full of surprises."

"What do you mean?"

"The girl Irish cheated on me with was there. It turns out she lied and then decided to keep up the pretense for twelve years."

"What do you mean she lied?"

"Irish didn't cheat on me after all. She made it up because she wanted him for herself."

Deafening silence.

He knows now why I needed this time to clear my head. It's not just because Irish showed up unannounced. It's because if I'd known then what I know now, we'd never have split up in the first place.

Eventually, he speaks. "Are you going to tell him?"

"No, and you're not going to tell him either."

Telling that truth won't help either of us. It won't change anything. We've both moved on.

"What about Fin?"

"I'll discuss that with the others when I get back. I appreciate the risks involved in Sophia knowing, but the way I see it, someone likely knows his true parentage anyway, so it's only a matter of time before it becomes public knowledge."

"The family may still ask you to keep up the pretense a little longer while they take stock of the Ruocco situation."

"Then we'll agree on a timeframe, but when it's reached, I'm telling Irish everything."

CHAPTER THIRTEEN

PADRAIG

The Hudson Dusters' HQ, Manhattan, New York

I THOUGHT MY EXISTENCE COULDN'T GET ANY WORSE.

It turns out it can.

Not only is the girl I'll forever be in love with going to take the vows with my eldest brother for a second time, but apparently they also share a child together.

I'm still processing the events of yesterday. From the unwelcoming reception afforded me by my own flesh and blood to this soul-destroying admission Dylan insisted on delivering on the phone last night.

Apparently, there's more, but that's all he felt able to share. The only reason he said anything at all is so I was prepared in advance.

Did Jaine fuck Eoin before or after she told me that she didn't love me? Did he spurn her in the end? Is that why she hated him so much? Not that it really matters.

This is simply a case of me being served my just desserts for cheating.

Apparently, Jaine had been passing Fin off as Ace's, and when he lost his life, and she returned to New York, she came clean and admitted that he's a Duster.

Eoin has a son. Something I'll never have because I'd only ever want to have a family with her, and now she's marrying him.

I'm worried if I let the reality of my situation sink in, I'll plummet so low that I'll never fucking recover. I'm barely surviving as it is. But what's the point in surviving when you have nothing left to live for?

And now I'm sitting in the meeting room beside my cousin, Aidan, having to pretend everything is okay. It's not. It never will be again.

I'm tempted to stand up, take center stage as the Paddy of old would have done before announcing that the fella in front of them who's trying his hardest to appear happy is a bare-faced fucking liar. That it's all just make-believe.

A pantomime.

Only this Prince Charming didn't get his Disney princess. In the end, he was forced to accept the hand of the wicked fairy, and the wish she granted him as a wedding gift was a shitty existence that he wouldn't wish on his own worst enemy.

But that's fine. Just you lot move along with your perfect lives. There's nothing to see here. Don't mind me being my usual mardy-arsed self because I'm stuck in an existence *you* inflicted on me.

I'll just sit back and watch while my reason for living lives her best life with my own fucking brother.

According to Dylan, she's in love with Eoin, and he her. What above my love? What the fuck do I do with that. Do I shelve it as it's now been superseded by his?

The bitter taste of self-pity laces my tongue, and it's causing me to feel resentful, more so because I can't say how I feel.

Pent-up emotions aren't my thing. I'm the type of fella who wears his heart on his sleeve. I always have been. I used to be able to talk to Jaine about these sorts of things.

Once upon a fucking time.

I want to feel sorry for myself, but I can't because, on the surface, I have to wear a painted-on smile and pretend to be happily married to Sophia.

I have to grin and bear it, but I don't know if I can right now. I don't know if I've got that amount of effort left in me after twelve fucking years of pining.

Eoin knew how much I loved Jaine. How much I still love her. Why would he do such a thing? I'm his brother. He should never have gone anywhere near her.

For now, I'll try my best to say nothing, but me and him are on a promise. That selfish fecker has taken away my reason for breathing. Jaine was *my* reason for being, not his. What do I do now that I have none?

Stop breathing?

"So, you say Luc traveled back with you and Sophia, Paddy?"

Da interrupts my thoughts as he sits there with his blank pad open in front of him. Some things never change. All eyes are now fixed on me.

"He did. Two days ago."

"And they've not mentioned anything about this new faction they're supposedly setting up?"

Dylan told me all about that fiasco too. The fact that my contract marriage was all for nothing in the end as Luciano is no longer don of the Sicilian mafia. I want to have a go at my family for that, but I can't.

And what would be the point? It wouldn't change anything. My complaint would fall on deaf ears since they don't seem to give a fuck about me anymore.

"Nothing."

"Surely, they must have mentioned something over the past twelve months." Jaine frowns at me as she voices the reasonable question. I can understand her frustrations. Ace was murdered. Eoin almost lost his life taking a bullet with Fin's name on it.

What she doesn't realize is that I spent my days alone trying to heal and get over her. It's clear she never had any problems getting over me or getting under my eldest brother.

"I never paid any attention to what they discussed."

"Jesus Christ. Did you not think to listen in?"

"Did you not think to not cheat on me with my own fucking brother?"

The bitter words slip from my mouth. Whether it was actual cheating or not, it still feels that way. She looks emotional. The dark circles around her eyes a clear indication that she's not slept a wink.

That makes two of us.

I feel Eoin's fury radiate across the table. If that fucker wants to take this to the containers, bring it on. There's a key difference between me and him. I was born the way I am. He was made the way he is.

Paddy, the emotional sibling. Happy-go-lucky Paddy. Paddy, the life and soul.

I'm all of those things until I'm pushed. And right now, I've been pushed so fucking far I'm worried I'll never find my way back.

I smile at him. He knows it's a silent offer. An offer he won't accept unless he has a death wish.

Jaine puts her hand on his arm, and he turns his head in her direction. I don't want him calmed down, and definitely not by her. I don't want him fucking touching her. She's mine. Not his.

Self-pity infuses with jealousy.

Right now, sibling or not, I want to kill the fucker with my bare hands.

He turns his attention back to me. We both know this is unfinished business. Everyone around the table realizes that.

"Don't speak to Jaine like that ever again."

I stare at him before turning to look at her once more. "I apologize, Jaine. I should have paid more attention. I'll be sure to listen in to my wife and brother-in-law's private conversations more closely moving forward."

I don't let on that it will be nigh on impossible for me to do so, given Sophia and I don't even live together.

Jaine stares at me, her expression unreadable.

The tension in the room is now so thick you could cut it with a knife. I take that as my cue to leave.

CHAPTER FOURTEEN

JAINE

The O'Connell Home, Darling, New York

IRISH HAS AVOIDED ME SINCE HIS RETURN A WEEK AGO. I REALIZE he's been licking the wounds of betrayal. Even though he's moved on, he still feels let down by Eoin and me.

He's also been spending time with his folks, trying to salvage a relationship that was fractured when the welcome they showed him was lukewarm at best.

I didn't take offense to what he said in the Duster meeting. How could I, when I completely understood the reason behind his cutting comeback?

In just under two months, the truth will be revealed to him. We'll unearth what we can in that timeframe, and if we're no further forward, then all bets are off. There will be no extension of time. I refuse to lie to Irish beyond that. I refuse to keep the knowledge from him that he has a son.

I appreciate the risks to my boys and me if Sophia and Luc are involved, but the way I see it, there will always be threats in this life. Maybe not so big, blatant, or directed quite so personally at me and my family, but they'll always be there all the same, covert or otherwise.

When all is revealed, Irish will then know that I never cheated on him, like I know now that he never cheated on me.

So, no, I wasn't offended by his adverse reaction. I was surprised more than anything. Irish has always been easygoing, everything always with a joke and a smile.

It took me back to three years ago.

When I first saw glimpses of his Duster side. He displayed even more of that at the meeting. With one silent look, he threw down the gauntlet at his eldest brother. A man who I know has Death himself at his right-hand side. A man Irish showed no fear of.

It has me wondering what Irish is like once he's flicked his internal switch to Duster mode. I've seen him kill. I watched him cut the throat of Sokolov. But I've never witnessed him do so on his own terms and on his own turf.

And I want to.

I can hear the sound of laughter the moment I enter the house. It's Fin. The sound so childlike and perfect it always makes me smile. It's met with a grown-up's laughter, and I recognize it straight away.

Irish.

Father and son.

Tears prick my eyes at what I'm about to witness. A sight I've been waiting to see for over two years now. I stand outside the family room and listen in.

"Padraig, you'll make him sick if you keep throwing him around like that," Roisin lectures.

"And what's a little sick between nephew and uncle, eh, Fin? I reckon we should tell your grandma to mind her own business, or else you'll throw up on her fancy rug."

More laughter, and I can't stop the smile from spreading across my face. God, how I've fucking missed my Irish.

"If he vomits on that rug, then you'll be the one cleaning it up, Padraig O'Connell."

Irish snickers. "It's all lies, Fin. I'm Grandma's favorite, not that she'd ever admit it because she knows fine well I'll record it and play it back to my brothers. But as her favorite, she would never see me having to mop up baby sick."

Suddenly feeling guilty for eavesdropping, I make a noise before entering the room.

I'm dressed in a suit, whereas Irish is wearing navy sweatpants and a white fitted t-shirt. Perched on his shoulders is a smiling Fin, his chubby little fingers gripping tightly on to Irish's hair, his face a picture of happiness.

They look so alike. A sob escapes me, but thankfully, it becomes more of a snort.

"Uh-oh. It looks like your ma's about to start having a go now, Fin. I reckon we'd best quit while we're ahead, lad, before both of us end up in trouble." He reaches up to grab him, tickling him as he does and leaving Fin giggling so hard he can scarcely catch his breath.

I can't help but laugh along.

No sooner has he put him on the floor, Fin's grabbing his leg and wanting more.

Walking over, I pick Fin up, kissing him on the top of his head. I'm conscious that Irish is now watching me interact with my little boy.

Our little boy.

"No more, Fin. Grandma's right. You'll make yourself sick." It's my turn to be the responsible adult.

"Let's get you in the bath, Finian O'Connell before Padraig teaches you any more bad habits." With a small smile, Roisin rolls her eyes exaggeratedly at Irish as she holds her arms toward me for Fin. Irish smirks cheekily in response.

It's obvious she wants to give me and him a chance to talk and clear the air. She's no doubt already heard about what went down.

We both watch as she leaves the room with Fin before closing the door quietly behind her.

And then it's just me and him.

I take Irish in as I stand directly in front of him. All of the O'Connell brothers are handsome, but Padraig is breathtaking to look at. He has a certain something that's impossible to put your finger on. It's like an inner spark that makes him different from anyone else I've ever met. Maybe it's something only I can see.

Then again, maybe not.

He's always grown a female fanbase wherever he goes. Mr. Gift of the Irish Gab has had to beat women off with a stick his whole life. By the time I reach his face, eyes of sparkling blue are laughing at me.

"Are you blatantly checking me out, darlin'?" Always so cocky and sure of himself. It's one of the traits I love most about him.

"You flatter yourself way too much, Irish," I smirk.

But we both know that's exactly what I was doing.

"Jaine, I'm sorry about before." Frowning, he runs his hand through his messy black hair. "I had no right saying what I did."

"It's fine. I didn't take offense."

"Unlike my brother." A glimmer once more of his alter-ego. The bite is far less this time around, but it's still there.

"He's protective."

"Possessive, you mean."

"That too."

There's a long pause. It's not awkward. It's just that, right here, right now, we're both having to adapt to a relationship that's changed. We're both having to figure out how to converse again. Just me. Just him. No longer me *and* him.

Once friends.

Once confidants.

Once everything

Now strangers.

Now parents.

Now nothing.

"I'd like for us to be friends, Jaine, if that's all right with you." He rocks back and forth on his feet.

An olive branch with a hint of anger. It's understandable. On one hand, it will take time for him to process what he thinks happened. On the other, he realizes neither of us can hold a permanent grudge because even if it did take place how he imagined it, it's been superseded. We've both moved on. Me with Eoin. Him with Sophia.

"I'd like that."

"And I'd also like to hang out with Fin sometimes, and JJ too, if he's around. I'll never have any wee ones of my own, so I'd like to be able to dote on any nieces and nephews that I'm blessed with. If I get too needy at times, then you can just give me a swift kick."

The guilt is suddenly overwhelming. I've had to live with this knowledge for over two years now. Surely, I can cope with another couple of months?

"Anywhere in particular?"

"Where I spend time with them, or where can you kick me?"

"Idiot." I chuckle.

He grins proudly, and then his smile fades.

"And I'm sorry, Jaine. About Ace. He was a good man."

"I appreciate that. Thank you." I drop my gaze to the floor as my thoughts drift back to when we were taken by the Bratva and to the events that followed. Noticing my mood change, he immediately places his finger under my chin and tilts my head up.

"I didn't mean to make you feel melancholy, darlin'."

"I know." I blink back tears that he won't be able to miss.

"And I'm also sorry for deceiving you the way I did. You know. When I pretended to be our Dylan."

I stare into eyes of ice blue and immediately get flooded with a plethora of emotions, memories, regrets, and what-ifs. I couldn't look away even if I tried.

"Why did you?"

His response is immediate. "Because I didn't want to let you go."

So open. So honest. So Irish.

"I'm glad you did." My voice is a whisper.

"And why is that?" His is low.

"Because…."

Because I love you. Always have. Always will.

Deep down, he must know that. He must be able to feel it.

"Interrupting something?" We both spin around to take in Eoin. We must have been so distracted by each other neither of us heard the front door open and close. I realize how condemning this must look. Irish and me standing close together, staring into each other's eyes. His finger under my chin, tilting it as though to kiss me.

"Not at all, brother. I was passing on my condolences about Ace, and Jaine was feeling a little melancholy, that's all."

"I can take care of Jaine's needs."

"I'm sure you can." Irish's tone is flat.

The tension is thick. It's my guessing what took place at the meeting is unfinished business between them. Not over me, per se. More so over the festering wound of disrespect.

"Anyway, I'm about to head off." Irish turns his attention back to me. "It was good chatting with you, Jaine."

"You too." I nod, offering a weak smile.

My phone vibrates around an hour later.

Padraig: *It's good to be back on my old number. You never finished what you were going to say.*

Jaine: *Should you be messaging me?*

Padraig: *We're family. I can't see any reason why we shouldn't unless you'd rather I didn't?*

Jaine: *I didn't say that.*

Padraig: *Finish the sentence then, darlin'. Because…?*

Jaine: *Because I didn't want to let you go either.*

I'M LYING IN BED WITH MY HEAD ON EOIN'S CHEST, LISTENING TO the steady thrum of his heart. I know he's got something on his mind, and I suspect it's because he found Irish and me in such a compromising position earlier.

To stake his claim, he fucked me three times in quick succession, and I'm not sure he's done with me yet.

"Do I have anything to be concerned about, Jaine?"

"What do you mean?" I ask, even though I already know the answer.

"You and Paddy."

I rest my chin on his chest, staring up at him until his aquamarine eyes connect with mine. "I love you."

"You love him too."

"True, but I still love you. I was honest about my feelings for both of you from the beginning, Eoin."

"It doesn't mean I have to like them."

"Nope, but it does mean you have to accept them for what they are because they'll never change."

"I do accept them. It was just difficult to see you standing so close to my brother."

"He was sympathizing about Ace, and I got a bit emotional, that's all."

"Are you sure that's all it was?"

"Yes."

No, but what else can I say when I don't know what the fuck it was?

It was *nothing because it can't ever be anything.*

"He shouldn't have said what he did to you."

"And he's apologized for it twice now. Anyway, once Fin's true parentage comes out, he'll know there was no cheating involved. It's understandable why he reacted the way he did. As far as he's concerned, I told him I didn't love him, then slept with his brother. You disrespected him by fucking the same woman you insisted he stay away from."

"I'm glad he apologized."

"He also apologized for all the deceit over the two years. I accepted both apologies."

A pause.

"Who would you choose, Jaine? Who would you choose if you could have only one of us?"

"Are you feeling insecure all of a sudden, Mr. O'Connell?"

"Not at all, Miss Jones. I'm merely curious."

Liar.

"I'm not going to answer that question."

"Why not?"

"Because I'm engaged to you."

"Are there any other reasons?"

"Because Irish is married to Sophia. Both those facts mean there's no choice to be made, so will you please quit with all the nonsensical questions and fuck me?"

"Again?"

"Again."

Rolling me onto my back, he pins me down with the full weight of his body. I groan my appreciation when his hand circles my throat.

"Such a demanding, greedy woman."

I don't want him having those thoughts because, regardless of what he says, I can tell he *is* worried about it, or at least it's playing on his mind.

Irish is happily married. What Eoin should be more concerned about is me deciding to draw a line under what we have because of his controlling nature.

When it comes to his brother and me, he has nothing to worry about.

CHAPTER FIFTEEN

PADRAIG

The O'Connell Home, Darling, New York

ANOTHER WEEK HAS PASSED.

I can still taste Jaine's bitter betrayal. I reckon I always will, but I can't dwell on it. Not when on the surface, I have to appear to be loved up with my Sicilian wife.

I'm lying flat on my back on the family room floor, wearing a t-shirt that's now covered in grubby, sticky handprints. Ma's just taken the two little scoundrels responsible to put them in a much-needed bath.

Who knew wee ones could be so exhausting? Little JJ is fairly quiet and placid, but Fin is a million miles an hour and likes to talk your ears off at every turn. I'm not sure where he gets that from as, while they're far from being introverted, neither Jaine nor Eoin is what you would call outgoing.

That's my tag.

I turn my head to look at Jaine as she lies on her back on the sectional in a pair of white jean shorts and a matching tank. I'm pretty sure the tatty high tops she's wearing are the same ones she wore back when she was nineteen. She looks just like she did on that final day. The day she rejected me that one last time, and just before I cheated on her.

My thoughts drift back to when we used to lie side by side on her student bed, talking about everything and anything. We'd spend hours mapping out what our future together would look like.

Maybe it was a bit premature as we weren't together that long, but I guess you just know when you've found your soul mate.

We never went so far as to talk about what we'd name our children if The Almighty decided to bless us with any. Finian may well have been my first choice too.

Back in our Yale days, everything was about the future because we actually had one. We were so young that it stretched out endlessly in front of us. These days, all we talk about is the past because we have no future, or at least not one together.

Looking at her now, it's like time stood still. I wish it had so I could have a do-over and not fuck up my entire life by making one silly mistake.

Regardless of where we've ended up, I'm still grateful for every moment that I got to spend with her. I wouldn't change it for the world. I wouldn't change her either.

"Do you remember the day we first met, darlin'?" I break the amicable silence.

She groans out loud and turns her head to look at me. "You mean the day the contents of my pencil case rolled down the auditorium and landed at Professor Young's feet?"

I laugh heartily at the memory. "I thought he was going to have a heart attack."

"I was worried his hairpiece was going to fall off." She sniggers.

"That wasn't the first time we met, though."

"Wasn't it?" She frowns.

"You had just walked into the admin office."

"The room that stank of lavender." She wrinkles her nose.

"That's the one. You were collecting your new class schedule from Miss Houser, and you almost knocked me over in your rush."

"Sorry." She smiles.

"I thought you were the most stunning girl I'd ever seen, with the most beautiful accent I'd ever heard, and you didn't even know I existed."

We stare at each other as our thoughts drift back.

"I knew you existed," she admits quietly. Her expression is thoughtful, almost like she's traveled back in time to the precise moment when our fates collided.

I raise a questioning eyebrow at her, and she smiles and rolls her eyes exaggeratedly.

"Well, you were always so sure of yourself, and I didn't want to feed that massive ego of yours, but I used to sneak glances at you when you weren't looking."

"So you *had* seen me before that day?"

"You were all I saw, Irish."

"I was *all* you saw?" I raise the other eyebrow.

She shrugs. "I'd been admiring you for a while. All the girls had." She fidgets with the cushion. "You were so handsome and popular and funny."

"I have to agree with you there, darlin'. I *am* all of those things." I smile smugly, laughing when the cushion she was distracting herself with connects with the side of my head.

"You missed out vain."

"That too. So, tell me more about this covert admiring malarkey. The fact that you couldn't keep your eyes off my handsomeness."

She laugh-snorts. "I'd liked you for ages, but I was plain Jaine. I never thought you'd be interested in someone like me."

I roll onto my side, watching as her cheeks stain pink at all these admissions.

Pushing myself to my feet, I stretch. I have to stop my lips from curving upward when her gaze drops to my groin. As much as it shouldn't, my dick twitches in response. Our eyes connect, and her cheeks redden further at having been caught ogling, just like she admitted to doing way back then.

I walk across and look down at her. I hold out my hand, and she places hers in mine, then I yank her to her feet. I want to gaze more closely at all of her fucking perfection. A perfection that isn't mine and never will be.

We stand there, handholding, like we did that very first time.

"You were never plain. And I more than liked you, darlin'."

I loved you. Always have. Always will.

I gently tuck her blonde hair behind her ear. We step apart when we hear the front door opening then closing. Both of us turning to stare at Eoin as he enters the room.

Impressive. Intimidating. Commanding.

There are a lot of powerful words you could use to describe my eldest brother. He's a scary motherfucker, or at least he is to those who don't know him.

I'm not sure why my parents insisted on marrying me off. He's probably fucked more women than I have, but then he cut back on his sexual shenanigans and reduced it down to a handful of females, whereas I was stuck in an endless loop, going around in the same vicious circle and showing no signs of ever stopping.

It's my own fault. I've no one to blame but myself.

Eoin had his pick of any woman in New York, though. Further afield if he wanted to venture there.

Why Jaine?

Did he deliberately try to steal the love of my life instead of searching for one of his own? Was I just too blind to see the signs because I trusted him with her? Trusted that my own flesh and blood would never betray me or cross that line?

I think back on their love-hate relationship. They fucked. Three years ago. Was it a one-time thing? I'm guessing it must have been, as Jaine hated him for some reason.

Did she love him, and it was another case of unreciprocated feelings? Was that why? And when did it all change? When they married for the first time? Then again, they share a child together. I guess that changes everything.

She walks over to him, and he snakes a possessive arm around her waist, looking down at her like she's the jewel in the crown. I can see the love in both their eyes, and it causes all sorts of emotions to flow through me.

Anger. Regret. Betrayal. Jealousy.

I need to accept it, but it's easier said than done. Jaine Jones is the love of my life, but I'm not the love of hers.

It's the hardest thing in the world, witnessing the person you love love someone else. A brutal reminder that they don't love you.

We share a past. They share a future. They'll no doubt marry soon and have even more children together.

How will I cope seeing Jaine's belly rounded with my brother's offspring when it should have been with mine?

This right now is the rest of my life. Me having to witness them being together. There's no escape. And this all stemmed from the fact that I dropped the ball and cheated.

I watch as he kisses her on the forehead. I'm sure their greeting is usually way more heated, but I suspect it's been cooled down for my benefit.

They won't want to rub it in.

The fact that they're happy. The fact that I'm miserable, as much as I have to pretend not to be. What happens when the pretense is no longer needed? When Sophia and I announce that we're estranged, or when she finally grants me the miracle, and we have the marriage annulled. What happens then?

Nothing, I guess.

Because my cheating was just the catalyst. The crux of the matter is that Jaine doesn't love me.

She said as much three years ago.

CHAPTER SIXTEEN

JAINE

The O'Connell Home, Darling, New York

MOST DAYS, I COME HOME TO FIND IRISH WITH FIN AND JJ. I KNOW it's just Fin today. Duke has taken JJ out.

My youngest adores Irish almost as much as his older brother does, but when he's tired or unwell, it's Eoin he seeks comfort from. Their bond is so strong.

At times, I feel guilty that JJ won't have any relationship with his real daddy, but I know Ace would appreciate how Eoin has stepped up to be there for our little boy.

Irish and I have fallen into our own routine over the last few weeks. When he's here, we talk at length about the past and our shared memories. Recently, we've progressed to safe topics.

There are several areas we don't discuss. Subconsciously, we both seem to have created identical boundaries constructed to cordon off certain subject matters.

We don't talk about how Eoin and I came to be. We don't talk about Irish and Sophia's relationship either. Those conversations can take place if and when we ever decide to open Pandora's box.

There's one bridge we'll have no choice but to cross imminently—that of Finian's parentage. If Irish has any axes to grind, he can do so once he's in possession of all the facts. Everything I've ever done was for him. Whether he views it that way or not remains to be seen.

I'm as honest with him as I can be for now. It's my guess that he's being exactly the same. That there's stuff he's holding back too.

I hear the voices as soon as I enter the house. Fin. Irish. Roisin. My blood runs cold at the sound of the fourth. Sophia.

What's she doing here?

Usually, I'd hover outside the room and laugh at Irish and Roisin's entertaining back-and-forth conversation over his and the kids' daily antics, but today, I walk straight in.

The conversation stops.

His past. His future. Colliding in the same room.

It's been a year since they married, and the memories of that day have decided that now's the right time for them to slideshow through my brain in minute fucking detail. Sophia knows where my thoughts have gone, as she's staring at me smugly. Because she won.

"It's good to see you again, Jaine." It's a blatant lie.

"It's good to see you too, Sophia." Ditto.

"I hear congratulations are in order. That you and Eoin are to marry for a second time and that you are to become the next Ma Duster." She smooths down her red fitted skirt that compliments her tight black shirt. As usual, she looks immaculate.

"That's the current plan." I remain standing.

"Current?" She looks pointedly at Roisin, who's sitting to her left, then arches one sleek eyebrow.

"Yes, current, Sophia. It all depends on whether I survive long enough. My husband was murdered, and we believe my son was the target of a recent drive-by shooting, which is why we have no choice but to live here. Given that my immediate family is being targeted, I can only assume that I'm at the top of the marksman's hit list too."

We stare at each other. I was hoping my blunt admission might see a reaction from her, something to indicate that she was involved in some way, but there's nothing. Her face is completely impassive.

"And can I ask, did you enjoy our wedding, Jaine?" With a smirk, she flicks her long dark hair over her shoulder.

Perfect silence.

An attempt to humiliate me by outing me as some pathetic loser who would show up to their ex-boyfriend's wedding without an invitation. Unfortunately for her, aside from Fin, the other parties present know precisely why I was there that day.

"I survived." As did they.

She knows what I'm saying. That the cozy tete-a-tete she arranged between me and Fergal, the one that saw me dance an Irish jig with Da Duster himself, backfired.

I lived to tell the tale.

"And how's married life?" It's my turn to ask a blunt question. Not that I really want to know that answer.

She smiles as she glances lovingly at Padraig, who's sitting to her right and looking like he'd rather be anywhere else than here. "We're still in the honeymoon period, so we have many sleepless nights. Unlike you, it's not because we're being kept awake by crying babies, but all in good time."

I'm sure I can taste vomit in my mouth.

My thoughts drift to the recent comment Irish made. He said he would never be a father. What did he mean by that, as Sophia's words are contradictory? I had just assumed it was because she had a medical issue, but that doesn't appear to be the case unless she's just trying to rile me.

"And how is business?" I continue. "I heard the unfortunate news from Leo. That Luc decided to step down. A new venture on the cards, perhaps?"

He didn't step down. He was let go. Fortunately for him, with his life intact. Unfortunate for the rest of us.

"That is why we have returned."

Disappointingly, she doesn't expand further.

An awkward silence follows, interrupted by Fin letting out a noisy yell. Irish uses it as his opportunity to vacate the sofa. Standing, he scoops up a giggling Fin before tossing him high in the air.

"He's a beautiful boy." Sophia smiles at Fin and Irish, the latter no longer paying any attention to what's being discussed.

"Yes, he is." I smile for the first time.

"He's very hyper. Much more like Padraig than Eoin, wouldn't you agree?"

She knows.

"Children Fin's age are always hyper." I force the smile to remain fixed on my face.

She nods, her unblinking gaze holding mine. "His eyes are also identical in color to Padraig's."

"They're the same color as Fergal's."

"Would anyone care for a cup of tea?" Roisin cuts in.

Has she also realized Sophia knows the secret we've been trying so hard to keep from her? For how long? And who told her? Not that it matters.

Five weeks from now, all will be revealed anyway.

The kids are in bed, Eoin's still at the office, and I'm sitting on the sofa in the safe space on the phone to Jessie.

My conversation with Sophia has been eating away at me ever since she and Irish left. I would never have suspected that she and Molly were allies, but after today, I'd be willing to bet my last dollar that Sophia knows Fin's true parentage. Those comments were laid out deliberately. She wanted me to know that she knows.

"Were Molly and Sophia friends?"

"Why are you asking, partner?"

"Because I strongly suspect Sophia knows who Fin's biological daddy is. She mentioned that his personality is more like Padraig's than Eoin's."

"Well, that doesn't really prove anything."

"I know, but she then went on to mention that his eye color matches Padraig's too. I know it's not proof paramount, but it wasn't so much what she said but the way she said it. It was as though she was laying out these facts on purpose because she wanted me to know that she knows."

"And you think Molly told her?"

"Who else could have? It's not common knowledge. Rodolfo doesn't know. Leo doesn't know. If this information were in the public domain, they would know for sure. They never take their finger off the pulse of this life."

"True. I mean, Molly and Sophia used to have regular girly get-togethers with Roisin at The Palace, and I did overhear one particular conversation."

There's a pause.

"Don't keep me in suspense, Jessie."

"Hold on. I'm just trying to recall what was said. It was back in the day when I used to hide out in the restroom and shut myself inside the cubicle."

"Because that's what people of a sound mind do." I snort.

"I never once said I was of a sound mind."

"True. Go on."

"So, they entered the restroom together while I was doing my thing in the cubicle."

"Hiding from Dylan."

"That's it. Anyway, they mentioned something about Roisin and a task. I'm not sure what the task was, so maybe you'd be best to ask the current Ma Duster for that little tidbit of information, but by all accounts, Paddy was refusing to sleep with Sophia, and she was getting a little irked by his constant rejection. More so as Molly was getting plenty of action from your current fiancé."

"Too much information."

"Jealousy's a curse, I know."

"I'm not jealous," I snap.

"I believe you." Clearly, she doesn't, and she's right not to because I am goddamn jealous.

"Anyway, Sophia was convinced it was because Paddy still loved you. She said that if she was going to be stuck in a loveless marriage facing a lifetime of solitude and misery, then it was only fair that she affords you the same courtesy. They also mentioned something about taking the law into their own hands."

Air escapes my lungs, and I suddenly can't breathe.

"Jaine?"

"Why didn't you tell me any of this at the time, Jessie!"

"I'm sorry, I didn't…."

"Think! You didn't goddamn think!"

"I thought it was just restroom gossip." I'm annoyed that she sounds upset. What has she got to be upset about? Her husband wasn't the one who was murdered in cold blood.

"Restroom gossip that could potentially have saved Ace's life had we known!"

I feel sick. I know it's hearsay. I know it's not concrete evidence of any wrongdoing. I know it probably wouldn't have changed the outcome. If Ace were in their sights, they would have gotten to him sooner or later. It's not the fucking point.

"You should have told me, Jessie!"

I disconnect the call.

CHAPTER SEVENTEEN

PADRAIG

Padraig's Apartment, Hudson Yards, New York

"You've known the whole time, yet you've said nothing."

I stare accusingly at my wife. Today's the first time I've seen her since we returned to New York three weeks ago. After visiting my family's home with me earlier, she then insisted on coming back to my apartment, no doubt, to search for signs of any random females I may have hooked up with.

I watch as she struts around my home like she owns it, picking things up, then putting them down in the wrong place.

"You insisted you didn't wish to hear about anything that wasn't business related. I was simply doing as you asked, Padraig." She looks smug. We both know she deliberately didn't tell me.

"I'd have wanted to know if my brother had gotten married." I'm trying to remain calm because we both know she wants me to react adversely.

She tsks. "Oh, come now, Padraig. If Eoin had married Molly, you wouldn't have cared less. It's the fact that he married your former flame that's causing you the problem."

I don't respond. She's right, and she knows it.

"It's time you got over your pathetic little infatuation with Jaine. She's re-marrying your brother. Surely that's all the proof you need to confirm that she doesn't care about you and probably never has. She loves him. Not you. It's time to get over it now."

"And do what exactly?"

She strolls toward me. It's meant to be seductive, but it does nothing for me. *She* does nothing for me. She stands so close that I'm met with the clawing stench of her perfume. It's almost as repugnant as she is.

"Well, perhaps the news I'm about to share is perfect timing. Luciano has had a change of heart about us. He wants you and I to be seen as a happily married couple. He believes it will help promote the correct image for our new organization and attract higher-quality individuals.

"Most of the people he is trying to entice have wives and children. It would appear that family lies at the heart of most organizations of our type. That means there can be no more living apart or pretense."

"I will never be your husband, Sophia." I glare at her.

She pouts at me, no doubt trying to make her mouth look inviting enough for me to want to kiss it.

"But you already *are* my husband."

"In name only. I will never perform the intimate duties expected of a husband."

"Come now, Padraig. You're part of the Ruocco family now. Luciano expects us to behave like a young couple in the first throes of love. As head of our family, we must follow his instruction and do what is expected."

"I'm a Duster. I answer to my da. I will never be a Ruocco. I will never answer to your brother. I will also never love you, Sophia."

"I can live with that if I must, but Luciano now also wishes for us to provide him with a Duster heir."

My heart sinks in my chest. I expected Luciano to move the goalposts, but not to this extent.

"Then we can use IVF."

"That process will take too long."

"Take it or leave it because I won't fuck you, Sophia," I hiss.

"You managed once before." She bats her eyelashes at me. Like that will make any difference.

"I was drunk."

"You still must have found me attractive enough."

"And that was also before I found out that you're not a very pleasant person to be around."

She smirks, no doubt proud of the fact that she's a complete bitch. "I'm not asking for you to be around me any longer than it takes to get me pregnant, Padraig."

"I won't do it."

There's a pause. She's about to play her trump card.

"It was an interesting conversation today, don't you think? That your precious Jaine believes herself to be at such high risk of an attack. I wonder who from?"

"Don't you dare fucking threaten her," I snarl.

She smiles wickedly. "I'm not a fool like Molly. I would never blatantly threaten anyone, especially not the future Da Duster's very own fiancée. But accidents happen all the time. Jaine must have many enemies considering the clients she represents. I'm sure if something were to happen to her, while it would be unfortunate, it wouldn't be entirely unexpected."

She places a manicured finger on my chest before dragging its blood-red tip slowly down to the top of my sweatpants.

"And speaking of fools, I wonder what ever happened to Molly. One minute, she was Eoin's fiancée, and the next minute, she was replaced by Jaine. She seems to have vanished into thin air. It's all a little suspicious, don't you think?" She raises one perfectly shaped eyebrow at me before removing her finger, turning, and walking toward the door. "Think about it, husband." She calls over her shoulder. "You know Luciano doesn't appreciate it when his plans are thwarted. It will just see him take his bad mood out on the unfortunate people you tried so hard to protect."

"If I agree to do this, then in return, I want an annulment on the basis that the marriage was forced."

"We'll see." She turns and smirks before opening the door and leaving.

"Sophia wants me to get her pregnant." I lean back on the sectional and stare into space, my phone balanced against my ear.

Fuck. My. Life.

"Isn't that traditionally the next step, Paddy? You court, you marry, you procreate, and your children repeat the process to continue the family line."

"I don't want to taint our blood with theirs. Theirs is toxic."

"Well, since we're mobsters, I'm not sure ours is much better."

"We have values, Dylan. We treat our people fairly. The Ruoccos have no values. They simply trample over others to get what they want."

"What do you mean?"

"They talk down to their people, humiliate them, and torture them emotionally and physically just because they can. I witnessed it with my own eyes. I half-expected Luciano to mistreat them, but I witnessed my own wife behaving in the same manner and, in many instances, toward innocent young children.

"I don't want to be bringing a little one into the world and have them raised to behave that way toward others. Trust me, as much as the child would be an O'Connell in name, that loathsome pair would ensure it has the heart of a Ruocco."

"But how will you be able to stop her from getting pregnant? She just has to stop taking birth control. Unless you're going to insist on wearing a rubber."

"I've never consummated the marriage," I mumble the admittance.

A pause.

"Did I hear you right? Did you say you've never touched your wife intimately since you married?" He sounds shocked.

"That's exactly what I said, Dyl."

"Jesus Christ. I mean, not that your sex life was front and center in our family discussions, but we all assumed that Luciano would have insisted on you getting your dick wet. That he would have held a gun to your head if you'd even attempted to resist his little sister's advances."

It's time for me to admit the truth. If I can't tell, Dyl, who can I tell?

"Between you and me, mine and Sophia's marriage is in name only."

"What do you mean?"

"It's all a front. We don't even live together. As for Luc, he wasn't bothered. I was simply a trophy husband—someone who could give him access to a strong alliance. When we were out of sight and mind in Sicily, it didn't matter because no one was to know. I'm guessing now we've returned to New York, questions are being asked. Why Sophia and I aren't being seen out and about together? Why we've not taken things to the next stage? After twelve months, most would have expected her to return with a babe in arms or at least be heavily pregnant.

"As we know, most factions are family-run businesses. With Luciano unmarried and Sophia and I estranged, it doesn't promote the right image to entice family-minded members to sign on the dotted line of their new organization, hence why I'm now being put under pressure."

There's a pause as he digests everything.

"But how will you get out of… you know… having to perform?"

"I've offered Sophia my own personal fortune in exchange for an annulment."

He lets out a low whistle. "That's a hefty price to pay."

"My freedom is priceless, Dyl."

"I'm not sure how our parents would react. You know how strongly they feel about marriage."

"It's not a divorce, so legally, it would be the same as if the marriage had never taken place."

"I know what an annulment is. It's what Jaine and Eoin had. Jaine cited that she had been forced into the union."

"Why did they get married in the first place?"

I have so many questions, but I'm not expecting to get many of them answered.

"For the protection of Finian. After Ace was killed and after what took place at St. Patrick's, everyone was on high alert. Once it became common knowledge that Fin was a Duster, he would have immediately become our Achilles heel. You know that. It was the only way."

"Then why annul it?"

"It's a long story and one that's not really mine to tell." He sounds sheepish. He's hiding something, but then Dylan's always been the one who's had to be the keeper of secrets. Most of them mine. "But they love each other now. You can see that, can't you?"

I know they do. I've witnessed it with my own eyes.

"Why her, though, Dylan? When he could have had anyone he wanted?" I ask the burning question.

"They fought it for a long-time, Jaine especially, but in the end, they caved. We don't get to choose who we fall in love with. You and I both know that. So, what are you going to do about Sophia?"

"I'll have no option but to do their bidding."

I don't tell him it's also because I've been backed into a corner by a veiled threat made against Jaine. Sophia's sharp. If she catches on that I've spilled my guts, she may retaliate by carrying out her threat regardless. It's not a risk I'm willing to take.

The way I see it, at the end of the day, I need to get her pregnant to gain my freedom anyway.

CHAPTER EIGHTEEN

JAINE

The Hudson Dusters' HQ, Manhattan, New York

"LUCIFER CALLED THIS MORNING. IT LOOKS LIKE IT'S SHOWTIME. He's had three brothers come forward in just over twenty-four hours. Apparently, they've been approached by the Colombians in much the same way Abel was. Same threats, same everything. I've told him to call church with Ghost to make sure all of Colton is singing from the same hymn sheet."

I make eye contact with everyone around the table from where I sit on Eoin's right-hand side. Jessie's notably absent, no doubt avoiding me after our recent run-in. We've since made our peace, but things are still a little tense between us.

"I'll speak to Rod and Delaney after this meeting. In fact, I may take a ride to the Scorpions' clubhouse and have a face-to-face with Delaney. I have a few documents I need signing anyway."

"You're not going anywhere on your own."

A menacing growl from my left utters words that are fast becoming a permanent echo around here. Just who the fuck does Eoin think he is?

Anger immediately spirals through me, an emotion that's becoming way too familiar nowadays. Since we've started semi-living together, his possessive streak has gotten out of control. A reality that's causing things to deteriorate between us. Something he's either ignoring or thinks I won't act on.

If he believes the latter, then he really doesn't know me at all.

I glance around the faces once more. As I suspected, everyone is now waiting for my adverse reaction like this is all some sort of game.

Ace is dead. Abel is dead. Raf is dead. It's no goddamn game.

I turn to face him. "We've had this conversation several times. You don't get to tell me what to do. You don't get to tell me how to live my life." My response is clipped.

"I'm your fiancé."

"That doesn't mean you own me. That doesn't give you automatic control over me."

"I took a vow to protect you."

"A vow that was taken as part of our marriage. A marriage that was subsequently annulled. The protection clause has therefore been removed."

"An annulment that should never have taken place!"

I ignore his raised voice, choosing to remain calm. "But it did, and so it's now my choice, and my decision is that I don't want your protection, nor do I need this possessive bullshit."

"Jaine, Eoin does have a point," Fergal interjects.

Like father like son. I realize the risks, and they're mine to take. They can both go fuck themselves.

"It's not a point I'm interested in hearing."

"Jaine is more than capable of looking after herself." We all look at Irish as he voices his opinion. He shrugs. "I've seen what she's capable of on more than one occasion, so if we need to take a show of hands, I'll gladly raise mine in favor that says she doesn't need to be wrapped in cotton wool."

"Mind your own business, Padraig!" Eoin hisses.

"I've known her for twelve years."

"You didn't see each other for eleven of those years!"

Irish is unperturbed by Eoin's blatant dig. "Moot point. We spoke on the phone multiple times a day for over nine of those years, and we messaged back and forth over two. I would argue, therefore, that I know Jaine Jones almost as well as she knows herself and way better than anyone else sat around this table, yourself included. She's…."

He makes eye contact with me, and I give him a subtle head shake. He immediately knows why. He thinks everyone present knows about my alter-ego. They don't. Only Dylan does.

"She's what?"

I turn my head to find Eoin narrowing his eyes at him.

"She's… a bit of an expert with a rifle." Irish continues with a cocky smile and Dylan snickers.

"She's not always going to be carrying a weapon, Paddy. You've been told what happened with Malky. What Jaine had to do."

"And I'm pretty sure it's not something that she hasn't done before, brother. Anyway, I thought the whole point was to have a wife who could roll up her sleeves and get stuck in. Jaine's the future Ma Duster. That's a hands-on role. It's not a job you can undertake with your arms tied behind your back, which is what you're attempting to do to her. What are you going to do? Lock her up in an ivory tower and throw away the key if she doesn't do your bidding."

"I might."

"On your head be it. I wish you well with trying to get Jaine to do something she doesn't want."

Enough is enough. I slap my hand on the tabletop. "Can you both please stop conversing about me like I'm not goddamn here!"

I pack up my briefcase. I've said all I came here to say, and now I know exactly what it is I have to do.

He's left me with no choice.

Jaine's Apartment, Upper East Side, New York

"I hate you."

He bites my bottom lip as his strong hands slide my skirt up to my waist. My apartment's cold, stale air bites my bare skin, causing me to shiver. No one's lived here for months.

Dec dropped me off, and Eoin followed me into the building. I pressed the button for my office, he pressed the button for my apartment, and now here I am with my back pressed against the wall as he manhandles me like it's his God-given right.

"Liar." His voice is hot against my ear, and I groan as he turns his attention to what's inside my panties, his hand pushing inside the damp material to cup my pussy.

"You're an arrogant bastard."

"That may be true, Miss Jones, but the truth of the matter is, you don't hate me. And why is that exactly?"

Pushing my panties to the side, he thrusts two fingers deep inside me, then finger fucks me hard and fast, the heel of his hand pressing deliciously against my clit. I grind against him. I need more. I always need more from him. I can never get enough.

"I asked you a question, Jaine." His mouth moves to my neck, and he nips on the delicate skin with his teeth.

"Because you're an asshole."

"That cussing little mouth of yours just can't help itself, can it? No, Jaine. You don't hate me. You love me."

I hear the sound of a zipper moments before he lifts me off the floor so I can anchor my legs around his slim hips, then, with one brutal push, he's inside me.

I link my hands behind his neck so we can both watch his dick deliver each punishing thrust.

"Look at your pussy soaking my cock, Jaine. My, my, aren't you such an insatiable little thing?"

"Shut up and fuck me, asshole." I dig my nails into his neck until I can feel blood and watch his nostrils flare. He's still fully dressed, and the marks I'm inflicting above his collar line will be visible for the world to see, which is just how he likes it. Eoin O'Connell wants me to own him as much as he wants to own me, and he wants the world to witness my claiming.

Positioning my legs so I'm jack-knifed against him, he grips my ass and fucks me hard and fast. This is his equivalent of a quickie. A twenty-minute fuck that will leave me raw and bruised.

My back hurts, but nothing matters apart from the feel of his cock inside me and the painful grip of his fingers as he holds me in place.

Harder. Faster. Deeper. He pistons into me like a machine.

"More." It's barely audible.

"Such a greedy, evil woman."

He curses when I clench around him, his breath hot against my neck as his movements become erratic. He raises his head, green eyes blazing into mine as his impressive length swells inside me.

With a growl, he embraces the first licks of his pleasure, the feral sounds he makes pushing me over the edge. With one punishing thrust, I shatter around him, my clenching walls taking him for everything he's got. I rest my forehead against his as he empties deep inside me, his eyes never leaving mine.

We stay there. Hot. Sweaty. Sated. I breathe him in. He breathes me in.

He's right. I do love him.

His lips find mine, his tongue sweeping deep. I can taste his love for me from his mouth, but it's not enough.

I feel caged. Suffocated. Drowned.

He lowers me to my feet, tucks in his dick, then zips up his pants. Aside from the bleeding scratches on his neck, he looks immaculate once more and not like he's just ruthlessly fucked me up against the wall.

I go to the restroom, clean myself up, straighten my skirt, then stare at my reflection in the mirror. I know if I don't make a stance, I'll lose my identity and become Eoin O'Connell's possession. I'm worth more than that.

Way more.

Love is no longer enough. Not after everything I've been through. I refuse to be compromised any longer.

I leave the restroom and take him in. Mr. Dominating. Dangerous. Deadly.

Mine.

I don't have to give any explanation. He knows why I'm saying what I'm about to. I've warned him enough times.

I love him. I will always love him, but we'll only be compatible if we can find a balance. I'm not cut out to be a mobster's trophy wife. Not even his.

Yes, I could tell him about my alter-ego, but the way I see it, that reveal shouldn't make any difference. If I don't want to be protected, and if I don't want to be possessed, then he should respect my decision rather than try to stifle me with his own.

He's left me with no choice but to utter the two words I didn't ever want to have to speak. I stare at him, and he stares back. He knows exactly what I'm going to say.

"It's over."

CHAPTER NINETEEN

PADRAIG

Padraig's Apartment, Hudson Yards, New York

I STARE AT MY WIFE ACROSS THE ROOM.

She looks pristine in black pants and a white silk blouse, her dark hair hanging in a sleek wave down her back. Most men would find her beautiful, but the surface is just a façade hiding her true ugliness. Then again, most men wouldn't care about what lies underneath.

I'm not most men.

The last time we spoke, she asked me for a baby. I tentatively agreed on one condition. That she grants me an annulment.

I don't want to introduce a child into their environment, but if I'm to be given no choice in the matter, then we can co-parent. That way, my son or daughter can live a relatively normal existence half the time with my own family instead of a toxic one full-time with the Ruoccos.

"Have you given any thought to what we discussed, Padraig?" She glances at her nails absent-mindedly like she has other places she'd much rather be. She doesn't.

"I have."

"And?"

"One pregnancy for one annulment."

"I haven't discussed the annulment side of things with my broth…."

"One pregnancy. One annulment. We then co-parent. The child lives with me fifty percent of the time. I'll personally handle the legal side of things to ensure the utmost privacy and confidentiality. That's my final offer. Take it or leave it, Sophia.

"The alternative is that we continue on as we are. If your brother doesn't like my final decision, he can pass me the gun, and I'll happily pull the trigger myself. Given how much his new organization needs the alliance with my family, I very much doubt he'd want it to come to that."

She sashays across to me, using her walk of seduction once more in an attempt to gain my interest. It will never work.

"I'm sure I can convince Luciano to accept your terms, so I think, since I'm already here, that we should just get started."

Fisting her hair, I yank her head back, leaning forward until my lips hover over hers, my breath hot against her mouth. I deliberately stare at her lips, and she licks them in silent response. I smirk down at her. "After we sign a new contract… wife."

I release her, and she stumbles backward. She's pink-cheeked and flustered because she thought I was going to kiss her. I wasn't.

"There's one final condition."

A typical untrustworthy Ruocco already attempting to move the goalposts.

"And what might that be?" I stare at her.

"I want you to stay away from Jaine Jones." She tilts her chin defiantly.

She must be aware that Eoin and Jaine are currently on a break. She'll be worried I may fall for Jaine's charms again, thus thwarting her procreation plans. What she doesn't realize is that it will be nothing more than a temporary blip between them.

"Don't disrespect me on this matter, Padraig." She doesn't say the words *or else*, but we both know they're silently implied—an unspoken reminder of the veiled threat issued in Jaine's direction. "I will have it added to the contract," she adds.

I say nothing. We both know my lack of response is my acceptance. It's not like I have any other choice.

"Then we're verbally agreed. One pregnancy. One annulment. Yes?"

This time I do answer. "Yes."

"Give me your word, Padraig."

"Subject to contract, I give you my word, Sophia."

"Then I shall discuss the matter with my brother and have our lawyers draw up the necessary paperwork for your perusal." I watch as she leaves.

It's my thinking that we'll be reviewing said document within a matter of days because it's clear Sophia wants me any way she can have me, and it would seem her brother wants my offspring even more.

The O'Connell Home, Darling, New York

It's been one day since Sophia paid me my visit. I'm expecting the contract to arrive from the Ruoccos imminently. At present, I have the upper hand, but I know it's only until Sophia falls pregnant.

Then all bets are off.

Luciano will no longer need me for an alliance with my family when Sophia hands him his very own Duster heir. Achieving her desired result is not an act I'm looking forward to participating in, however, which speaks volumes about how much I detest the girl, given I've fucked my way across Manhattan.

It's also been three days since Eoin and Jaine split up.

My eldest brother immediately took himself away to the containers to lick his wounds in private. No one's seen him since. Jaine's pretty much locked herself away in the safe space with the kids. She's been working from home, so no one's seen much of her either.

Is it a temporary split or permanent?

It isn't easy to predict. They're both stubborn. They're both set in their ways. They're both more alike than they realize, not that either would ever admit as much. Neither will back down. They're extremists. It's either black or white with them both.

What they need is an infusion of grey—something to balance them out.

He wants to protect and possess her, and she wants neither. He's trying to tame the untamable.

Eoin always left the handling of the MC side of things to Cillian, so he has no real experience when it comes to dealing with bikers. What he doesn't realize is that they're a different breed. They're free spirits. Jaine will never be a mobster's moll. She will never be content wearing finery and being surrounded by the luxury and trappings of wealth.

Like Molly would. Like Sophia would.

Given her vast personal wealth, Jaine doesn't need a man to provide her with such comforts. She needs so much more. Eoin's been trying to squeeze a square peg into a round hole, and for the first time in his life, something's backfired on him. I knew better than to attempt to change her, as did Ace.

I think back to the recent meeting. She's clearly never told Eoin about her alter-ego, and now I suspect I know why. Subconsciously or otherwise, she's had doubts.

About him. About their relationship. About their future together.

It's evening when I knock on the door to the safe space.

If Sophia has it inserted into the contract, I'll have no choice but to cease face-to-face contact with Jaine. Maybe even all communication. At least temporarily, and until Sophia's pregnant.

I need to speak to Jaine before then. To make sure she's okay. To be there for her if she needs someone to talk to or vent at. Because it's true what I said in the meeting. I *do* know Jaine Jones almost as well as she knows herself.

Her life raft. Her sounding board. Her confidant.

I was all three for her once upon a time, as she was for me. I want to offer to be all of those things for her today if she needs me to be.

The door swings open.

"Irish." It's barely audible.

Does she have a nickname for Eoin? Ace had one. I have one.

I have so many unanswered questions, but now is not the time because if I ever doubted Jaine's love for my eldest brother, then I was wrong to.

In three days, she's lost weight, her eyes are red, and she's pale. I'm not sure how it makes me feel. That I was never her first thought or her last thought every day like he clearly is, so letting me go didn't make her weep.

She was able to walk away from me without a backward glance or second thought because she never loved me the way she loves him.

My heart physically aches in my chest at the realization. That I was never enough. That I was never her end game the way she was mine.

"Are the kids in bed?"

She nods.

"I just wanted to make sure you were all right, darlin'," I utter the unnecessary words, as she's clearly not all right.

"I'm fine."

A typical female response, which means she's the opposite.

"Well, if this is how you look when you feel fine, then I'd hate to see the state you're in when you're upset."

She motions her head for me to step inside, and I do. It looks similar to how it did the last time I was in here. The only real difference is that it now looks lived in with the toys and children's stuff scattered around the place.

My mother hated her. Both my parents did. It's gone a complete one-eighty because she's given them Fin and JJ. Then again, she also saved my ma's life, even though I'm told my da almost ended hers.

I turn around to take her in. Her bottom lip quivering gives her away. I hold out my arms, she walks straight into them, and they instinctively wrap around her. Because it's where she was always meant to be. In my fucking arms.

And then she cries, and I soothe her as best I can. I know from how heart-wrenching each sob is that they're not just for Eoin.

That they're for Ace. That they're for her pop. That they're for everyone she's ever lost and for every negative life-changing event she's ever experienced.

This rare moment of weakness is a culmination of all the regrets and losses she can temporarily rid herself of. A release she can embrace because she's with someone who understands what she's been through because he lived through most of them with her first time around. Even if it was only at the end of a phone or as part of a message exchange.

I close my eyes as I inhale the scent of wildflowers from her hair.

Then I find myself praying that there's at least one tear in there for me. Over what we shared. Because even though it meant so little to her, it meant every-fucking-thing to me. She means everything to me.

And then my own silent tears mix with hers. Over my single biggest regret and my single biggest loss. Her.

Although, how can you lose what was never truly yours in the first place?

CHAPTER TWENTY

JAINE

The O'Connell Home, Darling, New York

To fix something, it first has to be broken.

I never realized just how broken I was until Irish started putting me back together using something I never thought I'd get to share with anyone again.

Memories.

We laughed and cried as we reminisced. I think, in some ways, he needed fixing as much as I did, although he seldom gives anything away about his life with Sophia.

It's been six days. Eoin and I still haven't spoken.

We've both needed time to mourn what we had and ponder over why it never worked out for us. My heart physically aches, but he's alive and well. He's not dead like Ace, and that's all that matters. My world will keep on turning as long as he's on it.

I'll survive. So will he.

I love him. I will always love him. Same as I do his brother. But in both cases, love just wasn't enough.

I can't be what Eoin wants me to be. I'm a biker. It's written in my DNA. The freedom of the open road is part of who I am. I need to be able to ride my hog. To inhale the scent of road dust mixed with exhaust fumes into my lungs.

I'll gladly meet my maker sooner rather than later by taking my chances so I can do just that because what's the point in living if you're already dead inside?

Eoin wanted to lock me up in a gilded cage. He wanted to clip my wings so I could never fly off even when he let me out. I don't want to exist. I don't want to be an extension of him. I want to live. I want to be me.

Plain Jaine Jones.

Maybe things will change for us. Maybe we'll both bend and compromise, but for now, we're broken. For now, we don't share a future.

I glance at the clock as I sit on the sofa. It's the last Sunday of the month, so the whole family is upstairs. It's the first time Eoin has been back to the house since it happened. I've decided to remain out of sight so he can spend quality time with the kids and his family.

Baby steps until we reach some normalcy.

I don't want to jeopardize his relationship with my boys. They need him as much as he needs them, especially little JJ.

Hopefully, we can reach some level of friendship in due course. My only concern is that it would quickly turn into a *with-benefits* scenario, and then we'd be back at square one. All we can do is take it one day at a time, I guess.

I remind myself to have a chat with Roisin about the task she set for Molly and Sophia. Any time she's tried to converse with me recently, I've deliberately kept the kids as the main topic of conversation. I know if I give her an inch, she'll start giving me relationship advice and telling me how to mend things with Eoin.

It needs to be a two-way street. If he's not prepared to change his single-minded direction, there's nothing to mend.

This time, it really is checkmate.

Jaine: *Can I use the shooting range?*
Dylan: *You got the keys?*
Jaine: *I have the spare set.*
Dylan: *You don't need my permission, but it's dark outside.*
Jaine: *I stopped being scared of the dark when I was five years old. Any night vision goggles?*
Dylan: *There's a pair attached to a helmet inside the first shooting table. Da's rifle is where you left it if you want to practice shooting at pretend heads.*
Jaine: *I miss my alter-ego.*
Dylan: *I'm sure you do. My big brother misses you.*
Jaine: *We agreed not to go there.*
Dylan: *I don't like seeing him in pain.*
Jaine: *Better a little pain now than a lot more later. We tried. It just didn't work out for us.*
Dylan: *You didn't try. Neither of you did. Not really. Anyway, I'd give it ten minutes before you head off.*
Jaine: *Any reason?*
Dylan: *Sophia and Paddy are just about to leave.*
Jaine: *Let me know when they've gone.*

Ten minutes later.

Dylan: *The coast is clear. They've just left. If you're quick, you won't re-trigger the external security lights. It'll be another minute before they switch off. The coast is* *clear on the inside too. Eoin's just getting JJ out of the bath.*

Tears prick my eyes, but I blink them back.

I'm dressed in the black attire I wear when my alter-ego takes out the two-legged trash, only this time, I've thrown some black cargo pants over the top.

The moment I step outside, something immediately feels off. I discount it. The security on this property is Fort Knox level. No one is getting in or out unless the family wants them to. I check my pocket to ensure I've got my phone and ear pods with me before skulking down the side of the building. Ten seconds later, the security lights switch off.

I'm plunged into darkness. I'm glad I layered up, as the clear night sky means the temperature is frigid.

Before making my way to the range, I reach into my puffer jacket pocket, pull on my black fingerless gloves, then yank my balaclava over my head. The only thing now visible is my warm breath colliding with the cold air.

I glance over my shoulder, still feeling uneasy, I keep to the shadows. I feel stupid being so overly cautious, but once a sniper, always a sniper.

Better to be careful than dead.

I find the goggles locked inside the first shooting table, exactly where Dylan said they would be. As expected, they're top-of-the-range military style—nothing but the best for the Dusters.

The rifle is where I left it inside the second table. It still has the suppressor fitted from last time. The scope isn't really suitable for night-time use, but I'll have to make do.

I don't bother switching on the accuracy checker. I can see if I've hit the target through the scope itself, and I know it will always be in the ninety-ninth percentile. I don't need an electronic reading to tell me how good I am at my second job. Having checked the elements, I illuminate the farthest away target before sitting down.

Line up. Check scope. Pull trigger.

It's a bit repetitive, but the same could be said when you're shooting skulls. For me, it's just offering a welcome distraction. Some much-needed sniper therapy and some *me* time.

I fire half a dozen shots before switching the target back off. I then glance around. It's similar to when I carry out a hit. I could be sat for minutes, or it could be hours. Boring for some, perhaps, but therapeutic for me.

My mind automatically drifts back to Nevada. To when I almost missed. To when Irish messaged me pretending to be Dylan.

Because I didn't want to let you go.

I'm glad we've managed to reclaim back some of what we lost. Maybe one day we'll be comfortable enough to dissect what's led us to this point, but for now, I'm just grateful to have him back in my life. He's been there for me recently. Like he always was in the past.

My confidant.

I can tell that all is not well in his world, but I don't want to pry. Both of us will move on to the more taboo subjects—some of them in around four weeks from now. I only hope we've built up enough of a friendship by then to survive the guaranteed fallout.

My ears prick once more. I'm sure I can hear something.

Or someone.

I shake my head. No one is going to be able to access any part of this property.

Unless someone's given them access.

Get a grip, Jaine.

I hear it again. My gut is telling me something's wrong. I quietly take my phone out of my pocket.

Jaine: *You there?*
Padraig: *Just got home, darlin'.*
Jaine: *Is Sophia still with you?*
Padraig: *She dropped me off. She has somewhere else she needs to be. Do you want me to call you?*
Jaine: *No. I'm outside on the range, and I'm sure I can hear something.*
Padraig: *Have you told the others?*
Jaine: *I didn't want to panic anyone. I also didn't want them to run out all guns blazing. Not when my kids are inside. If there is any danger out here, I don't want them getting caught up in the middle of it.*
Padraig: *Do you want me to go to Dylan's and check the surveillance? I can be there in ten minutes.*
Jaine: *Yes. It may be nothing...*
Padraig: *Better to be safe than sorry, Jaine. Don't move an inch.*
Jaine: *I won't.*
Padraig: *Pinkie promise?*
Jaine: *Pinkie promise.*

I wait, and I wait.

Jaine: *Dylan, once I give you the nod, you need to get everyone inside the safe space.*
Dylan: *What's going on, Jaine? Shall I call you?*
Jaine: *I think there may be someone on the property, so I can't talk. I'm at the range and armed, so I'm okay. Irish is heading to your apartment now to check the surveillance to make sure I'm not imagining things. I'm expecting an update imminently.*
Dylan: *Da and Eoin will want to go outside.*

Jaine: *The priority is to keep the children safe, Dyl. They're most likely the targets. To do that, you all need to stay inside with them.*
Dylan: *The system has thermal imaging.*
Jaine: *Then I'll get Irish to tell me how many and where they are because, trust me, I'm pretty sure I'm not alone out here. You need to get into the safe space as soon as I say. No arguments. No delay. I don't need to be worrying about what's going on in there when I have enough to worry about out here.*
Dylan: *Eoin will want to know where you are.*
Jaine: *Tell him I'm with Irish.*
Dylan: *I can't say that to him. You know what he'll think if I say that.*
Jaine: *Then what do you suggest, Dyl? If you tell him I'm out here or that I'm anywhere else, he'll open the front door and get his arrogant head blown off. Do it, Dylan. You say what you need to. If he thinks the worst, then so be it. I'd rather he hates my guts than be dead.*

I check my message from Irish.

Padraig: *Three intruders.*
Jaine: *Can you see them on the thermal imaging?*
Padraig: *Yes.*

I go back to my exchange with Dylan.

Jaine: *Three intruders. There may be more on the way. We don't know anything for sure. Get in the safe space now. You tell the family that I'm with Irish and that The Exterminator*

has just landed. Roisin knows about me, so you tell her to keep her mouth shut.
Dylan: *How does she know?*
Jaine: *I have no time to explain. Safe space, now. Let me know when you're all inside.*
Dylan: *How will you know where they are? We'll be able to access the system from the safe space, but it will be difficult for me to communicate their location to you without the risk of your identity being revealed.*
Jaine: *Irish can see them on the thermal imaging. He can guide me. I'm also wearing the night vision goggles. Message me once you're all inside. The priority is the children. I swear to God, if any of you step outside, I'll shoot you my goddamn self.*

Ten minutes pass.

Dylan: *All inside.*
Jaine: *Don't send any more messages.*

Jaine: *You there, Irish?*
Padraig: *I'm here, darlin.'*
Jaine: *I'm going to stick one ear pod in. Then I need you to talk me through exactly where they are.*

"Irish?" I whisper.

I stand up from the shooting table with the rifle in my hand. It's not the ideal weapon. It's not the ideal scope. It's not the ideal situation either, but what choice do I have? My babies are inside. Duke is inside. Eoin is inside.

If the grim reaper wants a soul, then let it be mine and not one of theirs.

"Head back toward the house, Jaine. There's one in front and one on either side. You'll collide with the one on the left-hand side on your way back from the range. None of them are moving right now, which makes me think they're waiting for instructions."

Sticking to the shadows, I make my way toward the side of the property. I must have passed this guy's sentry point unarmed on my way to the range with only minutes to spare. For once, The Almighty really was on my side. Let's hope he remains that way.

We don't speak until I'm on the approach.

"You're almost on top of him now."

"I see him." Irish is right. He's dressed similarly to me, and he's staring at the building but not making any move toward it. They're waiting for instructions.

I don't hesitate. I raise the rifle, fire, and he drops to the ground. A quick death, which is all we can ever hope for in this life.

"One down, two to go."

"Good girl."

"Let's be clear, Irish. I am not a good girl."

He laughs. "I think it's best you take out the fella on the far side now, darlin'. If they receive their instructions any time soon or catch on that they're being picked off one by one, then he has far more places to hide than the one out front. I don't want anything to happen to you if he takes you by surprise."

"I'm touched, Irish."

"I kind of like having you around."

Ditto.

Again, I stick to the shadows. As I walk past, I can see inside the house, and it's noticeably empty. Have the intruders realized the family has gone into hiding? That might be why they're waiting to be told what to do next.

I'm sure the windows are bulletproof, but they really do need to change them to reflective glass as, at present, it's like peering into a goldfish bowl.

I frown as I walk. Whatever I do, I need to stop them from getting inside the house. Fergal keeps an arsenal inside his office. With one shot, they can blow the door and get access to all sorts of weapons, including live grenades.

Panic sets in. This is not good. I always keep a clear head when I carry out a hit, but this isn't a hit. My family is being targeted. This isn't attack. It's defense.

"You okay, Jaine?"

"Don't speak to me," I snap.

I need to focus. I don't need Irish or anyone else distracting me. I move briskly, keeping my back pressed against the hard brick surface of the property, ducking below any windows in case I can be seen from the other side of the building.

I reach the next sniper moments later. Again, he's standing with his gun at his side. I prepare to commit cold-blooded murder for the second time tonight. That's when harsh reality decides to pay me a visit.

That this isn't my rifle. That the bullets won't be engraved. The O'Connells will know the shots weren't fired by The Exterminator, even though they were. I raise the weapon, fire, and he drops to the ground.

A groan.

It wasn't a clean shot. I was too distracted.

I walk over. Looking down at him, I watch as he clutches the side of his head, his lifeblood spilling all over the gravel. I have no choice but to do what I'm about to. Like me, he's wearing a balaclava. His eyes are wide and pleading as he silently begs for his life.

He would have killed my family.

I pull the trigger at point-blank range and watch as his brain leaks out, his eyes now fixed and staring.

I locate both bullets, covering my hands in blood and brains in the process. Taking his weapon, I quickly hide Fergal's rifle in the bushes along with the goggles. I'll need to get Dylan to pick them up later. I can't take them with me. Someone will notice they're missing for sure.

"Jaine, the intruder at the front is moving toward the building."

Clutching the replacement rifle in both hands, I start to run. I need to stop him from getting inside.

"I'm on my way." I round the corner toward the front elevation. "There's no one here, Irish."

It's then I hear the crunch of gravel behind me. I spin around, raising my weapon at the same time. The other sniper spots me and raises his. We stand face to face directly in front of the house that holds my entire world, our rifles pointed at each other's heads.

One of us is going to die today. Right now, it's a coin toss over which one. Then again, it's more likely to be both of us as, this time, my shot will be true, as will his, I'm sure.

Today's as good a day as any to die, I guess. My blood instantly turns cold as Death himself caresses my skin.

I'm suddenly flooded with regret. Is this what it was like for Ace when he knew it was his time? I have things I want to say, and now I'll never get the chance.

Ace. Eoin. Irish.

My babies.

I'll see my beautiful boy soon enough, so I can finally deliver the words I want to say to him face-to-face.

I'll never get the chance to say the words to Eoin that I want to. To tell him I love him and that I'm sorry. Should I have tried harder to make things work between us? Is love enough? Is love really all that matters?

I *can* say the words I need to say to Irish, though. Everything else will come out after I've gone. Fin's parentage. The fact that he never cheated. Those are truths someone else can easily reveal.

I want to return the words I took from him three years ago. Words that only I can return. He can do with them as he wishes. Ignore them. Laugh at them.

Reciprocate them.

"Irish."

"Jaine."

"Tell my boys I love them."

"You can tell them that your…."

"Tell Eoin that I love him and that I'm sorry."

"Jaine…"

"And Irish?" I interject because time is running out. "I love you. Always have. Always will."

Seconds. Minutes. Hours.

I'm not sure how long passes before I hear the shot. It takes a second to register that it hasn't been fired from a rifle. I watch as the intruder drops to the ground before slowly turning my head toward the door of the house I've been living in all these months.

Eoin.

The murder weapon is still in his hand, and it's now pointed straight at me.

He saved my life. Is he now going to end it?

We stare at each other. Right now, he has no idea that it's me. Right now, he's staring at The Exterminator for the first time in his life. Up until now, I was a ghost. A rumor. A figment of his imagination. But here I am in the flesh.

He can see me. And I can see him.

How exhausted he looks. How worn out with life. I choke back a sob. I did that to him, but what choice did he leave me?

Will he now walk over and rip off my mask, or will he allow me to leave with my secret still intact? I stare at him for a moment longer and watch as he lowers the weapon. He makes no attempt to move toward me.

He's letting me go.

I nod at him slowly, and he nods in silent response. I walk away without looking back. When I reach the gates, I message Dylan to tell him where Fergal's rifle and the goggles are located and that he also needs to locate the first bullet fired.

Eoin will be busy handling the clean-up, and the rest of the family will no doubt still be in shock over the fact that trouble brazenly knocked on their front door today.

Meanwhile, I'm not sure what to do next. I want to be with my babies, but I can't. I need Irish to come and pick me up, but I've just told him I love him.

Right now, I wish I really were dead.

What the fuck have I done?

CHAPTER TWENTY-ONE

PADRAIG

The O'Connell Home, Darling, New York

I WAS ALREADY WAITING OUTSIDE FOR HER, HAVING DOWNLOADED the surveillance software onto my phone by following Dylan's messaged instructions.

She hesitates when she sees me. We both know why. Because of what she just admitted to when she confronted death head-on. The only reason she said the words is because she thought her time was up, and she wanted to leave this life with no regrets.

I watch her as she gets into the vehicle.

Silence.

I'm still in shock. I have so many questions, but now is not the time to voice any or to expect any answers. She's just killed two of her own sniper kind. A third was about to kill her. She would have perished had Eoin not stepped in and saved her life. Not that he realized it was Jaine, of course.

"How did he know?"

"I told him. Or at least I told him via Dylan." I'm not going to lie. My big brother was her only chance of survival.

She spins her head toward me, her balaclava still in place, the rifle still clutched in fingers laced with dried blood.

"My hands were tied, darlin'. I couldn't help you. You'd already told them the *other* you was with me, so I couldn't turn up on my own. Not without revealing your identity."

"So, what did you say?"

"I told Dylan to tell Eoin that The Exterminator had taken out two of the bad guys but that he may need a little help closing down the third. Eoin never went into the safe space with the others."

"Why didn't he go in there?" She sounds panicked, likely at the thought that something could have happened to him.

He wants to protect her. She wants to protect him. Neither wants the other's protection.

You couldn't make it up.

"He was concerned that his headstrong ex-wife may turn up when she heard about what was going on. That she would insist on returning home to be with her children. Even though you dumped him for his over-protective stance, he was still insistent on providing it because your life will always mean more to him than his own."

It's hard-hitting but true. He loves her. He would do anything for her, including die.

My brother betrayed me. He disrespected me. They say what goes around comes around, and that's also true. It did. He lost her, and I didn't have to do a thing to make that happen. Karma delivered payback to him all on her own, just like she did me.

I shouldn't feel sorry for him, but I do.

He's still my brother, and I love him. He also saved her life, and for that, I will always be grateful.

"I only asked Dylan to tell them I was with you so Eoin wouldn't go searching for me."

"I know why you did it, darlin', but given our past, he's now going to think the worst of us."

"What else could I say? He'd have come after me otherwise, and you know it! He'd know I was safe if I was with you. I'd rather he thinks the worst of me than for him to be dead."

More silence. Both of us now lost in our own thoughts.

Dancing with death makes you say things you wouldn't normally. You can't live with your regrets if you're dead, so when the grim reaper comes calling, people tend to want to clear the air and get everything off their chests.

Jaine didn't die.

In hindsight, it would have been far better for everyone concerned had she left her confession unsaid. She and I can't ever act on it. Not just because I've verbally agreed to a contract with the Ruoccos but because I refuse to be my own brother's undoing. He may have wronged me, but two wrongs don't make a right. Plus, he and Jaine share Fin.

He will always hold the trump card.

I'm still reeling from the revelation but rejoicing in it too.

We were meant until we weren't.

But we are.

Our love was written in the stars until it wasn't.

But it is.

I went to Sicily and stuck my head in the sand, existing with my wishful thinking, foolish hopes, and pipe fucking dreams, not realizing that Jaine had married and fallen in love with my own brother.

We share a past. He can offer her a future. I can't. At least not now, and maybe not ever. As much as she loves me. As much as I love her. Jaine Jones will forever remain my end game that never will.

That's what karma delivered to me for cheating on her and losing her in the first place.

I drive to my apartment, then park the SUV in the car park underneath the building. I look at Jaine, but she's just staring straight ahead.

"Jaine," I say her name three times before she eventually turns to face me. I try to prize the blood-covered rifle from her hands, but she refuses to let it go. Finally, I manage to convince her to stick her balaclava and gloves in her jacket pocket and leave her jacket and rifle in the car.

She's in shock.

Who can blame her? I'm sure she needs to psych herself up when she's about to shoot someone in cold blood as her alias, regardless of how many times she's carried out the act.

As much as she's dressed for the part, it wasn't her weapon or her engraved bullets. She wasn't on a job.

She went outside to have a quiet shoot and to give herself time to think, and it turned into Armageddon. She'll want to be with her babies right now. She'll want to inspect them to make sure they both still have ten fingers and ten toes, but she's stuck between a rock and a hard place.

She didn't want to give her identity away today and with even more reason. It's not so much that the family would have found out. She must know she won't be able to keep it a secret for much longer. It's that the people orchestrating the snipers may have witnessed her unmasking.

If she already has a target on her back, it would be nothing compared to the size of one she'd earn if she were ever revealed to be the surreptitious sniper. She'd immediately have a price on her head. She'd be lucky to survive twenty-four hours with the countless enemies she'll have garnered over the years.

She can't go home. If they are still out there watching and waiting, they'll see her arrive in the middle of the night. Questions will be asked about where she's been. And that may lead them straight to me.

If Sophia finds out that she's been here? Well, that doesn't bear thinking about. She's already issued a veiled threat toward Jaine.

Padraig's Apartment, Hudson Yards, New York

She's been in the shower for the best part of an hour. I know she has a strict routine that she follows after she's carried out a hit. Even though that's not what this was, it's my guess she's following the same process. I know she uses bleach and whatnot and has her clothes incinerated.

She can't do that this time as she's got nothing else to wear.

As much as I'd love to see her in my shirt and jeans, I'm not sure Eoin would feel the same way, so she can't turn up at home dressed like that. He'll already suspect that something's gone on between us, even though it hasn't.

And it never will.

He may have betrayed me, but I would never betray him. He married her then fell in love with her. How can I blame him for that?

Jaine's love for me isn't something I can act on. I've filed her deathbed confession away for now, as it won't do anyone any good to dwell on it. I have to stick to my newly agreed plan with the Ruoccos for my sake as well as hers. For that, I need to continue to wear a mask of indifference.

The bittersweet words still ring loudly in my ears. I could cry with happiness and sadness at the same time. I won't do either. I will continue to grin and bear it for as long as I must.

Jaine loves me. Three years ago, she told me she didn't.

Why?

And why then fuck my brother behind my back? None of it makes any sense. I'm sitting on the sectional, staring into space, when she disturbs my thoughts.

"Sorry, I took so long."

I turn my head to find her swamped in my navy dressing gown. I can't stop my lips from curving up into a smile.

"I know you have your little routine, darlin'. I've thrown all your clothes in the washer."

"You know how to work a washing machine, Irish?" She snickers softly.

I laugh gently. "I've lived on my own most of my life, so I'm fairly domesticated."

"At least it doesn't smell like sex, feet, and dirty laundry in here."

I laugh again as she refers to my student accommodation, which she seldom visited due to Fletch's sexual shenanigans.

"Come sit with me, darlin'." I pat the seat beside me. I instantly feel her hesitation.

"We don't have to talk if you don't want to." About what she said. She knows that's what I'm saying. I'm sure one day we'll speak about those three little words that were kept secret for whatever reason. Words she no doubt regrets speaking out loud. Words that can't now be taken back.

In the end, it wasn't their time because it wasn't her time.

I can't explain how I feel. It's as though The Almighty granted me a miracle with one hand then immediately took it away with the other.

Should I be grateful that it was granted in the first place, or should I feel cheated that it was so brief I have to keep asking myself if it were real?

I love you. Always have. Always will.

Jaine Jones loves me, and that's all that matters. It's enough because it has to be.

I don't look at her as she sits down, I lift my arm, she slides herself underneath, and then she buries her face against my chest.

It's where she belongs. We both know it. But we also both know that it wasn't meant to be for us this time around.

Acceptance.

My thoughts are filled with what could have been as I hold the love of my life in my arms—a girl who's now the love of my brother's life.

I absorb every one of her silent sobs until she eventually cries herself to sleep. Then I scoop her up in my arms and place her in my bed.

The guest room is good enough for me.

CHAPTER TWENTY-TWO

JAINE

Padraig's Apartment, Hudson Yards, New York

I WAKE WITH A START, SITTING BOLT UPRIGHT AS THE MEMORIES OF the night before jolt me awake. Dawn is breaking. Its orange and yellow glow sneaks past the blinds to fill the space with a fake warmth.

I instantly know where I am, and I know it's his bed that I slept in as the sheets smell of him.

Irish's apartment. Old Spice.

The décor is navy and cream. It's a minimalistic, masculine space. There's no woman's touch in this room. In fact, I haven't seen any signs that a woman lives here. Even the toiletries in the bathroom are either unisex or for men. It's doubtful that Sophia would use a product that wasn't made exclusively for her and doesn't cost at least a billion dollars an ounce.

Why is there no trace of her? I understand that it hasn't been that long since they returned from Sicily. Maybe they live at her place? I was in such a state last night I never even stopped to consider that she could turn up at any moment.

I glance around, noticing that my freshly laundered clothes have been placed on the ottoman at the foot of the bed. Should I dress and leave? I'm sure he won't want me to be here any longer than is necessary.

He's married. I'm engaged.

I was engaged.

Eoin.

He saved my life, or at least he saved the life of The Exterminator. I need to speak to him. To explain. How do I even begin to explain? My thoughts are disturbed by a knock on the door.

"I've put the coffee on, Jaine."

Irish.

I feel awkward. I shouldn't be here. I shouldn't have compromised him. It was thoughtless of me. I shower and dress quickly, brushing my teeth with a new, sealed toothbrush that I found under the basin. I stare at my reflection in the over-sink mirror. I can see the souls of the two other snipers behind my eyes.

The third resides behind Eoin's.

My blood runs cold. I suddenly feel panicky again. A panic that caused me to wound and not outright kill the second sniper. I look at my hands, and they're shaking.

It wasn't attack. It was defense.

What if they return to the house and I'm not there? We could move back to Rising, but then it's not safe there, either. Ace was killed in Nevada. They'll find us no matter where we go. There's nowhere to run. There's nowhere to hide. All we can do is defend until we solve the goddamn puzzle.

Who?

I leave the restroom, sit on the end of the bed and place my head in my hands. I'm conscious of the mattress dipping and strong arms wrapping around me. Like it did all those years ago after I dispatched Lebedev, a feeling of safety immediately envelops me. I press my face against his chest. He's shirtless.

"You're still in shock, darlin', that's all." His voice is as soothing as his steady heartbeat as he strokes my hair.

"Is there any news on the snipers?"

"They were clean, Jaine."

Figures.

"Things aren't safe anymore, Irish." I sigh.

"This coming from the girl who didn't want any protection." He chuckles softly. I pull my head back to speak my mind but then forget what it was I was going to say.

Because it really is unfair to the rest of humankind how good-looking Padraig O'Connell is. Smiling blue eyes sparkle on a face that's wearing a cocky smirk at my blatant loss for words, his coal-black hair still wet and messy from the shower.

So beautiful. So perfect.

So not fucking mine.

I pull away. "It's not about my protection. It's about Fin and JJ. The shooters were on the doorstep of the goddamn house. What if I hadn't gone outside when I did? They could have wiped out the entire family. They were sitting ducks. I mean, how the fuck did they get on the property in the first place?" He squeezes my hand with his to stop my ranting, and I'm immediately grateful for its reassuring warmth.

"Irish, what I said…." I bite my lip, unsure of what to say next. I thought I was going to die. I needed him to know the truth. I don't regret giving back the words, but the timing could have been better.

But then, when exactly is the right time to admit to someone that you still love them?

"It was said in the heat of the moment, Jaine."

"Eoin."

"Don't worry. I won't breathe a word to him. Your secret is safe with me."

I stare at him. The reason I mentioned Eoin is because I know the thought of Padraig and me being together right now will be tearing him apart. He'll be thinking something is going on. I've stayed out all night.

Despite what Irish thinks my loving him isn't a secret. Not to Eoin or to the rest of his family. The only person it's ever been a secret from is him.

He stands and opens the blinds allowing the sunrise to welcome us to this new day. A day I should never have gotten to see.

My eyes drag over him. His inked skin contrasts against the glow of the morning sun, his upper body so defined it looks like he works on it all day, every day. I can't pull my gaze away. This time, my blatant admiration causes the atmosphere to change. Maybe it's the location? After all, I'm in his home.

In his bedroom.

On his bed.

Or maybe it's my frank admission?

I know if I look at his face, it won't be a smirk that I see. There's nothing remotely funny about this moment. I slowly raise my gaze, and my eyes connect with his dark, heated expression. I'd give anything to know what he's thinking right now.

He blinks, and the moment's gone. I watch as he crosses the room, opens a drawer, pulls out a t-shirt, and yanks it over his head.

Wise move. It's safer that way.

Thou shalt not give into temptation.

Easier said than done when you're faced with a shirtless Padraig O'Connell.

"I should…" I stand, and he nods in agreement. We both know it's best if I leave.

"Let me…"

We collide with each other on the way to the bedroom door. To steady me, his hands reach out and grab hold of my upper arms. I can feel their scorching heat the moment they connect with my skin. I stare up at him, my entire being now conscious of his.

I am him. He is me.

"Our souls have always been intertwined. You feel that too, darlin'?"

Right now, it's all I can feel. My eyes drop to his lips.

"Jaine…" It's a warning to us both. We can't cross the line. No good will ever come of it.

Lust. That's all this is, and it's perfectly understandable. We shared a past. The lack of mutual attraction isn't what ended us.

He cheated, but then he didn't.

We shouldn't have ended. We should have been forever.

The last twenty-four hours has us both seeking a release, but that can't be with each other. It can never be with each other.

I love him. He doesn't love me. He gave me his blessing to be with his brother.

Then stop looking at him like you want him to fuck you, as it really isn't helping.

Lust is called a sin for a reason. If not expertly handled, it can wreck lives and destroy people. I have to nip this in the bud before this thing between us spirals out of control. Reaching my hand up, I pull his head down to connect his lips with mine.

So soft. So familiar.

It's a closed-mouth, chaste kiss. A kiss of friendship. A kiss that says thank you. A kiss that says we can't. A kiss that says this stops right here, right now because people will get hurt otherwise. A kiss that draws a line in the sand.

Once. And. For. All

Nothing right could ever come from something so wrong.

I step back and stare up at him. "I'll skip the coffee. I need to get back."

He nods with a half-smile. "Liam's just called. He's downstairs waiting. Ma sent him to pick you up."

I nod back. "I'll see you soon, Irish."

I say soon because I'm not sure when it will be. Has my confession and our chaste kiss changed things between us? I hope not, but that remains to be seen. I leave his apartment and press the button for the elevator. I'm expecting the cabin to be empty when the doors open, but it's not.

"Sophia," I whisper.

"What the hell are you doing here?" she hisses.

If looks could kill, then I would be dead. This is not good. This is not good at all.

CHAPTER TWENTY-THREE

PADRAIG

Padraig's Apartment, Hudson Yards, New York

I REST MY HEAD BACK AGAINST THE SECTIONAL WHILE LETTING OUT a frustrated sigh. Sophia's just hand-delivered the new contract, and on her way to my apartment, she collided head-first with Jaine, who was on her way out.

"Fuck my life," I mumble after I answer my phone.

"It can't be that bad, surely." Dylan sounds surprisingly upbeat, given everything that's been going on.

"It's way worse."

"Explain."

"As you already know, Jaine stayed here last night, and before you ask, it was all strictly platonic. You know what she had to do. It's not like she could then stroll back into the house."

"I understand the reasons, and I have to say, I'm relieved to hear nothing happened between the two of you. I was worried that it might."

"Why would you be worried?" There's an awkward pause. *He knows.* "How long have you known Jaine's still in love with me?"

"A while." He sounds sheepish.

"What does that mean?"

I know exactly what he's going to say. The same thing Fletch did.

"You need to speak to Jaine."

"About?"

"That and several other things."

"What other things?"

"Paddy, it's not for me to say."

"Well, it will be difficult for me to speak to her about anything any time soon."

"How do you mean?"

"When Jaine was leaving, she bumped into Sophia on her way in."

"Jesus Christ. So Sophia knows Jaine spent the night at your place? Did you try to deny it?" He sounds worried, and with good reason. Sophia will have run straight home to tell her big brother.

"I told Sophia that Jaine just needed a place to stay after what happened back at the house and that nothing had gone on between us. She may have seen her arriving last night, so lying about it might have made the situation worse. She'd then have thought I *did* have something to hide."

"And the outcome?"

"She'd previously said she didn't want me to see Jaine face to face anymore. Now I'm not allowed to speak to her via any other means either." I run my hand through my hair in frustration.

Sophia hates Jaine's guts. Because she's my ex-girlfriend, or for some other reason?

"Ever again?"

"Not until Sophia's pregnant."

"So, you really are going to go through with it?"

"If it's the only way to buy my freedom, what choice do I have? I just need to read through the contract line by line to make sure I'm in agreement with everything."

"And how do you feel about the fact that you can't speak to Jaine?"

"Maybe it's for the best, at least for now," I admit.

"I never thought I'd hear you say that."

"She told me she loved me, Dylan. In fairness, she only told me because she thought she was going to die."

"Until her ex-husband saved her life."

"He didn't save her life. He saved The Exterminator's life. Anyway, how is he?"

"Not good. Unlike Sophia, he won't believe that nothing happened between you and Jaine."

"Jaine will speak to him. She had a little come-to-Jesus' moment after everything that happened. I think she now realizes that she was perhaps a bit hasty where he's concerned. I'm sure she'll try to sort things out with him now."

"I wish her luck with that because I don't think he'll be very receptive."

"How so?" I frown.

"I think he's had enough, Paddy. You've not been party to it, but their relationship has been a rollercoaster from day one, and that's putting it mildly."

"But they have a son. Surely, it's got to be worth putting in the extra effort for Fin's sake? And then there's little JJ. He already thinks Eoin's his da."

Another pause.

"What else, Dylan?"

"It's not for me to…."

"I need to ask Jaine, right?" I exhale in frustration.

"So Jaine stayed there last night, and nothing happened." He changes the subject.

"Nothing."

"Your tone doesn't sound convincing, Paddy. What the hell happened?"

"We got here, she showered while I dealt with her blood-stained clothes, she cried, then she went to bed. This morning, we had a chat, and then we kissed."

"You kissed!" I can't miss the disappointment in his voice. It's clear Dylan and Eoin have become close in my absence. Once he was understanding of my situation with Jaine, but now it seems he's far more understanding of Eoin's.

I feel betrayed, even though I have no right to. I left without either a word or a backward glance, so what did I expect?

"It wasn't that sort of kiss. It was nothing more than a peck and more of a goodbye than a hello."

"Either way, don't tell Eoin."

"I won't." I try to keep the bitterness out of my response.

"And how did you feel about the kiss?"

"I accepted the finality of it since there's nothing much I can do about my own situation. I know they betrayed me three years ago, but I agree that having them marry was the right thing to do, given Fin was the result of their one-time union. The lad deserves to have his da in his life. I can't blame Eoin for falling in love with her after they'd taken the vows."

Another noticeable pause.

"Don't you still love her?"

I laugh dryly, running my hand through my hair with a defeated sigh. "More than anything in the world, Dylan. You know that. But what can I do? I have to be realistic. My brother loves her, and she him, and they also share a child. I'm married to Sophia with no way out for the foreseeable future. I have to get her pregnant to escape, and during that time, I'm not allowed to see or speak to Jaine. I can't make plans. Not with her. Not with anyone. All I can do is wait for Sophia to conceive."

"And how do you feel about…. you know?"

"Fucking her? The thought of it makes me feel physically sick most of the time."

"It can't be that bad, surely. I mean, she's a pretty girl, and you did have sex with her once before."

"I was so drunk I can't even remember it. It was also before I discovered just how toxic she is."

"So what happens next?"

"Once I've agreed to the paperwork, she'll make an appointment with the ob-gyn. Provided they say there are no medical reasons why she can't fall pregnant immediately, it's just a case of agreeing a date. Obviously, I'll have to make an appointment with a urologist to make sure I'm not firing blanks."

This is a conversation for pauses it would seem. I know there's no point in asking any questions as I won't be given any answers.

"So, she'll move in with you?"

"I'll move in with her."

"Why?"

"Jaine slept in my bed. There's no way Sophia's ever sleeping in there now. Anyway, have you worked out how the security at the house was breached?" It's my turn to change the subject.

"I have."

"And."

"The alarm wasn't set after you left, so whoever had the controls for the car gates…."

"Sophia had them."

"We know that. Ma's already asked her why she didn't activate the security."

"And what did she say?"

"That she thought she had."

"And she believed her?"

"What else could she do, Paddy? To call her a liar would see her tattle tale to her big brother, and that's not a boat we want to rock right now. Not when we don't know what he's up to or what he's capable of. If we want to accuse her, we need physical proof."

"And how do we get that?"

"You tell me. Anyway, maybe she was being honest. Maybe she did forget. Maybe our enemies are watching our every move so closely they saw an opportunity and took it."

CHAPTER TWENTY-FOUR

JAINE

The O'Connell Home, Darling, New York

"CAN I HAVE A WORD PLEASE, ROISIN?"

Her shoulders immediately tense, and she stops what she's doing. Is it because I've approached her from behind? Is it a nervous reaction after what's happened recently?

Or has Jessie pre-warned her that I was looking to have a conversation about the girly chats she enjoyed with Sophia and Molly? Chats where I suspect I was the main topic of conversation.

I'm a biker. Roisin hates our kind. Having found herself pregnant at twenty-one, her biker baby daddy proceeded to abandon her in her time of need. In turn, she had no option but to give her newly born son up for adoption.

Fergal knows what went down, but her four boys aren't aware that they have an older half-sibling. That's not my secret to share.

Shit happens. You dust yourself down, and you deal. Instead, Roisin waged war against all bikers and against me in particular.

I'm not going to drag up the past. There's little point. I just want to gauge what damage has been done. I appreciate that I staged a personal vendetta against Eoin, but that was one-on-one. Roisin involved third parties in her attack against me.

One is now dead by my hand. The other could very well be directly involved in this very deliberate attack against me and mine. If she is, she'll meet her maker once I have proof.

Duke's taken the children to the summer house. I explained that I needed to have a private conversation with Roisin. He didn't ask any questions. He knows that if it's something he needs to be made aware of that I'll let him know in due course.

I've cornered her in the kitchen. She continues once more with her chopping. Having lived here a while now, I'm aware she likes to prepare Fergal's dinner in advance and at the same time every day. It's how I knew exactly when to make my move.

"About anything in particular?"

"Your chats with Sophia and Molly."

She stops what she's doing once more and slowly turns to look at me. It's been almost a week since the intruders were dispatched. She knows what could have happened had I not gone outside when I did. What my alter-ego subsequently had to do. She also knows that Eoin terminated one of the bad guys right outside the front door.

That's how close our enemies came to wiping out her entire family. And mine. The blood may have been washed away, but its invisible stain will forever remain. She's visibly aged since. We all have.

"Would you like a cup of tea?"

I shake my head and watch as she prepares one for herself.

"Sophia knows."

She's aware of what I'm referring to—Sophia's comments on how Fin is more like Irish than Eoin.

"I suspect she does."

"You suspect?" My tone contains just a hint of sarcasm.

"Okay, I know that she does!" she snaps, her worry now evident. I ignore it. Worrying won't add a day to any of our lives.

"Were she and Molly friends?"

"I wouldn't go that far." I can't miss the defensiveness lacing her voice. It's a clear sign of guilt.

She turns around to face me once more. She's wearing a beige lounge suit today that coordinates with her sheepskin slippers. She looks just like any other old grandma, but she's not.

"They must have been close enough for Molly to have told Sophia the news."

"It's speculation. We don't know anything for sure."

"How else would she have found out?"

Her silence speaks volumes. She and I both know there's no other way.

"And I'm pretty sure if Sophia knows, she'll have spilled her guts to her big brother by now."

More silence.

"So, these conversations," I say.

"What about them?"

"It was during them that you asked Molly to threaten me."

"It was meant to be a veiled threat." She takes a sip of her drink.

I snort. "Well, let's face it, Molly never did take instruction very well."

"Yes, it was during those conversations," she snaps back.

"And the task you set them was to keep your sons away from me, am I right?"

"In the main, yes."

"Did you antagonize her?"

"Which one."

"Sophia!" I'm annoyed with myself for biting back.

"I reminded her that it would do her well to remember that Padraig still loved you."

"Anything else?"

"That it would be in her own best interests to get him to take that precious purity of hers so there could be no going back from him."

I frown. After what happened with Malky, Roisin and I agreed to draw a line under the past. We're not friends. We will never be friends. But for the sake of the rest of the family, we agreed to a truce and to putting everything behind us so we could all move on.

What we share now is a mutual tolerance, much like the one Fergal and I share. I know her secret. She knows mine. I saved her life. She tried to end mine. And now, here we are.

"And that was her task?" I ask.

"Yes."

"And what was Molly's task?"

"To stop Eoin from falling in love with you any more than he already had done."

"By doing what?"

"His wish was her command."

I stare at the floor briefly and shake my head, shocked at just how much this small woman standing before me hated my goddamn guts.

"I'm sorry, Jaine." And she is. I can hear it in her voice. I shake my head again as words fail me.

"It's no wonder Eoin is such a misogynistic asshole," I mutter eventually as I turn my attention out the window. "So, you antagonized both to make sure they were working in tandem for the Duster greater good by keeping the hedonistic female biker away from your two God-fearing sons. A biker who was already happily married with two children and who had no interest in hooking up with either of your two precious boys."

"Something like that."

"Something like that." I let out a dry laugh. "If Sophia knew about Finian, then it wouldn't surprise me if she also knew about Eoin and me right from the start."

"I realize that."

"And that she may also have formed her own suspicions over Molly's disappearance. The fact that Molly was Eoin's fiancé one minute and me the next."

"I know that too."

"And it never concerned you?"

"She's family, Jaine."

"You can't trust a Ruocco! They'd stab each other in the back! Most of them are dead for that very reason!"

She doesn't respond initially. She lets me lash out, then waits until I rein it back in.

"Luc was the don of the Sicilian mafia. No one was to know he would get ousted from his own organization. We did all the background checks, and there was nothing sinister going on. Theirs was considered a good match," she says.

She's right, of course. I was as surprised as the next person when Leo told me the breaking news of the Ruocco's imminent departure.

I rub my hand over my face.

"I'm sorry, Jaine. I pushed the girl. Perhaps too hard when her hatred of you was already apparent."

I stare at her momentarily. She's right about that too. The wound of disrespect was created when I told Sophia I hoped one day Irish would love her as much as he did me. I regretted the words the moment they left my mouth. "I stuck the knife in. You merely twisted it."

There's a silence, each of us lost in our own thoughts. We both have regrets, but we can't alter the past.

"Is there anything else you need to get off your chest while we're having this heart-to-heart, Roisin? If there is, speak now. I may not be in such a forgiving mood if I find something else out at a later date."

She looks pensive for a moment. There is. What, I wonder?

Just as she's about to speak, the front door opens and closes. It'll be Duke with the kids.

"This conversation is not over," I warn her.

She nods. The frown I'm wearing is quickly replaced by a happy smile just as Finian rounds the corner into the room.

"Hey, little big guy." I scoop him up.

My thoughts then drift back to Irish. I haven't seen him since the morning I bumped into Sophia.

I guess my confession really did change things between us. Either that or his past colliding with his future did.

I LEAN MY HEAD BACK AGAINST THE SOFA AND ROLL MY EYES WITH a smile as I partake in a one-sided telephone conversation.

"Can you believe Mr. X-marks-the-spot was outside the house, partner?"

"He sure does get around, Jessie."

"How did he get there so fast? It's like he has some sort of sixth sense where the O'Connells are concerned."

"I guess he was in the right place at the right time." It's not all a lie. There is an element of truth to that.

"I didn't witness it personally because we were all tucked inside the safe space, but by all accounts, Eoin repaid one of his own debts by saving the sniper's life."

"I also believe that to be the case."

"Have you spoken to Mr. X?"

"You could say that."

"And what did he say?"

"Exactly what you just did. That Eoin saved his life."

"I guess Eoin was in the right place at the right time too, huh?"

"Maybe so." Definitely so.

"Anyway, speaking of big bad Eoin."

"What about him?" I know what's coming next.

"He refused to come into the safe space with the rest of us. He was worried you'd come back to the house."

"So I've been told."

Guilt swallows me whole. I didn't want his protection, but in the end, I'd be dead without it. If he had gone into the safe space with the others instead of staying put to look out for the other me, my number would have been up for sure.

"It broke him when Dylan said you'd gone to Paddy's apartment, Jaine."

"Nothing happened."

"Are you sure?"

"I was there, wasn't I?"

"Maybe you should tell Eoin that."

"I've tried calling. I've tried messaging. He won't answer either."

"Maybe you need to pay him a visit."

"So he can ignore me to my face?"

"I just think that aside from him being a bit over-protective, you guys had it all going for you."

"He was suffocating me, Jessie."

"I know that. I realize you're a proper female biker like Bailey, and you can look after yourself. That I'm just a pretend one, and I need a man to help me out most days. It just seems a shame to throw it all away on something he just needs to work on a little."

I snort. "A little? The man's a misogynist."

"Then work on changing him, Jaine. He'd do anything for you, you know that. Don't just butt heads with him all the time. This isn't all on him, partner? This is on both of you. You need to sit down and talk each and every time a problem arises, and then you need to compromise and find a solution. You're used to doing your own thing, and the men in your life have been accommodating with that, but Eoin's isn't like them. He's…"

"Possessive."

"Yes, but only because you're his everything, Jaine. You're his whole world."

"Even the world needs to be able to spin, Jessie."

"I'm sure he'll let you spin once he gets used to the idea. He's just scared. He's never felt this way about anyone before. You both went through so much to get to this point. Don't just throw it all away."

"I'll think about paying him a visit."

"You do that. Is it soon yet." She sounds hopeful.

"Soon?"

"You know? What my daddy spoke to you about. You said you'd tell me soon."

"It's imminent, Jessie." I chuckle.

"How imminent? Weeks? Months? Years?"

"Weeks, because I'm done with keeping secrets. It's time."

"That sounds ominous. Should I be worried?"

"That all depends on how you take the news. Maybe you'll be pleasantly surprised. Anyway, I had my chat with Roisin, and we both agreed that Sophia knows about Fin's true parentage and that she was the one who told Molly."

"Well, Hallelujah. It's great to hear you two finally agreeing on something."

"There's just one problem. We have no proof."

"Don't you have Molly's phone?"

"What do you mean?"

"Check her messages, partner. It's unlikely she ever took the time to delete anything, given the amount of time she spent with her head in the clouds."

I sit bolt upright. "Jessie O'Connell, did anyone ever tell you you're a goddamn genius?"

She lets out a smug snort. "Well, I always said that I got all the brains in the O'Brien family, but those brothers of mine wouldn't hear any of it. What did you call Eoin again?"

"A misogynist."

"That's my brothers right there."

"I could kiss you right now, Jessie."

"I'd rather you did something else for me?"

"What?"

"Go see Eoin."

"I will."

"When?"

"Tomorrow."

I disconnect the call, then rest my head on the sofa again.

Jaine: *Dec, can you take me to see Eoin tomorrow?*

I press send before I get chance to change my mind. I realize I won't get an immediate response. He'll have to check in with his boss first. I'm not naïve enough to think he'll take my instruction.

Will Eoin want to see me, or won't he? He's ignored my calls. He's ignored my messages.

Maybe he's still healing, or perhaps he's been busy. Either way, we can't continue as we are. When I was staring death in the face, one of my biggest regrets was that I should have tried harder to make things work between us.

There's no disputing how much I love him. Jessie seems convinced he can change. That we both can. I'm not so sure. Sometimes people are just too set in their ways. You also have to want to change.

As much as we're from the same life, our backgrounds differ wildly. Bikers are the lowest of the low in our world. Maybe we're just too different.

I stare at the phone. Still no response. Time passes. Tick fucking tock.

Maybe I should just go to the containers on my hog? Or maybe not. That would probably rile him further as he may see that as me flicking the bird at his protection once more.

A protection I tossed back in his face. A protection without which I'd now be dead. He saved the life of The Exterminator, but he was only in the right place at the right time because he was looking out for me.

Not that he knows he saved me, but he will eventually.

I reckon it's time for all of the reveals to take place. My alter-ego. Fin's parentage. My own parentage.

There's been way too much deceit for way too long. Looking death in the face has made me realize that you have to say what needs saying before the chance gets taken away from you.

How much did Ace want to say that he never got the chance to? Tears prick my eyes at my forever regret at not being there with him in his final moments, even if just to hold his hand and tell him how much I fucking loved him.

That I had to rely on Dylan telling me his final words.

But what if Dyl hadn't been there with him? What if there had been no one by his side that he could say anything to? What if he had been scared and all alone? I can't even go there. I can't even think about that. Dylan was there. Ace wasn't alone.

A sob escapes me.

I felt the very same regret that Ace may have done when I was staring down the barrel of that other sniper's rifle. When I was in that place between life and death. I had too many words for the too few seconds I had remaining.

How do you make each final word count? How do you choose?

I wasn't scared of dying. I was scared of the people I was leaving behind, the people I loved most, not knowing how much they meant to me. That they would never know because I'd never taken the time to tell them because, as I did with Ace, I just assumed I had tomorrow.

Each day you put things off, but what happens when tomorrow never comes? Your own regrets will turn into your loved ones' regrets because they'll never know your final thoughts and feelings, and they'll always wish they did.

Say it. Do it. Don't put it off. Live with no regrets.

"I love you, Ace. Always have. Always will," I whisper.

I stare at the ceiling. I would have been all alone had I not had Irish on the line. The regret I would have felt not telling him that I loved him is not something I would have wished to take to the grave with me. Yes, others could have told him, but would he have believed them?

I needed to say it out loud for that reason.

I took them from him, and I needed to give him those three words back, even though all he handed me were twenty generic ones.

It's three weeks until I spill my guts to him. Three weeks until my secret is laid bare. But how can I reveal anything when I haven't seen him? It needs to be done face-to-face. There's no other way.

I suspect Sophia is the reason for his absence. That my colliding with her at his apartment that day has something to do with it.

Not that I can blame her, even if there was nothing to hide. His ex-girlfriend leaving his place first thing in the morning can only ever look one thing.

Suspicious.

All that unfortunate collision will have done is add fuel to the fire and fan the flickering flames of hatred she holds for me that little bit more.

I think back to Eoin's comment at the meeting. That out of the twelve years Irish and I have known each other, how little time we've physically spent together?

I guess since Yale, aside from during the Bratva situation, ours has been a virtual relationship. One that's relied solely on messages and telephone calls, even though we lived in the same world and in the same city.

Was there a reason we never met up during all that time? When we resorted to being just friends at Yale, we only ever kept in touch via message. It was only after we left school that we picked up the phone.

Maybe he didn't think it appropriate to meet up when I started seeing Delaney, but I was single for five years before I met him.

The night of the attack was the first time I've ever been in Irish's apartment. He's never been inside mine.

Does that make our relationship less real or more? I think it's the latter because every single virtual moment we've ever spent together has been filled with real words.

You can't send a silent message. You can't make a silent call.

And he was right. He does know me better than anyone else ever has. But is the relationship truly real when no one knows you exist?

Things could have been so different had he told his family about me. He didn't. Maybe there was a reason for that.

Of course, there was. He never asked for anything more from me because he didn't think he deserved anything more. Because he believes he cheated. But he didn't. Not that it matters now.

I stare at my phone. At the absence of anything from him since the morning after the attack. He used to light up my screen a million times a day. I guess it's Sophia's screen he's illuminating these days.

They're happily married, Jaine. What do you expect?

More. I guess I expected more.

Declan: *I'll pick you up at 8.00 am.*

I stare at the message. I don't respond or acknowledge. There's no point.

I'll just be ready to leave at the stipulated time like a good girl.

CHAPTER TWENTY-FIVE

PADRAIG

Private Clinic, Upper East Side, New York

"YOUR WIFE IS A VERY FIT AND HEALTHY YOUNG WOMAN, MR. O'Connell. There's no reason why conception shouldn't be swift once you start trying."

I stare at Dr. Abella forcing a polite smile as I glance around his clinical white office. Its walls are adorned with proof of his qualifications, and the surface of his pine-colored desk is covered with images of him, his wife, and their two children. All perfectly displayed to assure his wealthy clients that he's the best man for the job when it comes to assisting them in all matters procreation.

In exchange for armfuls of their hard-earned cash, of course. I'm sure most couples sitting before him would be delighted to hear this *happy* news.

I am. I'm not.

I've gone through the contract line by line. If I provide the

Ruoccos with a Duster heir to allow them to maintain their alliance with my family, I'm effectively off the hook. That's all Luc was interested in.

Or so he says.

I suspect there's more to it than that, but that's all he was prepared to give away during our ten-minute telephone conversation. It's my guess the child is the second bite at the Duster cherry.

What was the first, I wonder?

I suspect Luc had known for a while that his days with the Cosa Nostra were numbered for reasons unknown to anyone outside the organization. That he manipulated the situation so he could retain the don ship until after Sophia and I had taken the vows, all so my family would be none the wiser.

I'm told Eoin unearthed the unwelcome news on my wedding day, and only because he backed the new don, Leoluca Di Matteo, into a corner, giving him no option but to admit the truth.

My wedding should never have taken place. It offered no political advantage to my family whatsoever. My life was ruined for nothing.

And now here I am, sitting staring at a balding, middle-aged pleasant enough man who's wearing a beaming smile as he tells me the news he thinks I've been desperate to hear.

That the love of my life will be able to bear the fruit of my loins and provide me with an army of mobster children.

I wish.

Instead, I have to impregnate the Sicilian viper sitting beside me. That's on the basis that I'm not firing blanks, of course. All my life, I've used a condom. The only time I didn't was with Jaine and then Sophia.

Jaine didn't get pregnant. Sophia didn't either.

Any child produced will permanently reside in New York and live with me or my family half the time. Given that Luc and Sophia are the last two Ruocco family members standing, the child need never travel to Sicily. If they wish to visit in the future, I'll take them personally.

I'm lost in my own thoughts when the doctor disturbs my concentration.

"How long have you been married, did you say?"

"Just over a year."

He frowns and then smiles at me. "Not that it's any of my business, but it seems a long time to wait to con...."

"Thank you, Dr. Abella," Sophia interrupts him. We both turn to face her. "My husband and I decided to delay starting a family. As you will appreciate, ours was an arranged marriage, so we wanted to get to know each other before taking the next step. We are both very pleased to hear that there is nothing preventing a pregnancy."

Lies fall so easily from her lips. What else has she been lying about, I wonder?

"I still have to get checked out medically, of course."

"I'm sure that won't be necessary, Padraig."

"There's no point in going to all that physical effort if I'm unable to uphold my side of the bargain."

"Well, I do have the contact details of a highly recommended urologist." Dr. Abella opens his desk drawer and pulls out a white business card. He reaches across the desk. Sophia attempts to take it, but I get there first.

I'll make the appointment to suit me. Knowing her, we'd be heading there now, and I need five minutes to get my head around all of this. We say our goodbyes, then leave.

I typically drive myself, as does our Dyl. As I had Sophia with me today, I roped Liam into bringing us.

I get in the back of the SUV, and Liam opens the door for Sophia. I watch as she closes the privacy screen.

"So, that is good news, is it not?"

I glance at her as she sits beside me. She's wearing cream pants with a matching top, the color perfectly setting off her olive skin. Her perfume is the same as before.

I realize the reason I dislike it so much is because it's lily based. It reminds me of our wedding day.

"I suppose so."

"You suppose so." She lets out a light laugh before placing her red talon-tipped hand possessively on my upper thigh. Putting my own hand over hers, I lift it off and place it back in her lap without saying a word.

"Have you spoken to Jaine recently?"

"You know I haven't."

"No calls, no messages, no more secret visits?"

"Her visit wasn't a secret."

"I beg to differ, Padraig. Her fiancé wasn't aware she would be alone with you in your apartment. I'm told he only found out when the intruders descended on the house, and he asked after her whereabouts."

I can't deny a thing. Jaine hasn't covered either of us in glory doing what she did. I know it was a spur-of-the-moment decision, but still.

"I heard they're still not on speaking terms. A pity when, according to you, nothing happened."

"Nothing did happen, and they had already split up. Jaine visiting me had nothing to do with their separation."

"Perhaps not, but it will no doubt be the reason they never get back together. Your brother doesn't strike me as the type of man who would ever accept sloppy seconds."

"As I said, nothing happened. Anyway, Jaine was mine first."

"And now you're mine." She places her hand on my thigh once more, and this time I leave it where it is. It's just not worth the effort. *She's* not worth the effort. She gets off on garnering a reaction from me.

"For now."

"For now."

We travel the rest of the journey in silence.

Sitting on the sofa, I stare across at the amber liquid. I've just been dropped off by Liam, the conversation with Sophia still ringing in my ears.

It's clear she wants me to believe myself responsible for the failure of Eoin and Jaine's relationship. That my covert rendezvous with Jaine was the final nail in the coffin.

It wasn't.

Jaine, Dylan, and I know the truth and one day when Jaine finally reveals all of her secrets, everyone else will know the truth too. That she came here because she had nowhere else safe to go.

It all boils down to trust. If Jaine were mine and she told me that nothing had happened, then I would believe her one hundred percent. Does Eoin not trust her, or does he not trust me with her?

Either way that says more about him than her. What's got him so worried? What she and I shared is in the past. Her future is with him, not me. Why would she want me when they're already a family unit?

I haven't spoken to him since the night of the attack. Maybe it's time to change that rather than listening to hearsay. Maybe it's time to be wrongly accused direct from the horse's mouth.

I continue to stare at my liquid nemesis. For the first time in a while, I'm tempted to give in to its silent call. I pick up my phone instead.

"How's it hanging, brother?" I smile as I speak. Dylan and I are slowly starting to repair our own fractured relationship. I had no idea how much my removing myself from the family affected him. We were joined at the hip. We did everything together before I abandoned him.

I realize now how selfish I was. That I could have and should have done things differently. Confronted my demons rather than running from them. Faced my problems head-on.

Maybe then I could have stopped the love of my life from marrying my own fucking brother.

"It's hanging just fine, Paddy."

He knows what I'm going to ask before I even say the words.

"How's Jaine?" It's been over a week since I spoke to her last.

"I'm not sure. She's been speaking to Jessie, not me."

"You sound a bit miffed about that."

"I thought she and I were friends."

"You are friends, but sometimes females just need to talk girly stuff."

"It's not just that."

"No?"

"I reckon it's partly because I kept telling her to do our Eoin's bidding. In the end, she'd had enough of me and him."

I chuckle. "She won't hold a grudge against either of you. She almost died. She'll just be taking time out and doing some reflection."

"I guess."

"You miss her?"

"Yes."

"Join the club. So, has Jessie not given anything away about what they've been talking about?"

"She's just mentioned one thing. That Jaine doesn't want to be a keeper of secrets anymore. She's going to spill her guts about everything."

"Even her alter-ego?"

"I reckon so. She can't keep it quiet for much longer."

A pause.

"Ma already knows. So, that makes three of us."

"How?"

"I'm guessing because the weapon Jaine used to dispatch Molly was the same one she used at St. Patrick's on your wedding day. She must have hidden it inside the venue because she didn't have it on her when Da collared her."

"That was fortunate for her and Ma."

"Indeed."

"Who was the actual target at the wedding?" I already know. It came up during a conversation with da, but he didn't go into any detail given he almost killed Jaine the very same day.

"Jaine showed up because she heard on the sniper grapevine that you were the target. She would never let anything happen to you."

"So, she saved my life?"

"Not exactly."

"What do you mean?"

"It wasn't you the two baddies were after. It was the rest of us. Jaine saved all of us that day."

"But she came for me?"

"She did, brother, and now you know why."

"Because she loves me."

"Partially that."

"What does that mean?" I'm not sure why I'm wasting my breath. He won't expand further.

"You…"

"Need to speak to Jaine. I can't, and you know I can't."

Frustratingly, he changes the subject like he always does when I start digging.

"How did it go at the clinic?"

"Sophia is primed and ready to go. If she'd had her way, we'd have fucked in the back of the SUV on the way back."

"That keen?"

"If I didn't find the whole thing off-putting enough, that was the icing on the cake. I'm not sure how I'll be able to go through with it."

"Lie back and think of your freedom?"

"I doubt there'll be any lying back involved. I'm pretty sure Sophia will make me work for every second of my freedom."

"Too much information. So, what happens next?"

"I need to visit the urologist."

"Putting it off?"

"Yes and no. As much as I want my freedom, I'm not sure it's worth it. Maybe I'll just remain a trophy husband for the rest of my days."

"But what if…"

"It will never happen, so it makes no difference."

"You don't even know what I was going to say."

"I know exactly what you were going to say. You were going to say what if Jaine never gets back with Eoin. You and I both know she will. It's just a matter of time. Anyway, they share Fin. I would never go anywhere near her while there's still a chance for them."

"Paddy…"

"Leave it there, Dyl. Anyway, I need to go and make this appointment. Regardless of whether I go ahead with this stupid idea of mine, I'd like to know if I'm capable of fathering a child or not."

CHAPTER TWENTY-SIX

JAINE

The Docks, Hudson Yards

I step out of the SUV and look around before pulling my suit jacket tighter around my torso.

After this, I'm going straight to the office, then I'm heading to my apartment to collect Molly's phone, which is currently locked up with my rifles.

Dec messaged me to cancel my pre-arranged appointment with Eoin. Then he did it again. Now, here we are, two days later.

I've been here several times now, but I still can't get used to how depressed it makes me feel. It's like the air is laced with a despondency that you inhale straight into your lungs until you physically can't breathe. Until you feel totally alone.

Most of the exposed stacked containers are either fully or partially stripped of paint and adverts, their exposed surfaces having long since been worn over time by the barrage of weather and the spray from the brackish water of the river.

Sometimes, a new one gets added, his surface both vibrant and enthusiastic when measured against the colorless backdrop of his long-suffering comrades. It's then he realizes what his future is going to be like.

Grey. Bleak. Desolate.

Same as theirs.

Same as ours.

Why keep fighting when the ending is inevitable?

I can understand why Eoin comes here at times. Sometimes, you need to escape life's burdens, even if it's just to stop you from going more insane than you already are.

Most of us are born of sound minds. It's our life experiences that slowly drive us mad. In our world, the negative experiences can far outweigh the positive ones, each new one delivering yet another hammer blow to what started off as an optimistic mindset.

I don't like that Eoin spends his time here, wallowing in the darkness inside his own head. It's not healthy. I want everything for him.

Contentment. Happiness. Even if it's not with me.

I don't like that I've pushed him so far that he's come here to lick his wounds.

I don't like that I'm one of his negative experiences. That I've had so many adverse effects on his life in our relatively short time together.

I love him, and I know he loves me. Is love really enough?

Do happily ever afters really happen?

Maybe they do. In fairy tales.

I follow Dec as he leads me between the containers once more. Am I going to one of the two I visited previously, or am I headed for another house of horrors filled with its own array of macabre delights?

I don't feel nervous. I don't feel scared. Maybe it's because I feel like I'm living on borrowed time these days anyway.

He saved my life. *He saved The Exterminator's life.*

In three weeks, he'll know exactly whose life he saved. In three weeks, I refuse to live a lie any longer.

I hope Eoin refuses to continue living his own lie. I hope he tells Irish the truth. The one thing that he *is* guilty of. Keeping us apart when he had no need to. Keeping us apart purely for his own selfish reasons. Not that it should matter anymore. Irish is happy now.

I want Eoin to be happy too.

Dec steps up to the door of the furnished container and motions his head for me to step inside. I hear the door close behind me.

This time, it's not pitch black. I look at the contents. At the sofa he fucked me over the last time I was here. At the other small pieces of furniture.

I'm guessing the sofa converts into a sleeping arrangement of sorts. Why does he come here when he has a perfectly good apartment?

I ask myself the question, but I already know the answer. His monster needs to vent and to do that, he needs access to the container next door and an assortment of unwilling victims. It's easier to remain on site, especially with the need for bloodshed riding you hard.

Having taken in my surroundings, I switch my attention to Eoin. He's dressed professionally with his back to me. Has he been to the office? Is he planning on going? Has he agreed to meet me here rather than there for a reason?

"What is it that you want, Jaine?" His voice is cold and distant, but even his unwelcoming tone doesn't stop my body from calling out to his. His shoulders tense.

He can sense it.

The physical addiction works both ways, even if the relationship never did.

"I don't know." I'm being honest. I don't know what it is I want from him. I'm not sure I ever have. Maybe that's part of the problem.

I used to think that when you loved someone, you worked hard at it because love was enough until I realized it isn't.

Maybe I'm just jaded with love. After Ace. After Irish. What's the point in working at it when it's so fleeting anyway? When in the end, it doesn't conquer all.

It simply conquers you.

He laughs dryly. "You don't know what you want?"

"I wanted to make sure you were okay."

"Did you come here to gloat?" He turns around slowly, his eyes burning green.

Anger. Arousal. Adrenaline. Which is the trigger, I wonder?

He crosses the floor like a panther readying to pounce on its prey. To do what?

Fuck me? Kill me?

He stops in front of me.

So perfectly imperfect.

His spicy cologne pulls me in as his tendrils of darkness wrap around me like a sensual caress. I've missed them. I've missed him.

I lick my lips unintentionally.

Or was it?

His gaze instantly drops to my mouth. We both hear my breath hitch as he grabs me and spins me around. Pulling my back against his hard body his hand circles my throat. A groan escapes me as the possessive human collar slowly tightens.

"Or is your greedy little pussy just hungry for my cock, Miss Jones?"

His other hand drops to the bottom of my skirt, which he then yanks up to my waist. I instinctively grind my ass against his groin.

He's hard.

He pushes me against the container wall, and my hands collide with the cold metal surface. His breath is hot against my neck, but he makes no attempt to kiss me.

I want him to kiss me. I need to taste his fucking arrogance.

Pushing my panties aside, he thrusts two fingers inside. Even though it hurts, I grind against them. I want more of this addictive, punishing pain only he can deliver.

He finger fucks me hard and fast as he scissors his fingers. I know what's coming next. I hear the sound of a zipper, then I feel the head of his cock against my slickness, and with one push, he's seated deep inside me.

My walls clench around him, welcoming him back.

Miss. Need. Love.

His thrusts are brutal and selfish, taking me back to our first time. When it wasn't about me, it was about him.

Right here is all about him. Right now, I don't care.

I push back against him, needing more. Demanding more. His fingers bruise my hips as he gives me exactly what I'm asking for.

The sound of my wetness echoes in the confined space, joined only by my groans and whines of appreciation as he fucks me hard against the wall.

There are no words spoken. This isn't intimacy. This is animalistic fucking. Provided it's a means to a mutually satisfying end, right now I don't fucking care.

I arch my back and spread my legs further, crying out in pain when he bottoms out. He curses me as his movements become jerky. With a low growl, he releases deep inside before pulling out. He knows I'm not finished.

"Beg to come." His hot breath is in my ear once more.

"Fuck you, asshole."

"That fucking mouth will beg." He presses his finger to my clit before circling it. I part my legs, but he just laughs darkly then moves his finger away. Asshole.

"Please."

"Good girl."

He slowly pushes his dick back inside my cum-filled pussy, causing his release to spill down my legs. I groan at the sensation as he tilts my hips and thrusts once, twice. I cry out on the third as I finally find my own release.

He pulls out once more and steps back, his fingers collecting his cum from my inner thighs before thrusting it back inside me.

I stand there with my skirt around my waist and his release oozing out of me. I don't turn around when I hear the sound of a zipper or when I hear footsteps.

He passes me a cloth to clean myself up. I stare at the wall as I do so, knowing now exactly what this is.

Payback. A pause, then he repeats the same two words.

"It's over."

CHAPTER TWENTY-SEVEN

PADRAIG

The Hudson Dusters' HQ, Manhattan, New York

We watch Jaine as she enters the meeting room.

She loves me.

Is it strange that it's all I can think about when I look at her? Jaine Jones fucking loves me. Padraig O'Connell.

Dreams actually do come true. Well, in part, at least. I'm no longer unloved. I'm just alone and unneeded these days.

She's dressed in a navy pantsuit, her blond hair hanging straight down her back. She looks good.

Confident. Assertive. Professional.

It's been a week since she and Eoin had their final showdown at the containers. No one knows precisely what went down. No one knows exactly what was said. My brother is an extremely private individual.

No one will ever know unless Jaine decides to tell them.

By all accounts, she's been there several times before now. She's witnessed my brother kill. Once is rare. Twice is unheard of.

The second time, it was a blood sacrifice in her honor. Malky McGrath.

He tried to end my ma's life, but that wasn't what resulted in his demise. It was the fact that he dared lay a hand on Jaine. Eoin ended him. Jaine ended Molly.

Seems pretty fair to me.

Molly's untimely demise happened at the venue I got married in. Jaine attended my wedding. She watched me take the vows with another woman. How did that make her feel? Is it wrong that I want to know?

Is it wrong that I want her to have hated every single moment of that day as much as I did?

I wonder when she's planning on telling everyone about her sniping sideline. Is that a reveal for today or for another time? She'll have it meticulously planned, I'm sure.

Who, when, where, and in which order.

Or will she launch a truth bomb into the family room with us all in it and wait for the explosion? Will the rest of them have a go at the ones who already knew? Will Da have a go at Ma? Will Eoin have a go at me and Dyl?

Looking at her, I think she's past caring.

We're family. We will always be family now, thanks to Fin and JJ. And that card trumps everything else, hence why Jaine is with us here today.

She won't attend every meeting. I'm guessing Jessie tells her what's on the agenda in advance so Jaine can make an informed decision.

Now that she's no longer with Eoin, could there ever be a chance for her and me? I push the unrealistic thought to the back of my mind.

Don't be daft, Padraig. Quit with all your wishful thinking, foolish hopes, and pipe dreams. Why would she be interested in you when you cheated on her? It's the reason she kept her distance all those years, and you know it.

Who can blame her?

If she loved me back then she never acted on it. Why would she do so now?

I've also got nothing to offer her. I'm currently trapped in a loveless marriage, having to play make-believe to the outside world until I impregnate my fake wife—an act that could take months or, knowing my luck, years.

"It's good to see you, Jaine."

"Fergal."

She doesn't give him the time of day. My da's actually fond of her, even if the fondness isn't reciprocated. It's my guess it's because of the scar she wears on her cheek courtesy of his blade.

"You're looking well today, Jaine." Aidan pipes up from my left-hand side. My cousin reminds me of what I used to be like back in the day before I stopped living and started existing. When everything was with a smile and a witty remark.

"As are you, Aidan."

We all watch as he places his hands behind his head, so Jaine can more easily admire him. She does so more for his male pride than anything else. He's of no interest to her. At least not in that way. It doesn't stop my jealousy from riling me. I want to punch him in the gut for flirting with her, but that won't fit in with my need to appear a happily married man.

Eoin glares at him but says nothing. Aidan's clearly pulled this stunt before. He does have a fancy for Jaine, but I reckon it's done primarily to wind my big brother up. Eoin shouldn't be reacting anyway.

When she did reach out to him, he slammed the door of second chances in her face.

His reaction came as a surprise to us all. We expected them to settle their differences and work together to find this missing balance of theirs. According to our Dylan, it's their third or fourth chance, not their second, so maybe Eoin decided there was no point in continuing to flog a dead horse.

"Dylan. Cillian."

She nods at both before turning her attention to me. "Padraig."

Her expression is impassive, but I can sense her disappointment in me. I've not been in contact with her since her frank admission and chaste kiss. She'll think they're the reason behind my prolonged silence.

Do I tell her about my pact with Sophia? Jaine and I used to tell each other everything, but that was before she became involved with my brother and before she became part of my family.

Where would her loyalties lie these days, I wonder? To me? To him? To them?

I've not told anyone apart from Dylan as I've no idea how the rest of my family will react to the fact that I'm trying to escape the clutches of the wife they went out of their way to hand-pick for me. And trying to preserve Jaine's life while I do so.

Then again, they didn't care about how I'd react when they entered me into an arranged marriage with her in the first place.

"Eoin."

She finally turns her attention to my eldest brother, and he stares at her like he wants to eat her alive.

He worships her. He adores her.

He may try to hide it from the others, but he can't hide it from someone who's worn that same look for the past twelve years. From someone who also worships and adores her.

"And what brings you here today, Jaine?" Da asks the all-important question.

He's had another chair brought to the table and had it placed on his right-hand side. The chair to the right of Dylan is also vacant, as Jessie is in Nevada visiting Lucifer. The chair to Eoin's right is also empty, as it's where Jaine usually sits.

She glances around, then takes her usual spot to Eoin's right.

He gives nothing away, but I know he'll be surprised by that move.

What he doesn't realize is that she's not doing it because she wants to sit next to his pompous arse. She's doing it to let him know that the fact that she dumped him, and then he dumped her straight back, has left her unaffected. She shelved her love for him the same as she's shelved her love for me.

She has far more important things to concern herself with right now.

"I've just had a meeting with Rod. It was local to here, so I thought I'd drop in to discuss the same matter with you."

"And that is?"

She side glances at Eoin before turning her attention back to Da. "A conversation I had with Nate Hawke."

"How is Nate?" I smile as I ask the question.

"Was that the conversation that took place the very same evening he intimated that he wanted to sleep with you?" Eoin tosses in.

"My, my. Two questions at once." Jaine smiles at me, but it doesn't quite reach her eyes. "Nate's the same as he's always been. As sharp as a tack and wondering what's in it for him."

She then turns her attention to Eoin. He doesn't even get the fake smile. "What wasn't in it for him was the opportunity to fuck me."

I watch Eoin's hand as he grips his Montblanc pen, no doubt imagining it to be the District Attorney's neck.

"So, what did you converse about, darlin'?"

Her attention flicks back to me. "Jaine will do just fine, Padraig."

I clutch my chest to pretend I'm mortally wounded that she's no longer referring to me as her Irish and that I'm no longer allowed to call her darlin'. I can't help but notice her lips twitching upward.

We'll repair. We always will.

Eoin glares at me. If looks could kill, I actually *would* be mortally wounded. What's got his panties in a bunch?

Jaine makes eye contact with each of us before continuing.

"I explained that I had some west coast clients who were experiencing a little unrest and raised my concern that the drive-by shooting in New York and outside Cillian's apartment could well be related."

Da frowns at her, no doubt concerned and curious as to why she'd want to involve the District Attorney, more so when he'd be after every one of us if the opportunity arose. Or then again, maybe not.

"Why would you do that, Jaine?" My eldest brother poses the next question.

"My concern, Eoin," she smiles politely at him, "is that this faceless faction may well be a larger entity than we first thought. The New York shooting may mean that their reach extends coast to coast. What we can't do is expose them and then not have the capabilities or manpower to deal with the numbers involved. We can't have any of their high rankers escaping the net then spreading out like a cancer, especially if they then find out who cast it in the first place."

"And what's Hawke going to do?"

"As they're now encroaching on his territory, I offered Nate a deal to work together to bring them down. He can handle the additional throughput by handing out convictions and jail time."

"So, by issuing death sentences you mean?" I toss in.

We all know that any high ranker in our life who earns himself a holiday spot on Rikers Island will quickly be welcomed by a wealth of enemies who are already sunning themselves there. Enemies who will be only too happy to ensure his extended vacation quickly turns into a mini break.

She nods. "He's agreed to do so, but on one condition."

"And what condition is that?" We turn to look at Da, but his face is giving nothing away.

"He wants exposure. Nate is all about enhancing that impressive legal resume of his and getting his face in the press. His argument, which is valid, is that if he's only handling the lower hierarchy, it won't earn him a great deal of publicity, or at least not enough for the amount of work he'd have to put in handling the potential numbers involved, so he wants their leader."

"And is that all he wants?"

"Yes."

"And do you trust him?" Eoin looks at her, but it's with admiration now because this is a solid plan, and everyone sitting here knows it.

If we can get Nate to work alongside us covertly, then maybe we can stop filling up the Hudson with so many bodies, and he can reap the rewards by destroying them legally in court.

Win-win for everyone, and the same end result for the dead person walking.

"I don't trust anyone, so why would I trust him?" She stares at him. "But I do know that Nate wouldn't lie to me about something like that. If he says that's all he wants, that's all he wants. It won't stop him from trying to pin anything he can on anyone else, so you do have to bear that in mind."

"So, this would be a case of good lawyer, bad lawyer?"

She smirks at me. "That's exactly the way I saw it too. Sometimes Robin has to work with The Joker and not Batman in order to get the job done. She smiles between Dylan and me, and Dyl lets out a laugh, earning himself a glare from Eoin, whose nose is out of joint as he's not party to the private joke. "Anyway, digest what I've said. I have to go as I have another meeting I need to get to."

"So, now we just need to work out who it is." We all look at Da again. He's shriveling away more and more each day. I reckon once this situation is resolved, we'll need to force him to retire and let Eoin take over the reins. He's more than capable. The only problem is that my parents won't be keen for him to do so without a wife.

"I have Molly's phone." We all turn our attention back to Jaine. It's never been openly discussed, but we're all fully aware of who ended the other girl's life.

"And what do you propose to do with that?" Eoin frowns at her.

She stares at him. "Molly shared a secret. I want to see if there's proof of who she shared it with. If there is, I want to know what else she shared."

Aidan snickers. "I'm sure she'll have shared plenty with our Eoin."

"I'm sure she will have," Jaine mutters, her eyes never leaving Eoin's.

Eoin's frown deepens. He won't want Jaine to witness his private communications with his ex, but he won't tell her not to go through the phone either. Not if it helps the cause. It's my guess that Molly sent him a lot more than work-related correspondence going by the foul mood he's currently descending into.

She breaks eye contact with him and then stands to leave. I watch my brother as he stares after her, his face filled with regret over what could have been.

I know exactly how he feels.

CHAPTER TWENTY-EIGHT

JAINE

The O'Connell Home, Darling, New York

I STARE AT THE HANDSET. IT'S THE SAME MODEL AS THE ONE I USE.

What secrets does it hold behind its blank screen, I wonder? A phone that could give up a plethora of truths or none at all. A device, the contents of which could be the answer to all our problems or could just add to them. Since it belongs to Molly McGrath, it's most likely the latter.

I guess I'm about to find out.

I think back over my conversation earlier today with Roisin. We finally finished our little tete-a-tete while Fin and JJ were watching a movie. I'm almost certain the first time around she was about to add something else, but this time, she didn't offer to expand further.

She's hiding something.

I can't point the finger. I have secrets of my own I've yet to reveal. If everyone had been aware of my alter-ego on the night of the attack, I wouldn't have had to compromise Irish the way I did. Then again, had I confessed, Eoin's protective streak would likely have kicked in and prevented me from doing what I had to.

What would the outcome have been then I wonder?

By keeping our secrets, we're forcing others to do the same, whether they're willing to or not, which isn't really fair.

Is there anyone else harboring Roisin's secret?

All she did add was that she continued to fuel the torches of hatred Sophia and Molly both carried for me in order to achieve her goal of keeping her two boys away from a biker. A bit nonsensical, given her other two sons are already married to our kind.

In the end, when she wanted the opposite for her eldest, it resulted in the McGraths declaring outlaw war on the O'Connells. Such blatant betrayal opened up a wound of disrespect. We all know those never heal in this life.

Those just become infected.

Malky's death. Molly's death. A close-run thing for both Roisin and me. All of that was as a direct result. Is that war truly over? What of the rest of the McGraths? Will they show up on our doorstep?

Is any war ever over? Isn't it just a case that a white flag is raised as a truce to create the pretense of peace in order to allow time to regroup? Fighting will always flare up, and conflict will always resume, more so in instances where the debt has not been repaid.

Sophia.

I started that war. I can point the finger at Roisin for provoking her as much as I like, but I uttered the silent words, 'Let battle commence.'

I charge Molly's handset on my laptop and the screen flickers to life within minutes. It was a thumbprint lock, but I changed the settings the day I ended hers. It's just as well, as I never thought to hack the digit off at the time. I also made sure to turn the location finder off.

I think back on the recent Duster meeting. At Adrian's lewd comment about the messages Molly may or may not have sent to Eoin. Jealousy courses through me. That she had access to something that's mine.

Was mine.

That day at the containers was payback. Nothing more, nothing less. We fucked, and I uttered those two words. We fucked, then he did the same.

Checkmate.

The slate may have been wiped clean that day regarding our turbulent relationship, but the memories will never fade—just more pages to add to the story of my life.

Same with Irish. After all those years apart, when he returned, I thought we could have a future, even if only as friends. But having not spoken to him for weeks, aside from at the meeting, it's clear he doesn't even want that.

What did I expect? I compromised him by selfishly doing what I did. I'm sure he won't want history repeating, hence the necessary distancing. I belong firmly in his past because I jeopardized his future with Sophia.

I look at Molly's phone once more. It hasn't got much power, but it's enough for me to access what I need and to download the entire content to my laptop.

There are a few missed calls. Numbers I'll ask either Jessie or Dylan to analyze. I move straight to the messages.

As Jessie suspected, they're all still there and filed neatly in name order. Molly was clearly a better administrator than she ever was a mobster or a lawyer.

My finger hovers over Eoin's name, but I don't look. It would be an invasion of privacy. They were together for over a year. They were planning on getting married. If they had intimate conversations or sent photos back and forth over that time, they're for their eyes only.

I scroll down until I see Sophia's name.

Does she realize I have the phone? She must know Molly is no longer with us, given the time that's lapsed, surely? Will she suspect I had any involvement in her demise? I don't bother scrolling back any further than necessary.

For now, I just need an answer to the question that's been bugging me for weeks. Does Sophia know about Fin, and if so, did Molly tell her?

Molly: *The boy is Padraig's. Eoin's just told me so. He says he married the biker to protect Finian, but it's all a lie. He's in love with her. It's just as Roisin predicted.*
Sophia: *It's as I feared, then. What happens now?*
Molly: *I don't know. I've just been dumped, so I'm about to leave the building.*
Sophia: *Your father will be furious.*
Molly: *If he reacts badly, then the O'Connells have brought that on themselves. Eoin disrespected me, and Roisin betrayed me, and as for that biker...*
Sophia: *She'll be executed mobster-style?*
Molly: *You read my mind.*

There's then a time gap. The last message was received only two days ago.

Sophia: *I've had a message from an unknown number. They say they've left a gift for you at St. Peters. It's in the safe room under the first sectional. I'm not sure how they got in there. Maybe one of the high-rankers let them in? Or maybe* *it's just a hoax? Either way, I thought I should pass on the message.*

Hoax or not, that's where I'm now headed.

What's the worst that can happen inside a church? I message Duke to let him know I need to go out, then shoving Molly's phone in my pocket, I place my dead one on charge.

I'm sure I won't need it. It won't take me long to get there and back.

St. Peter's Church, Upper East Side, New York

I park up my hog on the same grass verge I did last time I was here. I'd just married Eoin. I'd just kissed Eoin. And the guilt I felt for betraying Ace by doing both caused me to throw up.

It was over a year ago now.

The waves of grief don't get any smaller. They just get farther apart, so you can at least breathe in between each one. I feel guilty that I don't think about him every minute of every day like I used to. That I don't make time to talk to him each morning like I did.

It's not that I don't still love him or miss him. It's because I've had no choice but to move on with a life without him in it.

I wipe the tears from my cheeks. I know they're falling. They always do when I think of Jason Steele. I swallow the lump of words unspoken as I stare up at St. Peter's.

Unlike the rest of the family, I don't frequent this establishment, although the children do from time to time. Well, they did when it was safe for them to do so. I figured The Almighty wouldn't want me stopping by pretending to beg for his forgiveness for the number of souls I've personally collected over the years.

Let's face it, he doesn't have time to waste, and neither do I.

It's dusk, and the sky's laced with varying shades of blue and pink. Even though darkness hasn't fully descended, the bats are already out, and I can't help but smile as they flit playfully around my head.

I stare at Irish's church—a place he holds closer to his heart than any other.

I told him I loved him, and then he was gone. He clearly doesn't want my love in any shape or form.

I understand.

In a week, I'll tell him that Finian's his son. It seems wrong to keep it secret since his wife already knows, but I agreed to the two months timeline with the family.

Will he hate me? I can't change the choices I made back then. Would I if I could?

Yes. No.

I've had to live with my decisions. He's had to live with them too, even though he wasn't party to any that concerned him.

The same feeling of déjà vu washes over me as I face the ancient grey stone walls, my gaze dragged to the sky by the proud spire sat atop. This time, the earthy smell of freshly dug soil is absent.

Is the small graveyard with the uneven headstones finally full?

I make my way toward the imposing entrance, my hand connecting once again with the black circular handle before turning it and pushing the door forward. I switch on the lights, blinking as my vision adjusts to the contrast of the darkness I leave behind.

My eyes then glance over the tall, vaulted ceilings, the ancient wooden pews, and the abundance of stained-glass windows that no doubt look breathtaking with the sunlight streaming through.

Maybe one day I'll get to see this place in the daylight.

My gaze drops to the scaffolding over the altar. Are they renovating? Is Father O'Reilly here? I curse inwardly when I realize I have no idea where the safe room is.

Who can I ask if not him?

God himself?

I walk around, my hand skimming over each surface like Irish's would have done his whole life. I smile when I think of his son growing up and doing the same. Of his small hand touching all the places his daddy's did as a boy. Will Finian grow to love this place as much as Padraig does?

I reckon he will.

I raise both hands to my cheeks.

More tears. More regrets.

He never cheated. Life could have been so different for us.

I walk past the confessional booth, and that's when I notice the reflective glass window. I remember it from last time.

More tears. More memories.

I think back to Sarah and Cillian's wedding. Irish surrounded me then.

Watching. Listening. Ever-present.

Kiss Me was playing, and I was so sure I could feel him behind this very window.

It was just wishful thinking, idiot.

I walk toward it, gazing at myself in the reflective surface as I step forward. I take in the blonde biker who will always be too thin no matter how hard she tries to gain weight. She has a few more scars and lines these days, but she's relatively unchanged. On the outside, at least.

She's a single parent now. She's also a widow.

Self-pity causes my eyes to well up again.

More tears. More grief.

Holding my breath, I reach out and touch the surface of the glass. Nothing.

Cold. Hard. Unfeeling. The connection gone.

I sigh in disappointment and let my eyes drop. It's then I see it —the handle. This is the safe room.

I reach out, pull the handle down, and what will no doubt be an everything-proof door clicks open. Stepping inside, I let it self-close behind me. It's a white-walled room that's just large enough to accommodate two black sectionals. I turn back toward the window. As I thought, you can see the outside clearly from the inside.

I wander around. A toilet. A small shower. There's also a store cupboard, but the shelves are empty. There are just two large bottles of water sitting on the floor.

The gift.

Turning my attention to the sectionals, I reach under the first one and pull out a small wooden box. It's nothing special. I open it. It's a music box.

Chopin's *Marche Funebre* plays.

The funeral march.

Putting the box inside my jacket pocket, I take one final look around, then walk back toward the door and pull the handle down once more.

No click. I try again. Nothing.

I'm locked in, and for some reason, I don't think it's accidental.

CHAPTER TWENTY-NINE

PADRAIG

Padraig's Apartment, Hudson Yards, New York

"What do you mean Jaine's missing?" I sit bolt upright on the sectional.

"Just what I said, Paddy. She told Duke she needed to run an errand and hasn't been seen since. That was over four hours ago."

"Has she not got her phone with her?" Jaine takes her phone everywhere. Why would she not take it with her with everything that's been going on?

"We found it on charge. She won't have her burner with her, either. She doesn't carry it around so much as she seldom leaves the house these days unless it's to go to the office. Her extra-curricular activities have been shelved, as she was never allowed to go anywhere unescorted. The fact that she's missing doesn't necessarily mean anything bad's happened to her, but…."

"For whatever reason, she's one of their primary targets, Dylan! You know it as well as I do!" I snap, then immediately feel guilty. It's not his fault. He's just passing on the unwelcome news.

"Anyway, the rest of us are meeting at the house in thirty minutes."

"I'll be there."

"What about Sophia's ban?"

"Fuck Sophia and fuck the ban. If it means I have to put up with her for the rest of my days, so nothing happens to Jaine, then so be it. That's my cross to bear."

"Paddy…."

"I mean it, Dylan! Do you honestly think I could go on in a world without her in it?" I can hear the break in my own voice. Surely to God, he must fucking realize that my world will stop spinning if she's not on it. "I'll see you there."

"Paddy, before you set off. There's something I need to tell you."

"Now's not the…."

"It's important, Paddy."

"What is it, Dyl?"

"I accidentally told Eoin that you and Jaine kissed."

"You did what!" What the fuck has he done?

"I'm sorry, Paddy."

"When did you tell him?" I close my eyes in frustration.

"The day after you told me. He was putting me under pressure and asking what had gone on between the pair of you, and it just sort of slipped out."

"It just sort of slipped out. Jesus Christ, Dylan. You were the one who told me not to tell him!"

"I know."

"And what if Sophia finds out? She already hates Jaine's guts.

Do you really want her and Luc gunning for her? Why the hell do you think I've been distancing myself from her all this time? Through fucking choice?"

"Do you think they would?"

"I wouldn't put anything past them. Why do you think I want out of this toxic arrangement? A marriage my own family forced me into."

"No one knew, Paddy. It was seen as a good match."

"That's just the same shite they've been feeding you since day one. The Ruoccos were deemed untrustworthy even back then. The union was hinged on the fact that Luc was the don and that he was always going to remain so."

"Paddy…"

"Enough, Dylan."

It's no wonder Eoin looked at me like he wished me dead. He thinks something is going on between me and Jaine. He thinks I'm trampling on his toes.

Like he did mine.

I would never do that. Not to him. Not to her.

"In fact, Dylan, change of plan. Given that our big brother will now be baying for my blood, it's probably best I stay away. I'll conduct my own search."

"What are you going to do?"

"First, I'll pray to The Almighty, and then I'll scour the streets until I find her because find her I will."

"I think that might be for the best, Paddy. Please, be careful… and I really am sorry."

"I will, and I know you are."

"Do you want me to send a car? Liam still has yours."

"I'll sort myself out."

St. Peter's Church, Upper East Side, New York

Here's me criticizing Jaine, and I've done exactly the same thing.

I check my pockets once more, having now vacated the cab, but I've definitely left my phone at home.

"Fucking eejit." I run my hand through my hair in frustration as I stare at St. Peter's, allowing the familiar sense of calm this place always affords me to descend.

Father O'Reilly is away at present. He's taking a well-deserved vacation while some essential remedial works are undertaken inside. Two weeks of repairs started two days ago. In the meantime, the congregation has been asked to attend St. Gabriel's just up the road or to pray at the end of their beds like they used to do when they were in kindergarten.

Neither option is for me.

This little church is part of my soul. It's where I always saw myself taking the vows with Jaine. It's where I always saw our children being baptized.

It's also where my final resting place will be.

The little graveyard is full now, but the O'Connells have bought a substantial plot at the rear of the church, where each now holds our own invisible grave marker.

Is it morbid that it gives me a sense of peace knowing I've picked out exactly where I'll be laid to rest?

Maybe it is for some. I'm an organized person, so to me, it makes perfect sense when the only thing we're ever guaranteed in this life is death.

It's dark. Frigid. I watch my breath as it curls in the night air, smiling when its white trail is dispersed by the bats as they flit around my head.

Making my way to the door, I turn the circular metal handle before pushing it forward. It's always unlocked. No one in their right mind would ever dare disturb this place. This church may be the house of The Lord, but after him, it belongs to the Dusters. It belongs to me.

Anyone who harms it would feel my wrath.

The lights are on. The workers must have forgotten to switch them off. My eyes immediately take in the familiar vaulted ceilings and the ancient wooden pews, most of which I've carved my initials under.

I smile to myself. If old Father O'Reilly knew about that, I'd get a clip around the ear, even at the grand old age of thirty-one, and even if he does know precisely what atrocities I'm capable of considering how often I have to spill my guts to him.

I make my way to the front pew. It's the one where the family sits, or at least those of us who attend. Ma and Da would never miss a Sunday sermon unless they were ill, and my brothers and I have been brought up much the same.

If we pretended to be sick when we were younger, we'd have just earned ourselves a boot up the backside from Da. As we got older, it was easier to turn up rather than be on the receiving end of a lengthy lecture.

According to Ma, The Almighty has all-seeing eyes. I pray every day that he closes them whenever I'm on the wet work.

I'm told Jaine never attends church. Is it because of the security risk, or is it because she's an atheist? Maybe she thinks her soul's already condemned, so what's the point in asking for forgiveness?

I like to think that the people we issue the outlaw red card to are deserving of it. That we're ridding the world of the types that would never make it to the promised land anyway. That we're doing our bit to keep the population level down so the world can be filled with the great and the good rather than the insignificant and the bad.

It's each to their own when it comes to religion. I have my faith. Others have theirs. Live and let live is my approach. If it gives you something to cling to and gets you through each day in one piece, then that's good enough for me.

I have faith in the power of prayer. I used to have it in the power of love, too, but look where that got me.

Nowhere.

I sit in my own spot, even though I have the entire row to myself, and then I bow my head and pray for her.

My Jaine Jones

I hear my sob echo, then the next one, and the next. Pain. Anguish. Regret. Anger. Repeat.

Why me? Why her? Why us?

I'd have given up everything for her. I *would* give up everything for her. Why can't my everything have been enough?

Because you decided hers wasn't. If she had been enough, you would never have cheated on her.

And there he is. Even in this place of worship, the devil is on my shoulder, telling me the reason why she and I will never be.

It's all your own fault, Paddy.

I wipe the tears from my cheeks and sit upright, breathing in deeply before exhaling.

"Where are you, Jaine? Give me a fucking sign, darlin'." I whisper the words aloud, and then I sit there. Drowning in tears, memories, and regrets.

I'm unsure how long passes before I stand and slowly approach the ancient doors. The moment my hand makes contact with the cold metal, I feel the pull. The connection I tried so hard to bury is making itself known. Why now? It's like she's suddenly here with me.

I inhale, then exhale on a shaky breath.

Don't be daft, Padraig.

I push the door, and it pushes back against me until, finally, it relents and lets me out. Standing outside, I suck the night air deep into my lungs before walking. I stop in my tracks.

Go back.

My gut's yelling at me, but why would she be here of all places?

Running my hand through my hair, I storm back inside. I may as well check seeing as I'm already here.

CHAPTER THIRTY

JAINE

St. Peter's Church, Upper East Side, New York

Have I been abducted again? In a roundabout way, it would appear so.

Did Sophia send that message to Molly's phone on purpose? Does she know I have the handset?

Was there ever anyone else involved?

I'm not sure how long I've been locked in here. Six hours? Twelve? More? It's difficult to know as the church lights are on, so I can't tell if it's fake or natural light.

I've inspected my surroundings several times. It remains unchanged, as do the available supplies. Two large bottles of water, one of which is now half empty, and no food.

I ignore the angry growl coming from my stomach. I can live without food, but I won't survive long without water. I've checked both the shower and the toilet. Neither work. Maybe they've been disconnected because of the renovations.

Or maybe it's to make sure you run out.

I'm sure Father O'Reilly will show up soon. Can the door still be opened from the outside? Did someone set it up so it locked with no way in or out?

The funeral march.

If the choice of music were related to Molly's unfortunate demise, then the considerate party responsible for leaving her *gift* will be aware that she wouldn't have been able to collect it personally.

Will the family be concerned that I've still not returned? Will they have sent out a search party? Then again, they'll hardly think it suspicious, so why would they? It's not the first time I've gone AWOL, but it is the first time I've gone anywhere without my phone.

Idiot.

I stare out the window at nothing. Even if someone walks past, they won't be able to see or hear me.

There are no weapons in here, and even if there were, a bullet would no doubt just ricochet off the glass and end up buried in my own skull. All I can do is wait and hope that someone finds me. I lay back on the sectional and close my eyes.

Conserving energy is a must when I have no fuel to replace it with.

For the second time in a matter of weeks, I need saving. Maybe Eoin was right. Maybe I needed the protection I threw back in his face after all.

"Jaine."

I frown when I hear the familiar voice.

It can't be.

Slowly opening my eyes, my gaze connects with his. He's kneeling beside me, his finger gently stroking my cheek, his face inches from mine.

I can't speak. My nose tingles as my eyes fill with tears of self-pity. He smiles down at me, eyes so blue, face so perfect.

This time, the Disney princess has been saved by the prince and not the king.

"Irish." My voice is shaky. I can be weak with him. I can be anything I want to be with him because he knows every single kaleidoscopic part of my fucking soul.

I am him. He is me.

I finally feel the connection being reciprocated.

My mind then shifts to the immediate problem at hand. Sitting upright, I stare at the door. It's closed. Getting off the sectional, I pass him and walk across the room to pull the handle down.

As I knew it would be, it's locked.

"Shit," I hiss.

Irish walks over to where I'm standing. "It should just…." He pulls the handle down repeatedly. Nothing. A frown mars his brow. "It's meant to open automatically from the inside."

"If it did, I wouldn't be trapped in here." Walking back, I sit down, then watch Irish try the door again. He eventually gives up. My eyes track him as he makes all the other recent discoveries I did.

The fact that there's not much water. The fact that there's no food. The reality that the pretty much non-existent rations will now have to be split between us both.

"This place was always stocked with enough supplies to last six people for a week at least."

"I was sent here on a lost cause, Irish." Surely, he must realize it's me the bad guys are really after.

"What do you mean?" He turns to look at me, his frown deepening.

"What I mean is, whoever's sent me here on this fool's goddamn errand has deliberately removed everything in advance. They've also turned off the water supply." I look at him as he sits beside me, so close I can feel the warmth of his thigh against mine.

"I was going through Molly's phone. The last message she received suggested that she'd been left a gift under the sectional in here. I wanted to know what it was. If it was something that could help us track down this faceless faction we're up against. So, I came straight away."

"Without telling anyone where you were going?"

"Yup," I admit reluctantly.

"And without your phone?"

"Yup." I swing my head to look at him, hope, no doubt, written all over my face. He shakes his head.

"I caught a cab. In my haste to leave, I also left my phone at home." A pause. "And was this gift something that could help us track them down?"

I shake my head as I pull the small wooden box out of my pocket before passing it to him. He studies it before lifting the lid, recognizing the music instantly, just as I did.

"The funeral march." He closes it. "So, it was a setup."

"It would appear that way."

"And you have no idea who it might be?"

I shake my head. How can I tell him that I think his wife may be involved? I can't. He loves her. He's happy. I won't destroy that for him, and definitely not without proof.

"So, what do we do now?"

"We conserve energy because we have no food and very little water, and we wait. There's not much else we can do." Leaning my back against the sectional, I pull my knees up to my chest, then rest my chin on top.

Minutes pass as we both consider our predicament.

"You want to play I Spy, Jaine?"

It's a sentence that should make me smile. It does, and it doesn't. It takes me straight back to when the three of us were being held by the Bratva.

And then there were two.

I blink back the resultant tears before positioning myself so I'm lying down with my head resting on the armrest. It doesn't surprise me when Irish lies down beside me like we always did in our Yale days. We'd lay side by side on my student bed, planning what our future together would look like.

A future that was snatched from us by a lie.

He didn't cheat.

He pulls me across so my head can rest on his chest, and I sigh with contentment as I listen to the steady thrum of his heart. A heart I know was synchronized with my own long before we ever met. I inhale the familiar scent of his cologne.

"Only if I get to go first." The same condition as I had way back then when Pandora opened her box to reveal her nine-year-old secret. That for all that time, Irish had loved me too.

He chuckles. "You drive a hard bargain, darlin'. Go on then, seeing as it's you."

"I spy with my little eye, something beginning with D."

I can feel his thick swallow as we replay the past.

"Devastatingly handsome Irishman." Same answer.

A pause.

"Jaine." A hesitant whisper.

"Irish."

"Can I change the game?"

"To?"

"Truth or dare."

It's my turn to swallow thickly, as I know I have far more truths to reveal than he has. Is here and now the right time or place?

"Okay, but only if I get to go first."

"Out with it, then. Pick your evil."

"Truth." I pause. "How did you know where I was?"

He sighs deeply before replying. "Dylan told me you had gone AWOL, so I decided to come here to pray before starting my search for you. You know, being the good Irish Catholic boy that I am." We both chuckle. "I could feel your soul reaching out to mine just as I was leaving." He pauses. "Do you remember what I said to you all those years ago, Jaine?" His tone is serious now.

I nod. I know exactly what he's referring to.

"Our souls have always been intertwined. You feel that too, darlin'?"

"I still believe that. I felt the connection today. The last time I felt it was at St. Patrick's on my wedding day. I knew you were there."

I'm not sure when I realize that the material of his shirt is now wet with my silent tears. "I know you did. I saw you searching for my face in the crowd."

"What the fuck happened to us, Jaine?" I can hear the break in his voice—the raw emotion at the sheer unfairness of it all.

"Life happened." A sob-whisper.

"I cheated on you, that's what happened."

I pause. It's time for the first reveal. "Ask me to tell you a truth, Irish."

"Tell me a truth."

I pause. "I'm sorry."

"Sorry for what? You didn't do anything wrong."

I nod my head slowly. "I did." I wipe the tears from my eyes as I try to find the right words. "I'm sorry that I made you feel so unwanted. When I told you about Ace, I never realized that my constant rejection would then make you feel I loved you less than him because I never ever loved you any fucking less, Irish." My voice fades, drowned by tears, as I cling to the front of his shirt.

'He'd just managed to convince himself that you didn't love him back.'

Guilt. That I took a confident person and turned him into such a doubting Thomas. To be loved is strength, and to love is weakness. I made him weak because he loved me so much, and I offered him no strength because, in return, he doubted my own love for him.

"I thought I wasn't enough," he whispers.

"You were always enough."

He pulls me tighter against him.

"You didn't cheat on me," I utter the five life-changing words.

He immediately tenses beneath me, the words remaining suspended in the air.

"What do you mean?"

"Brittany admitted it at the reunion. Nothing happened between you and her."

"But she said…"

"She lied, Irish. She said you were drunk and upset because you thought I didn't love you. She took you upstairs to put you to bed and let you sleep it off, but then she saw an opportunity and took it. She staged everything because she wanted you for herself. She held on to the lie for twelve years. They all did. Fletch, Brittany, Skylar. All this time, they knew, and they never said a word."

Silence. I'm not sure how long it stretches as we both think back to an event that changed the course of both our lives. An event that never even took place.

"Jaine…. fuck… I…"

I know what it's like when you can't find the words. After Ace died, I struggled to find my voice as every word seemed inadequate compared to how tortured I felt inside.

How can a single word measure emptiness? How can a single word quantify loss? Because that's exactly what this is.

Loss.

What Brittany didn't realize is that she destroyed part of him that day, and she destroyed part of me too. For twelve years, I thought the worst of him, and he's thought the worst of himself. He's had to live with guilt as his bed partner all this time.

An outcome he didn't deserve because he didn't do anything fucking wrong.

Our future could have been so different. *Would* have been so different. What we had. What we shared. It was beyond anything.

We were timeless. We were ageless. We were a tale as old as fucking time, and they took that from us.

My arms tighten around him as the emotions hit hard, and I absorb every sob as his tears mingle with my own. We lie there, wrapped around each other like we always did as we let our tears run dry. No words are spoken. We're each lost in our own thoughts.

"Truth," he says eventually.

"Go on?" I sniff.

"Why did you tell me you didn't love me three years ago?"

How best to answer? Given the name of the game, I guess truthfully is best, or at least as far as I can.

"Your family entered you into an arranged marriage with Sophia. A contract there was no getting out of. I thought it best I didn't confuse things between us or become a distraction, so I removed myself from your life. It was the only way to stop you from reaching out."

I can feel his tension. He's not happy with that response, but it's not for me to tell him what his family did. That they pretty much ran me out of town. It's for them to explain their reasonings.

It's for Eoin to explain.

"I may be an emotional kind of fella, darlin', but I'm no fool. I would never have antagonized the Sicilians. While I may have vented my frustrations in front of you and my family because I trusted you both with them, I would never have done anything that would have put you in danger. My trying to remove myself from that contract would have done just that."

"I'm sorry."

He snorts. "You're sorry! Really? That's all I'm getting?" He stands and starts pacing the floor, running his hand through his hair like the other men in his family do. "I'm disappointed, Jaine. I'm disappointed that you, of all people, thought me so fucking weak that I'd be unable to cope with the reality of my situation. That I would allow my heart to rule my head. Do you have any fucking idea what you taking yourself away did to me? One minute you're telling me you love me, the next you're telling me you don't and that you never want to speak to me again!"

He stops and stares at me, his expression doing nothing to mask his pain. He yanks on his hair as he lets out a roar of frustration. More tears fill my eyes when he drops to his knees defeatedly and lets out a heart-wrenching sob.

"You fucking gutted me, darlin'! I loved you so much, and you ripped out my fucking heart!" His voice is wracked with pain and emotion as he drops his face into his hands, his shoulders shaking as he silently cries.

He's crying for me. For him. For us. I want to cry for us too, but this isn't about me. It's about him.

His anger. His grief. His truth.

I kneel beside him on the floor and try to wrap my arms around him, but he pushes me away.

"You don't get to fix this with a hug, Jaine. All these years, I thought I didn't matter. You destroyed me with a handful of fucking words, and then you walked away without a backward glance. It led to me living a life of deceit. It led to me pretending to be my brother so I didn't have to let you go. A pretense that almost ruined his fucking life too."

We stay where we are, both kneeling, both within touching distance. I'm so close I can feel the roulette wheel of his emotions spin. I know exactly which color it's going to stop on next.

Leaving me kneeling, he stands and paces the floor once more. What he's about to say will lead straight on to the next reveal. I know it will.

"If you loved me back then, why did you fuck my brother?"

He runs his hand through his hair repeatedly. I can feel the red-hot rage emanating from him.

He's getting more and more wound up, so much so the room is starting to feel decidedly smaller. I've never seen this side of Irish before. Maybe I should be worried about being trapped in here with him, but I'm not.

I stand and walk across the room before turning around and looking at him. "I didn't." I tilt my chin and wait. I can't blame anyone for this next reveal. This one is all on me.

He stops pacing and stares at me with eyes that have never been bluer. A deathly silence follows as we stare at each other. He knows what atrocities lurk behind my gaze. I swallow as I'm finally allowed to delve into the part of his soul I've never seen before.

I don't see individual faces. All I see is blood. Flowing. Vibrant. Pulsing. A sea of red made up of so many diseased souls they could never be fucking counted.

He doesn't make a move toward me. It's the distance that scares me most.

Scared.

Cocky. Handsome. Funny. My Irish. My confidant. What exactly is he? Right now, I don't know. Do I even want to know?

Psychopath.

I don't speak. I can't. How to say what I've wanted to say for over two years?

My crime. My punishment. My confession. My penance.

"What do you mean?"

I walk toward him until we're almost nose to nose before pushing my hair back from behind my left ear. His gaze is instantly drawn to the tattoo, the scrolled letter A now accompanied by the much smaller J.

He knows.

Gripping my chin painfully, he slowly turns my head and pushes back the hair covering my right ear. Time stands still as he takes in the scrolled letter I, accompanied by the much smaller F.

CHAPTER THIRTY-ONE

PADRAIG

St. Peter's Church, Upper East Side, New York

After all those years of being envious that Ace had his initial inked on her perfect skin, my brand marks her, too, now.

Finian's mine.

I have a two-year-old son that no one's bothered to fucking tell me about. Not Jaine. Not my own family.

I've been treated like a leper since I returned, and now I know why. I disrupted their perfect lives. Jaine had been slotted into the family to stand side by side with my eldest brother, and that left no room for me.

They didn't know what to do with the actual baby daddy when I turned up unannounced, so they just brushed me and my sad little existence under the fucking carpet.

She kept Fin from me. That's not love. What should have been some of the happiest moments of my life have been stolen from me.

Moments that are irreplaceable.

I never got to witness Fin entering the world. I never saw his first step. I never witnessed his first tooth. I never got to console him when he cried the first time he fell over and grazed his little knee.

When he said Da for the first time, he said it to someone else. Not to me.

Tears prick my eyes at the unfairness of it all. All I've ever wanted was to be a husband and a father. All I ever wanted was all of that with her.

It wasn't too much to ask from life, was it?

I'd have given up everything because that meant everything. She meant everything. Nothing else has ever mattered to me.

Instead, she sat on the sidelines and watched me existing as she moved on with her life with someone else.

First Ace, then with my own brother.

What did I ever do to her that I was deserving of that? Was it because she thought I cheated? Was this her idea of payback?

Betrayal.

There's no other word fitting to describe how I feel right now. Its bitterness laces my tongue, and it's turning my vision red as it courses through my blood. It's been a while since I felt the urge to kill, but I'm feeling it right now.

Not Jaine. I would never harm her. She's the mother of my son. Right now, though, I fucking hate her.

That she thought it right to walk out of my life without a backward glance. That she found it acceptable to keep my son away from me for all this time.

I've been back in New York for almost two months. I've been interacting with the child on a pretty much daily basis. Only now, I'm finding out why we're so similar.

It's because Fin and I share the same fucking DNA.

She's changed. The girl I knew would never have betrayed me like this. Jaine was never fake. Jaine was never dishonest. Why?

Undiluted rage. I never wanted her to see me like this, and definitely never in close proximity with no way to vent. The me that exists in the concrete tomb under Play.

I was born a psychopath. God saved the best for last when he created the final O'Connell brother. I pray most because I sin most.

Blood red.

My favorite color. I would bathe in the blood of my enemies. I would paint a fucking picture with it. Right now, I want to paint a room with it.

I stare at her. This girl I no longer know. The mother of my fucking son. I want to hurt her like she's hurt me.

Defiance. Regret.

Right now, she portrays a mixture of both because she doesn't know if she did the right thing or the wrong thing. Either by him, by me, or even by herself. But here we are. She made the decision on behalf of us all.

The wrong fucking one.

"Truth." Her gaze drops to where I'm repeatedly clenching and unclenching my fists. Is she scared? "Why."

There's no hesitation. "I was worried you would call off the wedding to Sophia and insist that we marry."

I dry laugh. "You are no fucking better than them, Jaine, do you know that?" I whisper-hiss.

"Who?" She frowns.

"My family! They made decisions on my behalf based on their assumptions, and you did exactly the same."

She stares at me. She knows I'm right.

Violence. Death. Murder.

I need to make someone bleed. Spinning around, I punch the

glass between us and the outside world before proceeding to tear the room apart.

Blood.

I need a blade and someone to blame. I need to hear the constant dripping sound of the place hidden so far below ground no one can hear my playthings fucking scream.

Panting, I face her with my blood dripping on the floor, and all the while, she stands there watching me. She wants me to react. To say something to her. To do something to her.

I will not salve her conscience for her.

I wipe the spray of my own blood from my face with the back of my hand and watch as her gaze tracks my every movement, her tongue flicking out to lick her pouty lips.

Aroused.

Jesus Christ, she's aroused by what she's just witnessed. It would appear Jaine gets off on fear. She gets off on violence. She gets off on me.

And it's why she also gets off on my brother.

I want her to see me kill. Not him. Because he's nothing compared to me. Not when it comes to creating a bloodbath.

I say nothing as I watch her use our limited water supply to wet a towel and then tend to my cuts. When she's done, I grip her chin hard, forcing her to look at me. She doesn't pull away. Green eyes bore straight into mine.

"You had no right," I hiss.

"I had every right to protect my son," she bites back.

"From his own father?"

"From his father's enemies. We already have reason to believe that Finian was targeted because someone is aware of his true parentage."

"Who knew?" I frown at her.

"Molly."

"And who would she have told?"

"That's what I'm trying to find out and why I've been going through her phone."

We stare at each other. It's not enough. It still doesn't excuse what she's done. Nothing ever will, she must know that.

"Dare."

She utters the word she knows she shouldn't. She knows she's deliberately dancing with Death himself now that she's stared into the depths of my fucked-up soul.

Dare I what?

Kiss her? Kill her? That's the only two options available to me.

My gaze drops to her lips, and she licks them in response. Does she want me to kiss her? My mouth waters as I remember the unique taste of each soft moan and sigh. A taste that was once all mine. A taste which now belongs to my brother.

I won't because even though they're not together, it's likely due to a misunderstanding over just that. Me and Jaine kissing.

I will never betray my brother because it turns out that he never betrayed me after all. He was given no choice but to marry Jaine, and it was undertaken to protect my son. Then he simply fell in love with her.

He never betrayed me.

She did.

CHAPTER THIRTY-TWO

JAINE

St. Peter's Church, Upper East Side, New York

ASIDE FROM THE SECTIONAL WE'VE BEEN USING, EVERYTHING ELSE in the safe room has been destroyed, the window to the outside world now smeared with fresh blood after being punched several times.

I take him in. His blue jeans, his long-sleeved white Henley, and his face are splattered with his own blood. His mussed hair is also streaked due to him repeatedly running his bleeding knuckles through its coal-black length.

"Dare."

I throw it out there. I don't know what I'm daring him to do exactly.

Kiss me? Kill me?

Given his current mindset, it's most likely to be the latter.

Undiluted rage. He hates me for what I've done and also for

what he thinks I've done, and he's struggling to hold it back right now.

I went with dare because in this dangerous game we're playing, there have been enough truth bombs for now, at least while we're confined to a safe room that will potentially kill us both.

He continues to stare at me before dropping his gaze to my mouth. My insides turn molten as I lick my lips in response.

I realize that he won't kill me. Love me or hate me, I'm the mother of his son. I also realize that he won't kiss me. Not when he's happily married to Sophia. I can taste my own disappointment at that realization.

In the end, he releases my chin, and I turn and walk back to the sectional.

Taking off my jacket, I lie on my side and sleep.

I'M NOT SURE HOW LONG HAS PASSED WHEN I FINALLY WAKE. I know exactly where I am, so I don't bother opening my eyes. There's no point. The visual will still be the same as it was when I closed them, and I still won't know whether it's night or day. Our situation will also have remained unchanged.

I lay down alone, but that's no longer the case. I'm now cocooned. My back's pressed against his front, his arm is thrown across my waist, and his hot breath is fanning my ear.

I know it's where I was always meant to be. In his arms.

Deep down, we both know it.

"I'm sorry about the way I reacted, darlin'."

He's awake. For some reason, I was sure he wasn't, having convinced myself that he wouldn't consciously be holding me this close if he were. That he must think I'm Sophia.

"You had every right to react the way you did. In truth, I'm not sure what I expected your reaction to be. I made the decision about Fin based on what I thought was best at the time. It was never going to be entirely right. It was never going to be entirely wrong. I don't regret what I did. I just wish I hadn't had to make the choice in the first place."

There's a pause while he digests what I've said. "I wish I'd been there with you… to see Finian being born. To witness all of his firsts…."

Raw emotion. Regrets. All infused with him trying to find it in himself to forgive me for what I've done.

"I know. I took pictures and videos of everything…." My voice fades as the tears start to fall. "I'm so fucking sorry, Irish. It was the hardest thing I've ever had to do. Every day, I hated myself for it."

He ignores my feeble apology because it's nowhere near enough salve for the damage I've inflicted on him.

"He looks just like me."

"He's you in every way, just in miniature form." I laugh-sob.

"Ace?"

"He knew he was yours from the moment he was born. He made sure he loved Fin enough for both of you. It was his dying wish that you be united with your son." A sob escapes me, and he pulls me closer to him.

"I'm sorry about Ace."

"Me too."

"What we went through together."

"He held you in high regard. He always did. It was Dylan who was there with him in the end. I was in New York. It was when…."

"I remember, darlin'. And you saved my family? At the wedding?"

I nod. "Delaney heard a rumor that it was you who was the target. That's the only reason I went. I would never have returned to New York so soon otherwise. In the end, I almost let the other sniper kill Eoin. I was convinced he was involved in Ace's death."

"Trust me, if Eoin wanted Ace dead, he would have undertaken the act personally, and he would never have denied his involvement," he says without hesitation.

"I realize that now."

"You love him? Eoin?"

"Yes," I admit. "Although I hated him at first."

"You pair always did have an unconventional relationship."

"That's putting it mildly." I chuckle.

"And you love me," he whispers.

"I never stopped."

His hand drops from my waist to my flat stomach, then he splays his fingers. I know he's trying to imagine what it must have felt like rounded with Fin.

Guilt eats away at me. At everything he's missed out on. Did I make the right choices? Because he's right, I am just as bad as his family. I did make decisions based on assumptions the same as they did. And he's the one who's had to live with the consequences.

"So, he was conceived when we had to perform for the camera?"

"Yes."

"Did you keep the tapes?"

"I keep them locked up beside my engraved bullets."

"Have you ever watched them?"

"No."

We both know I'm lying.

"What if we die in here?" I whisper.

"There's no one else I'd rather die with."

He kisses my tattoo, and then we lie there, each of us lost in our own thoughts once more.

"I love you." I'm not sure why tears prick my eyes as I say it this time.

Maybe it's because I may not get the opportunity to for much longer, or maybe it's because, even though we're in dire straits, I still wouldn't change this moment for anything in the world because I'm with him.

"I know."

He doesn't say it back because it's no longer reciprocated.

We sleep most of the time as one day rolls into the next.

I'm not sure how long we've been here, but we ran out of water around twenty-four hours ago, or was it forty-eight?

Will we die in here? Who knows. There's no one else I would rather die with either.

My Irish.

We've yelled. We've cried. We've stopped speaking. We've said sorry. We've put the world to rights and then undid it all again. We've avoided anything that could potentially lead to intimacy even though the temptation is there.

I guess we're still clinging to the hope that we'll be found in time. That if we kissed or fucked, then it would feel more like a betrayal. Yet another hurdle to get over when we've already completed a full fucking course.

He won't want to betray Sophia, and even though we're not officially together, I wouldn't want to betray Eoin. Nor would he. If Irish and I were ever to be together, I would have to ask Eoin for his blessing, the same as Irish had to give me his blessing to be with his brother.

My conscience would never rest otherwise.

I realize Irish blames me for everything, and that's fine for now.

Maybe we'll take that with us to the grave. If we do make it out of here alive, then the truth must be told.

No more lies. No more secrets.

I refuse to live the rest of my life trying to remember who I've told what to. No deception means there's no chance of slipping up.

Fin's parentage is now known. Mine will be made known. My alter-ego will also be revealed to the rest of the Duster family.

To Eoin.

And the O'Connells must own up to the part they played in the wrongdoings when it came to Irish. That I didn't abandon him without a backward glance. That I didn't let him go willingly. That they used my love for him against me, knowing I would always put his needs and well-being ahead of my own.

I understand why he's pissed off. That we made decisions on his behalf like he wasn't capable of making them for himself. That we made them because we assumed he'd behave in a certain way.

They had no right to do that. I realize now that I had no right to do that either. He's right. I'm just as bad as they are, but what's done is done. We can't change the past. All we can do is come clean and start a new future if the option is still available to us.

I hope it is.

No one did what they did to deliberately hurt him or cause him pain. There will be no re-do over the time that's been lost, so all we can do is let bygones be bygones and make the most of what's left.

I'm standing at the window, staring at the same daylight view I've been looking at for I don't know how long. I turn my head to look at Irish as he lies on the sectional with one arm behind his head. He hasn't changed physically. A few more lines and a few grey hairs, but he's still the same boy I fell in love with when I was nineteen years old. He's lost his exuberance, though, or at least he's buried it away.

He looks tired. I want to ask him about his life with Sophia, but

I know it's not something he wants to discuss. Is it because we have a past or for another reason?

"I can feel your eyes admiring me, Jaine."

"You're so vain." I snort at his smugness.

"I'm so handsome, is what you were really trying to say."

"On planet Padraig, perhaps."

He smiles, but it's a sad one.

"They'll find us, darlin'. Don't worry."

I don't respond because I'm not so sure that they will, or at least not in time.

CHAPTER THIRTY-THREE

EOIN

The O'Connell Home, Darling, New York

"Jesus Christ. It's been six days."

I'm pacing the floor and running my hands through my hair. At this rate, Da's office isn't going to have any carpet left.

"We're all aware of that, Eoin. It's one day more than it was yesterday, don't you know. Trust me. I'm an accountant."

I glare at Jessie and then at Dylan. Dylan looks at me apologetically.

"Jessie, why don't you go and help Sarah and Ma look after the little ones," he mumbles awkwardly. He won't want to piss her off, but he'll want to piss me off even less.

"I know when I'm not wanted." She rolls her eyes and sticks out her bottom lip as she leaves, but I've had just about enough of her. I realize it's her way of dealing with things, but her smart-mouthed remarks are making me reactive. I can't be at the docks when I'm needed here in case my wife decides to turn up.

Ex-wife.

I wait until Jessie closes the door before I speak further. "Paddy must be with her. He must have found her."

"I reckon so."

We keep having the same back and forth. Dylan hasn't mentioned anything about the repetitive nature of our conversations. He understands that his constant reassurance that she's not on her own is the only thing keeping me sane. I can't bear the thought of her being alone,

"But how?"

"Because…"

I hold my hand up to silence him, cursing myself for asking the question out loud. I don't need him to remind me that they share some sort of intangible fucking connection. Jaine's already told me all about it.

She loves him more than me.

"She doesn't."

I then realize I also said that out loud.

I sit on Da's chair, then lean back before resting my feet on top of his desk. "And what would you know, Dylan?"

"I know, Jaine. I know she doesn't love Paddy more. She loves you as much as him. She just loves you both differently."

"I don't have the same connection with her."

He shrugs. "Maybe not, but then neither did Ace, and trust me, if he were still alive, neither you nor Paddy would have had a look-in with her."

He's right. It still doesn't stop me from feeling inferior that Paddy was able to find her when I can't. I don't even know where to start looking. She's not taken either of her phones, and she went on her hog, and there's been no sighting of that either. Same with my brother. His phone is at home. We can only suspect he hailed a cab to wherever he was going.

"I love her, Dylan."

"I know you do."

"I sent her away."

"Over a kiss that meant nothing."

"It must have meant something."

"Paddy described it as a peck and that it was a farewell kiss rather than a hello kiss."

"He wanted to kiss her, and she him."

"They love each other and share a past, so maybe that's true, but they didn't act on it out of respect for both you and Sophia."

He pauses, but I know exactly what he's going to say.

"You need to tell him that you deliberately pursued her."

"I know."

"I'm not sure how he'll react."

We both know exactly how he'll react. He'll never forgive me. He'll also want bloodshed for my blatant disrespect. Both are quite understandable.

"We can worry about that when we find them." Because we will find them, and it won't be too late. I refuse to even consider that outcome, let alone discuss it.

"You should get some rest."

"It's easier said than done, Dylan."

We sit in silence, my head playing every conversation I've ever had with Jaine on repeat.

"And we've checked the boating lake?"

"Twice."

I rub my hand down the stubble on my face once more.

"And what did Paddy say again?"

"I've told you several times already."

"So, humor me once more!" I hiss.

"He said, 'First, I'll pray to The Almighty, and then I'll scour the streets.'"

I stare at him as it finally falls into place.

"I know where they are," I whisper.

"Where?"

"St. Peter's."

IT'S DARK WHEN WE ARRIVE, BUT THE CHURCH LIGHTS ARE ON. Is that a sign, or have the workers accidentally left them on?

Apparently, the renovations have been delayed due to the wrong type of wood having been received, so there's been no one on site for over a week now.

I don't stop to take in my surroundings. Dec drove us. Behind us is a black private ambulance being chauffeured by Liam and currently occupied by both Dr. Kelly and Tim.

Paddy and Jaine may not be here, but if they are, they may need urgent medical assistance given the time that's passed. I'm not prepared to take any chances.

Not with him. Especially not with her.

The medical team will remain in the ambulance until they're needed. If they are needed.

If it's not already too late.

Dylan follows me into the church. I can't help but whisper a silent prayer that they're in here. Even if the worse has happened, I'd sooner they be found.

We search everywhere, but there's no sign. We then sit on the family pew and stare up at the vaulted ceiling.

I feel hopeless.

For the first time, I'm confronted with a problem, and I have no solution. My person is going to die because I can't find her. I curse myself that I don't have the same in-built connection with her that she shares with my brother.

I think back to the raw pain and emotion that we witnessed at Cillian and Sarah's wedding. Paddy was inside the safe room. Jaine knew he was there, their bond so strong.

I broke him that day. I broke her too.

The day I used their love for each other against them for my own selfish gain, and all because I wanted her for myself.

"The safe room," I whisper. We run past the confessional booth, my eyes trained on the reflective glass. "Please, God."

We push the door open, and my hand automatically reaches up to cover my nose. It stinks, but it's not the smell of death. It's the smell of human waste.

Dylan and I stop in our tracks as we take them in. As they lay there with their arms wrapped around each other as though to offer the same comfort in death as they did in life.

For never was a story of more woe than this of Juliet and her Romeo.

Tears prick my eyes as I stare at them. Were they always destined to be star-crossed lovers?

A love so pure. A love so simple. A love where nothing else matters. Where no one else matters. *Not even me.*

Dylan places his hand on my arm, then approaches them.

I run my hand down my face. I can't let my emotions get the better of me. "Don't move them, Dylan. Fetch Dr. Kelly and Tim."

If they survive or don't, the person who did this to them will pay. But what do I do when I was partially the catalyst? When my own love for her played a part in destroying them both?

I stand and stare, not sure what to do next. I watch as Dr. Kelly checks both of them over. I make eye contact with Tim as he stares down at Jaine. They grew close.

He looks upset.

It seems like a lifetime has passed before Dr. Kelly turns to us. “They’re alive.”

I know my cheeks are wet with tears. For the first time since I was a small boy, I’m crying.

CHAPTER THIRTY-FOUR

JAINE

The O'Connell Home, Darling, New York

"TIM." I SMILE UP AT MY NURSE FRIEND WITH HIS UNRULY MOP OF red hair, his complementary freckles, and his beaming smile. A man who's seen me at rock bottom more than once, and now, here he is doing so again, only this time, I'm the patient.

"Have you been doing as I asked, Jaine?" He pushes his round black glasses further up his nose as he stares at me, no doubt trying to gauge whether I'm lying.

"As much as possible, but I'm not really a bed rest kind of person. You know that."

"You were less than twenty-four hours away from death."

"I've been much closer to death than that, trust me." I smile.

He rolls his eyes at me. "I'll be close to death myself if we don't see a marked improvement soon. Your ex-husband will be baying for my blood."

He's right. Eoin will be interrogating him several times a day. It's unfair of me to put him in such a compromising position. I decide honesty is the best policy.

"I got out of bed for an hour because I wanted to spend some time with JJ. He's been feeling unwell. We didn't do anything strenuous. We just cuddled on the sofa and watched a TV show. I did eat and drink everything I was asked to."

"I'm glad to hear it. It's all for your own good."

"Yes, Mom."

He chuckles as he checks my blood pressure and glucose.

"How is he?" I ask the same question I always do so he knows exactly who I'm referring to.

"Padraig is doing exactly what's been asked of him and so is recovering far more quickly." Tim's stock answer.

"Goody, two shoes," I mumble as I roll my eyes. I then stare at him.

"Go on." He stops what he's doing and looks back at me.

"Has he asked about me?"

"He asks about you as often as you ask about him, so every time I visit. I'm going there next. Do you want me to pass on a message?"

I shake my head.

"Then maybe you should give him a call, Jaine."

"Maybe." But we both know I won't. I'll just continue to ask after him.

Apparently, we were found unconscious with our arms wrapped around each other as we faced death head-on. I just remember going to sleep as usual then waking up here. As soon as I woke, I missed his arms around me. I missed lying side by side, talking like we always used to.

That was two days ago now.

Everyone has visited since, and the children have been enjoying all the attention. They especially liked meeting their new little cousin, Caireann, Sarah, and Cillian's new baby girl, who was born the same day we were found.

Even Eoin's dropped in a couple of times. He doesn't say much. He just stands there looking brooding in that dark, menacing way of his. Dylan said he'd never seen him so distraught as he was when he found us. That they both thought we were dead.

Tim and I make small talk as I let him finish poking and prodding me in order to do what he has to satisfy Eoin's demands.

"I'll be off then, Jaine."

I nod at him.

"You sure you don't want me to pass on a message to Padraig?" He raises an eyebrow at me.

I shake my head.

"I've left a list of dos and don'ts on the side."

"Sir, yes, sir." I salute with a grin.

With a chuckle, he leaves the room and closes the door behind him.

I rest my head against the pillow, taking in the almost clinical surroundings. Like everywhere else in the safe space, the main bedroom is finished in white and cream and is spatially furnished.

Alone and restless once more. I really need to get up. While no food for seven days and no water for three took its toll on my body, I have things I need to do.

I'm not dead. That means life goes on. I can't just lie here and do nothing.

I stare at my phone. Should I message Irish? Call him? I'm not sure what to do. Before saferoomgate, we hadn't spoken for weeks. Do we just revert back to the same? How can we when he knows Fin's his son? We can't just ignore each other now. Has he told anyone that he knows? I haven't told anyone that I've told him.

What a fucking mess.

I stare at my vibrating phone. "Dylan," I answer. It's only the second time I've spoken to him since he and Eoin found us at the church. He's no doubt been warned not to disturb my rest.

"How are you feeling, Jaine?"

"I feel fine, but no matter how often I explain that to Tim, he still expects me to stay in bed."

"You almost died, Jaine."

"In this life, that sort of comes with the territory, Dyl." I chuckle.

"It's not funny."

"It sort of was," I mumble.

"What the hell happened?"

"Has Irish not told you?"

"He says to speak to you, but you've been so poorly, Eoin would have crucified anyone who dared disturb you."

"I went through Molly's phone and found proof that Sophia knows what happened between me and Eoin. That Molly was dumped for me. She also knows Fin is Irish's biological son."

"Have you told anyone else?" He sounds shocked.

"Not about what I found on the phone, but he knows, Dyl. I told Padraig about Fin."

A lengthy pause.

"And how did he take it?"

"Badly at first. The reaction wasn't what I expected. He tore the place apart."

"I wondered what had happened."

"He calmed down afterward, but that was a side of him I've never seen before."

"Like everyone else, he has two sides. The happy-go-lucky persona that everyone knows and loves, and then there's the psychopath."

"He's that bad? Worse than Eoin?"

"I don't know. I've never seen Eoin kill, so I can't compare the two, but I'd imagine they'd be different."

"In what way?"

"Paddy's way more bloodthirsty. It's why he was always on the wet work. We've lost count of how many he's killed. It's also part of the reason he only deals with the internal goings-on. So he can't pick a fight."

"You're being serious?"

"No joke. I've seen him kill. If he's feeling generous, he'll gut them after he's hacked off various bits and pieces. If not, he'll bleed them dry, then carve them up into works of art, a bit like Hannibal Lecter does."

"He doesn't…."

"No, he doesn't eat them, Jaine." He laughs.

"There's so much I don't know about him."

"You spent most of your lives hiding behind messages and calls, that's why. It wasn't…."

"Real life?"

"Something like that. I guess it was similar to you and Eoin. You spent years with your back and forth. You probably thought you knew him quite well, but I suspect the reality of the complete package that made up my eldest brother wasn't who you expected."

He's right, of course. All I'd ever seen was Padraig's Mr. Gift of the Irish gab side, much like I'd only ever witnessed Eoin's Mr. Smug. Selfish. Pompous side. Mr. Dominating. Dangerous. Deadly didn't make an appearance until after we got married. I want to see the other side of Irish.

"It wasn't. You're right," I admit.

"Anyway, Paddy's not mentioned to me that he knows, so it's unlikely he's told anyone else. Maybe it's for safety reasons since you and Fin seem to be the ones being targeted."

"Maybe."

"I'm glad you told him, Jaine. I'm glad it's finally out in the open."

"Do I tell the others that he knows?"

"Let me speak to him first to see how he wants to play it. You've done your part now, so there's not much else you can do."

"I just thought he may have wanted to see him."

"He was seeing him most days before you went AWOL, Jaine."

"What do you mean?"

"He was going to the house when you weren't there."

"Why?" I'm suddenly annoyed that he went to such lengths just to avoid seeing me.

"After your run-in with Sophia at the elevator, he's been banned from communicating with you."

"But surely that's extreme? I mean, she knows we share Fin, even if she hasn't admitted it to anyone."

"That may be part of the problem."

"What do you mean?"

"She wants him to get her pregnant. She wants a baby."

I'm not sure how I feel about that. In some ways, it feels final, and I don't want things to ever be final between us.

"I'm not sure what difference that would make. They'd just be stepsiblings."

"It's not quite that simple."

"I don't know what you mean?"

"It's not really for me to say."

I can't argue. What goes on inside someone else's marriage isn't any of my business. He continues when I don't respond.

"What are you going to do about Eoin?"

"Again, I don't know what you mean. His last words to me were that we were done."

"I know why he said that." He sounds sheepish.

"Enlighten me."

"Paddy told me you and he kissed, and I accidentally told Eoin. He wanted to know what happened between you when you went to his apartment. He was putting me under pressure. I couldn't tell him the real reason so it just slipped out."

I frown at the handset. "It wasn't that sort of kiss."

"I know that, but he didn't give me any chance to explain further."

"So, what are you saying exactly?"

"That maybe you could attempt a reconciliation."

"But we're not compatible, Dyl. We've tried so many times."

"Trust me, Jaine. He'll try to change, if you will. When he saw you at the church, he cried. I've never seen Eoin emotional before. He thought you were dead. We both did. I'm not sure he could survive losing you." I wait for him to continue. It's obvious he's got something else on his mind. "Did anything happen between you and Paddy?"

"Are you asking if we kissed or if we fucked?"

"Well, I wasn't going to be quite so blunt."

"No to both."

"That's good to know."

"My jacket, Dyl?"

"Eoin's picking it up from Paddy's, and then he's going to drop it off."

"And my hog? It's parked up outside the church."

"That's the thing, Jaine, and that's why you were pretty much impossible to find. There's been no sign of it."

My heart sinks in my chest. Please, God. Not my goddamn hog.

"We need to find it, Dyl. I've had that ride since I was eighteen years old." I can hear the break in my voice.

"We'll find it. Don't worry."

What he doesn't add is that he can't guarantee what condition it will be in when they do.

CHAPTER THIRTY-FIVE

PADRAIG

Padraig's Apartment, Hudson Yards, New York

SOMETIMES, I WISH I'D NEVER WOKEN BACK UP. THOSE DAYS SPENT with Jaine were the best days of my life, even if they were brutal. They gave me a taste of what married life with her could be like.

We argued. We apologized. We laughed. We got angry. We joked. We got melancholy. We drove each other up the wall. I wouldn't change any of it for the world.

I saw her. She saw me. I want more. I want all of her.

But I can't have her.

I never cheated. She loves me. We share a child. But I have nothing to offer her. I'm trapped in a marriage for the foreseeable future with a woman who wants me to get her pregnant. Only then can I have my freedom.

That's if she doesn't turn into the Sicilian equivalent of a praying mantis once she's achieved her goal.

My eldest brother, on the other hand. He loves Jaine. She loves him. They sort of share a child together in the shape of little JJ. He can offer Jaine the world. And the world is what she deserves. She's been through enough as it is.

If you love someone, set them free.

I can't dwell on it. That's exactly what I need to do.

There's a knock on the bedroom door. I smile at the ginger lad as he enters the room.

"It's good to see you, Tim."

"You too, Padraig."

Apparently, Tim was the nurse in charge of Eoin when he was shot by the bullet intended for Finian.

My son.

I still can't quite wrap my head around it. I haven't told anyone that I know yet. I thought I'd get this thing sorted out with Jaine first. That's why I need to see our Eoin.

"Jaine was asking after you."

"Was she now?"

I try to appear disinterested, but he's not daft. He knows I want to know almost as much as I don't. We were found unconscious and wrapped around each other by Dylan, Eoin, Dr. Kelly, and Tim.

It was clear to all present that Jaine and I share a past. It wasn't a hold of friendship. It was a hold of lovers.

Of two people who loved each other in the last life, who love each other in this life, and who will love each other in the next life and the one after that.

The latter is what I cling on to. That we'll find each other again next time around.

If I have to go through the rest of my days with Jaine married to my brother, then so be it. He hasn't done anything wrong. It's not his fault he fell in love with her once they were forced into close proximity. She's easy to fall in love with. I should know.

"And what did you tell her?"

"That if she wants to know how you are, then maybe she should just give you a call."

She won't. We had gone weeks without talking before we got trapped, and it was me who ceased communications. For them to resume, I'd need to be the one reaching out, and I won't do that. At least, not until I've got her and Eoin back together.

I don't want anything that happened in the safe room to have caused any confusion, as there can be none. At the moment, she clearly thinks I'm happily married and that our closeness was as a result of the circumstances we found ourselves in.

It needs to stay that way.

I can't have her thinking there's any future for us when a future's not something I'm even guaranteed.

I need to switch the conversation away from Jaine. As much as I want to know about her I don't want Tim to feel caught in the middle. I witnessed firsthand what that did to our Dylan.

"Another couple of days, and you'll be up and about, I reckon."

"And Jaine?"

"She'll need a day or so more. She was already undernourished. She spends all her time looking out for everyone else when, really, she needs to start looking after herself properly."

"She not the type of girl you can tell what to do."

"Yeah, I get that. Headstrong and then some. Have you known her a long time?"

"Since I was nineteen. We studied at Yale together."

"And were you a couple back then?"

"For a few months. Why do you ask?"

He shrugs as he packs his things away. "If I didn't know you were married to someone else or that Jaine used to be married to Mr. O'Connell, then I would have thought you were a couple."

"Is that because of the compromising position you found us in?" I laugh.

He stops what he's doing and turns to face me. "It wasn't compromising. Mr. O'Connell said you looked like star-crossed lovers, and he was right. You looked like you were protecting each other."

I smile sadly. "What Jaine and I had was over a long time ago. She's back with Eoin again, or at least she will be soon."

"It's big of you." He turns his attention back to what he was doing.

"What is?"

"Putting her needs ahead of your own."

This lad can see right through me. My smile is betrayed by the single tear that runs down my face.

"I always will, Tim."

I STARE AT MY BIG BROTHER FROM MY SEATED POSITION ON THE sectional. I didn't want to have this conversation from my bed. I would have felt weak, and right now, I need to be stronger than I have ever been in my life.

We've never been close, Eoin and me. Maybe it's the eight-year age gap. Maybe it's the fact that he's always told me what to do like I wasn't capable of mustering a sensible or rational thought in my own head.

I'm a lawyer. I'm both sensible and rational when I need to be.

"How are you, Paddy?" He's not pacing like he would normally do. He's standing and staring straight at me. He's comparing himself to me. I know he is.

It's because he knows she loves me too.

He's trying to work out what she sees in me, but he never will because it's not visible on the outside. It's inside. What Jaine and I share isn't based on just the physical. It's deeper than that.

It's soul deep.

"Fine." I need to give myself a shake. One-word answers won't help. I should be grateful to him. Without him putting two and two together and working out where we were, Jaine and I would be dead. "Tim says I'll be up and about in a couple of days," I add.

"That's good to hear."

There's an awkward silence. This is the first time he and I have been alone together since I returned from Sicily.

Since I found out he had married the love of my life instead of finding one of his own. Since I found out that Jaine now loves him too. Since I found out he's been playing da to my son.

I stare back at him. Eoin's an impressive individual, but then, he always has been. Tall, lean, and good-looking. Appearance-wise, we're much the same. That's where the similarities end.

Eoin has a menacing presence that deters people from approaching him. With him, it's a case of what you see is what you get. That's just the way he likes it. He can converse and mingle, but it's not really him. He much prefers to control and orchestrate, and he's extremely good at it. He was born to head our family and organization.

He's the best brother for the job.

With me, it's more a case of not getting what you see. I'm what they call a smiling assassin. I'm your best friend until I decide that I'm not. And the not part typically involves me brandishing a blade in my hand, just so there's no confusion about how unfriendly I can be. Aside from my legal duties, it's why I'm on constant wet work.

I'm the best brother for that job.

"I know about Fin."

"And what is it that you know, exactly?"

"That he's mine. Isn't that enough?" I snort.

He nods. "The plan was to tell you two months after you got back. To let you get settled…."

"And to allow the family time to decide how best to reveal the secret they've been keeping from me."

"We didn't know how you'd react."

"You had no right making decisions on my behalf! None of you did! You had no right making assumptions that I'd behave in a certain way because I'm the emotional sibling. Do you honestly think I would have done anything to put him or Jaine in danger?"

"I'm sorry, Paddy."

And he is. I can tell.

"Sorry is not fucking good enough, brother. He's two years old. Time I won't ever get back, and for his whole young life, he's been calling someone else Da. You tell me, Eoin. How the fuck would you feel if that were your son?" I rest my head back against the sectional, suddenly exhausted.

"We only found out after the wedding. You didn't want to be contacted about anything. You weren't in the right head space. We couldn't take the risk."

"My head was fucked because I was forced by my *loving family* to do my Dusterly duty and marry the bitch from hell, and for what? It turns out it was all for nothing!"

"Paddy…" I can hear the guilt in his tone, and the silent admission makes me go straight for the jugular.

"Whereas you were forced to marry the love of *my* fucking life! Mine! And then you fell in love with her!"

Silence. He can't deny the fact that he loves her, so he won't.

"She told me that she loves me too, Eoin. That she never stopped. All this time, I thought she didn't and that she never had. That right there is what destroyed me most. For three years, I've been struggling to make it to the end of each fucking day. She walked away without a backward glance, and I resorted to lies and deceit because I couldn't let her go, and now, she's decided to tell me that she fucking loved me all along. Why the fuck would she do such a thing?"

My words are strangled by sobs. "What was the point in all this torture and misery? We had been friends for years. We could have remained friends if that's all we were ever destined to be. She took herself away for nothing, and when she did, she took away my only reason for fucking living."

And then I weep.

And as he did three years ago, my big brother sits down, wraps his arms around me, and tries his best to comfort me.

CHAPTER THIRTY-SIX

EOIN

Eoin's Apartment, Hudson Yards, New York

"He told me, Dyl." I throw back the whiskey in one as I stare across the room, welcoming the burn in my throat. It's my third one, and it won't be the last.

I was meant to leave Paddy's apartment and go straight to the house to talk things through with Jaine, but I couldn't. Not with guilt clawing away at my insides. Guilt I'm now trying to drown with whiskey.

"He told you what?"

"That he's having to get Sophia pregnant, and in exchange, Luc will allow him to annul their marriage."

"Ah."

"So, you already knew." I'm not sure whether to be annoyed or not.

"I've known for a while, yes."

"On what grounds can he possibly ask for an annulment?" It's my guess he'll go down the same route Jaine did with me. That he'll claim he was forced into the union by his family, which he was.

"Well, right now, he currently has two routes available to him. The same one Jaine went down."

"And the other?"

"While Paddy may have taken Sophia's purity under the haze of a drunken stupor, an act he can't even remember carrying out, he's never consummated their marriage. That route will no longer be available once he does the deed, of course."

"Jesus Christ."

"He can't abide her, Eoin. While they were in Sicily, their unhappily ever after wasn't noticeable to anyone, but back in New York, it is. Luciano wants them to start behaving like the newlyweds in love they're supposed to be. To seal the deal, he wants them to produce a Duster heir. He says it's to encourage family-orientated high rankers to sign on his new organization's dotted line…."

"He's simply panicking at Paddy's refusal to welcome Sophia into his bed. The fact that he'd rather sleep with a bullet in his skull than his sister. He's now worried that Paddy's membership in his family may only be temporary, and so he wants a permanent *in* to ours. The only way to achieve that is for Sophia to birth an O'Connell."

"That's the same conclusion I reached. Provided Paddy gets her pregnant, he'll be allowed to have the marriage annulled on the basis that he was backed into the union."

"They'll never let him leave, Dylan."

I pour myself a fourth whiskey, far larger than the previous ones.

"Again, I reached the same conclusion. Even though it wouldn't be a divorce, Luciano still wouldn't welcome the adverse publicity."

"Once the Ruoccos have the child, they'll have no further need for Paddy. They're simply dangling a carrot to get him to do their bidding."

"In fairness, I think Sophia's hoping that once they have a baby together, he'll finally stop pining after Jaine and settle down with her. What she's not understanding is that Jaine's not the problem. She is. By all accounts, she's not a pleasant person to be around, so much so that Paddy would rather have a gun put to his head than spend the rest of his life with her."

"Jesus Christ. What have we done, Dylan?" I whisper.

"No one was to know, Eoin. Luciano was don. It was seen as a good match at the time. And we can't change the past."

"Paddy's divulged far more to you than he did to me. What's his plan?"

"This 'child for an annulment' business has been drawn up as a new contract. Paddy had a few queries. As they insisted on having their family lawyer handle matters, Sophia headed back to Sicily to have them answered face-to-face. That's why she wasn't aware of Paddy's recent disappearance."

"I did wonder where she was. The fact that he was missing for a week, and she didn't notice, is representative of the fact that they live two very separate lives. Had she known, she would have been frantic that the Ruocco plans were potentially about to be scuppered. Surely, Paddy must suspect he'll never get out of the marriage alive?"

"I'm sure deep down he does, Eoin, but he's clutching at the very last straw available to him."

"Have you seen the contract?"

"No."

"We need sight of it."

"He'll refuse. He'll argue that we signed the last one without him being privy to it. His life. His decision."

"His death."

"He already feels like his life is over anyway."

"But it's not over. He knows about Fin. He knows he has a son."

"That will only make matters worse. Sophia knows. Jaine found the proof in Molly's phone. Paddy will be determined to keep Luc and Sophia away from Jaine and Fin."

"That's exactly what he's attempting to do. He wants me to mend things with her. To get remarried and do whatever is necessary to care for them and protect them because, right now, he's in no position to do so himself. Right now, he thinks he has nothing to offer either of them because he's trapped in a toxic marriage."

"He won't want Sophia anywhere near Fin. Apparently, they had a plethora of wee ones working on their estate back home, most likely illegally. Her nastiness extended to children, and it was verbal as well as physical. Paddy called her out on it, but instead of it improving her behavior, it just made it worse."

"And he wants to bring a child into that?"

"She's his wife. She wants a child. The contract stipulates joint custody and that the child must reside in New York at all times. He'll be hoping that she'll treat her own child better than she does the children of others."

"It's a bit of a gamble."

"The child will be an O'Connell. I'm not sure the Ruoccos would be stupid enough to harm a hair on its head."

"It's not the physical damage I'd be worried about."

"He's trapped, Eoin. He wants out. He's going to agree to the child and also to giving her all of his personal fortune to undo the destructive path his own family set him on."

I pause. "He was a mess when I saw him, Dylan."

"In what way?"

"The same way he was when Jaine first left to return to Rising. He thinks she walked away without a backward glance. That it was her choice and her decision."

"Did you not correct him?"

"He wasn't receptive to listening. He wanted to get everything off his chest." I swallow down more rising guilt with the help of the fourth whiskey.

"He needs to know that it wasn't her choice, Eoin. That it was the family's decision. That we separated them and pretty much ran her out of town."

"I realize that."

"Because Jaine won't have corrected him. You do know that. That's our news to spill, not hers."

"You're telling me what I already know!" I snap. He ignores my spike in temper.

"You'll also have to tell him about the other matter. Right now, he thinks you fell in love with Jaine only after you married her. He doesn't realize that you were infatuated with her for a long time before then. That you kept them apart to suit your own purposes."

"He'll never forgive me, Dylan." Closing my eyes, I run my hand over my face.

"Maybe not, but he still needs to know. Come what may, it's time for all of the secrets to be revealed. Now that Jaine's part of the family, and now that Paddy's back, we'll start tying ourselves in knots trying to remember what we've said and to whom otherwise. If he's not told, we would also be doing Jaine a disservice. Because you know as well as I do that everything she's ever done has been for our Padraig, and right now, he doesn't see it that way."

He pauses.

"There's one other thing you should know."

I'm not sure that I want to know any more. I don't encourage him, but he continues regardless.

"When Jaine went to the reunion, the girl Paddy cheated on her with was there. It turns out he didn't cheat after all. The girl lied because she wanted him for herself."

I didn't think it could get any worse, but it can and has. The reason they split up twelve years ago no longer exists.

"Does he know that?"

"I'm not sure. They've just been locked up together for several days, so they could have spoken about that and much more besides. It was Jaine who told me."

"You never said." Again, I don't know whether to be annoyed or not.

"You and she had gone your separate ways, so there seemed little point. What are you going to do now?"

"Try to sort things out with Jaine."

"What if she doesn't want to? Maybe after spending time with Paddy…."

"That's what he's worried about, Dylan." I interrupt. "That he's confused things with her, and he wants there to be no confusion. He wants her to know there's no future for him and her."

"Even if it breaks his own heart?"

"You can't break something that's already broken." Tonight, I witnessed with my own eyes just how broken he is. It's a visual I'll carry with me for the rest of my life.

"One other thing. Jaine went to the church on her hog, and now it's missing."

"So, they never wanted her to be found, or at least not until it was too late. It was a deliberate setup."

"It's certainly looking that way."

CHAPTER THIRTY-SEVEN

JAINE

The O'Connell Home, Darling, New York

I watch as Eoin throws a giggling Finian in the air before catching him safely in his strong hands. My smile turns to a grimace as Fin then proceeds to vomit his dinner all over the living space floor not ten seconds later.

Running across, I grab JJ around the middle and lift him before he can start to pick out the colored pieces from the puddle of glop, which is exactly what he did last time.

"Hey, little guy. We don't want to be touching that now, do we? Why don't we get you two stinky butts in the bath."

Eoin and I share a smile as we switch children. We both know when he's here, JJ will cry if Eoin doesn't bathe him, his attachment to him is so strong. Finian doesn't care who has to deal with him as long as they don't mind listening to his constant chatter as he splashes the lucky individual with water before honoring them with a crown of soap suds.

Eoin washes JJ thoroughly. They then play with toy boats, which Fin deliberately sinks. Fin then takes a water-filled sponge and squeezes it out over JJ's little head. JJ cries and looks at us with soulful tear-filled eyes, his bottom lip sticking out.

My gaze, as always, is drawn to his quivering chin, the little dent the same as the one Ace had. I stare at it as tears fill my own eyes when I think of his daddy and everything he's missing out on.

We've repeated this process so many times, but I'm determined never to take one precious moment I spend with them for granted ever again. I almost died for a second time. I just drifted off to sleep with Irish, so I'm not sure I'd even have known.

Is that the best way to go?

I'm not so sure that it is. At least when I was staring down the loaded barrel of the other sniper's rifle, I got the chance to say goodbye.

To Irish, at least.

My eyes connect with Eoin's once more. Has he been with anyone else? Not that we've been split up all that long, but it had a finality to it this time that it's never had before. I guess he's single and free to do as he wishes.

I also guess it's none of my business.

He's stopped by the past three evenings, although he's never stayed over. Then again, the kids have worn me out. I've missed them, and they've missed me. For the past three days, we haven't gotten out of our pajamas. We've spent the whole time building pillow forts, watching Disney movies, and eating a combination of healthy and unhealthy snacks. I've even gained some weight. Something that I'm sure will make Tim happy.

Eoin hasn't been very talkative when he's been here. He clearly has something on his mind. Something he's not quite sure how to say. It isn't like him.

Mr. Smug. Selfish. Pompous is never at a loss for words.

We focus on the children as we put them to bed before returning to the living area. I watch as he takes his usual seat on the sofa. He's been home first, as he's dressed down in dark blue jeans and a cream turtleneck. Clothing that best displays the true perfection hidden underneath.

I admire him from where I'm standing, my eyes drinking in every delicious, deadly inch. It's blatant. I don't attempt to hide it. He knows I want him. I know he wants me. That's never been the issue. If a relationship could survive based on fucking alone, we've got it in the bag.

It can't, though. It's not enough. Nowhere near.

"I want to apologize, Jaine."

"For what?"

"For how I treated you at the docks. It was unnecessary. I was being reactive."

"What were you reacting to?" I already know the answer, thanks to Dylan.

"The fact that you kissed Paddy." And there it is.

"It wasn't that sort of kiss."

"I still didn't like the thought of it."

"Irish is happily married. Why would I attempt to kiss him any other way?"

I don't miss the fleeting frown that crosses his face. Over what I did, or something else?

"I was still jealous. I'm sorry."

"It doesn't matter. It's in the past."

"What about the future?"

"What about it?"

"Do you still wish to share one with me?"

I walk across, taking the seat beside him. He doesn't wrap his arm around me like he usually does because he knows he doesn't have my permission to do that right now.

"I wouldn't have a future if it wasn't for you, Eoin. If you hadn't worked out where we were… That aside, it still doesn't mean we should spend it together."

"If you choose to spend it with me for that reason only, then I'd much rather you not." He runs his hand through his hair as he stares across the room, and my eyes are instantly drawn to his face. It's more lined these days. His cheekbones are more pronounced, but then they never filled back out after he spent the best part of a week in a coma after saving Fin.

The stress of this life is really starting to show, and he's not even forty yet. The stress of our on-and-off relationship won't be helping either, the dark circles around his eyes a clear indication that he's not been sleeping.

I saved him twice. He's saved me twice. We're even.

"We have compatibility issues."

He remains silent because he can't deny it.

"I don't mind your possessive nature per se, but your over-protectiveness is another matter. I realize I need protection, but not to the extent where I can't function as my own person. I need more freedom."

I'm asking a lot of him. I know I am. Even more so after what's just happened. I'm asking him to change as a person to accommodate me as a person.

"I'll do my best to give you that. It's difficult for me. I can't let anything happen to you."

"And why is that?" I already know why.

"Because I love you." Aquamarine eyes finally meet mine.

I link my fingers through his calloused ones. "I love you too and I don't want anything to happen to you either. Does that mean I get to dictate when you go out and who you get to see? Will it work for you if I insist you can't go anywhere on your own?"

Silence. Maybe now he understands the point I'm trying to make, but then I'm not so sure it's the understanding that's the issue. It's just that he can't help himself. It's second nature.

He's been raised to protect the woman in his life and to lay down his own life for her. I can't fault him for that, but we're opposites in that regard. I protect me.

My life. My death. My actions. My consequences.

And therein lies our problem.

Moving to straddle his lap, I face him. His hands shift to my hips as I watch his eyes turn green. He's staring at me like he wants to eat me alive.

"I think we need to take things one day at a time."

He nods slowly, staring at me like he's trying to imprint me to memory somehow. Why is that?

His hand fists my hair, pulling my head down so my lips hover over his. I stare at his mouth, then drown in his gaze. I lick my lips, and his eyes drop.

He says nothing as his thumb drags roughly across my bottom lip. I suck it into my mouth and then bite down. Hard.

The conversation is now at an end because, right now, Eoin O'Connell would agree to anything I want. He's currently visualizing my mouth wrapped around a different part of his anatomy. A rock-hard part that's throbbing directly underneath me.

His hand releases my hair, his strong fingers moving to wrap around my throat before gripping it so tightly I'm struggling to breathe.

I've fucking missed him.

Green eyes worship my face as his thumb tilts my chin down, then with a low growl, his lips capture mine, his tongue immediately taking ownership by thrusting deep into my mouth.

Searching. Tasting. Remembering.

He attempts to yank my top over my head, but I stop him. "Not here."

We don't need Finian walking in on us. I anchor my legs around his waist as he walks us to my bedroom. Throwing me on the bed, I watch as he pulls his sweater over his head to reveal the mouthwatering map of ink and scars hidden underneath. With a body like his, he should be on the cover of a mobster magazine.

So perfectly imperfect and all fucking mine.

For one day at a time.

He unbuttons his jeans but leaves them on before yanking off my pants and pulling my top over my head.

Naked in seconds.

His gaze drifts over me, stopping to admire every one of my own scars, each one letting him know that he's found his match. That I can stand by his side and survive in his world because I'm just as much of a fuck up as he is.

Holding his gaze, I sit up and drag my nails down his chiseled torso. His abs tense when my fingers dip inside the front of his opened jeans to connect with the slick head of his hard dick. I spread the precum around the crown, smirking when it jerks in response.

Moving from the bed, I kneel on the floor before him, my mouth watering as he frees his cock from his jeans. I watch as he strokes himself, pre-cum quickly coating his clenched fist.

With one hand, he grips my hair, then, guiding his dick to my parted lips with the other, he thrusts deep. I gag as the blunt head connects with the back of my throat, my eyes instantly tearing up. He doesn't stop. This is exactly where he wants me.

On my knees and submitting to his every demand like a good girl.

He fucks my mouth hard and fast, causing a mixture of saliva and precum to drip from my chin. I stare up at him, my fingers digging into his thighs. I suck harder, my hands moving to grip his balls.

He curses me as he closes his eyes and throws his head back. My insides instantly turn molten when he lets out a low, feral growl, letting me know he's getting close. With a loud pop, he pulls his dick free.

I watch as he strokes his slick length. He grunts his approval when I trace my fingertips around my nipples, his hand movements becoming faster at the visual. Leaning forward I suck on one of his balls causing it to tighten in my mouth.

Fisting my hair, he yanks my head back, then, with a curse, he releases hot ropes of cum all over my face. He stands over me, and we stare at each other. I dip my finger into his release before sucking it into my mouth, causing him to grunt his approval once more.

Something's off.

He's here physically but not mentally. I've felt the disconnect all night. It's just been compounded by the fact that Eoin is always vocal with his demands during sex, and for the first time, I've sucked him off in utter silence. Is he here because he wants to be or because he has to be?

Right now, I'm not too sure.

I stand, then make my way into the restroom before doing something I never do. I lock the door so he can't follow. I'm not sure why I bothered. Something tells me he won't anyway. Turning on the shower, I stand under the scorching water until it starts to run cold before slowly drying myself, then brushing my teeth.

When I return to the bedroom, the lights are already off—another unusual sign. Normally, we'd lie by lamplight and share truths and memories.

When he reaches for me, I use the age-old excuse that I'm tired as it's been a long day. He doesn't argue. He simply rolls over and faces the other way. Is he relieved?

I'm not tired. I don't even sleep.

Instead, I lie awake all night, wondering what the fuck is going on.

Maybe it's for the best that I only agreed to a day-at-a-time relationship with him because, right now, I have a feeling mine and Eoin's days together really are numbered.

CHAPTER THIRTY-EIGHT

PADRAIG

The O'Connell Home, Darling, New York

IT'S BEEN TWO WEEKS SINCE JAINE AND I ALMOST PERISHED IN EACH other's arms. In that time, it's been confirmed by the urologist that I'm not firing blanks. Given I've already fathered a son, I wasn't expecting the result to be anything different.

I shouldn't be here today. Or at least not at this time of day.

Not when Jaine's home.

She now knows about my Sophia-inflicted ban. Even though I'm not permitted to, I had to see her one last time.

I haven't signed the contract yet, but I'll have no choice now that Sophia's back from Sicily. All of my requests have been accepted. Nothing is now stopping me and her from creating a child together.

But I don't want to.

I want to go back in time because I demand a do-over. I want to see the girl standing in front of me, pregnant with my offspring, because I didn't get to witness it first time around. I stare at the love of my life as she stands at the front door of my family home. At the girl I willingly pushed back into the arms of my brother to keep her and Fin safe.

My gaze drifts to her hand. It's absent of the obscene engagement ring I thought Eoin would have insisted she wear once again. All so he can show off to the world that she's his.

By default.

"How have you been, Jaine?" Those words seem wrong. They seem insignificant when compared to everything we've been through together.

I watch her. She looks as confused as I feel. She's searching for something worthwhile to say in response to my mediocre question. Like me, she's struggling to find words when there are none suitable.

Although under a fucked-up set of circumstances, we lived together for several days at the church. We shared a lot. Even though I almost died, that whole experience was one of the best times of my life.

How pathetic is that?

In the end, she doesn't respond. She simply motions her head for me to enter. Once inside, she closes the door behind me then slowly presses her hands against my chest. I instinctively wrap my arms around her. She's missed them. I know she has. And they've missed her.

I think back on what Tim referred to us as. Star-crossed lovers.

Will tragedy befall us because of an ending chosen for us by my own flesh and blood? It will for me, I'm sure. Deep down, I know my chances of escaping the union with Sophia with my life still intact are slim to none.

But then I've always been the type of fella who clings on to foolish hope. It's the only reason I'm still here. That I didn't just give up existing a long time ago.

Because without hope, all is lost. But without Jaine, there is no hope.

At least not for me.

"That good, darlin'?" I chuckle sadly against her hair as I inhale the smell of wildflowers, my fingers moving to trace the tattoo on her wrist. She watches my movements as I circle the poppies and then the four-leaf clovers. I don't need to ask. I know one is for me, and one is for Ace. Tears prick my eyes.

How could I have ever doubted her love for me?

She steps back, making no attempt to hide her wet cheeks. Jaine's never been anything but herself when she's with me. She's never hidden from me because I've never hidden from her.

"I'm sorry I've not been to see Finian, Jaine… I…"

She shakes her head. She understands, or at least she thinks she does. About Sophia not wanting me here. About me being so madly in love with my wife that her wish is my every command.

I want to tell Jaine the truth. I would have had she not been in love with me, but I have no idea how she'd react if I were to admit that her love is reciprocated.

And here's me doing to her what she did to me. Making decisions. Making assumptions.

I understand now why she didn't want to take the risks because when the shoe is on the other foot, I don't want to take them either.

Not with her. Not with Fin.

"He's in the family room."

I follow her through to where Fin's sitting with Ma. She and I make eye contact, and her eyes well up.

Guilt.

We've not spoken about the deceit. I've only discussed it with

Eoin and Dylan, but I'm aware the rest of the family now knows that I know.

Fin lets out a mighty yell as soon as he sees me—his favorite uncle.

His da.

"Hey there, trouble." I can't stop the tears from spilling down my cheeks as I lift him and spin him around—my carbon copy.

My son.

Jaine walks over to us as I hold him in my arms.

Our son.

"Finian."

He looks at her before leaning over to press a messy kiss against her cheek. She smiles at him and then at me.

"Finian, this is your da."

She turns to look at me with tear-filled eyes. "He's never called anyone that before… I…" She swallows thickly, her voice filled with raw emotion. "I would never have allowed it." Shifting him to one arm, I wrap my other around her, and we stand there. A small family unit. For now, at least.

Jaine and I shed silent tears, and it's then I hear my ma sobbing in the background because now she realizes this was how it was always meant to be.

Me and her. Her and me. Not the fucked-up mess we're in now.

I have my arms wrapped around the two most important people in my life. The two people that represent my whole fucking world. For how much longer is anyone's guess.

I understand now why they call it the present because these two right here are the best fucking gifts I've ever had. Who needs tomorrow when you can have today?

Padraig's Apartment, Hudson Yards, New York

"Would I be able to see a copy of the contract?"

I frown at my phone—a question from out of nowhere from our Dylan when we were talking about work. "Why do you want to see it?"

"I just want to know what they're making you sign up for."

"They're not making me sign up for anything."

"Okay, I want to see what you're willingly signing yourself up for."

"Only if you swear you won't show it to anyone else."

"I swear."

"You're a proficient liar these days." I snort.

"Only because you made me one."

He's right. I send him a copy of the document that's currently still open on my screen. I know he'll send it to my big brother. That they'll try to talk me out of it. At the end of the day, it's my decision. My life.

My existence.

"Have you signed it yet?"

"No."

"Because you don't want to?"

"Leave it, Dyl."

I change the subject to another one I don't really want to talk about.

"So, did Eoin and Jaine sort out their differences?"

"He did what was asked of him."

"Like it was any hardship." I snort once more.

"Padraig, I won't ask what went on in the church between you and Jaine, but you wanted her to not be confused over you. She's not. She thinks you're happy with your lot. That you're in love with your wife."

"Why, Dyl? It's the only thing I don't understand. Why did she do what she did?"

"Did you not ask her?"

"No. I just chided her on the fact that she walked away without a backward glance."

"Then you need to have a conversation with Eoin."

"About what?"

"That's all I'm saying, Paddy. It's not my story to tell."

I hear what he's saying, but I'm in no mood to talk to my eldest brother any time soon. I'm grateful he's doing what I asked him to do, but that doesn't make it any easier to accept that he will be living the happily ever after with the girl who was supposed to be my end game, not his.

CHAPTER THIRTY-NINE

JAINE

The O'Connell Home, Darling, New York

I LIE BACK ON MY BED, FULLY DRESSED. I'M HAVING A REFLECTIVE sort of day over the shit show that is my life. I then think about the little wooden box with its morbid music.

What does it all mean? Does it relate to Molly's demise or mine?

Am I the target? Fin? Irish? The O'Connell family? All of the above?

Aside from the approaches made to Lucifer's men, nothing untoward has happened on the west coast since. If it is the same faction involved, they seem to be focusing their attention on what's going on in New York, specifically in crossing my name off their hit list.

I answer my flashing phone, still wearing the same frown.

"How are you feeling, partner?"

"Melancholy." I sigh.

"That good, huh?"

"Someone tried to kill me. How would you feel?"

"Did they, though? Do you know that for sure?"

"They took my hog so it wouldn't give away my location. I think that speaks for itself."

"I'm sorry about your bike, Jaine."

"Not as much as I am. It was one of the happiest moments of my life when my pop passed me the keys to that classic on my eighteenth birthday."

"Maybe it'll still show up."

"It'll either be a burnt-out wreck or parked up at the bottom of the Hudson by now."

A biker's hog is like an extension of their own person. I'm not sure I'll ever find another that means as much to me as that one did. I'm actually praying that it doesn't turn up. I admire Jessie's optimism, but if it does, it won't be in the pristine condition I left it in.

When and if it's returned, it will be used to make either a threat or a statement.

"So what happened in your forced proximity situation? I know what happened in mine." She snickers. We all know what happened in hers. She's told us all enough times.

"Nothing happened."

"At all?"

"We argued, made up, put the world to rights."

"Do you still love him?"

"It's not the kind of thing you can just switch off. Then again, he did, so who knows? Maybe it's just me who's cursed."

"Loving someone's a curse?"

"When your name is Jaine Jones, it would appear so."

"Maybe he does love you, and he just doesn't want to say it."

I snort. "I admire all the wishful thinking you've got going on."

"Dylan told me that Paddy never cheated after all."

"That was nice of him to share that with you."

"You and he would never have split up if you'd known that."

"No shit, Sherlock."

"How does that make you feel?"

"Confused as well as melancholy."

"So he never cheated, you share a child, and you love him."

"And he's happily married and in love with someone else, so your point is?"

"And how are things with big bad Eoin?"

"We're taking things one day at a time."

I don't tell her I think something's going on with him. Eoin's not being Eoin. Is it because I'm trying to change him, or is something else going on?

"Communication and compromise. That's the answer."

"Thanks for the relationship advice."

"You love him still?"

"Why do I feel like I'm being interrogated?"

"I'm just trying to find out where your head's at these days, partner."

"When you find out, then be sure to let me know. Yes, I still love him. I love them both. I will always love them both. Same as I will always love Ace."

"It's all so complicated. I'm glad I'm a one-man woman. Anyway, did you find out anything else from Molly's phone?"

"I haven't had time to check. In fact, I'm glad you mentioned that, as I need to put it back on charge."

I walk into the living space to get the phone. I left it beside the little music box on the dresser in the hallway. I stare at the empty space when I get there.

"It's gone."

"What's gone?"

"The phone. It's gone. Along with the music box I found at the church."

"Did Eoin take it?"

"No. He brought them here then passed them to me, so why would he take them away again?"

"Roisin?"

"She seldom comes down here, and even if she did, she wouldn't take something without asking. She knows I'd notice."

"The only people who've been inside the house recently have been family, partner."

I pause. "Jessie, can I tell you something in the strictest confidence?"

"Of course."

"I'm convinced Sophia has got something to do with all of this."

It's her turn to pause. "You can't just accuse her, Jaine."

"I realize that."

"So, what are you going to do?"

"Go through the rest of the data from Molly's phone. See if I can find any proof."

"But if you don't have…"

"I downloaded everything to my laptop before I left for the church. If the person who took the handset thinks I can no longer see everything that was on there, then more fool them."

I STARE AT THE MESSAGE EXCHANGE BETWEEN SOPHIA AND MOLLY. I'm not really sure what to do with this new piece of information. It's probably irrelevant now anyway.

Should I tell anyone? I mean, they're happily married. Why would I want to rock the boat?

Because he deserves to know the truth. He's been told enough lies as it is.

It may be a case of history repeating, but what's done is done. It's old news. It's for Sophia to come clean about, not me. Perhaps she's already told him. Maybe I'd just look like a tattle tale for telling him something he already knows.

I dial Jessie's number.

"Twice in one day. I should feel flattered, but instead, you've got me worried, partner."

I can't stop the smile from crossing my face. "Jessie, I've found something else on the message exchange between Molly and Sophia, but you can't breathe a word if I tell you."

"I never breathe a word about anything we discuss, Jaine. You know that. I know you have a good relationship with Dyl. That if you wanted him to know you'd tell him yourself."

She's right. I would. "I need to read something out to you."

"Go on."

Molly: *Rumor has it that things progressed between you and Padraig last night.*
Sophia: *Let's just say I played the only card I had left.*
Molly: *I don't understand.*
Sophia: *Roisin wanted me to carry out her task. I couldn't.*
Molly: *That's not what I heard.*
Sophia: *Padraig was drunk.*
Molly: *What did you do?*
Sophia: *I got into bed beside him, of course.*
Molly: *But how did he manage to perform?*
Sophia: *He didn't. It wasn't my virginal blood on the sheets. It was pig's blood.*
Molly: *Sophia! I can't believe you did that. Won't he find out?*

Sophia: *How will he ever find out? Only you and I know. He was so drunk he couldn't remember a thing, and when he woke up to find me naked in bed beside him with blood between my legs and on the sheets, he accepted what had happened without hesitation.*

There's a pause as Jessie digests the information.

"I don't think you should keep this to yourself, Jaine."

It's the opposite of what I expected her to say.

"But they're happy now, so what good will it do to drag it up? Surely, it would just be seen as bitterness on my part? I mean, they're obviously sharing a marital bed as they're trying for a baby. Or at least, that's what Dyl said."

"Yes, he told me the same. Still, it doesn't seem right not to mention anything. I mean, their whole relationship is based on a lie."

"The keyword is *their*. I don't think we should get involved."

"Don't you think he's been fed enough lies as it is?"

"I was lied to, too, remember?"

"Not as much as he was."

"Are we point-scoring now?" I huff. "Anyway, I tried to deliver justice for him."

"And ended up falling in love with the person you held solely responsible. Have you explained all of that to him?"

"No. It doesn't seem right to tell him about my personal crusade on his behalf. Not when he's in love with someone else."

"Have you asked him if he still loves you? Just because he's not said the words doesn't mean he doesn't still have the feelings."

"No! I can't ask him that when he's married to someone else! That would be wrong on every level."

'Maybe."

"Would you want another woman asking Dylan that?"

"There's never been another woman. I was the first and only woman ever to conquer that O'Connell."

"If there had been, I'm not sure you would have appreciated it. Anyway, I'm with Eoin now."

In an uncommunicative relationship that exists day by day with a man who's now making excuses not to see you.

"Who would you choose, Jaine?"

"Jesus Christ."

"You must know."

"You want the goddamn truth?"

"I do."

"I wouldn't be able to choose, so I'm only glad I'll never have to. Sophia will be pregnant soon. She and Irish will be doing their family thing soon enough."

"But what if she is behind everything?"

"The only way she could ever be confronted would be with concrete proof."

"And how do we get that?"

"I'm not sure because, unlike Molly, Sophia will have the highest level of security on her phone and everything else she uses."

"So you're not going to say anything about her virginity?"

"Not unless I have reason to, and right now, I'm not sure what good it would do anyone, least of all Irish. Anyway, he may already know."

"I suppose." She doesn't sound convinced.

"And you're also missing out on one very important fact, Jessie."

"And that is?"

"If Irish had feelings for me, then why would he have given me his blessing to be with his brother."

"I guess there is that."

CHAPTER FORTY

JAINE

The O'Connell Home, Darling, New York

I CAN HEAR LOUD LAUGHTER AS SOON AS I ENTER THE HOUSE. I know it's Irish. His laugh is so infectious it instantly brings a smile to my face in the same way Finian's does.

I'm surprised he's here today. Sarah and Cillian have taken Fin and JJ to spend time with their new baby cousin. But then it is his parents' house.

I'm just a temporary resident who now seems to live here permanently.

My thoughts immediately drift to Sophia.

Tell Irish? Don't? You have proof.

He loves her. He's married to her. They're going to have a baby together. Keep your nose out of other people's goddamn business, Jaine.

I walk into the family room to find Irish and Duke sitting side by side on the sectional.

"Something funny?" I ask the question out loud to no one in particular as I look between them. Not surprisingly, both look shocked to see me. I left work earlier than usual today, so they won't have been expecting me.

My bad.

"We were just reminiscing about Ace."

My eyes well up as I look at Irish. I keep forgetting that he knew Ace before he ever knew he and I had a past. How many memories does he have that he could share with me, because I'll never have enough. I'll take any spares I can get.

"Jaine, darlin'." Irish stands and walks across to pull me straight into his arms.

"I'm sorry. I seem to have turned into an emotional wreck." I wipe the tears from my face with my hand.

"It's only to be expected. In a matter of weeks, you've almost died twice."

I raise my head and stare into eyes of sparkling blue. For the first time, I notice that even though his mouth has the upward curve it always has, ready to turn into an infectious smile at any opportunity, his eyes hold a sad, almost defeated look.

He's not happy. Why is that?

"Anyway, I should head off."

"You don't have to leave on my account," But I know he does have to leave for that very reason. Because he's not allowed to be anywhere near me. More tears prick my eyes.

"Jaine."

I disentangle myself from his arms, turn and leave.

There's a knock on the safe space door not ten minutes later. I open it to find Duke standing there.

He's looking older now, his hair rapidly becoming more peppered with grey. What's been happening on our own doorstep won't be helping matters. We're all aging because of what's been going on.

Now that Roisin takes the kids most afternoons, Duke's been spending his free time at the Scorpions' clubhouse. With Delaney now the proud father of a little boy he and Bailey have named King, he's been happy to relinquish a little control to the other council members.

As Duke's a former prez of his own club, he's been roped in to help out—something he's only too happy about.

His look is sympathetic, causing more tears to prick my eyes. I motion my head for him to step inside, and he does, taking a seat on the sofa. I immediately curl up beside him, and he wraps his arm around me.

"We've not had much chance to talk since your ordeal at the church."

"I know." I sigh.

"How was it spending time with Padraig again, even if it wasn't under the best of circumstances?"

I shrug. "Is it wrong to say I enjoyed it?"

"Nope. Nothing wrong with that at all. He was saying you argued and yelled at each other, and then you made your peace."

"We did."

"So, are your feelings for him still as strong?"

"I love him. I will always love him." My voice fades out.

"Say what's on your mind, Jainie."

"Irish never cheated."

"And who told you that?"

"The girl he supposedly cheated on me with."

He lets out a low whistle "Shit. So she lied all this time. Well, I guess that changes a lot of things."

"It actually changes nothing."

"It does mentally. You must be wondering what your life would have been like. There's every chance you and Padraig may never have split up."

"But then I'd have never gotten back with Ace."

"Things happen for a reason, Jainie. I figure you were always meant to end up back with Ace for the time that you did. Fate works in mysterious ways. Who's to say you're not meant to end up back with Padraig after all these years? That it's the reason the truth has only now come to light."

"He's married. He also gave me the green light to be with his own brother."

"But you love him."

"He doesn't love me."

"Have you asked him?"

"He's married. Why would I ask him that?"

"Out of curiosity."

I snort. "It's not the sort of thing you ask someone out of curiosity, Duke."

He chuckles. "I guess you're right. And how are things between you and the eldest Duster?"

"We're taking things one day at a time."

"You love him still?"

"You know I do."

"But?"

"I just worry that we're not compatible. That we're too different. I don't mind how possessive he is, but I don't like the overprotectiveness. I mean, if I ever want to do my sideline again, how will I be able to? He never lets me out of his sight."

"You could just tell him about it."

"I plan on doing that, but it doesn't guarantee me any leeway with him, and you know it. He could then just see me as a trophy, lock me in a gilded cage, and throw away the key."

"Or he may not."

I pause. "Things have been different between us lately. I don't know if it's because I've asked him to change or if it's for some other reason, but we've stopped communicating. I'm worried we've been through so much what we shared is no longer salvageable."

"So, what's the plan, then? Because with two little boys in tow, you can't just live your life one day at a time, Jainie."

"I realize that. I guess we need to find something to balance us."

"Maybe it's not something you need for balance, but someone."

I stare at him. "Like relationship advice?"

"Nope."

I frown. "I'm not sure what you mean."

"Do you know the reason your birth parents split up?"

"Nope. Do you?"

He places a kiss on the top of my head. "That's a question for your birth daddy to answer, Jainie, not me. I'm sure you'll figure things out with Eoin in time. The man loves you, and sometimes, when you almost lose the thing that matters most, it can temporarily tilt your world off its axis. I think that's all this is. You're asking him to stop protecting the person he loves most. All he can see is that person almost died when he did just that."

Duke does have a valid point. "We'll figure it out."

"One day at a time."

We both chuckle.

"So, what else is happening? I can tell you've got something else weighing on your mind."

"I mentioned to you about the message on Molly's phone and about me finding the music box."

"You did."

"I was speaking to Jessie today, and she suggested I look through some of the older messages. When I went to look for the phone, both the handset and the music box had vanished."

"Are you suggesting someone came in here and took them without your permission? That's a serious accusation, Jainie."

"I realize that but what other explanation is there? They can't just disappear?"

"And you think that someone may have been Sophia?"

"Only family members have access to this space, and I'm guessing Irish doesn't come to the house on his own every time."

"You guess right. I've seen Sophia here once or twice. So, you couldn't find out anything else because you no longer have access to the handset?"

I shake my head. "When I opened Molly's phone the first time, I downloaded everything onto my laptop."

"Good thinking. So did you find anything else of interest?"

"I haven't gone through everything yet, but what I did unearth was that Sophia told Irish that he'd taken her virginity the night of Dylan's engagement party. Turns out that she lied. He didn't. Turns out he was drunk, so she set it up to look like he had by using pig's blood on the sheets."

"And he fell for it?"

"Yup. Same as he did the first time when Brittany accused him of sleeping with her too."

"That boy needs to steer clear of whiskey."

"He does."

We both laugh once more.

"What do I do, Duke? Do I tell him even though it's in the past and it's none of my business? They're trying for a baby, so whether he took her virginity that night or later, it's no longer relevant if they're married and happy."

"Are you sure they're happy?"

"If they're trying for a baby, then they must be? I don't want to open up a can of worms or be seen to be sticking my nose in their relationship."

"Then, I think for now it's best to keep it to yourself and just continue to look for proof that Sophia and her brother may be involved in some way in what's been going on. Because, if they are, then it doesn't matter whether Padraig took her virginity or not. She's a dead woman walking."

"And how do I find that proof, Duke?"

He chuckles. "You're the lawyer. I'll let you figure that one out."

CHAPTER FORTY-ONE

PADRAIG

Padraig's Apartment, Hudson Yards, New York

"I THOUGHT IT BEST WE MEET FACE TO FACE, PADRAIG." LUCIANO slaps me too hard on the back, causing me to grit my teeth.

I've not done any wet work since returning to New York, but he's making me itch to have him as my first unwilling victim. He's only slightly more detestable than his baby sister.

I take in my brother-in-law. Thirty-one years old, tall, olive-skinned, with black hair tied back at the nape of his neck and well-groomed facial hair. He smiles at me with a face full of veneers.

No doubt someone knocked out his original teeth for being the untrustworthy fecker that he is.

Even now, we don't know what he was involved in that saw him kicked out of the Sicilian mafia. It must have been something of note. They obviously couldn't wait to be rid of him if they let him leave with his life intact.

The main concern is that he's about to recommence whatever the fuck it was with the Dusters as a visible ally.

"Is that right, Luciano."

I remain sitting on the sectional as he helps himself to a whiskey.

"So, this contract."

"What about it?"

"I believe you have yet to sign it." He throws back the whiskey in one before pouring himself another.

"I'm still reviewing it."

"You have insulted my sister."

Here we go. "In what way? I married her, which is all that was ever asked of me. Your sister's vile behavior insults me."

"You disrespect your wife with such comments."

"I didn't ask for her to be my wife."

"No. You would rather be married to the biker who gravely insulted her. I'm not sure why you are so anxious to achieve your freedom when Jaine has already chosen to marry your brother."

"I'm sure your sister won't be too insulted when I pass her my fortune."

"We do not need your money."

"I beg to differ. You have property and land, but having had my brother carry out an extensive background search, it would appear that you don't have much by way of cash reserves. It doesn't take a rocket scientist to work out why you wanted Sophia to wed an O'Connell. We have billions of dollars in liquid cash over and above an extensive business and property portfolio. We also have a credible reputation. Something you don't. You need something of note behind you to poach high-rankers from other factions to join your less-than-credible organization. You also need funds with which to pay them."

I watch as he pours himself a third whiskey with now less than steady hands. I've clearly hit the nail on the head.

"I would speculate you were already aware when the initial contract was signed between you and my da that you were already on shaky ground with your old organization. I'm sure if we wanted to, we could have Jaine confirm this with the new Don Leoluca. As you know, she represents them legally these days. Could it perhaps be the case that the original contract was signed under false pretenses?"

His fist clenches around the glass. I'm right. I know I am, and depending on what was contained within the initial contract, that could make it null and void, and he knows it.

"You stole my sister's virtue before you were legally wed. As used goods, she is worthless to my family now. I would have to pay someone to take her off my hands," he spits.

He's right. Had I not taken her purity, I could have proceeded down the contractual route, but I will not dishonor the girl.

"At least she won't be a divorcee. And you don't have much of a family to concern yourself with when it's only you and her."

"And a future Duster heir."

He smirks and I immediately want to cut it from his face. "A meal ticket, you mean? Someone to ensure you always have an alliance with my family."

"In return, we are giving you what you asked for. Why are you refusing to sign a contract that you yourself requested?"

He's right. I've been putting it off, as signing it means the clock will then countdown to me upholding my side of the bargain. I then need to get Sophia pregnant. Have I also been putting it off because I hoped Jaine and me…

Don't be stupid, Padraig.

I lean forward, pick up the printed copy from the table, sign it, and pass it to him.

He rolls it up and places it in his inner jacket pocket. "You have seven days to commence the contract, or it becomes void. You will then have to part with your fortune while remaining married to my sister indefinitely."

I stare at him. "Unlike you, Luciano, money means nothing to me. Now get out."

"What do you mean you signed it?"

The clock clicking down to my doom has me pacing the floor. "Luciano came to collect the contract personally, so I signed it, handed it over, and told him to get out."

"How did he react?"

"Like he wanted to hold a gun to my head and pull the trigger."

"Paddy…"

"Relax. He needs me to get his sister pregnant so his family and ours are tied for life. The baby will then be his cash cow."

"Great."

"It's what Da and Eoin wanted, isn't it? I aim to please."

"Everyone but yourself."

"I'll be happy if I get my freedom."

"Paddy."

I can hear the worry in his tone. That freedom isn't something I'll ever achieve, at least not alive. "I realize it's unlikely, Dylan, but I've got to at least try."

"So, when do you have to do the deed?"

"I have seven days from when I signed. If I don't, then the contract is null and void, and I still have to hand over the contents of my bank account. I'll also be stuck with Sophia for the rest of my days."

"And what will you do when you get your freedom?"

"Spend the rest of my life thinking about what could have been."

"Then why push Jaine into the arms of our brother?"

"Because she needs someone to be there for her. She loves him. He loves her. They want to be together. And it could take months before Sophia falls pregnant. Knowing my luck, maybe even years. Anyway, what does it matter what I want? It didn't before."

"It matters to Jaine. She loves you."

"I don't doubt her love for me, but my feelings didn't exactly matter to her then. She got together with my brother with no consideration as to how it would make me feel, so why should it matter now?"

"Paddy."

"It's best I just let her get on with her life, Dylan. Of course, I'll be there for Finian, but it will only ever be friendship for Jaine and me."

"You need to speak to Eoin."

"And I will. I just don't want him to look smug."

"Why would he do that? You gave her up when you asked him to mend things with her."

"It doesn't matter. He'll still see it that he won."

"He won't. Trust me. You need to speak to him."

"I will." I won't.

CHAPTER FORTY-TWO

JAINE

The O'Connell Home, Darling, New York

Everyone's here, with the exception of Sophia and Sarah. The latter because she's taken all the kids to the summer house for the duration. The former, as she probably has much better things to do with her time, like continuing to plot how to kill me.

I'm the last to arrive, having come straight from a meeting at JFK with a client who had flown in specially. There's a warrant out for his arrest, so discretion was the priority—that and haste.

All eyes turn to me as I make my way into the room.

Is this a family meeting or a business one?

There's no agenda been issued, and nothing's been said verbally. I suspect, like me, the others were sent a message late last night requesting them to be here at ten a.m. prompt.

Everyone's dressed professionally, so I don't feel out of place in my navy pantsuit. If it's a business meeting, I'm guessing it's taking place here to allow Roisin to be present. Tongues would wag should Ma Duster show face at HQ.

Eoin makes brief eye contact with me, as does Padraig, then both turn away. My blood immediately simmers with annoyance.

I'm annoyed with Eoin because I'm reaching the end of my tether with how distant he's been lately. Our relationship has gone from a two-way street to a one-way street to a stationary car park. That's if it can still be referred to as a relationship. A relationship typically involves two people interacting. We don't seem to do too much of that these days.

We don't see each other that often. The physical side of our relationship, while still frenzied, is silent and disconnected. We're only really fucking as our bodies are insistent that we do because of this insane physical attraction that neither of us can switch off.

Eoin's blatant step back can't just be over my insistence that he tone down the over-protectiveness. There's something he's not telling me. I guess that's fair enough. We all have our secrets. But I haven't changed as a person as a result of mine.

He has.

I'm pissed off with Padraig because, while I appreciate his wife hates my guts, the fact that we're not allowed to communicate is ridiculous. We share a child. We have no option but to talk.

You managed perfectly well for two years, Jaine.

I glance around the room. I'm not sure how I feel about a meeting being held here. This is supposed to be my home, even if it is only temporary—a place where I should be able to switch off.

All eyes are waiting to see where I sit. In the end, I take the seat beside Aidan. I can feel Roisin's eyes boring into me. She misses nothing. She'll now know something is amiss between me and her eldest. I don't make eye contact with her. Now's not the time.

"I'm sorry I'm late. I had a pre-arranged meeting with a client at the airport that I couldn't get out of."

They know what I'm saying. That having briefed me, my client is now on his way to an unknown destination to avoid having to holiday on Rikers Island any time soon.

"Thank you for joining us, Jaine." Fergal smiles at me and then looks around the room. "Roisin and I have asked everyone here today for a reason." We watch as he reaches out and squeezes her hand. "We thought it only right that we apologize to Padraig formally for all the lies and deception we've subjected him to. As you know, I may be many things, but I've never been a liar, and to be drawn into that minefield is not something I ever plan on doing again."

He turns to look at Irish. Tears fill my eyes as I watch them fill his. He's always so fucking emotional. It's one of the things I love most about him.

"We're sorry, son. The moment Jaine told us about Finian, we should have told you. We should have asked how you wanted things to play out and considered your thoughts and feelings. We can't change the past. We can only apologize for it." We all watch as Roisin and Fergal hug their youngest.

Tears. Apologies. Forgiveness.

I suddenly feel overwhelmed by this whole situation. I feel like I'm attending some sort of Liar's Anonymous Meeting, where I'm expected to stand up next, say my piece, and get it all off my chest too.

I deceived the entire family for sixteen months. I know all eyes are now looking at me expectantly, silently suggesting that I say something to Irish. Are they expecting me to apologize for my own lies and deceit? What they don't realize is that Irish and I have already made our peace in private when we faced death head-on in the church.

Today might be the time for truths, but I'm not ready to spill my guts about anything else. The remaining secrets I have to reveal must be divulged to certain individuals first. They're not just for public announcement.

I'm glad Roisin and Fergal have made their peace with Irish. If the O'Connells want to stay here and hug it out as a family, that's up to them. I have things to be getting on with. Just as I'm standing to leave, Dylan speaks.

"There's a large delivery just arriving at the front gates."

I can't be The Exterminator today, so I'll be expected to wait inside with the rest of the womenfolk like a good girl while the big brave O'Connell men take care of business.

I already know what it is. I can feel it in my fucking bones. Tears prick my eyes, and worry fills my gut.

They knew I'd be here.

I discreetly try to take a deep breath in and then out. I feel like I'm on the cusp of a breakdown most days. Eoin. Irish. Almost dying twice. I know Fergal meant well, but this house is meant to be a place of refuge for me, and today, it felt the opposite. It's a reminder that I'm only a temporary guest here. That I have no real say in who comes or goes.

That I'm not actual family.

I'm lost in my thoughts. I'm not sure how long passes before I eventually notice that I'm inside alone. That everyone else has drifted outside to see what this delivery is.

Don't go outside, Jaine. You already know what it is.

I eventually make my way out to the front of the house to take in the long pine wood coffin that's been placed directly in front of the building.

Everyone is standing back and staring at the nine-foot-long by three-foot-high wooden box like it's a bomb about to go off.

"Don't open it." It doesn't even sound like my voice, even though the words tumbled from my mouth.

"Do you know what it is, Jaine?" I look at Dylan and nod silently.

"We need to open it. We need to know if there's a message inside…."

I glance at Eoin. "The coffin *is* the goddamn message."

Everyone continues to stare at it because, unlike me, they don't know what's inside.

I can feel it. I can smell it.

I watch as Eoin uses the crowbar provided to prize off the wooden lid, the sun immediately glinting off the familiar black metal. It's no longer pristine. It's now all twisted and scratched. I squeeze my eyes closed. I can't look any longer.

"Oh, my God." It's Jessie's voice. She now realizes what it is.

"Jaine, darlin'." Irish whispers.

I open my eyes, and with tears running down my cheeks, I walk straight into his arms, and he wraps them tightly around me.

"What is it?" Aidan asks.

I hear the sadness in Jessie's voice when she replies. "It's her hog. It's been crushed."

Jones & Associates Legal, Upper East Side, New York

I left.

As soon as I extracted myself from Irish's arms, I wiped the tears from my eyes and then had Dec drive me straight to the office.

I couldn't deal.

I couldn't face being the center of attention. I couldn't stomach their looks of pity. Most of all, I couldn't handle having to stare any longer at my hog's crushed carcass.

I had to get out of there.

I'd already decided that I didn't want to have to live any longer in a home that's not my own, but today's delivery was yet another warning.

What choice do I have?

My beautiful fucking hog, reduced to a piece of twisted metal.

I press the button under my desk that locks my office door from the inside as more tears cascade down my face. I'm sick of crying. I'm sick of being on the receiving end of both veiled and blatant death threats.

I'm sick of Eoin. I'm sick of Irish. I'm stuck on a melancholy treadmill that I need to get off, but I don't know how to. Why did Ace have to leave me? He'd know what to do. He'd be able to comfort me.

Instead, Irish did.

I squeeze my eyes closed in frustration. He shouldn't have done that. We shouldn't have done that. How must that have looked to everyone else?

To Eoin.

My life is such a fucked-up mess right now. I really am living from one day to the next, going by the special delivery that no doubt had my name written all over it.

Tomorrow really isn't guaranteed for me.

My burner vibrates. It's the only person with the number who doesn't realize who the phone actually belongs to.

"Jaine, I'm sorry."

Sorry for what? For opening the wooden coffin holding my hog, or for barely acknowledging me for weeks aside from with his dick?

"You did what you had to do."

"How did you know what it was?"

"Call it a biker's sixth sense. I've had that ride since I was eighteen years old." I curse myself when my voice breaks.

"I wanted to comfort you. I..." I can hear the break in his voice too. Is it guilt over how he's been treating me or because I publicly chose his brother's arms over his? I suspect it's the latter.

"I've got another call coming in, Eoin. I have to go." We both know I'm lying. I disconnect the call. I'm not sure what he expected. He can't pick and choose when he wants to be in a relationship with me.

Putting my office phone on do not disturb, I open my laptop and start perusing the information from Molly's phone once more.

CHAPTER FORTY-THREE

ROISIN

The O'Connell Home, Darling, New York

REGRETS.

At my age, you try to avoid them because, when you're in the winter of your life, you don't have much time to right your wrongs, and the longer you carry them with you, the heavier they become.

I was wrong. I realize that now.

Fergal and I have been made aware of what our youngest's life was like during the year he spent living in Sicily. A life that I willingly signed him up for because I thought I knew what was best for him.

It turns out that I didn't.

I made assumptions and decisions on his behalf, and now here he is prepared to give up his fortune and sacrifice his life to escape the chains of the arranged marriage I thought best for him. In exchange for his freedom, Padraig will give Luciano what he wants and give me and his da what he thinks we want.

A Duster heir.

Let it be said, if God never gifts me another grandbaby, I would be happy with that, provided I can have my happy-go-lucky son back. A boy that spent a year living as a recluse in another country, trying to piece together the shards of his broken heart.

He was betrayed and let down by his own family. He was all alone. He had no one to turn to.

I'm responsible for that.

What sort of a mother am I that I put my needs before his? That I put my needs before any of my sons'? I convinced myself they aligned with my own, even when I knew they didn't.

I was quick to condemn the girl, but I could take a leaf out of Jaine Jones' book when it comes to raising a family. Her boys will make their own decisions. If they choose wrong, she'll be there to dust them down and pick up the pieces.

Why couldn't I have been happy doing the same?

I was so filled with anger and hate over my own past that I almost destroyed my boys' future happiness, all because the women they chose were bikers.

Padraig loves Jaine. Jaine loves him. They share a son. They would never have split up had she not thought he cheated. It turns out he didn't. The truth will always out, and it did.

Twelve years later. Twelve years too late.

Fate robbed them of their happiness, but then so did his own family.

So did I.

Anyone who sees them together knows they were destined, just like me and my Fergal were. When I see them with young Finian and JJ, it brings tears to my eyes.

What have we done? What have I done? A mother doesn't always know best. I realize that now.

My poor boy returned to an unwelcoming home, all because we were tangled in our web of lies and deception. After twelve months of solitude, he came home needing to be embraced by the arms of his loving family, and we pushed him away.

He felt like he no longer belonged, that no one cared. He felt like he had no one and nothing.

We needed to apologize to Padraig. To explain that, although they were wrong, our intentions were good. We wanted to keep everyone safe, but once more, we made decisions on his behalf because we assumed how he'd react.

We had no right to do that.

Finian's his son. He's already missed out on so much of his young life.

Fergal was so sure that Jaine was the right female for the Ma Duster role that we manipulated the situation to our own advantage by forcing our eldest to marry her, and his obsession with her turned to love.

She loves them both. They both love her.

I watched Jaine as she entered the room earlier. I saw the detached look both my boys drew her as each tried to show complete indifference.

But they can't hide from me. They both adore her. They both worship her.

Now that Paddy is back in New York, guilt is eating away at my eldest. He knows Jaine is only his by default. He had to work hard for her love, whereas she gave it to his youngest brother freely because it was always his.

I take a sip of tea as I look around my luxurious home. It's all material. It's all meaningless. Family is all that matters, and my concern is that I've now destroyed mine. Because what I always feared would happen will happen, and it's all my own fault.

My two boys will go head-to-head over the same woman, and it's then the final lie will be revealed.

A lie that is mine alone.

Dylan has sent Fergal and me a copy of the new contract that Padraig had drawn up between him and Luciano Ruocco.

It was signed three days ago. I now know what I need to do. The final decision will then rest with Jaine.

Will she act, or won't she?

CHAPTER FORTY-FOUR

EOIN

The Hudson Dusters' HQ, Manhattan, New York

I STARE OUT MY OFFICE WINDOW.

The sky is grey and bleak, which perfectly reflects my mood. I have the best office, the best view, the best of everything that money can buy, but what does any of it matter when I'm going to lose her?

Then how can you lose someone who was never truly yours in the first place? A woman who was only yours because the love of her life was taken from her.

By my family. By me.

Paddy had it all, or so we thought. The looks, the charm, the wealth, the beautiful women. But he would have traded all of it for her.

I get it.

Because I would now do the same. I would forgo everything for

Jaine Jones because I love her. She's like a drug in my veins that I can't get enough of.

My own perfect addiction.

My first thought when I wake and the last before I sleep. I would do anything for her, and I know she would do anything for me.

I can't shake the sight of my brother from my mind as he wept once more over what he had lost.

Her.

He will always be her first choice. I will always be second. Her love for him was given freely. Her love for me was only given because I wore her down.

She admitted as much.

I was never destined to love you, Eoin. You made me love you.

I saw what they meant to each other when they were facing certain death. Loving each other, comforting each other, protecting each other from what they would face in the next life.

For never was a story of more woe than this of Juliet and her Romeo.

If Fate meant for them to be together, then let it happen for them. I may have been fated to be hers. I realize now she was never fated to be mine.

A knock on the door disturbs my thoughts.

"Come in."

I already know who it is. I could feel him watching our interactions yesterday morning at the house. Between me and Jaine. Between Jaine and Paddy. Between Paddy and me.

I turn to watch him as he takes a seat on one of the tan-colored executive chairs that face me. He remains silent.

Walking across, I take my own chair then look at him across the desk. Dylan has the easiest life of the lot of us. The only sign that he's aging is the one or two grey hairs that now scatter the sides of his black hair.

I've grown used to his presence and to using him as my sounding board. It's not something I've ever had before—another male to discuss things with, or at least not in any great depth.

I realize now that I was only borrowing him too. That he also belongs to Paddy and not me. They were always thick as thieves until Paddy left.

You've fallen for the same woman as your brother. So, tell me, how will you explain all of this to him? That you've effectively stolen his life?"

Molly was right. That's exactly what I did do. Unintentionally, perhaps, but I did all the same.

"How are you feeling?" I know he's referring to when Jaine blatantly chose Paddy's arms over mine in front of the entire family.

"Accepting."

He frowns at me. "What does that mean exactly?"

"Accepting of the fact that Jaine will always choose Paddy."

"That's not true, Eoin."

"I think it's time we both stopped pretending, Dylan. It's not the first time she's chosen him over me. The night of the attack, she decided to spend time with him rather than reach out to me. Let's face it. It was always inevitable. She was never truly mine. I was only ever allowed to borrow her."

"She is yours."

I slam my hand on my desk and watch him recoil. I'm not angry. I'm frustrated more than anything. Annoyed with myself that I thought I could have it all. That I thought I could have her.

"You're pushing her away, Eoin. I can see what you're doing."

"I have no choice, Dylan."

"But Paddy wanted you…."

"It's not about what Paddy wants. And if Paddy were

completely honest with himself, he'd admit that it's Jaine that he wants. He always has."

"But he can't have her."

"Maybe not right now."

"He wanted her to be with you."

"For now, he does."

"You need to explain, Eoin."

Standing, I walk back across to the window. "Right now, Paddy's focus is on getting out of the arranged marriage. There's a reason for that."

"And that is?"

"He has hope. For the first time, there's a chance that he and Jaine can finally be together if, by some miracle, he can extract himself from the marriage in one piece."

"So, that's why you've been pushing her away."

"I'm not pushing her away. I'm merely withdrawing from her life so she has freedom of choice. I'm not prepared to do Paddy's bidding. It's making decisions for other people that's gotten us all into this mess in the first place."

"Eoin…"

"You saw them, Dylan. The same as I did. They were meant." Silence. He knows I'm right. "Did you know that she keeps a photo of the pair of them in her phone case?"

"How do you know that?" his frown deepens.

"I saw something sticking out. When I took the phone out to tuck it back in, there it was. It was from their Yale days."

"Eoin," he warns.

"She doesn't carry a photo of me around with her, so surely that's proof enough."

"So, what now?"

"How many days before Paddy's contract needs to be commenced?"

“Four.”

“I want you to send a copy to Jaine. Maybe there’s some way she can extract him from the arrangement legally or at least talk some sense into him.”

“But then she’ll know all about him and Sophia.”

“I’m aware of that.”

“But…”

“Send it, Dylan!”

I realize I may be digging my own grave, but Jaine should have the right to choose between us. I don’t want her to live the rest of her life filled with regret.

I stare once more at the bleak sky and try to consider a future without her in it.

I can’t.

CHAPTER FORTY-FIVE

JAINE

Jones & Associates Legal, Upper East Side, New York

It's late, and I'm exhausted. I rub my tired eyes as I continue to trawl through the data when my phone starts ringing.

"Are you still at the office, partner?"

"I am."

"It's almost midnight."

"Thank you for stating the obvious. I'm going through Molly's phone."

"Found anything of interest?"

"Not really, but I'm only halfway."

"Is the data on the office server?"

"It is now."

"Well, sorry, but I'm going to have to stop you right there. Someone's trying to hack in. I need to update the security and run a few checks. I've let everyone know via email that the system will be down overnight. They've all acknowledged. I thought I'd call you direct just to let you know."

"Thanks, Jessie." I yawn as I close the lid on my laptop.

"How are you feeling about... you know?"

"About the fact that my hog is currently a garden ornament at Chez O'Connell? I feel goddamn great."

"I'm sorry."

"I know you are."

"If I had one, I'd let you have it." Her gesture brings tears to my eyes because I know she would.

"That's kind of you, but you don't."

"Will you have Ace's ship…."

"No, I won't," I interject. "Ace's hog will never leave Rising."

"What will you do?"

"I'll speak to Delaney and see if he can find me another Softail. It won't be the same, but then nothing ever is the second time around."

"How are things between you and Eoin?"

"You mean after I sought comfort in the arms of his brother?" I close my eyes once more in frustration at myself.

"Yes, after that."

"I haven't spoken to him since yesterday. I told him I had to go as I needed to take another call."

"And you lied."

"Yup."

"Could he tell you were lying?"

"Yup."

"But why lie?"

"Because we're drifting apart, Jessie, that's why. It's my guess there's a reason behind it, but he's not saying what it is."

"Have you asked him?"

"Nope."

"We've had this conversation before. About communication."

"I'll ask him." I don't want to tell her it's unlikely to do any good. The problem is much bigger than communication.

"When?"

"Once I've finished going through the data from Molly's phone."

"And how long's that going to take?"

"Maybe another day or so. I figured I'd glean every piece of information I could. I can then pass the details to you and Dyl for you to peruse at your leisure."

"Did you go through her communication with Eoin?"

"That's the only correspondence I won't be looking at."

"Aren't you curious?" She snickers.

"We all know what that did to the cat."

"You're jealous."

"I am not." I snort.

"Liar." She's right. I am a liar.

"I don't do jealousy. You know that."

"You may not act on it, but you feel it all the same. Maybe he sent her clips of him jerking off."

"Jessie," I warn.

"Your voice sounds green."

"How the hell can a voice sound green."

"It just can."

"Anyway, he won't have sent her any of those."

"Has he ever sent you any?"

"No! That's why I know he won't have sent her any."

"Maybe she sent him some, and he returned the favor."

"Jessie," I warn again.

"You'll never know unless you check."

"That would be an invasion of privacy."

"He knows you have the phone, and he's expecting you to look, Jaine."

"Jessie." I grit my teeth. I can taste the jealousy in my mouth.

"All right, all right. Stop repeating my name using that green tone of yours. Anyway, I need to go and sort out this hacking situation. Are you heading home now?"

"Roisin has the kids, so I'm going to stay at my apartment tonight."

"Be careful."

"Yes, Mom."

"Later, partner."

"Night."

"Jessie."

"Go easy on me, partner. I've barely slept." She yawns exaggeratedly down the phone.

I'm sitting at my desk, staring at my laptop screen. "All of my emails are marked as read, and they weren't all read. Now I can't decipher which is which."

"Ah, yes. There was a slight issue with yours. I forgot to ask you to log out. I'm trying to reinstate it now."

"How long to resolve?"

"Give me a few hours."

"I have meetings, Jessie!" I glance at the wall clock. "And I'm already late for the first one, Jesus Christ."

"Prayers might help."

"Jessie!"

"Who are you meeting with?"

"Rod."

"He won't mind if you're a little late. Just tell him it's my fault.

Then while you're waiting on little old me, why don't you collect the Duster order from him and drop it off with big bad Eoin?"

"I can't just barge into HQ unannounced." I'm making excuses. I just don't want to face the inevitable.

"You're Eoin's fiancée. You can do whatever the hell you like."

"I'm his day-by-day sort of girlfriend," I argue, knowing even the term girlfriend is stretching it these days.

"That still sounds like you don't need an appointment."

"Maybe I'll call on ahead anyway."

"You do whatever you feel you need to do but speak to him."

"Okay!"

"Promise?"

"Promise."

I disconnect the call before making my way out of the office. I appreciate what Jessie's saying, but it seems pointless. My gut's telling me that Eoin's already thrown in the towel where our relationship is concerned. I get that she says we need to communicate, but that's easier said than done when I'm not the one who's holding back.

I can only listen if he's prepared to talk, and I think Eoin's done talking.

Private Dining Room, Palace Hotel, Manhattan

"How have you been, Jaine?"

We're in a private room in our regular overpriced, ostentatious haunt.

I smile at my handsome Mexican friend. "I'm doing fine, Rod. More importantly, how have you been? You've been frequenting New York quite a lot recently. It can't just be to personally hand-deliver each Duster order. Is there something that keeps bringing you back to our concrete jungle, or should I say someone?" I smile as I raise an eyebrow at him while sipping my extortionately priced water.

"You legal types are always so inquisitive."

I snort. "That's what makes us so good at our jobs, and being good at my job is the key reason you hire me."

That and the fact that he knows he can trust me with anything, illegal or otherwise.

"I may have met someone, but it's extremely early days. Well, I may have met two women, actually." A coy smile.

"A love triangle." I raise my second eyebrow. "Take it from me. Those are never good places to be, at least not from the female's perspective."

I pause briefly. Rod normally brings up anything he's heard on the outlaw grapevine. Has he learned about my near-death experiences at the house and at the church? Leo hasn't mentioned anything, but that doesn't mean others haven't heard.

It's unlikely La eMe would be involved, but you just never know. I trust Rod more than most people, but in this game, it pays never to trust anyone one hundred percent.

Trusting someone too much opens you up to being let down or killed.

"There's no reason for you to be in that situation again now you're dating your ex-husband."

My smile is forced, which Rod doesn't miss.

"Is all not well in paradise, Jaine?" It's his turn to raise an eyebrow.

"Let's just say, perhaps Eoin and I should have taken more time to learn from past mistakes rather than diving headfirst into the sea of second chances."

"Salvageable?"

"Anything is salvageable. It all depends on how much you want it to work. Anyway, enough of our relationship woes. Do you have anything new to report?"

"Nope. Since the Colombians approached Lucifer's men and he sent them packing, there's been nothing. Have you still got the District Attorney on standby?"

I nod. "Nate is chomping at the bit. Not at doing his job per se, just at all the publicity it will attract for him."

"He does like to have his mugshot in the press."

"He does." I laugh.

"Maybe you need to have a private word with the DA over our way to see if he'd be interested in the same deal."

It had already crossed my mind. I nod. "I may just do that."

It's not like Eoin will stop me from heading to the opposite coast. I'm still chauffeured everywhere, but would he kick up a protective stink since he seems to have lost all interest?

I'm not so sure that he would these days.

The Hudson Dusters' HQ, Manhattan, New York

My stiletto heels click on the marble flooring as I pass the reception quartet. The color of the day?

Burgundy.

I find it quite a morbid color. It's sort of black with a hint of red, like death infused with blood.

Will they or won't they let their mobster boss know that his ex-wife, day-by-day girlfriend is on her way up? I don't stop to find out.

I press the call button for the elevator. Once inside, I take in the appearance of the professionally dressed girl who's living on borrowed time in the all-mirrored surface. I have an almost defeated look these days.

When I reach Eoin's office, I'm surprised to find that Candice isn't sitting outside.

It's then I feel it—the hammering of the final nail. I don't hesitate to open his office door.

I know exactly what I'll find.

Their mouths are an inch apart, no doubt only parting to take in the intruder who has the audacity to interrupt their make-out session. I don't doubt their kissing will quickly escalate into full-blown desk sex the moment I'm gone.

Eoin has discarded both his jacket and tie and his shirt sleeves are rolled up.

I guess he means business.

My traitorous eyes can't help but feast on his powerful, veiny arms, their dark ink artwork contrasting magnificently against the brilliant whiteness of his crisp shirt. Arms that are currently snaked around the slim waist of Candice as she stands with her groin pressed firmly against his, her fingers remaining tangled in his black hair. Hair I've fisted so many times I've lost fucking count.

Jealousy bowls through me, so powerful it almost knocks me off my feet, but I remain impassive. In the time I've taken the order from Rod out of my briefcase and thrown it on the top of his desk, my jealousy has turned into rage.

Burgundy rage.

A rage that I embrace. A rage that's been missing for months.

I ignore her. She's not worthy of my time. Instead, I make eye contact with him. Aquamarine. Why not green?

I walk over to them and wait while he releases his grip on his PA before turning to face me. He gives nothing away. There's not a shred of guilt, and there's no apology.

Asshole.

I press my hand over his heart, feeling the familiar strong, steady thrum beneath my fingertips. Even now, my body wants his. Well, fuck my body and fuck him.

As long as it beats, it's yours.

I stare at him, ignoring the mixed bag of emotions that are screaming to surface. "You're a goddamn liar."

Removing my hand, I walk toward the door. Just before I close it, I glance over my shoulder, my eyes dropping to the leather-topped surface of the desk. My desk.

"Don't forget to wipe."

The final click of the door signifies the end of a relationship that was doomed from the start.

CHAPTER FORTY-SIX

PADRAIG

Padraig's Apartment, Hudson Yards, New York

Two days.

And to make matters worse, Sophia wants to move in here.

I stare at the entrance to my apartment, which is steadily filling up with moving boxes. I'm told my place is both larger and in a nicer area.

Fuck. My. Life.

My phone rings. Dylan. To answer or not? He's tried me a few times, but I've let it go straight to voicemail each time.

It'll be about the copy of the contract I sent him. I'm guessing he was waiting for feedback from Ma and Da and my eldest brother. I know he'll have sent it on to all three, even though he swore he wouldn't.

Either that or it will be about what happened the other day at our parents' house. When a distressed Jaine walked straight into my arms rather than seek solace in my eldest brother's.

He'll likely want to broach both subjects, and I'm not sure I've got it in me to discuss either.

"Dylan," I answer. I may as well get it over with.

"Padraig, I've been trying to get hold of you for days!"

"I've been busy."

"Doing what?"

"Helping Sophia move in."

"But I thought you were moving in with her?"

"She insisted. Apparently, my place trumps hers."

There's a pause.

"Paddy, why are you doing this?"

"Why am I doing what?" How many times can I be asked the same question?

"Why go through with his?"

"I have no choice, Dylan. Sophia wants a baby."

"We don't always get what we want."

"She backed me into a corner." I reckon it's time I told him the whole truth. "Between you and me, she also issued a veiled threat toward Jaine. Jaine made reference to the fact that she currently has a target on her back. Sophia subsequently commented to me that given accidents happen all the time and given the clients Jaine represents, if something were to happen to her, it wouldn't be entirely unexpected."

"She actually said that?" He sounds gobsmacked. Maybe now he'll appreciate what I'm up against.

"Yes. I added the annulment as a condition to get something out of it, but now you know why I have no choice but to go through with getting her pregnant. Because she's right. If something were to happen to Jaine, it would be impossible to hold anyone to task over it."

"Jesus Christ. You never mentioned any of that before."

"And I probably shouldn't have said anything now. It's my cross to bear. Do you honestly think I'd willingly bring a child into this? I'm trying to make the best of a bad situation while keeping Jaine safe."

"You need to tell Jaine. You need to tell the others."

"What difference will that make? I'll still have to go through with it. Something could happen to Jaine if I don't."

"Don't you see, Paddy? It almost did. The message on Molly's phone that saw Jaine head straight to the church was from Sophia to Molly."

I sit down on the sectional. "Jesus Christ."

"Unfortunately, there's no proof that Sophia was involved in what happened. It was worded in a way to suggest that she was merely passing on an anonymous message."

"Without proof, we have nothing." I exhale in frustration.

"Paddy, given what you've just told me, you can't go through with this. This is blackmail."

"You tell me what other choice I have, brother?" My question is met with silence. "Exactly. I have none. Telling the rest of the family would make no difference. We can't accuse the Ruoccos of anything without concrete evidence. There's also the small fact that I took the girl's purity. If I hadn't, we could have contested the original contract. I'm almost certain it was signed under false pretenses. Luciano already knew his position with the mafia was in jeopardy. I've not bothered to look into it because there's no point. It's been superseded by me sleeping with his sister. He's right. She's worthless to him now. He would have to pay someone to take her off his hands."

"So, he wants a Duster heir in return for you taking her virginity?"

"Yes, and if I don't…"

"Something might accidentally happen to Jaine."

"In a nutshell, yes."

"So we need proof."

"And given how manipulative and cunning the pair of them are, it's not something I'd expect to unearth any time soon, if ever."

"So, you're doomed."

"Unless The Almighty grants me a miracle."

"He granted one for Cillian and me."

"I'm the brother that has to repent most. He's unlikely to do the same for me."

I can smell her vile lily-based scent before I even see her. "I need to go, Dylan."

"But…"

I disconnect the call just as my wife enters my apartment. I look up from where I'm sitting on the sectional to take in her smug expression as she stands and inspects her red-talon-tipped fingers. She has a keycard now. She can come and go as she pleases.

She's already started moving things around. She's also insisted that we use the main bedroom. I knew she would, so I moved my bed to one of the guest rooms in advance.

There's no way she's lying in it after Jaine.

"We still have two days, Sophia. I wouldn't get comfortable just yet."

She smiles coyly at me as she smooths down her black pants. "Come now, Padraig. The next stage in our relationship is inevitable. There's no need to wait any longer. I can move in now and transfer the rest of my belongings later."

"We don't have a relationship. All we're doing is undertaking an act to fulfill the terms of a contract, or at least that's all I'm doing."

She narrows her eyes but doesn't reply. In a way, I feel sorry for the girl. She's still clinging to the hope that this 'relationship' will work out. It may well have done had her true colors shown her to be a half-decent person, but she's not.

"Two days, Padraig." She smiles seductively. "I may even buy some special lingerie for our delayed wedding night."

I stare at her but say nothing. If she thinks gift-wrapping herself will make her more appealing to my dick, then she's very sadly mistaken.

Even he has standards.

CHAPTER FORTY-SEVEN

JAINE

The O'Connell Home, Darling, New York

I HAD MY HOG SHIPPED BACK TO RISING IN THE END.

I'm not sure what I'll do with it, but one thing's for sure, I'll never toss it on the scrap heap. It may be nothing more than a hunk of twisted metal now, but I'm sure I'll find a use for it. The heart of my Softail is still in there somewhere, even if, like mine, it's been badly crushed.

My mind drifts to Eoin. I knew he was pulling back, but I never expected to witness what I did.

Did he ever love me?

I suspect he did in his own arrogant way, and definitely more than he ever has anyone else, aside from himself, that is. I guess when you have selfish, narcissistic tendencies, it's difficult to put anyone else's needs ahead of your own for any length of time.

I've gone through our relationship line by line.

In many ways, Eoin was trying to change me into what he wanted me to be. He wanted to make me reliant and dependent. I'm neither of those two things. In the end, trying to please him would have resulted in me not being true to myself. He wanted me to slot into his life with as little disruption as possible simply because he refused to compromise.

Maybe you refused to compromise too, Jaine.

I refuse to cry over a cheater. My crushed heart will mend. It always does. If it can survive losing Ace, it can survive anything this life of ours has to throw at it.

I'm in the kitchen, lost in my thoughts, and staring at nothing in particular. The thing I miss most living here is windows. The safe space is below ground level, so there are none. Sometimes I feel like I'm trapped. Like I'm going to go stir-crazy stuck behind these four walls. I feel like I'm buried alive.

I guess, in some ways, I am.

I can't stay here any longer. Not after everything that's happened with Eoin and Irish. This is their family home, and I'll never be family.

I need to find a safe space someplace else. I mean, let's face it. This property didn't offer much in the way of security when the attack took place. I'd have been just as secure hiding out in the purpose-built safe room at the rear of my own apartment. It's not very large, but enough that, with a few alterations, Duke, the kids, and I could survive in there for a few days.

Maybe that's the answer.

As much as Eoin was hemming me in, this place, this family, is doing exactly the same. I've been letting others make decisions for me because it's been easier. If I allow that to continue, I'll end up losing my identity. I'll lose me.

I can't allow that to happen.

I stare at my vibrating handset. Dylan. Does he know now, I

wonder? Did his big brother tell him that he cheated on me? That I walked in on him just as he was about to fuck his PA over the desk that I gifted him?

Jealousy floods my veins.

It will ease up soon enough. Mr. Smug. Selfish. Pompous is no longer entitled to take up space in my head.

"Dylan."

"Jaine, I need your urgent help." He sounds worried. "I sent you an email the other day. Did you see it?"

I frown when I realize that I didn't, or at least I haven't yet. "Let me double-check. I had an issue with my inbox. Everything was showing as having been read. Jessie was looking into it for me."

I return to the living space, sit down, open my laptop, and scroll through the most recent correspondence.

I frown when I see the email from Dylan. It deepens when I then see one from Roisin sent on the very same day. The attachments are identical. I know before I open the document that the content will be life-changing.

"What is it, Dylan?"

"Read it. It's too complicated to explain."

Dylan doesn't disconnect the call. He stays on the line as I spend the next half hour skim-reading a contract that effectively has Irish signing his life away. Sophia gets everything, including shared custody of a child it would appear he has no option but to provide her with.

Reading between the lines, Luciano wants a Duster heir. In return, Padraig can have his singledom.

That's if he lives long enough to embrace it.

"Dylan… I'm confused. I thought he loved her."

Just because he's not in love with her doesn't mean he's in love with you.

"He hates her, Jaine. So much so he's never even consummated their marriage. As a parting gift, Sophia wants a baby, or should I say Luciano does. To ensure they get what they want, they've also issued a veiled threat against you. Paddy won't allow anything to happen to you. He'll do whatever it takes to keep you safe."

So, Irish criticized me for keeping secrets as I didn't want to risk him, but he's doing exactly the same.

"But it's no longer a veiled threat, Dylan. It's reality. Whether he goes through with this pregnancy or not won't change the fact that the Ruoccos are already gunning for me."

"He also feels beholden to her, Jaine. He took her purity. She's used goods…."

"He didn't," I interject.

"What do you mean?"

"I found an exchange between Molly and Sophia on Molly's phone. The whole thing was a setup. Sophia used pig's blood and convinced Irish that it was her virginal blood. I never mentioned anything before as it wasn't really any of my business. I also thought that they'd moved on, given they were trying for a baby together."

"And he believed her because he was so drunk that he can't remember a thing."

"Exactly. It's the same as what happened with Brittany."

"Wait a minute, that means he's never been intimate with Sophia. Or at least, not yet he hasn't."

"I realize that. How long have we got?"

"About thirty-six hours. What are you thinking? Sophia's moving into his apartment as we speak. He said she's even considering selecting some sexy lingerie for their delayed wedding night."

Jealousy. This time over a different brother.

"If she does, she'll need to take it back for a refund because over my dead body will she be laying one manicured Sicilian fucking finger on him."

"What are you suggesting, Jaine?"

"I need access to her phone. There were communications between her and Molly that hinted at several things, but they were too one-sided to be used as concrete evidence."

"How will you gain access?"

"I need to be in Irish's apartment in approximately thirty-six hours. I imagine Sophia's mind will be elsewhere then. She'll think she's finally got her man, so her phone will no longer be her top priority."

"Then what?"

"I'll download the content and send it to you."

"Am I okay to involve Jessie? Two heads will be quicker than one at trying to decipher the data quickly."

"Yes. I'm fine with you involving her, but no one else. And Irish doesn't find out until I tell him."

"Jaine, there have already been way too many secrets." He sounds reluctant, and I get it. He's had to be the keeper of most of them.

"And they are all about to be revealed, Dylan, I promise you. But it needs to be done in the right order."

"So, not even Eoin?" It's my guess his big brother hasn't mentioned that we're over and that he's reverted back to his philandering ways.

"Not even him."

"What if Paddy sees you?"

"He won't. I have a plan."

"Are you sure you don't want me to sneak in instead? You may see or hear…."

"I'll do it, Dylan." My head's already on the chopping block. Plus, if it doesn't go according to plan, then I've got no one to blame but myself.

CHAPTER FORTY-EIGHT

PADRAIG

Padraig's Apartment, Hudson Yards, New York

I'M NOT SURE WHAT SORT OF MOOD I'M IN.

It's similar to the one I was in the day my life ended. Bewilderment that my day of reckoning is finally here. I suppose there's a silver lining this time, although is my freedom just a carrot being dangled to make me jump through Ruocco hoops? That it's not something I'm ever likely to achieve.

Probably.

At least Jaine is back with Eoin, so she and Fin are safe, although it does concern me that she's not taken to wearing that obscene engagement ring he bought for her.

I look at my watch, then switch my attention to the ceiling. Sophia will be here in ten minutes. We've agreed to get tonight over with, and then she'll move the rest of her stuff in over the next week. I hope she's not expecting me to wine and dine her before the big event because I won't be.

I'm sitting here in blue jeans and a white tee. Everything's coming off. There's no point in me pretending otherwise. She'll want to get straight down to business, I'm sure.

There's been no one since Jaine apart from once with Sophia that I don't even remember. I'm not sure why I feel guilty, but I do. I feel like I'm cheating on Jaine all over again, even though we're not together.

She's going to marry my brother. She'll be my sister-in-law.

Forever forbidden.

The rest of my life will be spent watching from the sidelines as she lives her best life with Eoin. I'll have to watch as they take the vows. As they have kids. As they celebrate anniversaries. As they grow old together. I can feel tears running down my face.

Angry. Sad. Disappointed.

That's how I feel when I think about my lot.

My thoughts drift to Jaine. To our time together at the church. I wish I were back there right now, even if we were slowly dying. As we lay side by side like we did way back then, putting the world to rights and talking just because we love hearing the sound of the other person's voice.

I hear the knock on the door. I locked it from the inside. For now, this is my home. I'm not sharing it until I have no choice. I walk to the kitchen, turn on the faucet, then wash my face with cold water.

I need a miracle.

Raising my face to the ceiling, I whisper a silent prayer, then with a sigh, I walk across and open the apartment door. Sophia stands there looking smug because she knows this is it. I can't run anymore.

I have to put out.

Given that we're not going anywhere, she's completely overdressed in a cream pantsuit. Maybe she thinks I'll take my time unwrapping her like a gift.

I won't.

She walks past me, filling my nose with her lily-based stench. Funeral flowers. The smell of death. I may not die tonight, but I'll surely wish for death several times over as she demands her pound of flesh.

She turns to look at me. If she were a nice person, I'd feel guilty about how indifferent I'm being, but she's not, so I don't.

I'm not going to sit around and make small talk. I motion my head toward the bedroom, and she spins in that direction.

"Handbag." I motion my head toward the sliver of cream leather that she's grasping tightly in her hand.

"But my phone…."

"Does not belong in the bedroom. A bedroom is not a place for social media, for television, or for distractions of any kind. A bedroom is for sleeping or fucking."

I watch her neck redden as her then flustered hands clumsily drop the bag on the coffee table.

She's aroused.

At least that makes one of us.

CHAPTER FORTY-NINE

JAINE

Padraig's Apartment, Hudson Yards, New York

IT'S TYPICAL OF THE DUSTERS THAT THEY OWN THE APARTMENT directly below the penthouse. They did at Dylan's too. That's the one Jessie bought and still owns.

I came dressed as my alter-ego. The only difference is I'm wearing my biker jacket, having left my puffer in the back of Irish's car.

I'm also armed, but it's a Glock instead of a rifle. I don't expect to have to put it to any use, but from experience, I know it's always safer to expect the unexpected.

Burner. Check. Newly purchased night goggles. Check. Download device plus spare. Check.

Putting in one ear pod, I quickly pull a balaclava over my face. Dylan can see and control everything inside Irish's apartment. Apparently, Padraig had switched off the security function, but Dyl sneaked back in today and set it all back up again. The only place he can't see inside is the bedrooms, for obvious reasons.

As soon as he told me this, I immediately thought of me and Eoin.

Does the same apply to his apartment? We fucked everywhere. Sometimes we barely made it inside the front door.

Maybe it's not something you need for balance, but someone.

What did Duke mean by that exactly?

Jesus, Jaine. Now's not the time. Plus, he's an asshole. He cheated on you. You witnessed it with your own eyes," I chide myself as I welcome the familiar feeling of rage that descends when I think of him these days.

"Can you hear me, Dylan?"

"Loud and clear."

Closing the door of the empty apartment, I make my way to the elevator. "Where are they?"

"They've just gone into the bedroom."

I pause as I digest that unwelcome information.

"Can you see me?"

"You're the ninja walking toward the elevator."

I chuckle. "That's me. You remember the plan?"

"Unlock the door. As soon as you get inside, switch off all the lights apart from inside the main bedroom, that's if they're still on. Have you got the device?"

"Got it. Are you sure it will crack the code? I don't want to get there only to find I need Sophia's thumb. I'm sure it will ruin the moment if I interrupt to hack it off."

"It will do everything it needs to. You just have to plug it into the charging point on the phone. Best of luck, Jaine."

I raise my arm with my own thumb up to confirm all is understood and also to let him know there's to be no further communication.

We both know the risks. I don't need any distractions.

I stand outside the door. It's grey. Same as Eoin's. Will it be everything-proof too?

Switching on the nighttime goggles, I click open the door with the gun raised. The lights are already off. I glance around, knowing they're already in the bedroom.

I spot Sophia's handbag on the table. A mobile handset rests beside it. Shoving the Glock down the back of my pants, I make my way forward, pulling on the thin pair of gloves I brought with me.

I pick up the phone and open the case, causing the piece of paper trapped inside to fall to the floor.

Fuck.

I pick it up and stare at it. It's not Sophia's phone. It's Irish's. A lump forms in my throat as I take in the image captured from our Yale days. The very same one I carry in the back of my own case.

Now is not the time, Jaine.

I push the image behind the handset before closing the case and placing it back on the table. Lifting the bag, I take out Sophia's phone before putting the bag back on the table.

I go to the kitchen area and plug the download device in to her phone.

Two minutes. That's how long he needs.

Two minutes feels like the equivalent of two years when you're in a hurry. When you're trying to prevent someone you love from having to stick his dick in a woman he'd much rather not because he's looking out for your best interests.

Eventually, my burner vibrates. We're done. Removing the device, I make my way back across to the table before placing the phone back inside the bag.

I hear the bedroom door click.

It's then I notice the handset is still illuminated and that I can see it clearly through the soft leather of the bag.

Fuck.

Seconds tick by. How long does it take for the screen to go dark?

"Padraig, did you switch the lights off?" It's Sophia.

"I can't remember." Good answer.

I can hear footsteps. Please, God, switch off the goddamn screen.

Tick tock. Tick tock.

The screen switches off just as the stench of her lily-based perfume reaches my nostrils.

I sink down behind the sofa. There's nowhere else for me to go. I pull the Glock from my pants as I wait. Sophia won't be able to see me unless she walks toward the front door.

She's running water.

I stay where I am until I hear her footsteps retreating toward the bedroom. I wait until I hear the bedroom door click once more before standing and making my way outside. Usually, I'd take the stairs, but for what I've got planned, time is of the essence, so I press the button for the elevator.

"Any luck, Dylan?"

"One word, Jaine."

Please be a fucking positive one for a change.

"Bingo."

I don't ask any questions. I make my way straight to ground level. Still wearing my get-up, I hit the fire alarm, dragging off my balaclava before I reach street level.

"Take that, Sophia."

"Jaine, you didn't." I can hear Jessie laughing in the background.

"I goddamn did."

CHAPTER FIFTY

PADRAIG

Padraig's Apartment, Hudson Yards, New York

I COULDN'T BRING MYSELF TO TOUCH SOPHIA.

Many men would have killed to be in my position, but I'd rather have ended myself than be intimate with her.

I escaped to the restroom then stared at my reflection in the mirror for a full ten minutes while trying to talk myself into doing the necessary. I was never going to be granted an immaculate conception. I was always going to have to get my dick wet.

Lie back and think of the Dusters. All I could think about was Jaine.

When I returned, I suggested Sophia fetch us both a glass of water. I knew I was simply delaying the inevitable. I could tell she was anxious to get on with it. Just when I was about to bite the bullet, the fire alarm went off.

For once, God really was on my side.

We made our way out of the building and waited for the firefighters to arrive. Eventually, Sophia had had enough, and I had Liam take her home. I remained on the sidewalk, rejoicing in my victory while freezing to death. In the end, it was a false alarm. There was no fire.

Did someone set it off deliberately?

Regardless, my victory will be short-lived. I'll still have to uphold my side of the contract tomorrow and the day after.

Purgatory. That's what this is.

It's now two a.m., and I'm lying in bed wide awake. I can hear my phone vibrating in the other room. To get up or not? It's not like I'll be sleeping anytime soon.

"Dylan." I lie back on the sectional in the darkness. "It was deliberate, wasn't it?" He knows I'm referring to the fire alarm.

"It was."

"It's just delaying the inevitable. You do know that?"

"We'll see."

"What do you mean?"

"We've obtained the contents of Sophia's phone. Jessie and I are just going through the data now."

"And how did you manage to do that without the physical handset? Luciano will be able to trace anyone who tries to access the number remotely."

"We had access to the physical phone."

"How? She takes it everywhere with her." And then it falls into place. "The lights went out earlier. Was someone in my apartment?"

"Yes."

"Who?"

"One of our high rankers."

"And do you have everything you need?"

"It's looking that way. We've created a checklist. Events and dates, that sort of thing. We're just cross-referencing it all now."

"So, Sophia and Luc are involved?"

"We don't want to count our chickens until we have all the facts, but it's looking that way."

"And when will you know for sure?"

"Give us twenty-four hours. There's a lot of data to go through."

"What you saved me from yesterday, Sophia will now expect to take place today."

"I appreciate that, Paddy. We're going as fast as we can. We have to be completely certain."

"Can I help in any way?"

"There is one thing you can do."

"Anything."

"Pray."

"Consider it done."

"One other thing, Paddy."

I know what he's going to say before he says it.

"You need to have that conversation with Eoin. It's time for everything to be out in the open once and for all. No more secrets."

CHAPTER FIFTY-ONE

JAINE

The O'Connell Home, Darling, New York

I STARE AT THE TWIN METAL PIPES OF THE BRAND-NEW HARLEY Davidson Softail in all-black that's parked up in front of me. I then inhale the welcome smell of leather and grease.

My biker soul is itching to sit astride the custom-made machine, turn the keys, watch the pipes vibrate with exhaust fumes, and then ride off into the sunset.

"Who sent it?"

I turn my attention to Dylan. In the absence of anyone else being at home, he drew the short straw and had to come to take delivery. He called as soon as he realized what it was.

"Your fiancé."

I turn to look at him. He's wearing grey sweatpants and tatty sneakers. His white t-shirt is crumpled, making it look like he's slept in it. He probably has. Going by the dark circles around his eyes he's been up all night working on the data from Sophia's phone.

"He hasn't told you that he cheated on me? That I walked into his office and found him locking lips with his PA?"

I watch as shock registers on his face.

"I guess not."

I toss the keys at him, and he catches them with one hand. "I can't accept it. Not from him. There's no forgiving what he's done."

He doesn't speak. Given how close he and Eoin are these days, I'm surprised he doesn't already know. Then again, maybe Eoin's pulling back from Dylan too now.

"That stays between you and me. It's for your big brother to announce the news to the rest of the family."

He nods slowly.

It's my guess he'll be on the phone to Eoin as soon as he leaves here.

"Any updates on the phone data?" I turn my attention to the hog again, taking in the custom finish that's been added to make it look as much like my old ride as possible.

Why would Eoin go to so much effort for someone he obviously cares very little about? You can't just walk in off the street and buy this level of detail. This machine has had to be pre-ordered, then hand built.

"We're almost done. Jessie was just finishing off when I was called away."

I nod. "I won't hold you up, then. I'll wait here until you get back."

He walks across and leaves the keys of the hog on the black leather seat.

Temptation.

I turn and walk back to the house.

If I'd never given in to that in the first place, maybe I wouldn't be in love with a narcissistic asshole who can't keep his dick in his pants.

I CAN FEEL EOIN'S EYES BORING INTO ME WHEN HE ENTERS THE family room. Does he expect me to look at him? Why should I make eye contact?

After what they witnessed the last time they looked in his direction, he doesn't deserve my eyes being anywhere near him.

As usual, the rest of the family watches our silent exchange. There's no amusement this time. Not because they know he and I are through but because the subject about to be discussed is no laughing matter.

I make brief eye contact with Roisin and Fergal, then watch as Eoin sits beside his da so he's directly facing me. Roisin looks between us both. She now knows that we're over, or at least she suspects as much.

As is the norm, Sarah has taken the kids to the summer house, this time so Duke can be present. He's sat to my right while Jessie is on my left.

Duke deserves to be here. This conversation may well contain information about Ace. More importantly, who was responsible for his death and why.

We sit in silence.

"Is Paddy on his way?"

I'm still aroused every time I hear Eoin's dark, menacing voice. I hate him as much as I love him, not that he's deserving of either emotion. Asshole.

"Sorry, I'm late." I turn to look at Irish as he enters the room. His eyes connect with mine, and he shoots me a small smile. He's obviously just showered, as his hair is still a wet mess.

I've had no heads-up in advance. I pray to God that, for his sake, today's findings see him off the hook and no longer party to the contents of the contract with the Ruoccos. I watch as he takes a seat between Cillian and Aidan.

As much as he's more withdrawn these days, Irish still has that something that's just him. It's what draws people in like a moth to a flame. A personality so vibrant you can't help but fall in love with him.

Just like I did when I was nineteen years old.

While his eyes still hold an element of sadness, they're filled with something else today. Hope.

And that's what has his mouth ready to curve upward at any available opportunity into a smile that could light up a room or a life.

Just like he did mine.

My eyes then drift to Eoin. I know he's been watching me watching Irish. Why? What does it matter to him that I'm admiring his brother? We make eye contact, and my insides flip over.

Green.

Anger. Arousal. Adrenaline.

The trigger won't be arousal. If I still had that effect on him, he wouldn't have fucked someone else.

Today, he looks his full eight years older than his sibling. It's reflected in the lines on his face and the grey in his hair. He's lost weight. His cheeks are more sunken than they were.

Why do I care? He cheated.

But you do care, Jaine.

I haven't seen him since that day in his office. Like Irish, he visits the house to spend time with the kids. They never run into each other. I never run into either of them.

I drag my eyes away from his gaze, and they connect with

Roisin's. I see worry in hers before it's gone. Worry over what exactly? More deceit? More lies?

Who am I to point the finger?

"I'm not sure what level of detail to go into." Everyone turns to look at Dylan. He's not a natural-born public speaker. That's why it's best he takes to the floor. It will have way more impact. "We had reason to suspect that Sophia may be involved in what's been going on," he continues.

"Who's we?" Typical Eoin.

"Jaine, Jessie, and me," Dylan responds. "For those of you who don't already know, the message that sent Jaine on the wild goose chase to the church was sent from Sophia to Molly."

"And where is this message?"

I stare at Eoin. "It was on the handset you passed to me, along with my jacket and the music box. The handset and the music box have subsequently vanished from the safe space." I turn my attention back to his brother. "Go on, Dylan."

"Anyway, although there were some other instances of wrongdoing on Molly's phone, there was nothing concrete, so we… Jaine and I that is… thought it might be best if we accessed Sophia's phone."

"And did you?"

"Yes."

"Who did exactly?" It's Padraig's turn to ask a question. He's no doubt curious as to who the intruder was in his apartment.

"Jaine did."

All eyes turn to me, but I ignore them. Who doesn't matter right now? What does matter is what was unearthed.

"What the fuck were you thinking, Jaine!" Eoin's Mr. Dominating. Dangerous. Deadly side has decided to join the party. I'm not sure why he's pretending to be interested in my physical well-being when it's clear he doesn't give a flying fuck about my emotional one.

"I was thinking that I might like to find out the truth."

"You could have gotten yourself killed!"

"By Irish?" I raise an eyebrow.

"You know very well what I mean. Sophia could have seen you. Luciano would have been baying for your blood."

I snort. "In case it's escaped your attention, he already is."

He glares at me before standing and pacing the floor.

"Go on, Dylan," he mutters.

It's clear Dyl would much rather not, but he does anyway. "So, Jessie and I deciphered the information between us as best we could. It's taken so long because we wanted to be…."

"We're waiting, Dylan!"

Dylan's face pales at his eldest brother's harsh tone. "We have reason to believe that Luc has been working in cahoots with the Colombians all this time. It seems he was attempting to take the Sicilians down the trafficking route. An idea they rejected, hence why they showed him the door."

Eoin stops pacing. "Jesus Christ. So, the Ruoccos were behind everything that happened in Nevada."

"Go on, Dylan!" It's my turn to hiss because, after all this time, I'll finally have my own truth.

He looks between Eoin and me. Then his gaze returns to me. "As we already suspected, we were all targeted at Paddy's wedding. The Ruoccos' thought process was that if the entire O'Connell family were wiped out after Paddy and Sophia said, 'I do,' Paddy would instantly become Da Duster, making Sophia Ma Duster. They made a second attempt right here at the house, as we all know. Both attempts were thwarted thanks to the timely intervention of The Exterminator."

"And Eoin," I add.

Well, it's true. He may be a cheating asshole, but he saved my life while taking out the third sniper.

"That's when they decided to focus their attention on the contract with Paddy. A contract he had no option but to agree to after they issued a veiled threat toward Jaine."

I stare at Irish. He stares at me.

"Paddy, why didn't you say something?" Fergal sounds pained more than pissed that Irish has had to carry yet another burden on behalf of his family. On behalf of me.

"I couldn't let anything happen to Jaine, And it would have changed nothing, Da, so there seemed little point." His gaze never leaves mine.

"One of the contract conditions was that Padraig would have to oblige them with a Duster heir. Although, there's nothing to say they wouldn't have gone after the entire family once the child was born, including Paddy himself, but that's just speculation on my part."

"Can we see this contract?" Cillian asks.

Dylan turns to look at him. "That's up to Paddy. It's his business, so it's up to him if he wants to disclose it." He then swings his attention back to me. "Sophia obviously decided that she wanted payback for the comment you made three years ago, hence the attack on your life. She was also aware of Fin's true parentage hence the attack on his."

"What did you say three years ago?" Everyone swings their attention to Irish as he stares at me once more.

"That's Jaine's personal business and for her to disclose or otherwise, Paddy," Dyl replies on my behalf this time.

"So, if they're the silent faction behind the trafficking business, that means that the Ruoccos are inadvertently responsible for the death of Rafael Flores and the near death of Delaney." It's what I already suspected.

Dylan nods. "It would also make them responsible for my and Eoin's brush with death in Nevada. When I was saved by Jessie." He smiles across at her before looking at me once more. "And Eoin by The Exterminator."

I can immediately feel three sets of knowing eyes on me, which I ignore. My secret will be revealed to the O'Connell masses soon enough, but it's not a reveal for today.

"Their suggestion that they need to promote a family image to encourage quality high rankers is nothing more than a bloody ploy," Fergal mutters more to himself than aloud. We all wait for him to continue. "They want a child to gain access to our loyalty, our resources, and our wealth, nothing more. If they've been formed as an organization all this time, my concern is this nameless faction of theirs is far larger and more established than they've been letting on."

Padraig nods. "I mentioned the initial contract to Luciano. The fact that it was potentially signed under false pretenses, as his role with the Cosa Nostra was limited even back then. He didn't confirm or deny it, which makes me think the same."

Fergal slams his hand on the table beside him. I can understand why. He and Roisin have welcomed a family to join with theirs through the sacred sanctity of marriage. It turns out the family they embraced had been planning to kill them off the entire time so they could claim their Duster empire as their own.

If the only survivors were Sophia and her child, they would potentially inherit everything after any claims were settled against the estate by the rest of the O'Connell family that is. Notwithstanding, the child, if he were a boy, would instantly become Da Duster. A puppet to be forever controlled by the Ruoccos.

I listen as they all mumble between themselves. While this is all well and good, I need to know my own truth.

"What about Ace?"

The room falls silent once more. I already know what he's going to say.

Dylan frowns. "The data revealed that Luciano was visiting with the Colombians around the time of Ace's… you know. Anyway, it's not concrete, but we strongly suspect he may have been the second sniper. There were several references made to him avenging his sister around the date."

I can feel the blood drain from my face. Ace died because of a throwaway comment I made three years ago.

"Jaine." I glance at Roisin, the guilt evident on her face. She antagonized Sophia. She made her hate me even more. She'll feel responsible. But it's not her fault. It's mine.

Ace's blood is on my hands.

I don't remember standing. I don't remember going to the safe space to change into my biker attire, either.

What I do remember is turning the keys in the ignition of the gleaming new Softail and leaving.

IT'S THE FIRST TIME I'VE EVER BEEN HERE DURING DAYLIGHT hours.

It's an overcast kind of day, so there aren't too many people around to take in the female biker who's turned up to spoil the scenery at their respectable family boating lake.

Picking up a handful of stones, I gently skim them across the water's surface.

I pick up some more and keep on going because I don't know what else to fucking do. What do you do when you find out you're responsible for the death of the man you loved? I fall to my knees as

I suddenly forget how to breathe. The guilt is overwhelming. How the fuck can I ever come back from this?

How the fuck do I tell my son that I'm responsible for his daddy's death?

The lump in my throat releases as a sob, followed by another and another, as my packed-away grief slowly unravels, this time infused by immeasurable guilt. It'll be too heavy for me to ever pack away again. I know the weight of it will eventually destroy me.

Ace killed.

Eoin almost killed.

Fin targeted.

All because of me.

If she was going to be stuck in a loveless marriage facing a lifetime of solitude and misery, then it was only fair that she affords you the same courtesy.

I ignore my phone as it vibrates in my pocket. What are they going to say? It wasn't your fault. Bullshit. It was all my fucking fault.

I don't move from where I'm sitting on the ground, my head resting against the seat of a hog that isn't even mine. Eventually, I pull the handset from my jacket.

Missed calls from Dylan and Eoin. I'm not sure why the latter would expect me to speak to him. Surely, he's got good old Candice on speed dial these days.

I message Dylan.

Jaine: *Can you send me a synopsis of the data?*

Dylan: *For any reason in particular?*

Jaine: *I want to run it past Nate and see if he needs anything else.*

Dylan: *Give me ten minutes.*

Jaine: *And Dylan. This stays between us.*

No matter what I do, I can't bring Ace back, but at least I can seek retribution for him, Raf, and Abel.

"Jaine, I was pleasantly surprised to hear from you."

I lean against the doorframe of his apartment with my arms folded. "Pleasantly?" I raise an eyebrow. "What you're trying to say, Nate is that when you passed me your business card with your personal details on, you never expected me to put them to any use," I smirk.

"Something like that." He smiles warmly.

"I hope I'm not disturbing your evening plans?"

"Nothing I can't postpone until another time."

It's my guess he's having to put off the next in a very long line of hook-ups. Rumor has it ever since his Ivy League wife divorced him for allegedly fucking a teenage cheerleader, he's been playing the field.

Only women of suitable breeding and fit to be seen on the arm of the District Attorney, of course. Nate takes his public image extremely seriously—no more cheerleaders and, at forty-seven, definitely no more teenagers for him.

"Do come in." I watch his eyes drift slowly over my leathers as he motions for me to step inside.

"I'm a biker, Nate, but then you already knew that."

"Yes, of course. I must say, you look completely different in this get-up, Jaine. Next, you'll be telling me you arrived here on a motorcycle." He smirks at me.

"Why else would I be wearing leathers?"

It would appear I've rendered the DA speechless. It's understandable. He's used to seeing me in a tailored business suit and stilettos and, more often than not, being chauffeur driven around in an everything-proof SUV.

I walk past him, taking in the monochrome space. It's immaculate, which is what I fully anticipated. Workwise, everything with Nate is organized and precise. It's only to be expected that he carries that trait into his personal life too.

I turn to face him, watching as his eyes rise from my ass level. He makes no attempt to disguise the fact that he was checking me out.

He grins once more, his auburn hair perfectly groomed as usual, his eyes smiling and blue against a face that gets better looking with age.

"It's the first time I've seen you out of a suit too, Nate." I take in the black jeans and white fitted t-shirt he's wearing on his six-three athletic build frame.

"Please sit, Jaine." He motions toward the black leather three-seater couch. "Drink?"

"No, thank you." Taking a seat, I watch as he fixes himself a whiskey before sitting beside me.

"Firstly, I'd like to say how sorry I am, Jaine."

His sincere apology causes tears to prick my eyes. I know immediately what he's referring to. The fact that we now have a suspect for Ace's death.

I nod but say nothing. What's there to say? I opened my mouth, my husband got shot as a result, and now he's dead.

I wait for him to speak further. As soon as I received the brief synopsis from Jessie, I immediately forwarded it on, names, etc., withheld obviously.

"The document I received contains a great level of detail, Jaine, but if you want my unbiased personal opinion, it's not enough. It could see us drag these people into court only for them to then walk free. A lot of the information relates to a grudge held against you personally and to an ambition by these people to overthrow the Dusters and then assume their organization and their mantle."

His answer is what I expected. While it's enough for the O'Connells to know who is responsible, it's not enough for it to ever stand up in court.

"What do you need?"

"Ideally, a confession."

I snort. "And how do you expect anyone to obtain that, Nate?"

He smiles at me, displaying dazzling white teeth. "That's not really my problem now, is it? You want my help. Then you need to give me something tangible to work with. I'm not in the habit of taking on cases I have zero chance of winning. You typically represent these sorts. You know as well as I do that if it's not concrete, they'll walk. All we'll have succeeded in doing is rattling a mafia hornet's nest."

I close my eyes and rub my hand over my tired face.

"The alternative, of course, is that we let the mobsters handle it between themselves, but that could see a lot of guilty parties scattering to the wind. We both know what will then happen is they'll regroup and come back bigger and stronger and with an unquenchable thirst for vengeance."

He pauses. "I'm sorry, Jaine. I wish I had better news…."

"I understand. It's what I half expected you to say."

He stands, leaves the room, then comes back to join me, passing me a device as he retakes his seat. I stare at it in my hand. It's similar to a small round watch battery.

"Now, this remains strictly between you and me, Jaine."

"What is it?"

"It's a state-of-the-art recording device."

"What do you expect me to do with it?"

"I want you to get me a recorded confession."

I watch as he flips it over. "Just press the back, and the red light will come on. Then it's voice-activated. You can carry it on your person, or you can swallow it. Everything from the point of activation will then be recorded. It will also transmit to my phone in real-time."

"Just in case?" I raise an eyebrow. He knows what I'm asking. Just in case the host disappears without a trace.

He nods.

"What happens if it records other damning evidence?"

"Those parts will become unexplainably scrambled."

I stare at him. His expression is sincere. I trust him, at least on this.

"If we could also access the leader's phone in the same manner you did the other, I'm sure that would also hold some very worthwhile evidence."

"I'll see what I can do." I sound defeated. We both know what he's asking is for someone to effectively become a dead person walking. Whoever chooses to enter the Sicilian lion's den is coming out in a body bag.

I stand to leave, and Nate escorts me to the door.

"Meanwhile, I'll speak to my opposite number on the west coast. It's best we're prepared for any eventuality."

I'm about to speak, but he answers my question before it's even aired.

"Don't worry, Jaine. I agreed to work with you on this. Aside from the parties we're targeting, there will be no names mentioned. I give you my word."

"I appreciate that, Nate."

"Good luck."

I step into the corridor and listen to the click as the door closes behind me. I shove the recording device in my pocket beside the spare download one.

I guess it's time I started praying, as I'm going to need all the help I can get.

I TAKE OUT MY PHONE. THERE ARE NO MORE MISSED CALLS. DYLAN knew where I was headed, and Eoin must have given up trying. I stare at the messages from Irish.

Padraig: *I thought rather than call you so you could just ignore me that I'd send a message instead.*
Padraig: *Do you want me to tell you a joke?*

No, I want you to tell me that you love me.

Padraig: *I'll tell you it anyway.*
Padraig: *What do you call an Irishman with a bad case of chickenpox?*

I brush the tears from my eyes as I recall memories from a lifetime ago—our first message exchange as *friends.* I look at the time. It was sent an hour ago. With a laugh-sob, I message back.

Jaine: *A lepper-chaun.*

He messages straight back.

Padraig: *You remembered. I reckon it's because the old ones are always the best.*

As if I could ever forget.

Jaine: *You also reminded me at the time that your ma said if you haven't got anything nice to say, then don't say anything at all, hence why I'm going to ignore that last message about old being best.*
Padraig: *Ouch.*
Jaine: *Sorry, not sorry.*
Padraig: *Jaine?*
Jaine: *Yes.*
Padraig: *Come home, darlin'.*
Jaine: *That's part of the problem, Irish. I don't have a home anymore.*

Tears prick my eyes at my reality. I blink them back as I stare up at the night sky and let out a loud sigh. I have nowhere else to go apart from the O'Connell home.

I decide to make a detour on my way.

CHAPTER FIFTY-TWO

PADRAIG

The O'Connell Home, Darling, New York

Hours have passed, and there's still been no sign of Jaine.

What else can we expect?

She was told earlier today that, in a roundabout way, she was responsible for Ace's death. How does the family expect her to react?

Eoin has tried getting in touch with her, but she's not answered any of his calls, nor has she returned them. I can see the shadows under his eyes. He looks like he hasn't slept properly in weeks, and he most likely hasn't.

It's partly his own fault. This is where it all falls down between the pair of them. I appreciate that Jaine has almost perished a couple of times recently, but it's par for the course in this life. He's trying to dictate terms to her, and it's causing endless arguments. He'd be better off saving his breath.

The caveman approach doesn't work with Jaine. She's self-sufficient because she's had to be her whole life. He needs to relax the reins a little, but no matter how hard he tries, he can't. He loves her so much that he's scared to face a life without her in it.

I get it.

He's never felt this way about a woman before, but it doesn't matter what anyone says. Love isn't enough. I should know. I've loved Jaine Jones for years, and it's made no difference. She'll still never be mine.

And what's the point in having someone like her anyway if you're just going to lock her in an ivory tower?

"I'm going to head off," I say to no one in particular, as no one's really paying me any attention. Everyone's still too shell-shocked. They're all too worried about Jaine and her whereabouts, which is perfectly understandable.

She's a big girl. She'll turn up in her own time and under her own steam when she's good and ready, so there's no point in pacing the floor or worrying unduly unless a significant amount of time has passed.

No decisions can be made on how to proceed with what's been unearthed by Dylan and Jessie. Jaine's already mentioned that Nathan Hawke is involved. We need to know how to handle things while considering the sizable bite he'll expect from the Ruocco cherry.

I've already messaged Sophia to say something came up today and had no response. It's not like her. I'm worried it's a sign that something's about to kick off. That somehow, the Ruoccos know that her phone's been breached. At this stage, there's no point in worrying anyone else with my suspicions.

Eoin makes eye contact with me briefly, then looks away. He's hiding something. I suspect it's to do with Jaine. Surely, it can't be that bad? He should just get it off his chest. I have no more secrets.

Well, aside from the one where I'm in love with Jaine, and she doesn't know. But I reckon that's one I'll need to take to the grave with me.

I've already given my brother the green light where she's concerned. I can't very well backpedal now. It's up to him not to blow it with her.

I silently make my way outside, breathing the cold night air into my lungs as soon as the door has closed behind me.

Am I finally off the hook?

I'm not too sure any of us are while the Ruoccos are still at large. Despite being mobsters, we can't just rush in all guns blazing. Da's right. Luciano likely has a bigger army behind him than he's been letting on. They could quickly scatter to the wind if we're not careful.

I'm sure Nate will have a plan that sees Luc blamed for their downfall as opposed to the Dusters, provided, as Jaine mentioned, that he gets to drag the leading man himself through court.

As for my Sicilian wife? She lied. I didn't take her purity after all, so in the end, I owe her nothing.

In return for her attacks against Jaine and my son, I've decided I'm going to take her on a date night. Better late than never, I guess.

She'll finally get her wish. She will indeed become my next plaything. Unfortunately for her, however, it won't be in the bedroom. It will be in my concrete chamber of horrors underneath Play.

There, I will paint her with my very own palette of pain.

My phone vibrates. I pray to God it's Jaine. I read over my messages from earlier. Will she remember the punchline, I wonder?

Padraig: *I thought rather than call you so you could just ignore me that I'd send a message instead.*

Padraig: *Do you want me to tell you a joke?*

Padraig: *I'll tell you it anyway.*
Padraig: *What do you call an Irishman with a bad case of chickenpox?*

Tears prick my eyes when I see that she's typing.

Jaine: *A lepper-chaun.*

I laugh-sob as I message straight back.

Padraig: *You remembered. I reckon it's because the old ones are always the best.*
Jaine: *You reminded me at the time that your ma said if you haven't got anything nice to say, then don't say anything at all, hence why I'm going to ignore that last message about old being best.*
Padraig: *Ouch.*
Jaine: *Sorry, not sorry.*
Padraig: *Jaine?*
Jaine: *Yes.*
Padraig: *Come home, darlin'.*
Jaine: *That's part of the problem, Irish. I don't have a home anymore.*

Guilt.

Me. My family. We're responsible for that. If she'd never met me, Ace would still be alive, and she'd still be happily married. She'd never have had a confrontation with Sophia. Instead, she's pretty much on the run with a Sicilian price on her head.

I don't tell the others she's made contact. I doubt she'd appreciate them lighting up her handset or asking her countless questions.

Instead, I stick my phone in my pocket, then set off for the only place in the world where I can ever truly clear my head.

St. Peter's Church, Upper East Side, New York

I've driven rather than caught a cab. I'm hoping that in the unlikely event our enemies show up again, they'll find it much harder to shift an armored SUV than Jaine's hog.

Speaking of hogs.

I take in Jaine's new ride that's parked outside the church. Eoin bought it for her as a gift. Dylan said he had considered getting her another classic but thought that would be demeaning to the crushed one. Instead, he opted for a new one in the same all-black finish.

I wonder if he'd ever consider getting on the back of it. Not that I was ever on the back of the old one. I frown to myself, concerned that this will be me for the rest of my days. Comparing what Jaine and I did to what they'll do.

Maybe I didn't think this through? Maybe I should have fought for her? But why would I want anyone else to suffer like I am? More so, my own brother.

She loves him. He loves her. Just because my own situation is potentially about to change doesn't mean I should start moving the goalposts on him.

I appreciate that they're having problems again. I have no idea what they are. I won't pry, as it's none of my business. I gave him my blessing. I can't simply take it back.

I step inside the church, smiling as I take in the familiar surroundings. The workers are still on with the renovations, so old Father O'Reilly will still be off sunning himself somewhere while bashing that Bible of his.

Running my hand along one of the ancient wooden pews, I look around. Where is she, I wonder? I realize there's only one place she can be.

I make my way down past the confessional booth, taking in my image in the reflective glass as I walk toward the safe room. I don't think I've changed all that much over the years. A couple more lines and a few grey hairs. I'm a bit less jovial, but living this life will do that to you.

Falling in love with a girl who's destined never to be yours will do that to you too.

I smirk when I see that the door's been jammed open. She's not taking any chances after the last time. Who can blame her? I don't speak as I enter the room where we almost died, as she's currently fast asleep on the sectional.

Sitting, I look down at her. She's not changed too much either, but then, Jaine really is plain in that way. Everything about her is au natural. It always has been. Like me, she has a few more lines and a couple of scars, but that's about it. She still has the same big green eyes, pouty lips, and straight-up-and-down shape.

"I can feel you admiring me, Irish."

I laugh heartily. "And how did you know it was me, darlin'?"

She smiles, keeping her eyes closed. "Old Spice. No one else in the world wears it. Only you."

"My da used to."

"Used to. You see, even Fergal's moved on from a cologne that Methuselah himself used to wear."

She laughs with me, but it's gone as quickly as it arrived.

"It was my fault. At the time, I knew there would be repercussions, but I thought I'd be made to pay, not anyone else."

"That's the thing, Jaine. You *were* made to pay. She hit you where it hurt most. She hurt the people you love."

She nods. I can see her chin quivering. I quickly lie down beside her, pulling her across so her head is resting on my chest then I let her cry it out. She'll forever cry a river for Ace, which is only to be expected.

"Ma says she's to blame for antagonizing her."

She lets out a shaky sigh. "I said the condemning words. Roisin just fueled the fire."

I tighten my grip around her. "The Ruoccos are to blame, not you or Ma. Anyway, as Ace always used to say, when your time's up, it's up. There's nothing anyone can do to change that."

"I guess."

"What did you say to Sophia that got her so fired up anyway?"

I feel her tense. Maybe she doesn't want to be reminded as it's too painful. I mean, whatever it was snowballed into Ace losing his life.

"I said, 'I only hope Padraig grows to love you as much as he did me.'" Her voice is quiet. I'm sure she'd much rather never have told me, but there it is.

I roll on my side to look down at her. She's self-conscious as her confession has caused her cheeks to turn pink.

"Were you jealous, darlin'?"

A hesitant nod.

Is it wrong that my heart soars? That she lashed out at my future wife because she couldn't bear the thought of me being with anyone else?

"I'm surprised you let your professional image slip in public." I try to keep my tone as matter-of-fact as possible. I can't rejoice over a comment that resulted in Ace losing his life.

"It was the first and last time. It was foolish. I regretted the words the moment they left my mouth, but they were out there. I couldn't take them back."

"And when was this exactly?"

"It was at The Meeting Rooms, the night Sarah and I got

abducted by the Colombian trafficker. Now I come to think of it, he had most likely been invited along by Luciano."

"And what made you come here today?"

She shrugs. "I needed someplace to think."

"About Ace?"

"Among other things."

There's a lengthy pause. She's got something else on her mind. I wait for her to speak.

"Eoin cheated on me."

And there it is. What's also causing her distress and the reason my brother looks like death warmed up.

"Are you sure?"

She moves past me, then stands up. She walks toward the window to look out, even though the door's wide open.

"I witnessed it with my own eyes!"

"Why would he cheat? He loves you. Why would he have bought you the hog if he didn't?" I keep my voice calm. There's no point antagonizing her when she's clearly volatile.

She spins around, eyes flashing green. "It won't have been for my benefit. It will have been to lessen Mr. I Can't Keep My Dick In My Pants' feelings of goddamn guilt."

I chuckle. "It must be an O'Connell trait."

"You never cheated on me. He did."

"No. You're right. I didn't."

I stand and walk toward her just as my phone starts to ring.

"Dylan," I answer, then put him on hands-free.

"Have you found Jaine yet?" He sounds panicked. He's no doubt been getting it in the neck from our eldest brother.

"I'm here, Dylan." She answers.

"Jaine, are you…."

"I'm fine. I just needed some time to process everything, that's all."

A pause.

"I'll get off then. I just wanted to make sure you were okay. Everyone was worried sick." What he means is that Eoin was worried and making his life a misery.

I need to speak to Dylan about this cheating allegation. Did Eoin or didn't he? Now's not the time for that discussion. Not with Jaine so adamant that he did.

"I'll give you a call on my way home, Dyl."

"I look forward to it."

I disconnect the call just as our eyes are both drawn to the slip of paper protruding from behind my handset.

"I know what that is."

My lips turn upward. "So, you broke into my apartment and then went snooping." I remove the photo, and we both stare at the image.

I watch as she pulls her own phone from her inside pocket. She opens the case and lifts out the handset. We're confronted by the same image of us from our Yale days.

"Snap." We say it at the same time as though we're playing the childhood game, but this is now no game.

I stare at her before slowly backing her up against the glass we were once on opposite sides of because I know now that we're on exactly the same side and always have been. My gaze drops to her lips, causing her to lick their pouty surface.

She wants me to kiss her. Rightly or wrongly, there's no hesitation on my part this time.

She groans against my lips the moment they connect with hers. I silence her by thrusting my tongue deep into her mouth, tasting the perfection I've only been able to dream about all these years.

That's when time stands still. That's when the fates align. That's when everything suddenly makes perfect fucking sense. That it has always been me and her. Her and me.

I need more. Way fucking more. I need all of her.

Now. Always. Forever.

My hand fists her hair as I devour her mouth.

Mine.

You need to stop, Paddy. She's not yours.

I don't fucking care.

I growl as her small hands tangle in my hair. Sucking her bottom lip possessively into my mouth, I bite down hard. I'm rewarded with her groaning her pleasure and her front instinctively pressing against mine.

Wanting more. Needing more. Demanding more.

I smirk against her mouth, and in retaliation, she bites my lip until I can taste blood.

My favorite fucking flavor.

I lift her feet off the floor. The moment my hard-on connects with the heat of her pussy, I thrust against her. I need to be inside her. Her legs anchor around my hips, and she grinds back her acceptance until she's pressed tightly against my length with her nails digging welcomingly into my back—blood red.

My favorite fucking color.

Would we have willingly stopped? We'll never know. Our mouths only part when we hear the sound of the church doors being slammed shut.

We both stare in that direction. This time, we have our phones, and we're not locked in the safe room, so what's the worst that can happen?

CHAPTER FIFTY-THREE

JAINE

St. Peter's Church, Upper East Side, New York

WHAT JUST HAPPENED SHOULDN'T HAVE.

But you wanted it to happen, Jaine. My throbbing clit can't argue with that.

I can still taste Padraig's O'Connell's unique flavor on the tip of my tongue, mixed with the metallic taste of his blood.

I'm wet. I'm aroused. I want more. Way more. I wouldn't have stopped. I'd have kept right on fucking going.

Eoin and I aren't together. He cheated. But I can't just start something with Irish. Not without Eoin's approval. I owe him that, at least, regardless of what he did. Irish doesn't love me anyway.

Twenty generic words, remember, Jaine?

The only positive from the sound we both heard was that it stopped us from progressing from kissing to fucking. Because we would have.

My guts are telling me that my living on borrowed time may just have caught up with us both. That Irish was in the wrong place at the wrong time and has been caught up in my final countdown.

We run down the corridor past the confessional booth and into the nave. We glance around, but there doesn't appear to be anyone here. I watch as Irish walks to the entrance before pushing at the ancient doors.

"We're locked in."

"Not again."

"Yep." He places his ear against the wood and then sniffs. "Get Dylan on the phone, Jaine. Quickly."

"What's wrong?" I take my phone from my pocket as I walk toward him, and that's when I smell it. Gasoline.

I stare at him as I dial Dylan's number. "They're going to torch the place with us inside, aren't they?" I disconnect the call. "His number's just ringing out."

"Call Eoin."

I try his number, knowing he probably won't answer, but he does straight away.

"Quickly, Jaine. I can already smell smoke."

"Jaine, where the fuck are you?" Eoin sounds worn out with worry. I've had so many missed calls from him.

"St. Peters. Padraig is here too. They're about to torch the place with us inside. The door has been barricaded from the outside."

"Fuck!" I can hear the devastation in his voice, and then I hear the familiar sound in the background as he punches the wall. Guilt spirals through me. I've done this to him. He may have weakened me, but I've weakened him. We're each other's kryptonite. "I'm leaving now. I'll call the fire department on the way."

I disconnect the call. That's when I see the flames licking up the outside of the stained-glass.

"What about the windows? Can't we just smash them?"

"They've been treated, so they're everything-proof, Jaine."

"Irish." He raises his gaze to where I'm currently looking. The roof is on fire.

"How long will it take to burn to the ground?"

"It's difficult to say. Many of the oldest parts will be made of wood, so they'll go up like tinder." I watch a frown cross his face. This is his special place, and because of me, it's going to be burned to the ground.

"Irish… I'm so sorry." I know words don't help when you're about to lose something that means so much, but I don't know what else I can do.

Walking over, he wraps his arms around me. "It's only a building, Jaine."

"But the memories."

He taps his head. "They're all in here, darlin'."

We stand there with our arms wrapped around each other as the place slowly fills with smoke, and the roof creaks and groans as the wooden joists turn to ash.

"Let's get under a pew. It'll be safer there, and there'll be less smoke."

We crawl underneath the one farthest back and closest to the entrance. Due to how narrow it is, Irish lies on the floor, and I lie on top of him. All we can do now is wait.

"Tell me something, Jaine. Anything at all." His arms are wrapped around me, holding me tight against his chest. I know he's trying to distract me from the fact that the smoke is starting to form a thick cloud.

"I always feel safe when I'm with you." It's true. I remember the feeling enveloping me when I got into the SUV after killing Lebedev.

He kisses the top of my head. "That's because I'll do anything to keep you safe."

I tighten my hold around him, hoping in some way I can make him feel safe too.

"The first time I came here was for Cillian and Sarah's wedding. When I walked inside, I felt you. It's as if you were here."

He pauses. "Someone once told me that the eyes are the windows to the soul. That I should ask the woman that I was in love with face to face if she loved me too. I came here that night to do just that."

I stare at him. It was me who told Dylan to do that. Padraig, when he was pretending to be Dylan. We were talking about his cliché blonde Disney Princess. Me. My voice breaks as I look up at him. "You were here?"

He nods. "I was, darlin'."

"I could feel you," I sob-whisper. And now I know exactly where he was. "Did you see me from behind the glass?"

"I saw you. You were all I saw."

"And did you hear it?" Tears stream down my face.

Kiss me.

He tilts my face up and presses his lips gently to mine. "I heard it."

"Why didn't you come out?"

"Because I didn't want anything to happen to you. My coming out would have put you at risk. I needed to keep you safe."

A pause.

"They would have touched, Jaine."

"What would have?"

"Our fingers. If the glass hadn't been there, they would have touched." He strokes my back as he starts to hum our song. I can hear the roof slowly starting to cave in. I watch the flames dance until the acrid smell of the smoke burns my nostrils, and I can't see anything anymore. I'm going to die, but it doesn't matter because I'm with Irish.

"I love you, Irish."

"I love you too, darlin'."

He gave them back. Or is this now just an end-of-life dream?

I feel myself being lifted.

Smoke. Can't breathe.

I want to shout out, but I have no oxygen.

Arms. Strong. Familiar.

"I've got you, Jaine."

Eoin. I love him.

All he ever wanted was to keep me safe. I spurned him. Spurned his protection. How many times has he since had to save me?

I inhale enough oxygen to scream out one word. "Irish!"

"I'll go back for him, Jaine."

"Promise me."

"I promise."

And then there's nothing but blackness. When I wake, I'm lying on the grass outside the church. The whole building is on fire.

Where's Eoin? Where's Irish?

"Jaine."

I turn to see Dylan. "Where's Eoin?"

"He went back to get Paddy." I can see the worry on his face. He doesn't think they'll make it back out.

The fear I felt before at the containers is nothing compared to what I'm feeling now. I remember making Eoin promise to go back in for him. He promised with no hesitation. He'd do anything for me. I realize now that I issued him with a death sentence.

I scramble to get off the ground, hacking my guts up as I try to approach the burning building.

Dylan grabs me around the waist. I try to prize his hands off me. "I can't let you go in there, Jaine. I'm sorry."

"I need to help them!" My broken voice is drowned out by the sound of the rest of the church roof caving in.

We both turn to stare. We both know what this means.

I twist and turn, trying to escape as Dylan and Cillian both hold on to me. I struggle to get away as I yell my frustrations at the sky and at God him fucking self, and then I sink to my knees because I already know that it's too late. The building is a fireball. No one could survive it.

They're fucking gone.

Standing, I turn and walk toward the hog.

"Jaine." I turn to look at Dylan. He's crying, but then what do I expect? He's just watched two of his brothers die.

He sobs as I get on my hog, but he doesn't come after me. He's too lost in his own grief.

Ace. Eoin. Irish.

They're all dead, and it's my fault. I need to leave before anyone else gets killed.

I STARE ACROSS THE LAKE ONCE MORE.

Peaceful. Tranquil. Still.

If I start crying, I'll fill it. I feel numb. Too scared to even breathe in case I shatter.

I killed them.

Ace too beautiful. Eoin too protective. Irish too caring. I was their common denominator. I was their self-destruct button.

Dead. Dead. Dead.

How can I live without them? I can't.

My sun, my moon, my stars. Gone. My life is now dark.

Even my children will be safer without me around. It's in their best interests that I become the necessary dead person walking.

I don't want to be followed. Whether I succeed or not, I won't live to tell the tale. I take my burner from inside my jacket, remove the phone from the case then take the images from the back. Me and Ace. My two boys. Me and Irish. I pause to stare at it. It's the only image I have of us together. I stick them in the back pocket of my leather pants.

I don't have an image of me and Eoin, or I'd have kept ours in there too. After all those months, we never had a single picture taken together. I want that more than anything now that I can't have it.

I put my phone back in the case, throw it as far across the lake as possible, and watch it sink beneath the surface.

The Exterminator no more.

I blink back the tears. I can't allow them to fall.

There's just one last thing I need to do before I go.

Because I have to go, you see. Because when you've loved and lost as many times as I have, there's nothing left. I can't even stop to think.

I dial his number from my other phone, and he answers immediately.

"Nate."

"Jaine, is everything okay?"

"Everything's fine. I'm just calling to let you know that I'll be the one going in." He knows I'm referring to the suicide mission.

There's a pause. "You do know what that means?" He sounds shocked.

"I know exactly what it means, Nate, but it's the right thing to do. I'm the one they're after, so let's just give them what they want."

"You have the address?"

"I have it."

"And the recording device?"

I dig it out of my inside pocket, switch it on, then put it in my mouth.

"I've just swallowed it."

"Jesus Christ, Jaine."

"It's the only way, Nate."

I disconnect the call and then throw the phone into the lake to rest beside the other.

Jaine Jones no more.

Mounting the hog that doesn't even belong to me, I set off for the home of Luciano Ruocco. If he wants me dead, then he can be my guest, but I'm going to see him sent down for life before I go.

CHAPTER FIFTY-FOUR

JAINE

The Ruocco Home, Upper West Side, New York

SITTING ASTRIDE THE HOG WITH THE ENGINE STILL RUNNING, I STARE at the Italian-inspired mansion from across the street.

It's impressive, but so too is the extensive Ruocco property portfolio. Having run a background check, they have very little by way of cash reserves, so it's my guess that many of the buildings they claim to own are via off-the-record mortgages. That they owe some seriously big names some seriously big money, hence why they need their hands on the Duster's liquid billions.

Given that Sophia's now a widow, she will, of course, have access to Irish's personal wealth. Not that it's for me to mention anything.

I'm sure they'll already be aware. They'll no doubt have had someone take photographic evidence of Padraig and Eoin's bodies as they were pulled from the smoldering embers of St. Peter's Church.

The bile from my empty stomach rises to the surface, but I swallow it down. I can't vomit in case I throw up the recording device. It's not for much longer. Then it will all be over. I bite back tears of pain and devastation. I can't let them surface, or I'll never recover enough to do what I have to do.

I haven't spoken out loud on my way here. I know Nate can hear every word. It hasn't been intentional. It doesn't really matter what I say now.

My life has been rendered meaningless.

"I'm at the Ruocco property. Anything mentioned about either my clients or the Dusters is off the record. I need you to honor that. Anything said about me is irrelevant." He knows what I'm saying. That I won't be alive long enough to take exception.

I turn my hog in the road, then pull up outside the black metal gates. I press the intercom, and they immediately swing open.

Dismounting the hog, I leave the helmet on the seat, then make my way to the front door. The building is architecturally magnificent. A combination of brick and limestone, with wrought metal balconies in black and gold set over five stories.

I don't have to ring the bell. The door is immediately thrown open by Luciano himself.

"Come in, Jaine, please." Fake niceties. He has a gleam in his eye because the target he's been after all this time has willingly come to him.

I step inside. As I thought, the property is vulgar, with beige marble flooring and even more wrought iron. As much as the O'Connell family residence is ostentatious, it at least has a modicum of taste. The internal décor in this place is as vile as the owner himself.

We stare at each other.

He's handsome enough if you like the Italian mafia look, but his teeth are as fake as his pleasant personality. By all accounts, Luciano's favorite topic of conversation is himself.

Now that we're inside, he drops the pretend smile. "Would you mind if I search you, Jaine?"

"Not at all." I lift my arms as he runs his hands slowly over me. The only thing he could potentially find is the download device, but given he's undertaking the exercise to cop a feel more than anything else, it's doubtful he'll search for something so small. He'll be more interested in phones and weapons. I have neither.

I stand as he slowly runs his hands over my ass. I could snap his arm or neck, but that won't do me any good. I'm handing myself over as a solution to an ongoing problem. I'm not here to make the situation worse for those I'll leave behind.

"Thank you. Please come with me."

I follow him downstairs, leaving via what looks like an old servant's entrance. I'm guessing the people who exit this way won't be seen again. The cold air nips at my skin. For once, I relish it. Pretty soon, I won't feel anything.

We stop at an old wooden door. It's already unlocked. He pushes it, and it opens with a reluctant creak. He then flicks a switch. Lights flicker on.

As I suspected, it's a similar environment to what lies underneath Play. It will be soundproofed, of course, as, unlike that concrete tomb, it's not below ground level. I'm sure Luciano wouldn't want to disturb his wealthy neighbors when he has the urge to murder someone in cold blood like he's about to do me.

I don't resist when he binds my hands behind my back. Neither do I put up any resistance when he pushes me down on the plastic chair that's set out in the middle of the room. Once more, we stare at each other.

"Why did you come here, Jaine?"

"I want answers. Then you can do with me what you will. I am your main target, after all."

I know he'll give me answers because, having known Luc for as long as I have, I know he likes to brag.

"You murdered my husband."

"You disrespected my sister."

I feel sick as he gives me the confirmation we already suspected.

"Why?" I choke it out.

"Call it retaliation. My sister was faced with having to marry a man who was in love with another woman. A man who physically rejected her over and over again," he spits.

"That wasn't my fault."

He backhands me across the face. All I can taste is blood mixed with the taste of the acidic bile I had to swallow back earlier.

"You gloated, Jaine. Do not deny that."

"It was three years ago."

"Three years. Three days. What does it matter when you are entered into a hopeless marriage? Padraig disrespected her. He refused to accept her into his bed because he was obsessed with you."

"I did nothing to encourage that."

"Perhaps not, but you then proceeded to birth him a son, whereas my sister had to return from Sicily to face gossips suggesting that she was either barren or that there were already issues with her new marriage."

What can I say? His mind is made up. To the Ruoccos, I'm the cause of Sophia and Irish's marriage failing, even though, according to Dylan, it was more to do with her personality than anything else.

"And then, on the night they were finally supposed to consummate their marriage, you compromised Sophia's phone."

"How did you know?" I don't deny it. There's no point.

"It's fitted with technology that can identify if any new hardware has been added."

So, he was aware of the download device. "How did you know it was me?

"You were seen leaving Padraig's building moments after the fire alarm had been set off. Who could have pressed the alarm, I wonder?" He backhands me once more. So hard I almost black out. "I thought it only fitting that we start our own fire in response."

I shake my head in an attempt to clear my blurred vision. I need to remain alert until I get what I need.

"So, you committed arson by setting fire to St. Peter's."

"It was no less than Padraig deserved. To perish in the very building he holds closest to his heart."

"So what now?"

"We urgently need access to liquid reserves. Thanks to you, we have no option but to abandon the Duster heir idea and terminate Padraig's life so Sophia can access his wealth. Such a waste of an opportunity. We wished to make him Da Duster by eliminating the rest of the family, but The Exterminator kept getting in the way of our original plans."

I don't mention that there will be no need to kill Padraig as he's already dead, or did they not stop to check on the results of their handiwork at the church?

"And the trafficking?"

"So, now you know who is behind it." He smirks proudly. As I suspected, he's only too happy to brag. "A very lucrative business opportunity, and one the Dusters declined to become involved with." He shrugs. "No matter. We will continue using the Colombians as our front. We have access to another motorcycle club in the area that is only too happy to assist with the logistics, so we have no need to pursue any of the others further. You may know of them. The Punishers."

I shake my head, even though I know exactly who they are. I'm hoping playing the dumb blonde act will encourage him to spill more truths.

"Their president, Lucky, has a lot of hungry biker mouths to feed, so he was extremely keen to work alongside us." He looks at his watch. "His brothers will be doing their first transport run this evening, in fact."

Lucky's not going to be very lucky if Nate is picking up on any of this. I pray to God that he is.

"Women and children?"

"But of course. Not that children appeal to me personally, but there is a high demand for young, innocent flesh."

Bile rises in my throat once more. I swallow it down. I've never known anyone more deserving of an engraved bullet. He looks at his watch once more. As he does, I spit out the bile and blood that's accumulated inside my mouth.

"Anyway, Jaine. Enough chit-chat. It is time for us to go."

I look at him. I thought this would be the room where I would meet my maker. Apparently not.

"Go where?"

He smiles at me. "To meet with my sister, of course. She wishes to say her goodbyes to you personally."

CHAPTER FIFTY-FIVE

PADRAIG

St. Peter's Church, Upper East Side, New York

When I eventually came around, I was lying in the recovery position on the grass outside the church, and the firefighters were already in attendance.

Apparently, the roof had just caved in, and everyone thought Eoin and I were dead. Fortunately, he had already carried an unconscious me to the doors. He then had to move a burning beam from across the entrance to drag me out.

The first person we both searched for was Jaine, but she was nowhere to be found.

Dylan said she had a meltdown, then believing Eoin and I had perished, she rode off into the night. Razr has since confirmed that the last known location for her burner was at the boating lake.

That's where we're now standing. Cillian, Dylan, me, and an

extremely agitated Eoin, who's pacing the small jetty that's supposedly where Jaine last stood.

It's pitch-black, apart from the moon reflecting off the water. It's also deathly quiet, save for the sound of a lone owl hooting in the distance.

I take back what I said before as I stand here wondering what to do with myself. My throwaway thought that Eoin should calm down and just let her get on with living her life. Because I feel it now. His inner turmoil. His anguish. What he went through. It matches my own because I can no longer feel our connection.

Is it because she's dead? Is she lying at the bottom of the lake? The lake she's been returning to more and more frequently because it's our place? A place once filled with so many happy memories for me until now.

Tears prick my eyes as I stare out across the water. I keep my emotions in check for my big brother's sake. I know Eoin wants to jump straight in, but he'll see nothing in the murky depths. It would take professional divers to find her even if she is in there and he knows it.

It won't stop him from wanting to try at the first sign of any encouragement from us, though. To repeatedly go below the surface until his own exhaustion overwhelms him, and he's also claimed by the dark expanse of water.

If she is in there, it's already too late. Bringing her out won't bring her back. It will only bring the rest of us closure. I'd rather sit here with my wishful thinking, foolish hopes, and pipe dreams and pretend that Jaine Jones is just fine.

Because how could I survive in this world without her when I am her, and she is me?

I stare at Eoin. He's covered in debris and soot from the church, and his hands are burned from having to shift the burning beam to save my life for a second time. He refused to have them seen by Dr.

Kelly. Bandages would only restrict his hand movements, and he wants to be able to act without hindrance when and if we ever find Jaine.

My phone vibrates, but I know it won't be her. I have a feeling she flung both her handsets into the lake to signify the end.

I pull my phone from my pocket.

Razr: *Any news?*
Padraig: *Nothing.*

I watch Eoin pace like an expectant father. In a way, Jaine's acted selfishly. My big brother will never survive losing her because they haven't made their peace.

Why would he cheat on her when he clearly loves her more than life itself? What made their relationship so fucking complicated that they continually went out of their way to make life a living hell for each other? Why couldn't they just be happy?

But would I want that when their unhappiness could mean a future for me and her? If she's still around to have one, that is.

"Tell me again, Dylan," Eoin snaps.

"Cillian and I had to stop her from trying to get into the church. When the roof caved in, she thought you had both died. We all did. Having accepted it for what it was, she walked off, got on the hog, and left. That's it."

There's one word that Eoin desperately wants him to change like it will somehow affect the overall outcome. It won't, but maybe, like me, he clings on to foolish hope too.

Accepted.

He doesn't like the thought that she bowed down to acceptance. Jaine Jones would never just accept. She would never just walk away. What the fuck is her Swan song? Because there will definitely be one.

My phone rings, but I just ignore it. It will be Ma, Da, or Razr. Nothing's changed.

It rings again and again. Yanking it from my pocket, I stare at the number. I know then it's the sign we've all been waiting for. I answer the call.

"Where is she?"

"Luciano Ruocco has her. I'll send you the location. There isn't much time."

"We're heading to the car now."

I start running toward the SUV, and the others follow. Cillian takes to the driver's seat, as he knows these streets better than most.

"Who was it, Paddy?"

"It was Nate Hawke, Dyl. Luciano's got her. She's alive. For now, at least."

"How does Nate have your number?"

"It's a long story and one that's not important for now."

As soon as he keys in the location, Cillian takes off out of the car park like a bat out of hell.

We're four brothers who put family first. Always. What Jaine doesn't realize is that she *is* family, and we always look after our own.

This is her Swan song.

She was never going to go without making her final mark on our outlaw world. Nate obviously needed more to be able to take down the leader of the no longer faceless faction. Jaine is delivering him just that, even if it means paying with her own life.

I turn to look at Eoin. Even in the darkness of the vehicle, I can feel it, and it brings a small smile to my face.

Foolish hope? Yup. He relies on it too.

CHAPTER FIFTY-SIX

JAINE

Unknown Location

I'VE KNOWN FOR A WHILE THAT I WAS LIVING ON BORROWED TIME.

Having been blindfolded and tossed in the back of a van, I had no choice but to roll around the floor for what seemed like hours. I felt every bump in the road, and I'm no doubt displaying a bruise for each.

I was grateful when it came to a standstill and the engine cut off. My final destination has now been reached. My crime? Having been loved by Padraig O'Connell and choosing to rub his fiancée's face in it three years ago.

Still, there are no do-overs in this life. I'll gladly meet my maker, knowing Ace's killer will finally be behind bars with the Riker's Island clock ticking down until he meets his own end.

I hear the doors of the vehicle open. I don't struggle when they pull me from the back or complain when my knees collide with the ground. I inhale the pungent smell of earth infused with the familiar scent of petrichor.

The latter reminds me of home.

Tears prick my eyes, but I don't give in to them. I won't give the Ruoccos the satisfaction of watching me crumble.

It's undergrowth. Woodland. A bullet in the skull and thrown in a shallow grave is my thinking. Maybe they'll even make me dig it first.

The blindfold is ripped from my eyes, and I blink against the harsh light. The vehicle engine has been cut, but the headlights remain lit so they can see what they're doing.

There are two goons with Luciano now. He won't want to get his manicured hands dirty. The fourth person present is Sophia.

I stare at her as she smiles smugly at me.

"It's good to see you, Jaine."

"Is it?"

"You're looking… well."

She glances over my appearance. I'm aware my clothes stink of smoke, and my face is no doubt swollen after the backhanders I received from Luciano. I can still see out of my right eye, but only just. If I were to live until tomorrow, my eye would have closed up completely.

But I won't live until tomorrow.

She strikes without warning—another backhander. I remain silent as the pain radiates across my jaw. She'll get hers tenfold in the next life.

"What shall we do with her, sister?" Luciano already sounds bored.

She chuckles. "Why, kill her, of course."

I watch as he pulls out a Glock from inside his jacket.

She shakes her head. "No, not like that." She stares at the goons. "How deep is the hole?"

They look at each other.

"Around six feet." one mutters.

"Perfect." She smiles at me.

"Sophia." Luciano sounds impatient as he looks at his watch. He wants this to be over with. I've obviously spoiled enough of his evening.

"Position her at the end of the grave."

The goons grab me and stand me at the foot of my final resting place in some wood where I'll almost certainly never be found.

My thoughts immediately drift to the family plot at Rising. I wanted to be buried beside Ace and Pop. Where my boys could join us one day if they wanted to.

I won't be.

I'll be here in an unmarked grave. I'm suddenly overwhelmed with guilt that I'm putting them through this. I hope they realize I did this to keep them safe.

Sophia pushes me backward, and I fall into the hole. The wind is knocked out of me when my back collides with its cold, watery base.

It's then I hear it.

Chopin's *Marche Funebre*.

The funeral march.

"Don't forget your little gift."

The small wooden musical box lands at my feet, still playing.

"Bury her alive," she announces.

So, I'm to suffocate under six feet of dirt.

I feel each shovelful of soil as it lands on me. My hands are still tied, so I try to keep my mouth and eyes closed, but it quickly makes its way up my nose. I'm already struggling to breathe.

Tears of self-pity fill my eyes. It's not the ending I imagined, but then what is? I was never going to die of old age surrounded by family as we reminisced over the ninety-year life I led.

This is the reality of the life I chose to lead—the life I would choose over and over again. The voices fade, and finally, the music box is silenced.

I'm suddenly enveloped by cold. Is it the soil, or is it Death? Has my ex-husband's right-hand man come to claim me for himself?

More tears. Regret this time. That things with Eoin and me were so flawed. We never stood a chance.

If I could have done just one last thing, I'd have taken a photograph. Because I want one more than anything. I want to have it in the back pocket of my pants where I have all the others.

I can't believe we never took one.

That we never captured even one snapshot of our fucked-up time together.

The tears flow freely now. No one can see me cry. A sob escapes me—just one. And then I remember that Nate can hear me. I mumble the words, trying to prevent the soil from invading my mouth, at least until I can get them out.

"Tell Roisin I'm sorry about what happened to Eoin and Padraig. That it was just too much to come back from after Ace. Tell her to tell my sons that I love them. That sometimes, we have to make the toughest decisions to do what's best for our children. She knows that better than most."

The crushing weight of the earth lies heavy on my chest until my breathing becomes labored. Until the cold takes root in my bones.

Until there is nothing.

Until there is silence.

Until there is noise.

Until there are voices.

I struggle to breathe. Panic. I don't want to inhale the earth into my lungs, but they're suddenly burning.

I take a breath. Air.

Familiar strong arms wrap around me.

Eoin.

I take a second breath.

"I love you." The words exhale from my lips as the darkness envelops me once more.

CHAPTER FIFTY-SEVEN

PADRAIG

Unknown Location

"I LOVE YOU."

Three little words are uttered just before she loses consciousness. The intended recipient was my brother, not me.

I knew she loved him. I'd just never heard her say it. I know she loves me too, but witnessing her declare her love for him still feels strange.

I watch as he holds her in his arms. She looks lifeless, but she's not. Thanks to Nate, we found her just as she'd suffocated under six feet of earth.

Mouth-to-mouth and heart massage. I did the latter while Eoin breathed life back into her by doing the former. It took a solid minute to bring her back. Not that we would ever have given up trying. I would have given my own heart and he his final breath to bring Jaine Jones back.

I watch him cradle her like she's the most precious thing in the world. To him, she is. To me, she is. His love for her is so visible when she's not looking. As soon as she turns in his direction, his expression becomes completely indifferent.

Does he regret falling in love with her? All the trouble she's been?

He could have had his pick. He could have selected a mobster female who would kill when necessary and do as she's told the rest of the time.

Instead, he fell in love with a biker. One who still has a secret that she's not shared with him. How will he feel when it's revealed? How will he feel that I knew all this time and he didn't?

I kissed her, even after I gave him my blessing. I know he won't have cheated on her because he's wearing the same look I do anytime I look at her.

It's what unconditional love looks like.

You'll take anything she has to give because anything is better than nothing, and nothing is what you're left with when you don't have her in your life.

She's my reason for breathing, the same as his, so why is he pushing her away?

I turn my head, watching as Cillian and Dylan push Luciano's two goons into the now-empty grave we just freed Jaine from. She survived her ordeal. They won't.

Luciano and Sophia have been taken away by Liam. Are they headed for the containers or Play?

I found the download device in Jaine's jacket as I pressed down on her still heart that very first time. Dylan then did the necessary with Luciano's phone after he beat seven shades of shite out of him.

My brother, the recluse, is now my brother, the murderer. Someone tried to kill his friend today. The Robin to his Batman.

And he acted in a frenzied manner. We had to stop him in the end. We need Luciano alive, as Nate has first dibs.

Sophia, the wicked fairy, on the other hand, is all mine. She'll pay for what she did to my Disney fucking princess.

Padraig's Apartment, Hudson Yards, New York

"Any news, Dyl?"

I'm resting on the sofa with the phone leaning against my ear. Aside from smoke inhalation, I'm not too worse for wear after yesterday's ordeal. I'm not sure the same can be said for Eoin. His hands are in a right state.

"Nothing. We've all been warned to stay away from the house by Ma. She says Jaine needs time to reflect on what happened."

We all know that's mere speculation on Ma's part, of course. The reality is that Jaine's locked herself in the safe space. The only people allowed in are Duke and the kids and Tim, and the latter only because she knows Eoin will insist on having regular updates on her physical well-being.

Her mental health is my main concern. She lost the will to live yesterday. She gave up. If we'd arrived a minute later, we wouldn't have been able to save her.

"Jessie tells me that she has two new handsets being delivered today. Her burner wasn't on contract for obvious reasons, so I reckon it will be a new number for that." He continues.

"Will she give it to everyone who had it before?"

"Who knows? We'll just have to wait and see."

"And Luciano?"

"He and Sophia are being retained at the docks for now. I suspect Jaine will want to have a discussion with Nate before anything's decided. Whether Luc gets processed via the legal route as is hoped or whether we have to deal with him in our own way.

After everything she put herself through, I hope Nate has enough evidence to convict him."

"I can speak to Nate if necessary."

"I didn't realize he had your number. Not until he called you with Jaine's whereabouts."

I can understand his curiosity. Why would a mobster have the contact details of the District Attorney?

"I've known him for a long time. We're both legal professionals, so we were always going to cross paths." I give as little away as possible. It's Nate's secret to spill, not mine.

"I guess." He doesn't sound convinced.

I change the subject. "Jaine told me that Eoin cheated on her. That she and him split up as a result."

"He didn't cheat. It was staged."

"What do you mean?"

"He was trying to extract himself from her life."

"Why?"

"He thinks Jaine should be given the choice and not just have him inflicted on her like you wanted, so he's been trying to distance himself."

"But she loves him. She said as much yesterday."

"She loves you too."

"Have you told her what game he's playing? Jesus Christ, Dylan. She could have gone to meet her maker believing that of him."

"I haven't told her, but I will as soon as she has an active phone."

I know what he's going to say before he says it.

"You need to speak to Eoin too."

"I will." And this time, I mean it.

CHAPTER FIFTY-EIGHT

JAINE

The O'Connell Home, Darling, New York

"We need to stop meeting like this."

I smile at Tim's words, but I'm pretty sure it doesn't reach my eyes.

Is it all over now? I'm not sure I can go through another day like yesterday. A day I thought would be my last.

A wave of nausea suddenly grips me. I heave, and my head is expertly lifted so I can vomit bile into a white paper bowl. I've lost count of the number of times I've been sick. The first time around it contained the recording device which I immediately switched off.

All I can smell is dirt. All I can taste is dirt. As I suspected, my eye is fully closed up today.

"How is Irish, Tim?"

"Padraig is fine. He's suffering from the effects of smoke

inhalation, but he'll be back to his normal self in a couple of days. Like you, he's been throwing up regularly."

"And Eoin?"

"He has some damage to his hands. Running into a burning building to rescue a disaster-prone couple will do that to you. Thankfully the damage isn't as bad as we first feared."

"We're not a couple."

A pause. "If you say so."

"Where is Eoin?"

"He's upstairs. He's been returning the favor."

I frown.

"He's been your Florence Nightingale this time around. He's refusing to go home until he knows you're okay."

"Why?"

I say the word out loud unintentionally. If he doesn't love me. If he doesn't care about me. If he cheated on me. Then why?

"Perhaps you need to have a heart-to-heart, Jaine. With both of them."

"I will." And this time, I mean it.

"DYLAN."

"It's good to hear from you, Jaine."

Tears prick my eyes. I can tell he means it. How would my death have affected him and the others? At the time, it didn't matter. I didn't care. I just wanted the risks to my children to end. I just wanted the pain of losing Irish and Eoin to end. It turns out I didn't lose them after all.

They almost lost me.

"I called to update you. I've messaged Nate. He's confident he has enough ammunition to convict Luciano. He's agreed to deal with you moving forward. I've given him your contact details."

"The DA wants to speak to me personally? What if I say something I shouldn't?" He sounds nervous.

"You won't. If you do, he'll pretend he didn't hear it."

"That's decent of him."

"I'm in his good books. His opposite number on the west coast was able to intercept a lorry load of trafficked victims last night, thanks to Luc spilling his guts. I'm guessing the Punishers MC will be no more, given they were responsible for handling the logistics."

"Jesus Christ."

"The Ruoccos were behind everything, Dyl. In the end, they had abandoned their Duster heir idea. Their new plan was to kill Irish and steal his wealth, hence the fire."

"How on earth were you able to communicate with Nate?"

"I never expected to see the light of day again, so I threw both my phones in the boating lake, then swallowed the recording device he'd given me. He needed a confession. I got him one. He also needed the contents of Luc's phone. You got that for him."

"Teamwork."

"As always, Batman." I pause briefly. "I'm sorry, Dylan. I was so hellbent on ending my pain and protecting my kids. I never stopped to consider how my actions would affect anyone else."

"I felt responsible, Jaine. I should have reassured you." His voice breaks, and it causes tears to spring to my eyes. Dylan is the opposite of Irish. He seldom gets emotional.

"You thought they were gone too, so how could you? You were dealing with your own grief. I had just reached the end of my tether with it all. I couldn't see any other way out. I was putting everyone at risk—even my children. What Nate needed meant sending someone on a suicide mission. It made sense to kill two birds with one stone. It was me they wanted, after all." I pause again. "How is Irish?"

"He's fine. He's been asking after you. He's still feeling the effects of the smoke inhalation and has been placed on a very exciting diet of water and oxygen." He laughs.

"Eoin went back for him because I made him promise." I can hear the guilt in my voice.

"He went back for him because he's his big brother, Jaine, and that's what big brothers do. You asking that of him would have made no difference."

"How is he?"

"His hands are a mess, but it's superficial in the main."

"Will they scar?"

"I'm not sure." He chuckles. "Don't worry. He won't be bothered. Contrary to what you may think, Eoin isn't vain."

"No, he's just a cheater," I bite back.

There's a pause.

"Can I ask what it is you actually saw?"

"Him and Candice. Standing so close you couldn't have gotten a sheet of paper between them, and her hands were in his hair."

"It's quite common for women to get up close and personal with Eoin, Jaine, even more so at social events. He is what most would call an eligible bachelor."

Jealousy flares through me. "This was in his office, and I've never seen it happen at any event," I snap.

"You've never attended many where you and he were both in attendance, and you pair never did anything socially…."

"Because we spent all our time arguing, falling out, and having make-up sex."

"I couldn't have said it better myself. So much so…."

"We never did anything remotely normal." I interrupt once more. "Like take a photograph together," I whisper.

"Never?"

"Not even one. And it was my biggest regret. I had the photo of the kids, of Ace and me, of Irish and me. They were all in my back pocket. All I wanted was to have one of me and Eoin beside them, but in all the time we were together, we never did anything normal like just taking a photo together." My voice breaks.

"Speaking of photos, Jaine. He saw the one in your phone case. The one of you and Paddy."

I exhale loudly, knowing that it would have gone down like a lead balloon.

"I never knew that."

"He took it as the final sign that you and he were never meant. Not in the same way you and Paddy were. I tried to explain to him that you love them both equally, just differently, but he won't listen."

"Why?"

"Because his conscience is eating away at him. Molly's final words to him when they split up, were that he had effectively stolen Paddy's life. I know they haunt him, more so when Paddy still doesn't know what actually happened. The fact that Eoin actively pursued you."

"He needs to tell him, Dylan. It's not for me to say."

"He knows that, and he will, but for the record, he never cheated on you."

"I don't understand."

"He was pushing you away because he thinks you should be able to choose who you want to be with. That it shouldn't automatically be him just because you were already together."

"What if I want to be with him? He's being a goddamn martyr when no one asked him to be one," I bite back as my voice breaks once more. "Has he not learned anything during this whole shitshow? That we need to stop making assumptions and making decisions for other people? It's why we're all in this goddamn mess in the first place."

"So, what are you going to do?"

"I'll go see him in a couple of days."

"And Sophia?"

"Where is she?"

"At the containers for now, but she'll be moving to Play imminently."

"What will happen to her?"

"Paddy will happen to her."

"Can I be there?"

"I'm sure he will insist, Jaine."

CHAPTER FIFTY-NINE

JAINE

The Docks, Hudson Yards

I PULL UP AT THE CONTAINERS ON THE HOG THAT I'VE STILL NEITHER acknowledged receipt of nor accepted. Liam took me to the Ruocco property this morning. It was still parked up where I left it. No doubt it would have been crushed in due course had they had their way.

Fortunately, they didn't.

Luciano is currently being held for questioning. I've messaged back and forth with Nate, but we've not actually spoken. I haven't been able to face it. The fact that my legal nemesis was the person with me during some of the darkest moments of my life.

It turns out the recording device was also fitted with a tracker. As soon as I arrived at my final destination, he called Irish and told him exactly where I was. If the O'Connell brothers had arrived a few minutes later, it would have been game over.

It's been four days since churchgate, and this is the first time I've left the house. I can't face going to see the devastation the fire left behind, so I figured I'd come here and give the eldest O'Connell a piece of my mind instead.

Who the fuck does he think he is?

My life. My death. My actions. My consequences.

I'm not interested in his assumptions or his decisions. Hypocrite? Maybe.

So what if he's saved my life four times? It still doesn't give him any rights over it. Asshole.

In the absence of having much else to occupy my thoughts, I've spent the past four days with everything going around in my head.

Did Irish say he loved me, or was it just the smoke addling my brain? If he did, did he say it to give me peace of mind in my final moments, or did he mean it?

Because, ever since, those twenty generic words have just kept bouncing around in my brain.

You and Eoin have my blessing to move on with your lives together, darlin'. I wish you all the best.

I haven't spoken to him, but then I haven't spoken to anyone really. My business number is on divert to the office, and only Dylan and Delaney currently have my new burner number. Will I give it to Eoin or Padraig? I'm not so sure that I will, or at least not yet.

It's overcast once more. I'm sure the weather changes on the approach to this place until it becomes so oppressive that you can't physically breathe. I inhale the misty air deep into my lungs. I know exactly what it feels like not to be able to breathe.

I'll take this dense air anytime over none at all.

I cut the engine, remove my helmet, then shake my hair free. There's no need to take the keys out of the ignition. It's not like anyone will follow me here or attempt to steal the hog. They'd need to have a death wish turning up without an invitation, given Eoin's mood most days.

I dismount my ride and make my way around the side of the containers on foot. I want to surprise the eldest Duster. It's the first time I've come here uninvited. I've worn my fuck-off big boots to navigate the uneven surface more easily. We're still trying to salvage my leathers, so I've had to resort to wearing combats and a puffer jacket today.

I can hear him before I see him, or at least I can hear who or what he's hitting. I stand outside yet another container I've never been in. How many are in use? I don't even know. It's just another sad reflection on how little I really know about him compared to how much he knows about me.

I stand outside the rusty door. Is it locked? Should I knock? All I can hear is the thudding noise as he punches or kicks whatever he's taking his anger out on.

Pressing the handle down, I push the door ajar. Arousal flows through me at the sight I'm met with.

Eoin O'Connell is in nothing but a pair of grey training pants. His inked, toned upper body is covered in sweat, each rivulet running down and darkening the waistband. Veins protrude from his insanely lean build, a body he must work on all day, every day, to achieve the level of fitness I see in front of me.

I watch as he punches and kicks at the heavy bag, every hit hard enough to kill a man. I should know, I've used similar and done almost that.

He's not wearing gloves. He's not wearing footwear. He looks feral. Anger rolls through me that he never once told me he was trained in MMA or that we even had that in common.

He made me spar with Declan when, all this time, I could easily have sparred with him. What's even more infuriating is the overwhelming need I feel to lick the sweat from his body.

I stand and watch. Every punch, every kick, is making me wetter between the legs. I want to fight him. I want to fuck him. Right now, I don't know which I want to do more.

Fuck him.

I hate him. I love him. Right now, I don't know which is the overriding emotion.

Love him.

"Are you enjoying the view, Miss Jones?" I watch as he grabs hold of the heavy bag before letting it go and turning around to look at me, his eyes blazing green.

I'm breathless as I take him in. So powerful. So dangerous. So perfectly masculine. So imperfectly scarred.

My eyes drop to the toned V dipping into his pants. I silently curse myself as my tongue darts out to moisten my lips. His eyes track the movement.

"It would appear so."

"Fuck you."

"That. Fucking. Mouth," he says under his breath.

"You're a goddamn liar."

"I did what I had to do."

Dylan has obviously told him about our conversation. More rage barrels through me.

"You had no right." I stare at him across the room.

"I had every right!"

Guilt pours from him. I can feel it. He thinks he stole his brother's life, and now he's damned if he does and damned if he doesn't.

I nod my head toward the bag. "Why didn't you tell me you practiced MMA?"

"You never asked."

"You made me spar with Dec when I could have sparred with you," I hiss, feeling betrayed.

"I will never spar with you."

"Because you don't want to hurt me? Is that it?" I raise an eyebrow.

Silence.

"You're such a misogynistic asshole, do you know that?"

He clenches his jaw.

"Hit a nerve, have I?"

"Why did you do what you did?"

"Don't change the subject," I mutter.

"Why did you do what you did?"

"Stop repeating the question until you get a goddamn answer." I bite back.

"If you answered it the first time, I wouldn't have to repeat myself."

"Fuck you!"

"Why. Did. You. Do. What. You. Did!"

I stare at him. "I thought you were dead. I thought Irish was dead. I thought it would be better for everyone left if I were dead too." My voice breaks.

"Jaine…"

I shake my head. "Don't you dare show me any fucking sympathy! You don't get to make my choices for me. It's my life. Mine. It's not fucking yours to play God with. Fuck you, Eoin O'Connell, for trying to do just that!"

"You and Paddy are meant."

"I decide who's meant for me! Not you! You don't get to make decisions on my behalf all so you can ease your own goddamn guilty conscience!"

"That's not what I was..."

"I call bullshit! That's exactly what you were doing, asshole."

I turn to leave.

"I'm not done with you, Jaine. Don't you dare turn your back on me!"

I can hear the switch as Mr. Dominating. Dangerous. Deadly decides he wants to join the party. I glance at him over my shoulder and smirk. "Fuck. You."

I open the door of the container. It's raining. I lift my face to the sky as the thick droplets land on my skin, and then I run. If the fucker's not done with me, he's going to have to catch me before I reach the hog.

Anticipation surges through me. Will he chase me?

I don't go the direct route back, which is what he'll expect me to do. Instead, I set off in the opposite direction as the rain pounds against my face. For the first time in months, I feel alive. My heart pounds in my chest as my body ignites.

He's coming after me. I can feel him.

I run until I have no choice but to lean against a container to catch my breath. My skin prickles. He's close. I slide into a gap he won't be able to fit in, just as I see him pass. He's not running. He's walking. His long strides quickly eating into the distance between us. He's still only wearing his training pants. His feet are still bare.

I can feel his rage. I want it directed at me.

I squeeze out of the gap, and the hair on the back of my neck immediately stands on end. He's behind me. I know he is.

I don't look. I just run. I'm fast, but I know he'll be faster. I can see the hog in the distance. So close. Too far.

I'm sure I can feel his breath on my neck. I spin around to face him, raising my foot to kick at the same time. It connects with abs of steeled muscle. He grabs my boot and pushes me onto my back. I hit the ground with a thud.

From my position on the ground, I sweep his legs. It's his turn to fall to the ground. Scrambling to my feet, I run for the hog again, only to be grabbed around the neck seconds later.

"I. Said. Fuck. You." I try to elbow him in the gut, but he anticipates the move and uses his other arm to pin my arms to my sides.

"You're a fucking asshole." I curse and struggle. I kick and bite. He doesn't loosen his hold. I'm suddenly aware of the heat of his body radiating against my back. I can smell the sweat from his skin mixing with the rainwater. I want to taste him.

Not want. Need.

More. Than. Anything.

His monster can sense my arousal because he's hard when I press my ass against his groin. My legs almost give way as he spins me around and pushes me back against a container. Pinning my hands above my head with one hand, the other grips my throat.

I watch as he licks the rainwater from his lips, causing my eyes to drop to his mouth. I want it on me.

Licking. Sucking. Biting.

I raise my gaze to meet his. Rage mixed with lust. He wants to fuck me, but he doesn't.

Which will win?

I lean forward and run my tongue slowly up the strong column of his throat. Salt mixed with testosterone and every other addictive flavor that makes up Eoin O'Connell. I moan in appreciation as I swallow exaggeratedly like I've just licked my favorite popsicle. With a growl, he fists my hair and yanks my head back.

My lips part, and his gaze drops, his head cocking in that deranged way of his. Tendrils of darkness infused with spicy cologne wrap around me. I fucking welcome them. His breath is hot against my lips, his mouth so close I can almost taste the addictive flavor of his arrogance.

I can't move. I don't want to move. I'm exactly where I want to be.

His lips capture mine, and his tongue sweeps deep, drowning all my senses.

He releases my pinned hands, and I groan as my freed fingers connect with the ripped perfection of his torso. I can't get enough of the feel of his damp skin under my fingertips or the taste of its saltiness under my tongue.

He rips open the crotch of my combats, securing one of my legs over his arm so I can't move. With the other hand, he yanks his pants down before fisting his impressive cock. My mouth waters at the sight of him rubbing the pre-cum around the tip before stroking himself. Securing my other leg, he watches as I line up his dick, and then he thrusts deep.

I mewl my pleasure as he fucks me, my nails clawing at his back.

Fast. Furious. Frenzied.

The base of my spine scrapes against the metal surface of the container with every punishing thrust. His tongue licks the rainwater from my neck, and then he bites down hard.

Marking me. Claiming me. Making me his.

That's what he just doesn't get. I will always be fucking his.

I hiss my appreciation as my hands move to fist his hair, wanting more, needing more. In return, he bites down harder and fucks me deeper. Rainwater cascades over, and between us, as he pounds into me, each thrust alternating pain and pleasure.

One final push, and he claims his release with a roar, his liquid darkness filling me and pulling me over the edge with him.

I cling to him, our bodies a raging inferno against the cold, wet air. Resting my forehead against his, I look deep into eyes of aquamarine.

"Disobedient, evil woman."

His lips find mine once more. A kiss so searing it scorches my very soul. I love every side of Eoin O'Connell. I don't want a future where he's not in it.

CHAPTER SIXTY

JAINE

Play Gentlemen's Club, Manhattan, New York

I LISTEN TO THE FAMILIAR SOUND OF DRIPPING WATER.

Memories come flooding back of me and Fergal going toe to toe. My hand instinctively reaches up to touch the scar on my cheek. A souvenir from Irish's wedding day.

My very own hand-picked wedding favor courtesy of the blushing bride.

I stare at her as she sits on a plastic chair similar to the one I was made to sit on. She stares back. No words are spoken.

Sophia Ruocco is no longer immaculate or pristine. Her red blouse is stained, and her black trousers have ripped on both knees. She looks her age with no make-up and unkempt hair.

Nineteen. Old enough to die.

Her brother sentenced Abel to just that at the same age when he was made to let Luciano ride bitch to the Undertaker's clubhouse, all so he could shoot down my husband in cold blood.

Yes, Sophia Ruocco is old enough to die here today.

A woman who gave me the thumbs down three times. To die of thirst in an empty church. To burn to death in that very same building. To suffocate under six feet of earth in an unmarked grave.

I may have used up most of my nine lives, but I must have at least one left as I'm right here living it.

Since the last attempt on my life, her brother has been taken into custody, and she's been left to rot alone. First, at the containers. Now here. A disused area of the subway that doubles as a concrete tomb. A place where no one can hear you scream or beg for mercy. The only sound is the constant dripping that would slowly drive you insane.

The only smell is death.

For now.

I'm sure it will be added to soon enough by the metallic stench of blood and the stink of human waste. Maybe she'll welcome death as a preference to going stir-crazy.

Not that she'll get to choose.

My eyes drift to Irish. I watch as he polishes each potential murder weapon before placing them lovingly on the wheeled trolley.

Which one will he use to end his wife's life, I wonder? Or will he do the same as his brother did? Will he allow me to choose a fitting sentence?

His brother's domain is the docks. This is his domain. His house of horrors. His playroom of pain.

Like everyone else, he has two sides, Jaine. The happy-go-lucky persona that everyone knows and loves, and then there's the psychopath.

Is it wrong that I'm excited to witness his alter-ego in all his maniacal glory?

I watch as he steps into coveralls. And then he turns to face me. He looks exactly the same, but his eyes… they're gleaming. He looks unhinged. He smiles, but it doesn't connect with them because his mind is elsewhere. It's already bathing in the sea of Sophia's blood.

I watch as his gaze drifts slowly over me. Like he's playing spot the difference with how I looked last time. It stops on my neck. The bruising. The tell-tale sign that I've been claimed by his brother.

"You're fucking him."

That's when I know that Irish isn't in the room because, while he may have thought that before, he would never have said it aloud.

Sophia laughs. I'm not sure I would have been quite so brave. He turns to stare at her in brief contemplation. He's deciding where to start. Which shiny piece of metal will he put to use first?

Decisions. Decisions.

He turns his attention back to the trolley and picks up a switchblade. Reaching forward, he slices her right across the mouth.

"Stop fucking laughing."

She has stopped. Her laughter has turned to sobs. She's now been disfigured for life. Not that her life will last much longer.

She turns to me.

"Jaine." Her voice is pleading.

I stare at her. She must be as insane as he is if she thinks I'll put a stop to this.

"Would you like me to intervene, Sophia? Would you like me to stop your husband from gutting you like a fish?"

I walk slowly toward her, then lean forward and whisper in her ear. "You showed my husband no mercy. I will show you the same. What you don't fucking realize is that I'd gladly do the honors myself, but I'm not sure I'd do the act justice. You see, I use a different weapon when I kill. Can you keep a secret? Of course, you can because you're not fucking going anywhere." I smirk as I pull one of my engraved bullets from my pocket and hold it in front of her face.

Her gaze fixes on the engraving, and her eyes widen again. "You can't be."

I smile at her. "Oh, but I am. Sorry for thwarting your plans in Nevada and at the house. Now you know why I attended your wedding without an invitation." I smirk.

I let all that sink in before I make the next reveal. "There's one other little fact that you weren't aware of. When I came to your home to pay you a visit, I was wearing a recording device. The District Attorney heard every goddamn word." I stand upright and step back. "I hope your big brother enjoys his short-lived holiday on Rikers. I'll give him a week at most."

"You filthy biker bitch. I hope you rot in hell." She sprays blood as she tries to speak, and then her eyes widen in fear because she knows she's just antagonized her loving husband further. She turns toward Irish as he reaches for her mouth. She knows what's coming. She clenches her teeth shut. With a shrug, he picks up a hammer, parts her lips, and smashes them. I grimace at the sight.

She screams in pain, and he uses the opportunity to grab her tongue. Then with another flick of the blade, he slices it off. Blood sprays everywhere, and she immediately starts to choke.

I smile. Blood? Dirt? A choke for a choke.

"I don't want to hear any more from you… wife," he hisses in her ear.

With bulging eyes, she stares at me. Begging. Pleading. She's not asking for my forgiveness, though. Even with death imminent, it's still all about Sophia.

Irish searches through the trolley once more. "Hold her head, Jaine."

His tone is authoritative. With Eoin, it would get me riled, but with Irish, it has quite the opposite effect. He can tell I'm aroused by it as he smirks as I move to stand behind her.

"Hold it steady."

I grip her head in my hands. It feels hot and wet. Is it blood, tears, or sweat?

I taste vomit—my own.

"Tilt it back for me."

Again, I do as I'm told, and that's when I see what he's holding in his hand—a four-inch nail.

"Irish," I whisper.

"Do as I ask, Jaine." His tone remains assertive.

I nod, then close my eyes and swallow repeatedly as he prizes open her eyelid and shoves the nail straight into her eyeball.

The sound is nothing like I've heard before. A scream that doesn't sound quite human, along with a squelch when the nail sinks into the jelly-like fluid of her eye. I quickly release her head, spin around, and throw up the bile from my empty stomach.

It's too much for me, but for Padraig, I realize it's not even scratching the surface. I turn back around and stare at him.

Realization. Acceptance. Of what he is.

We stay that way until the screams turn to whimpers. Until the only sound is dripping once more.

Water. Blood. Piss.

I inhale, and the air is now thick with the stench of fresh shit.

"Now, the other one, Jaine." Commanding.

I nod slowly and take a deep breath before gripping her head again. It's hot, wet, and sticky now, and I'm still not sure with what. I gag as I close my eyes once more as he repeats a process that's not any easier to listen to the second time around.

"What now?" My voice is a whisper as I open my eyes to stare at the man before me. He looks like his usual self. He's just splattered with blood and eyeball slime.

Insane.

"I'll give you the choice, Jaine. We can either bleed her dry, or we can gut her."

"Bleed her dry." I'm not sure my stomach can witness the sound or smell of any more bodily fluids being spilled on the concrete floor.

He nods. I watch as he pulls down chains from the ceiling. Chains I hadn't even realized were hanging there. Is he going to suspend her by the arms? Then I realize he's not. I know exactly what he's going to do when I see that the chains are fitted with a six-foot narrow plank with buckle straps.

She offers only a weak resistance as he unbinds her feet and wraps one chain around her ankles. Walking to the rear of the space, he then pulls on a hoist until she's suspended head down and in mid-air from the ceiling with the chair still attached.

With an ease that tells me he's done this many times before, he cuts the bindings tying the chair to her. He discards it, then attaches her wrists to the slim plank using the straps.

The result? An inverted cross.

I watch as he pulls across a large plastic container and places it directly underneath her. She makes a small whimper when, with the precision of a surgeon, he cuts into her neck and inserts a tube before securing it with medical tape. He feeds the other end into the container just as her lifeblood starts to drip out.

He turns around, and we stare at each other. Reaching into my jacket pocket, I pull out the small wooden box and open the lid.

Chopin's *Marche Funebre* plays.

Walking across, I place it still open beside the container. It seems only fitting to return Sophia's gift.

I walk back across. I wait for Irish to speak because I have no words.

"I'm sorry if my methods are a bit extreme, Jaine, but people like Sophia must be made to suffer. They have sinned against us, and for that, they have to pay a penance." He points at her. "She killed Ace. She almost killed you. She tried to kill my son. Our son. Under normal circumstances, I would have tortured her for hours until she begged me to end her suffering, but since today was an introduction for you, I decided to keep it brief."

I watch as his gaze drops once more to the bruising on my neck. This time, he says nothing. This time, I can't help feeling both guilty and aroused.

I want him to tell me that he loves me. I know he did in the past. Does he still? I want to know that I wasn't imagining it at the church. I want him to supersede the blessing he gave me and his brother by telling me that he wants me for himself.

Then I realize I don't know what I want. It's quickly replaced by the realization that I do. I want them both, but I can't have them both.

"Let's get cleaned up, Jaine."

Right now, I don't think I'll ever feel clean again.

Having brushed my teeth, I stand in the shower and let the water rinse away the stench associated with Sophia. It was only to be expected that this place has wash facilities. You can't very well leave here covered in the lifeblood and bodily fluids of others.

It's not like I had an opportunity to look around when I was partaking in an Irish jig with Fergal, and I was hardly in the right frame of mind having just slit the throat of young Abel.

The washroom is floor-to-ceiling white tiled walls with mirrors positioned at every angle. Maybe it's so you can double-check to make sure you haven't missed any specks of blood.

After rinsing my hair for the second time, I step past the glass screen before wrapping a towel around my head and another around my body. I stare at thirty-one-year-old me in the mirror above the sink. I look much the same on the outside as when I first met Irish, aside from a small map of scars and a few more tattoos. I'm glad the mirror doesn't reflect what lies underneath, as my soul must be as black as the bowels of hell.

I'm a killer. Irish's ways may be more colorful and artistic than mine, but we are both willing servers of justice.

I am him. He is me.

It's no wonder you two were so well-matched.

Maybe Fletch was right after all.

I stare at the bruising on my neck inflicted by Eoin's monster. We fucked several times more, and I returned the gesture. Eoin O'Connell likes the world to know that he's been claimed.

Has he been? I'm not sure he has. I'm not sure I have, either.

Until he's revealed his truth to Irish and I've revealed my own to him, I'm not sure we can ever move forward. Our relationship is in limbo.

I towel dry my hair, then open and drag one of the several combs on offer through it. As they were in Irish's apartment, all the toiletries were for men, but then killing's not a very feminine act.

Maybe that's why Eoin struggles so much.

He pretends he wants a murderous spouse, but I suspect he really wants a traditional Catholic wife. One who sees to his every demanding need both in and out of the bedroom and one who will also bear him a small army of mobster children.

Is that me? I don't even know what me is anymore. My own confusion is likely what's confusing everyone else.

Since Ace, nothing in my life has made any sense. I feel like

I'm a pinball bouncing off the bumpers and being flipped back into the game, never getting the chance to stop and rest anywhere. At some point, it will be game over, and I'll fall through the gap at the bottom.

Maybe it's me who needs to find the balance. Maybe it's me who's out of alignment.

I run my finger down the side of a gleaming straight razor, cursing when the sharp blade kisses my skin, causing blood to quickly pool on the surface.

"Is everything okay, Jaine?"

"It's fine. I've cut my finger, but it's only a scratch."

Irish doesn't knock. He walks straight in, wearing nothing but a small white towel tied loosely around his slim hips. Beads of moisture cling to his inked skin, suggesting he's not even bothered to dry himself. I watch him lift my finger to inspect it, gasping when he sucks the bloody tip into his mouth.

I stare at him. He's still in his unhinged state.

My eyes drift unwittingly over his body. He's truly beautiful. Unlike Eoin, who has the ripped, veiny body of a cage fighter, Irish has the body of a god. Everything is in proportion and tweaked to perfection. Maybe Dylan's right. Maybe I've been wrong all along. Maybe it isn't Eoin who's the vain brother.

Maybe it's Padraig.

Normally he'd comment and make a joke about me blatantly admiring him, but he doesn't because he hasn't reverted back to his true self yet. Or maybe this is his true self. Maybe the other has been the smokescreen all along.

He's currently feasting on my blood. Do I like it? The wetness pooling between my legs suggests that I do. My arousal increases at the thought of tasting his too.

As if he can read my mind, he takes the blade and nicks his thumb. Then pressing it against my mouth, he drags it roughly across. My tongue flicks out to lick the surface of my now bloody lips, and as they part, he thrusts his thumb inside my mouth.

I groan as his metallic flavor hits. I suck hard. An action that produces a growl deep in his throat. What are we doing?

It's wrong. *It's right.*

He yanks my finger from his mouth before slowly drawing the bloody tip down his chest. Marking him. Staining him. Then he does the same to me with his before pressing both together.

Joined by fate. Sealed by blood.

Fisting my hair, he pulls my head back. He stares down at me, and I stare back. He's back. The unhinged look is gone. Can he see the total adoration? Does he realize how much I fucking love him? How everything I've ever done was for him?

I welcome his mouth as it connects with mine, his tongue thrusting deep. The taste of the fusion of our blood floods my senses.

He deepens the kiss as he turns and lifts me so I'm sitting on the counter, and then his mouth drops to my neck. He sucks hard on the tender flesh. I know exactly what he's doing. He's branding me in the same way his brother did.

I groan my approval as my hands tangle in his hair, my hips instinctively rising off the surface.

Wanting more. Needing more. Needing him.

I want him to fuck me. He knows I do, but we both know we won't go there.

I break our kiss, and he growls in warning when I bite down hard on his neck. It's a throaty sound that threatens domination. It's a feral sound that promises control. Does he not know that I'd already do anything for him?

"Look at us, Jaine." He runs his nose slowly up mine, his voice soft and sensual. I turn my head and stare at us in the full-length mirror.

"We look so fucking perfect together."

He's right. We do.

His lips find mine once more. I feel it—the connection. I've always known that Irish is my soul mate. I've never once doubted it. I want him to tell me that he loves me because the more I think I heard it at the church, the more convinced I am that I didn't.

How can we have a future if he doesn't love me?

CHAPTER SIXTY-ONE

PADRAIG

The Hudson Dusters' HQ, Manhattan, New York

JAINE AND I ALMOST FUCKED YESTERDAY. SHE FUCKED MY BROTHER the day before. What happens now?

It's the first meeting we'll all have attended since the fire at the church.

Has she been with him since yesterday? I have no idea. It's none of my business. She and I aren't an item, but then neither are they. If they were officially back together, we'd all have heard about it by now. My wife is dead. She's currently being turned into human soup, which is no more than she deserves. I'm a widower.

All three of us are single.

I gave him my blessing, though. What sort of a low-life brother does that make me that I would still then pursue the love of his life?

She was the love of mine first.

He stares at me across the meeting room table. His neck is bruised like mine. Everyone present will know the female responsible for his claiming was Jaine. For mine, they may well think the same thing.

They suspect. He knows.

If he's in any shadow of a doubt, he'll realize the moment she enters the room.

We hear her arrive. We then hear the mumble of conversation as she talks with Candice.

The door opens moments later, and her eyes connect with mine. She's wearing a navy pantsuit which perfectly flatters her straight-up-and-down shape. I thought she may have worn a complementary scarf today, but she hasn't. She's hiding nothing.

Her lips curve upwards as my gaze drops to her throat. It's a movement that's barely noticeable, but I saw it.

She stands while everyone inspects her to see if she's any worse for wear after being buried alive before being dug dead from the ground.

Everyone knows what she did. That she entered a situation there was no coming back from. At the time, it suited her just fine because she didn't want to come back.

In the end, her working in cahoots with Nathan Hawke saw a trafficking ring halted, a rogue MC in Nevada brought to its knees, my traitorous wife's life terminated, and my brother-in-law sent down. Countless members of his nameless organization and their Colombian sidekicks are also now behind bars.

All of that, thanks to Jaine.

Once Luc is dead, which I'm sure won't be too long given the plethora of enemies he has on the inside, the Ruocco estate will pass to me as the only surviving family member. When that happens, it would be my intention to pass it straight to Finian and JJ. I have enough personal wealth. I don't need any more.

Dare I hope for any more offspring when I'd only ever want them with her?

"It's good to see you, Jaine." Da greets her in his usual manner as she takes her seat to the right of Eoin.

"You too, Fergal."

"Jaine, I don't know what to… how to…." It's not like my da to be lost for words, but he is. And it's because he feels emotional.

What she did for the family went above and beyond.

Everyone around the table now knows just how much she loves me and my brother, not that it was ever in dispute.

There's just that one remaining niggle for me. That after everything she and I went through together, why she did what she did three years ago? If she'd fight tooth and nail for me, if she'd die for me, then why walk away without a backward glance or a second thought?

Dylan says I need to speak to Eoin about that. I intend to do just that right after this meeting.

"There's no need to say anything, Fergal. It's over. Sophia's dead and Luciano's hopefully imminent demise will mark the end of the toxic Ruocco line. It won't bring Ace, Raf, or Abel back, but at least we've delivered justice on their behalf. I've spoken with the others, more importantly, Rodolfo. As much as he would have liked to have played a part in Luc's ending, he appreciates that this is the best way forward for all concerned parties. He's only grateful he can finally lay Raf's ghost to rest."

We all show our respect to our fallen brothers with a short silence.

"You clearly had cause for celebration, Jaine," Aidan says it how it is, which is what he always does, as he raises an eyebrow at the marks on her neck.

She doesn't respond.

He then smirks between Eoin and me without saying another

word. Jessie whispers in Dylan's ear, but he just looks worried. Cillian and Da remain silent.

Eoin stares at me. He's aware he didn't inflict all those marks on her throat. He knows the other person to do so was me.

It's difficult reading his expression. Guilt. Jealousy. A combination of both.

There's one that's notably missing. Rage.

Why is that? I suspect I'm about to find out.

"TAKE A SEAT, PADRAIG."

He's looking out the window at the best view the building has to offer. It's my thinking that having the best view, the best office, and the best of everything no longer matters to him. The only thing that does is Jaine.

I take a seat on one of the tan-colored executive chairs. Both have been pulled out from under the desk, so I suspect Dylan will join us shortly.

My eyes drift to the leather-topped surface. By all accounts, the desk was a gift from Jaine. She insisted that the previous one was a health hazard due to the number of times Eoin had fucked Candice over it. She then proceeded to have it chucked on a bonfire.

I can only imagine my elder brother's outrage at the time. He loved that desk. It turns out he loves Jaine more.

Nothing else has changed in here. Same white background. Same wooden case filled with tomes on finance and economics. Same black and white images of our ancestors lining the walls. Past Dusters. At some point, my image will hang beside theirs, as will my son's.

Mine and Jaine's son. And little JJ's, too, of course.

I stare at Eoin. He's lost weight. He's clearly been working out a lot more than usual. The less polished look suits him. It makes him look more human.

Is he deliberately not talking, or is he contemplating what it is he has to say? We both know this conversation is well overdue, and there's a reason for that. A reason I suspect I'm not going to like.

"Sorry, I'm late." Dylan enters the room, closing the door behind him. He looks pale. Like he's worried something's about to kick off. He takes the seat beside me and fidgets.

Eoin eventually turns around, his gaze dropping to my neck. He'll think Jaine and I fucked. Will he mention the bruising? There seems little point, given he knows who inflicted it.

He takes a seat and then looks between Dylan and me. He's lost the air of arrogance that he used to wear like a badge of honor.

Jaine's changed him.

Normally, he'd start talking and expect everyone just to listen without interruption. This time, he's actually considering what he's going to say. Then again, maybe that has nothing to do with Jaine and more to do with the matter at hand.

"I need to apologize, Paddy."

I stare at him. There's only one thing he would have to apologize over. Jaine.

"Go on."

"The first apology is on behalf of the whole family." He pauses. "When you were entered into the marriage with Sophia, I was asked to pay Jaine a visit."

My blood runs cold in my veins because I now know what he's going to say. I'm finally going to get an answer to my niggle.

"We had no idea who she was or that you shared a past with her. All we knew was that you were in love with her, and she you. Da signed the contract with Luciano before we even knew about her. If it hadn't been entered into, we could have considered her, but it had. There was no going back at that stage. Any subsequent indication that you were involved with someone else would have resulted in war. You know that. You would have had a price on your head, and so would Jaine."

"What did the family do, Eoin?"

"Da asked me to warn her off."

I close my eyes, then slowly reopen them. "What did you ask of her?"

"To cease all communication with you until your marriage to Sophia had taken place."

I swallow as I try to digest what it is that he's saying. It tastes bitter. He told her not to speak to me for two years. Two fucking years.

"So, she lied when she told me that she didn't love me. She said it so I'd walk away, and then, to make doubly sure I knew there was no future for us, she left town."

"Yes. She stood her ground quite determinedly. She didn't want to let you go. In the end, I had to use her love for you against her."

"In what way?"

"I suggested that if you thought there was any hope of a future for you and her, you might refuse to go through with the arranged marriage, that it could then see you come to harm having disrespected the Sicilians."

"So, she backed down and returned to Rising. Where she'd be out of sight and mind."

"Yes. She did it for you, Padraig. Everything Jaine ever did, she did for you. I need you to know that."

"She was pregnant with my child."

"No one was aware of that. Even Jaine herself didn't know who the father was. Not until after Finian was born."

"And why would she have bothered to find out when you ran her out of town? She had my baby in her fucking belly!"

"I'm sorry, Paddy."

"You're sorry." I snort. "But my loss was your gain, wasn't it, brother? You got to marry the love of *my* life, and then you fell in love with her."

An even more pronounced delay. I know this is now the piece de resistance.

"Tell me."

He glances at Dylan and then looks back at me. "When you told me about Jaine, about you messaging her when she was headed to Nevada…."

"When she was about to give birth to my fucking son, you mean?" I interrupt.

He frowns and nods slowly. "I should have allowed you to be open with each other about who you were conversing with."

"And why didn't you, Eoin?"

I close my eyes in disbelief as I wait. Again, I know what he's about to say. Why the fuck didn't I see what was going on right under my nose? He was messaging her. He was talking to her. He even admitted to missing her when she didn't communicate with him.

Because you never expected your own flesh and blood to fuck you over.

"WHY DIDN'T YOU?" I slam my hand down on the leather surface of the desk.

"Because, by then, I wanted her for myself."

And there it is. The truth. The reason he's been trying to push her away. The reason behind my having to deceive her for two years.

The reason my life fucking ended.

"So, having conveniently navigated me into an arranged marriage, you then pursued the love of my life."

I curse the tears that fall. I curse being so fucking emotional at times.

"Every single day, I had to force myself to open my eyes because the only thing I had to look forward to was closing them again. She was my first thought. My last thought. She was my every fucking thing. You took away my reason for living."

"Paddy…"

I stand. "Tomorrow. Eight a.m. The Docks. Bring a Glock."

"Paddy, what are you doing?"

I turn to look at Dylan. "He knew how I felt about Jaine, but that didn't stop him from removing her from my life so he could pursue her for himself. Tell me I'm wrong."

"Paddy, it wasn't like that."

"TELL ME I'M FUCKING WRONG!"

Silence.

I look at Eoin once more. "Tomorrow. Be there. If you're not, I'll come looking for you."

CHAPTER SIXTY-TWO

JAINE

The O'Connell Home, Darling, New York

"What do you mean he's challenged him to a duel? Which century are we goddamn living in?"

I've only just put my babies to bed. Somehow, Fin got hold of some gum which he then managed to get all tangled up in JJ's black curls. I had no option but to cut some of them off. JJ cried his little heart out when he saw them all stuck together in a little pile. His pitiful tears saw me reduced to tears too. I rest my head back against the sofa.

"Just what I said, Jaine. Eoin told him what happened. About the family effectively running you out of town. About him pursuing you with no thought of him."

"I'm not sure what Eoin expected. Irish and I lost each other for three years as a result, and he also missed out on the first two years of his son's life."

"I know, Jaine, but we can't go back and change things. I'm sure the family and Eoin would if they could. I'm sure there are things all of us would do differently had we the opportunity of a do-over."

He's right. I have ten years' worth of regrets with Ace. Twelve years with Irish. And with Eoin, it's a daily event.

"Then I think it's time for the next reveal, Dylan."

"What do you mean?"

"The only bullet that will be fired tomorrow is an engraved one."

The Docks, Hudson Yards

I don't arrive on the hog this time. Being discreet is key, and a Harley is not in any way discreet. I also needed to bring a rifle. It's a new one, and it fires with the most precision.

I can't afford to miss.

It feels strange turning up as my alter-ego, but to perform as The Exterminator, I need to dress for the part. Because that's what it is —a part I choose to play.

As Dylan rightly says, we all have two sides. It's time for Eoin to meet the other side of me.

The last time I was here, we fucked outside in the rain after I found out one more thing about him. That he's an experienced cage fighter. I want to see him fight. I want to see him lose control. Then I want him to fuck me into oblivion while he's all bloody and sweaty.

There are still so many things I don't know about him. I told him everything there was to know about me bar this one reveal, but it's almost like he never expected us to go the distance, so he never saw any point in revealing any more than he had to. That the count-down would begin, and the final bell would ring time on what we shared as soon as Irish returned.

Today I'm just here to stop them from killing each other.

It's still dark. I'm two hours ahead of schedule, but I figured it was better to be too early than too late. I stick in one ear pod, pull on my balaclava, then grab the bag that contains my rifle from the back seat.

With a nod at Dylan, I alight the vehicle. He's the only O'Connell who can contact me today. I still haven't given Eoin or Irish my new number. There seems little point, giving I seldom use my burner. These days, The Exterminator only surfaces for family occasions.

Dylan's given me the heads up on where the gunfight will take place. It's exactly where Liam parked up that first time.

With my bag thrown over my shoulder, I skulk to the container he told me to use as my nest. I could shoot from a standing position, but the accuracy is greater when I use a stand. I'm not aiming at a skull today. I'm aiming at a much smaller target—another weapon.

Once I get everything positioned, I lie on my stomach, poised and ready. It's freezing, the breeze being carried off the river making it even more so. I know my body will acclimatize soon. It always does.

The conditions aren't favorable, so they make it difficult to see into the distance. All I can do is stare at the containers that surround me. I count them. I try to read the worn adverts—anything to pass the time.

The first car pulls up around an hour and a half later.

I recognize the plate immediately. It's the SUV Dec usually drives. I suspect he won't be doing so today. I watch as it pulls into the clearing. I then watch as Eoin steps out of the driver's door.

Even from here, I can feel his inner turmoil. He did wrong. He betrayed his brother, but as Dylan says, we can't undo the past. In as many months, he's saved Padraig's life twice and mine four times. I know that sort of payback doesn't automatically heal the festering wound of disrespect, but after what I put him through, he's paid his dues. To me, at least. I need to explain that to Irish.

I didn't make it easy for Eoin to fall in love with me, the same as he didn't make it easy for me to fall in love with him. It happened despite the obstacles we set for each other, not because of them. Subconsciously, have we both continued to fight our emotions?

Maybe it's not something you need for balance, but someone.

I watch as he disappears from view. I check my watch. Seven-forty-five a.m.

Not five minutes later, the second vehicle pulls up. Time passes. Is Irish regretting his impulsiveness? Is he having second thoughts?

I watch as he steps out of the vehicle. It's his other side that's with us today. I know immediately that he's not having second thoughts because I can instantly feel his rage. Dylan's right. He is bloodthirsty, and that's exactly what he's baying for today. He wants to spill his own brother's blood. That's what I need to stop from happening.

The time counts down. I know they won't start early. I know they won't begin late. I know the battle will commence at precisely eight a.m.

CHAPTER SIXTY-THREE

JAINE

The Docks, Hudson Yards

I WATCH EOIN COME BACK INTO VIEW.

Rubbing my hands together to get the blood circulating, I place my finger back over the trigger. I'm relieved when they stand side on to me. Had one given me their back, I would have had to move. That would have resulted in me having to change position, which could have led to me being too late to save the day.

I need to get their attention. I need to reveal myself. Then I need to talk some sense into them. Because I know Eoin won't offer any further reasoning for something he already feels so much guilt over. I also know that, in his current mindset, Padraig won't be prepared to listen anyway.

There's less than a minute to go. They stand facing each other. I watch as they both reach for their weapons. As soon as I see the sun glint off the partially raised Glock, I pull the trigger.

Mine is the only shot fired.

The gun flies from Irish's hand. I knew I had to take out his weapon. I knew Eoin would never have pulled his trigger.

I can feel Irish's anger envelop me from where I'm lying on the container top. He knows who made him lose the weapon. Right now, he'll feel even more betrayed. He'll think I chose Eoin over him.

I didn't. I chose neither.

I just stopped him from making the biggest mistake of his life. None of us need any more regrets.

I'm done hiding. I stand. Both sets of eyes swing toward me, but no one says anything. Only one of them knows who hides behind the disguise. The other will know imminently.

I pack my weapon away, sling the bag over my shoulder, then make my way down the metal rungs on the side of the container.

My feet hit the uneven surface of the ground. I'm nervous. I've interfered in something that was none of my business. I'm not in a relationship with either of them. I had no right. But if I hadn't, then Eoin would have ended up dead.

I turn the corner and walk into the clearing. I stand in my black combats and puffer jacket with my balaclava still in place.

I'm silent. To speak, I need to be Jaine Jones. Right now, I'm not. I need to remove my mask first. My heart pounds in my chest at the thought of it. The only person I've ever told willingly was Delaney. He was there when The Exterminator was born.

Irish, Ace, and Duke found out during the Bratva situation. Dylan found out, as I needed intel on Lebedev. Roisin found out when she saw the engraved bullet amongst Molly's liquified brains.

For some reason, to whip my mask off feels like a vanity in some way. Like it's some proud *ta-da* moment. It's not. I'd much rather not.

"Show him."

Irish's alter-ego is still in place, and his authoritative tone is making me wet. I look at him as he stands in black jeans and a long-sleeved black t-shirt.

I walk toward Eoin, taking in his dark blue jeans and leather jacket. I stop in front of him. Can he tell it's me under this guise?

"Take off the mask." Irish is talking to Eoin now. Eoin turns to look at him, and Irish nods. He then turns to look at me, and I nod.

The moment he reaches out, his spicy cologne envelops me. I have to hold back the groan as our physical connection fires up.

He must know now, surely.

I close my eyes as the balaclava is yanked over my head. I've never felt so exposed as I do right now. I keep them closed. I can't look at him.

What is he thinking? Is he hurt that I never told him? Angry?

"Jaine." My name is barely a whisper. I feel the tear roll down my cheek as I swallow thickly. I'm not even sure why I'm crying.

"Jaine, look at me."

I stand with my secret laid bare. The fact that I'm a mass murderer. The fact that I'm a serial killer. The fact that I've killed more people than he has.

But not as many as Irish.

I slowly open my eyes and look at him.

Betrayal. That's the only word that can describe the look he's wearing.

His forehead mars. "Why didn't you tell me?"

"I thought you'd treat me differently. That you'd wrap me up in even more cotton wool because you'd see me as some sort of trophy."

"Is that what you truly think of me?" His look of betrayal changes to one of hurt.

"I don't know what to think of you, Eoin. You've kept so much of yourself hidden from me that I'm not sure I know you at all."

We stare at each other, only breaking eye contact when I turn to look at Irish. His unhinged look has gone. He's back. I know the question he's going to ask before he even opens his mouth.

"Why did you shoot my gun away? Why not his?"

"Because he would never have pulled the trigger, and you would have. And you can't make life-changing decisions when you're missing most of the facts."

"So, tell me?"

Where to even begin?

"Eoin didn't want to marry me. I coerced it, so he had no choice. For the first time in my life, I wanted revenge. I set out to ruin his life because he ruined yours. In the end, I realized I was using him as a scapegoat because I needed someone to hold accountable for everything that had gone wrong. It was your parents who made the final decision when it came to your arranged marriage, Roisin mostly. She admitted as much. It wasn't Eoin. Yes, he should never have kept us apart. It was an infatuation, and he behaved selfishly. But if I'd known it was you I was messaging, that it wasn't Dylan, I would have put a stop to it. So, in the end, I'm glad it never came out because I needed you as much as you needed me, and we gained an extra year because of what he did."

"But you fell in love with him, darlin'."

"I fought it every step of the way. I never wanted that to happen. Eoin didn't either."

"So, you fought it, and then, what? You just gave in? Knowing how I felt about you? How you felt about me? Why, Jaine?"

Twenty generic words.

"You gave us your blessing, Irish," I whisper the words.

He frowns as he slowly shakes his head. "I would never have given my blessing to you being with my brother, darlin'."

It's good to be back on my old number.

That's when the realization hits me. He never gave his blessing. Someone else did. And I know exactly who it was.

"You're going to need to choose, darlin'. It's the only way to settle this once and for all. You need to choose between me and Eoin."

I frown at him. He's issuing ultimatums, but does he even love me?

I turn, and I walk away. Neither tries to stop me. There's no point. Everything that needed to be said has been. Both are trying to digest what's just gone down. That now makes three of us.

Walking, I message Dylan to ask him to pick me up. He calls me straight away.

"I'm already at the pick-up point, Jaine. I've just had Nate on the phone. He's been trying to get hold of you. Luciano's on the run. He's escaped."

CHAPTER SIXTY-FOUR

PADRAIG

Padraig's Apartment, Hudson Yards, New York

JAINE VANISHED WITHOUT A TRACE A WEEK AGO.

She left the docks that day, and we didn't see her again. Well, Duke knew her approximate whereabouts, and Dylan did too, but both were sworn to secrecy.

Ma and Duke mind the kids between them, with the rest of us helping out where we can while trying to locate Luciano.

Did Jaine leave because I threatened to kill Eoin, or did she leave because Luc managed to escape Rikers? I think it was a combination of the two.

She knew she would be Luc's primary target. If she hadn't left, she would have brought the trouble back to a doorstep that housed her kids. I'm sure my putting her on the spot also caused her to run.

You need to choose between me and Eoin. She'll have needed time to think.

Having now had time to reflect, I realize the arranged marriage was the catalyst that led to me simply existing. My entire family was responsible for signing me up for that all because I was going around in circles searching for a replacement for a girl they didn't even know existed.

Mistakes were made on both sides. Mistakes that will never be repeated. Lessons have been learned.

The bottom line is I would have ended up in exactly the same place at exactly the same time after the initial contract was agreed to. While some of us nearly died as a result of our signing on the Sicilian dotted line, in the end, we didn't. We lived to tell the tale. We didn't lose out. I didn't lose out.

Jaine did. Ace did. He lost his life. She lost Ace.

Her jealousy made her reactive, and she said something she shouldn't have to the Ruoccos, all because she was in love with me. Ace paid the ultimate price for her overreaction.

Eoin and I are back on speaking terms, but only after I sought the assurances I needed. It's been confirmed that he was planning on marrying Molly until Jaine threw her last-minute curveball. Once they had taken the vows together, she then went on a crusade on my behalf to deliver karma personally.

He didn't want to marry her. He reluctantly agreed to do so to protect my son. He had been infatuated with her, but in close proximity, he fell in love with her. I can't fault him for that. I can't blame him, either. We don't get to choose who we fall in love with. She then proceeded to love him straight back.

Would they have stayed together after Jaine delivered her payback?

No, they wouldn't have because her conscience and loyalty to me would never have allowed it. The only reason Jaine entered into a relationship with my brother was because she thought I condoned it. That I gave their union my blessing.

I didn't.

It's up to Jaine how she chooses to punish the sender of the twenty-word message. She knows who it is. All three of us do. The guilty party will have to wait for Jaine to return to New York before they're served their comeuppance. They're currently not aware she knows. That's Jaine's reveal.

It wasn't Jaine's fault. It wasn't Eoin's fault. It's a simple case of the truth coming out after even more lies.

Eoin went on to save Fin's life, resulting in him almost losing his own, and he's since saved Jaine's life four times and my own twice.

I owe him.

His betrayal saw me turn reactive. A reaction that would have led to me doing something I would have regretted for the rest of my life. Killing my own brother. I'm grateful Jaine intervened, even though I was pissed off with her at the time.

Jaine loves me. I love her.

Jaine loves Eoin. He loves her.

She can't choose either of us while she's on the run.

"Any news, Dyl?" I rest my head back against the sectional as I answer my vibrating phone.

"Nothing. Nate is starting to get agitated. The longer Luc is on the run, the more opportunity he has to set up something new. The risk to Jaine is also increasing daily."

"Has he got any suggestions?"

"Yes, but she's not going to like it."

"Then we don't tell her."

"Do you think more lies and deceit are the answer?"

"I'll do whatever it takes to draw a line under it while keeping her alive, Dylan. While Luc's on the run, that means Jaine has no choice but to be. What's Nate suggesting?"

"That you and Eoin go after her."

I frown at the phone. "Surely that will just see her run faster and further? In her mind, we'll be exposed if we're anywhere near her."

"As you say, she can't run if she doesn't know."

"When she sees us, it'll be the first thing she does."

"By then, you'll be close enough to follow. Nate thinks Luc is waiting for the Dusters to make a move. That it's only a matter of time before either you or Eoin reach out to her. He's as sure as he can be that if you follow her, Luc will follow you. That you'll lead him straight to the prize."

Nate's got a point.

"Let me have a word with Eoin and see what he thinks. Where is she?"

"She's on the west coast, trying to lure Luc as far away from New York as possible. If he wants her, he's going to have to catch her. She knows he'll go after her, so she's deliberately trying to steer clear of the places and people she cares about. I think she's hoping she'll spot him first. Her only problem will be if he's not alone."

"The west coast is a large area. It'll be like trying to find a needle in a haystack."

"Apart from tomorrow. We suspect she'll be in Rising."

"How do you know?"

"It's her pop's birthday."

"Then we're flying out there today."

Rising Cemetery, Rising, California

Eoin and I haven't said much on the way here.

While we're on speaking terms, I'm not sure our relationship will ever recover. He may have saved my life, but in our world, betrayal is typically met with a death sentence, no matter how much you repent. No number of rights will correct that sort of wrong.

He willingly went after the love of my life. The burden of guilt he carries is a testament to the fact that he knows what he did was wrong. I would never have done the same to him. Jaine was right. Having committed the greatest outlaw sin, he wouldn't have pulled the trigger on me.

We flew into LAX yesterday, stayed overnight at an airport hotel, hired an SUV, and headed straight for Rising this morning while it was still dark. We can't take the chance of missing Jaine.

I glance out the window, but it's too dark to see anything vaguely familiar. I've only been to Rising twice. Once during the Bratva ordeal and the second time when Jaine buried her pop.

Dawn is finally starting to break when I recognize the grey stone pillars in the distance. I'm hit by a melancholy moment when I think of Ace, who's also now buried here.

He was a good man—trustworthy and kind. The latter is an adjective not used to describe many in our world. He had a good heart. A big heart. And little JJ is shaping up to be just like him. I'm glad Jaine was given him as a blessing. A part of Ace that she got to keep.

A part that she will protect no matter what hence why she's been on the run for a week.

I glance at Eoin as he slows down the vehicle to take the turn. JJ thinks of him as his da. The little lad cries when Eoin's not there to put him in the bath or cuddle him when upset. How can I take that away from him when he's already lost one da?

Tears prick my eyes. As much as we both love the same woman, there's way more to it than just the emotion itself. Whatever decision Jaine makes will impact so many lives.

If she doesn't choose me, then I will forever remain alone because there is no one for me but her. I'll pine from afar as I have these past twelve years. I'll just carry on existing. I've already provided my parents with a grandson. I've done my Duster duty. Nothing more is expected of me now.

As the future Da Duster, Eoin won't be able to remain alone. Every da needs his ma.

He'll have no choice but to take a second wife. He'll also have to produce heirs. If Jaine doesn't pick him, he'll have to marry someone he doesn't love, just like I had to marry Sophia.

How can I expect him to do something that, in the end, I refused to accept for myself?

He won't argue like I did. He'll accept his lot because it's what's expected of him. It's just part of the role he was born into. A box on an endless list he needs to checkmark before he's awarded the grand title of Da Duster.

"Take this little road here, and then we'll park up." I point it out. "The plot itself is the one farthest from the entrance."

He nods silently and does as I've asked. We then pull up and wait. We'll hear her before we see her, I'm sure.

CHAPTER SIXTY-FIVE

JAINE

Rising Cemetery, Rising, California

NIGHT IS RELEASING ITS HOLD ON THE SKY, ALLOWING DAY'S vibrant shades of red and orange to finally streak through. I take in the overhanging black wrought ironwork twisted to say *Rising Cemetery* as I guide Ace's hog through the now all-too-familiar entrance.

It's Pop's birthday. He would have been sixty-two years old. I miss him. I miss Ace. But given that I'm currently on the run, I'm missing a lot of people.

My babies.

A week feels like a year. Children change daily at their ages. I'm missing out on so much. *Stop being selfish, Jaine. Look at everything Irish missed out on. Look at everything Ace is missing out on.*

I notice the parked-up SUV on my way down to the plot. My

gut is telling me it's safe. I want Luciano Ruocco to find me. Just not today.

Maybe it's someone else who's visiting their deceased loved ones before they have to hightail it out of dodge, leaving a trail of biker breadcrumbs for a Sicilian vulture in their wake. Maybe they're unable to spend any time with their living loved ones either.

Why am I running? I can't stay at the O'Connell house and bring trouble to their doorstep. Not with my kids living there. I'm the target. Even more so now. I hope Luc finds me soon because I won't rest until he's dead.

I promised Nate he could have first dibs, but the legal system failed me. He got out. And like an injured animal, he'll be even more unpredictable now. He'll also know that I got out too. That I was dug out of the suffocating hole in the ground he buried me in to die. He'll know now who exposed him. And given that she's vanished off the face of the earth, he'll suspect I'm also responsible for the demise of his baby sister.

I'm not. Her loving husband delivered her comeuppance.

I pull up the hog and dismount. I spoke to Father Reynolds in advance. The flowers I requested have already been placed on Pop's grave.

I pull the hand-written letter from my jacket pocket and lean it against the headstone. It doesn't contain anything other than a few heartfelt words telling him how much I love and miss him and how sorry I am for leaving him behind when I ran for ten years.

He may not have been my biological daddy, but he was there for me after my momma died and raised me as if I were his own.

He brought me here. To Rising. To Jason Steele. Tears prick my eyes as I turn to Ace's grave—my best friend. I love him. I will always love him.

And then I sit cross-legged on the ground. I tell them about Fin and JJ. I laugh. I cry. Then I reminisce while taking in the uninterrupted views over Rising.

I try not to feel sorry for myself as today's not about me, but it's hard not to. Two loved ones are in the cold, unforgiving ground, and the others are thousands of miles away. Loved ones I may or may not ever see again.

I'm not sure how long passes. When you have nowhere to go and nowhere to be, does time really matter?

I'm just saying my goodbyes and standing to leave when I sense them approaching from behind. I know who it is. I can *feel* them. I realize then that I do share a connection with both. It's just that with Irish, it was always embraced. With Eoin, it was always rejected.

By me? By him? By both of us?

If I'd allowed Irish to end Eoin's life, I know he would also have ended his own because he'd never have gotten over it. No matter how often he washed his hands, the stain of his brother's blood would have always been visible.

The three men I love are in the same place for the first time.

"What are you doing here?" I don't turn around. My tone isn't welcoming because they shouldn't be here. I'm on the run to keep everyone safe, including them.

Do they not remember what happened when I thought they'd perished last time around? I lost the will to live.

"We needed to see you, Jaine. To make sure..." Eoin doesn't know what to say. I turn around slowly to take them in. Irish was baying for his blood the last time I saw them together.

I look at the eldest Duster. He looks tired, defeated almost. My eyes trail up his exposed arms in his fitted white t-shirt. I'm not sure if arms can ever be defined as good-looking, but Eoin's are.

My gaze then drifts to connect with eyes of sparkling blue—my Irish. I'm about to speak, but he gets in there first.

"We were just passing by. We thought maybe you could offer to show us around your hometown, darlin'." He shoots me his winning smile.

"No one ever just passes by Rising, Irish."

He shrugs. "We got a bit lost and ended up here. Eoin's rubbish at map reading, you see. That's why he has to rely on Dec taking him everywhere."

Eoin draws him a glare. I can't stop my lips from curving upward.

Irish pounces on my reaction, his smile widening further. "What do you say, Jaine? We can tell you what's been happening back home as you show us around."

I know I shouldn't. I know it's too dangerous, but I've missed them. I nod reluctantly. "Only if you agree to leave town before sundown."

"Agreed." I stare at Eoin, looking for any signs that he's lying to me. He's not.

"I'll need to drop the hog off at the house. I can't leave it here in case it's seen. If anything happens…." I feel myself tearing up at the thought of Ace's beloved ride being crushed.

"Then let's take it to the house."

I nod once more.

"Can I just…?" I stare at Irish as he motions his head in the direction of Ace's grave. I step aside and let him approach. He reads the words aloud.

"Husband. Father. Son. Friend. Biker."

Tears prick my eyes. I walk away to give him some privacy. Irish knew Ace. It's only right that I allow him time with him without eavesdropping on his conversation.

I'm not alone for long.

"It's a pretty view."

I nod. "Everything you can see in front of you is Rising. My pop would have loved this view. It's why I picked it. Ace loved it too."

A sob of self-pity escapes me. I welcome his strong arms as they wrap around me, the scent of his spicy cologne offering me its own blanket of comfort.

"I've missed you, Miss Jones."

I sob-chuckle at his familiar pompous tone. "I've missed you too, Mr. O'Connell."

I look up at him, and he presses a kiss against my forehead before raising one eyebrow. "You must be feeling generous today. It's definitely a marked improvement on *asshole*."

I chuckle again as he pulls me closer grateful that I no longer feel so alone.

Jaine's Home, Rising, California

I'm not sure how I feel about bringing Eoin and Irish to my childhood home. I've always kept Rising separate from New York. I'm a different person there. Here, I'm just plain Jaine Jones—a local girl who grew up and married a local boy.

Ace's old lady. Ace's wife. Ace's widow.

My family home is nothing like the O'Connell's, but then their mansion-like property would look completely out of place in this vast space.

I park Ace's hog where he always used to. My crushed Softail is right beside it. The metal may be twisted, but it still has a heart, so there it will forever remain.

My eyes graze over the ranch-style property's white walls and dark, red-tiled roof. It's set in its own fifty acres of nothingness, and right now, every inch is covered in the white poppies that grow wild in these parts, their sweet floral notes filling the air.

The white-painted porch still has the same rocking chair my pop used to sit in alongside the little two-seater swing, all fenced off by the same old wooden railing.

I step down from the hog and look around, trying to see it through their eyes. The place I lived from ages seven to eighteen and the place I ran to when I was given no choice but to leave New York.

I watch them step out of the SUV to take in their surroundings.

Irish inhales, then nods like he's just discovered some great secret.

"This is your scent, Jaine. I always thought it was a perfume or lotion, but it's this. It surrounds you wherever you go."

Tears prick my eyes. "It's because it's in my blood. Rising is my home. It always will be."

"Finian wasn't born here?"

I shake my head. "He was born in Nevada, in the same hospital I was born in, and in the same hospital, Raf Flores died in. The circle of life took place that night. They crossed over at exactly the same time. For that reason, I like to think a little bit of Raf lives on in Fin."

"And JJ?" Eoin looks at me. He adores my little boy. I love that he's so curious about him.

"JJ was born in Rising. In the same medical center that his daddy was born in, and the same one that he…." I swallow thickly. I don't finish the sentence. There's no need. We all know what happened to Ace. "I'll show you on the way to the clubhouse. I need to go there today. I promised Clay I would make a start clearing Ace's room… if that's okay."

"What are those tracks, Jaine? All of those crisscrossing the land?" Irish immediately deviates away from the melancholy moment. He points at the one nearest the house.

I smile as I'm suddenly flooded with memories. "Ace and I made those. The grass was stomped down over the years by our ever-growing feet. It never did grow back."

Once we reach the house, I unlock and open the door. Nothing's changed. It's all still as it was just before I left for New York. Time has stood still here. I needed it to. The property is clean inside and tidy out. Jethro and his wife, Matilda, stop by most days. She's currently heavily pregnant with baby number four.

I watch as they look around the modern white and grey interior, their eyes stopping on the ancient cream leather sofa that I'll never part with and which looks so out of place.

I guess, in some ways, I'm welcoming them fully into my life by welcoming them into my childhood home—the place I shared with my pop, and then Ace, and then with my babies.

I watch as Eoin looks at the images of me and Ace. He then moves on to the ones of me as a young girl. Back when I was PJ to everyone who knew me.

I was always PJ to Ace.

Can he see the ten-year gap when I ran out on my best friend? Because it's all I see every time I look at those images.

I walk across to where Irish is looking at all the photos of Fin. I can see the tears shining in his eyes as he thinks about everything he missed out on. "Can I have a few, darlin'? I… don't have any." He lets out a sob—my beautiful, emotional Irish.

I take his hand in mine and squeeze it. Then I motion my head for him to follow me.

As soon as we step inside, he looks around the little bedroom in its shades of blue with its childlike motorcycle theme going on. He already knows it's Fin's room. I watch as he walks around. Touching things. Picking them up. Smelling them. Of course, I feel guilty. I will always feel guilty.

I open the little blue wardrobe and take out the storage box. I place it on top of the matching chest of drawers and lift the lid.

I struggle to speak at first as my own emotions get the better of me. "Every picture and video ever taken of Fin was always duplicated. They're all in here. All of his firsts are also in here. His first blanket. His first toy. His first soother. I don't need them. I was there. You weren't, so I saved them all for you. I know it's not the same, but I tried my hardest to capture every memory."

He looks inside the box with tears rolling down his cheeks before pulling me into his arms.

"I'm so fucking sorry, Irish," I sob.

We stand, offering as much comfort to each other as we can. He doesn't speak or acknowledge my apology. I know he still hasn't forgiven me. I'm not sure that he ever will. I did what I thought was best at the time, and sometimes that's all you can do.

I leave him looking through the contents, noticing that my childhood bedroom door is now ajar. I step inside to find Eoin staring out the window. I gaze around the pink-walled room with its four-poster bed and all of its sparkly, feathery, and glittery things going on before walking across to stand beside him.

"I told you I had a pink fluffy bedroom. I wasn't a total tomboy." I smile, but then it fades. "Ace and I never had the heart to take it apart. It held way too many memories. We figured if we ever had a little girl, it would be perfect for her."

I look up at him, and he turns to face me fully, cupping my chin in his strong hand. "You can still have that little girl, Jaine."

I realize now that I want that. I want more children. With Eoin or with Irish? Right now, it doesn't matter. Not when I'm once again living on borrowed time.

"I'd like that," I whisper.

He presses his lips gently against mine. It's a kiss of love.

At least I know Eoin loves me.

CHAPTER SIXTY-SIX

PADRAIG

Jaine's Home, Rising, California

I STARE AT THE BOX OF BABY THINGS.

In many ways, I was lucky. I've only had to live with the regret of not knowing I had a son for a short while. Jaine's had to live with her guilt from the moment he was born.

She's clearly always been thinking of me.

I stare at the first image ever taken.

I remember receiving it moments after Fin entered the world. It's of him and Ace. I smile at the size of the tiny bundle held ever so gently in the arms of the muscular, heavily-inked biker. A mop of black hair peeks out from the top of white swaddling.

I remember feeling jealous at the time. That Ace had everything I ever wanted. Jaine. A son. Ace knew he was mine, but he loved him unconditionally all the same.

I flick through the countless images. There are so many, and all were taken from the second Fin was born until her entire family was plucked from Rising ahead of time.

I gaze out of Fin's bedroom window. Jaine's family home is everything mine isn't.

Peaceful. Tranquil. Secluded.

You can actually hear yourself think because there's no one around for miles. You're surrounded by nothing but open space and fields of wildflowers and poppies. The same poppies that make up the tattoo on her wrist representative of Ace and Rising, contrasted by the circle of four-leaf clovers for me and New York.

Jaine is actually three-sided, not just two like the rest of us.

The images of the young, carefree girl I saw today are reminiscent of the girl I fell in love with at Yale. The Rising girl is different from the strong businesswoman who dominates the legal profession in New York. And then there's The Exterminator.

I take in the small garden and the sparkling water in the swimming pool. She obviously has the property regularly maintained, as it's immaculate. Even though the inside is modern, some of the furniture is ancient. Those will be the sentimental pieces that are held together by memories. Items she'll never be able to bring herself to part with.

And so many photographs.

I'm not sure if Eoin noticed, but I did. The gap in the images of her and Ace. When she went on the run for ten years because she thought he didn't love her. Back when she became my life raft. My sounding board. My confidant.

And I became hers.

I'm not sure why she thought her love for Ace was unrequited. His face is filled with complete adoration for her in every image they're in together, right from when they were in single figures.

He loved her. It shone from him. Not that I'd say that to her now. She's filled with enough regrets as it is.

Over him. Over me. Over Eoin.

She would have traveled between here and New York if Ace were still alive. I'm not sure why she doesn't still consider that. If she and I were together, I would encourage it. I'm a city boy, I always will be. But I'd love to call both places home. Rising is the perfect location to raise a young family.

Would she want that with me? A family? More children?

I leave Fin's room with a smile on my face, a box full of memories in my hands, and for the first in a long-time, actual hope in my heart. It's then I see the other ajar door.

I walk toward it, pausing when I hear Eoin speak.

"You can still have that little girl, Jaine."

"I'd like that."

I step back from the door, suddenly feeling like I'm intruding. I guess Jaine doesn't want a family with me after all. It's Eoin she wants one with.

It was just more foolish hope on my part.

The Angels of Hellfire Clubhouse, Rising, California

Jaine rode shotgun as Eoin drove us to Rising.

They didn't hold hands, but I'm sure the conversation that had taken place back at the house had them itching to be tactile with one other. They couldn't because I was playing third wheel.

She wants to have a child with Eoin. She said as much. A daughter. What happens if they have a son? Will they keep trying?

I'm not sure how I feel. I've become accepting of their love, but talk of them having a family. Does that mean she'd choose him over me?

I know I shouldn't have listened in. You never hear anything good when you eavesdrop, every fool knows that. I should have pushed the door open when I heard him speaking because it wasn't so much what Eoin said that was the problem. It was what Jaine responded with.

I'd like that.

I look out the window. It's a picture postcard pretty little town. The main street comprises a row of shops, local businesses, and a post office. There are, of course, the essential buildings every place needs, no matter the size. A police station, a church, and a school. Jaine points out the medical center where Duke, Ace, and JJ were all born and where Ace sadly passed away.

Aside from houses, there's not much of anything apart from bikers. There are plenty of them around. The main group congregated outside the cigar shop, each sitting astride a gleaming hog.

I immediately recognize the Angels of Hellfire patch on their cuts. It's the same one Jaine's worn on her jacket since she was nineteen.

The bikers stare at us. They won't recognize the vehicle or be able to see their former Prez's old lady through the darkened windows. They're probably wondering who would dare visit their sleepy little town uninvited.

The menace on their faces is to encourage us not to stop. They're telling us that there's nothing to see here, so we might as well keep right on going.

Rather than wait for them to approach or follow us, Jaine motions for Eoin to pull over. When he does, she steps out.

I watch a huge blonde-haired biker walk over to her. I've seen him before. He was there when I killed Sokolov. My eyes drift to his cut. Enforcer.

They embrace, then Jaine motions her head to where we're sitting in the vehicle. He doesn't come over. He nods at her then looks menacingly at us once more.

Eoin and I both stare as she walks back to the SUV. She's dressed head to toe in black leather. It's my guess that we're both thinking the same thing. That she belongs here. That these are her people.

She gets in the vehicle. "Follow Jefferson. He'll lead you to the clubhouse."

WE DIDN'T TALK MUCH AFTER THAT. NOT THAT I CONTRIBUTED much to the conversation before, given the melancholy mood I'd descended into.

Eoin drove while Jaine and I just stared out of our respective windows, taking in the vast expanse of nothingness on the way there. My memories are vague from my previous visit, but it was over three years ago.

I stare at the unattractive black building as we approach. The windows are covered in bulletproof sheet metal, then fitted with bars over the top. Even though it's in the middle of nowhere, everything is fenced off and electrified.

We watch as Jefferson pulls up, then, lowering his feet to the ground, he waves across to another biker with long red hair. He's young. Maybe twenty-one. He lifts a hand in acknowledgment, then jogs across before keying in the code and swinging open the creaking gates.

Eoin lowers his window, and the young lad looks past him to salute Jaine.

"Lincoln." She laughs as Eoin draws him a death glare. He needs to be careful. He has to remember that she wasn't just any old lady to these bikers. She was Ace's wife.

She was *the* old lady.

We park up in the compound. I get out, inhaling the smell of the flowers planted in the several tractor tires scattered around the place.

I raise my face to the sky. It's a pleasant day. Warm and sunny. I take in the group of rowdy children of varying ages playing tag. This will be their life. Their future. All they will ever know. They'll be born bikers, and they'll die bikers. Just like Ace.

No doubt, if Jaine still lived here, Finian would be one of them. I smile at that thought. That my son is half biker. It's then I notice the group of scantily clad females sunbathing on deckchairs and recliners. They're out of sight, but not.

I chuckle to myself. "Are they…"

"The cum sluts," Jaine whispers in my ear before I can even finish my question.

We both laugh as we recall our conversation from way back about the two-legged perks the bikers were rewarded with as part of their remuneration package.

"They're not allowed inside the communal area until after eight p.m. So, they stay in the bedroom area, the kitchen area or they come outside."

"Why eight?"

"That's when the old ladies and the kids need to make tracks. Any old lady here beyond then will likely witness something she'll regret."

"And that is?" Eoin steps out then turns to look at us.

"Her old man fucking a cum slut."

"So, bikers cheat on their wives?" Eoin raises an eyebrow.

"Hedonistic. Promiscuous. Heathens. Those are a few of the choice words your ma uses to refer to our kind. She's mostly right. It's the reason she wanted to keep me away from her two precious sons. She was worried I'd lead you both astray." She smirks until her eyes land on a particular hog, then her good mood evaporates.

"Is there a problem, Jaine?" I frown at her.

She shakes her head. "Lucifer's here, is all."

Eoin and I look at each other. Lucifer is family in a roundabout way. He's Jessie's da, which makes him Dylan's father-in-law. He's also Bailey's da, so he's Paul Delaney's father-in-law too. I've never met him, but I've seen Dylan's wedding video and many images.

"Is that a problem, darlin'?"

She shakes her head to indicate not, but the slowness with which she does says otherwise.

We step inside the clubhouse. It's the same as before, with its dark wood tables, chairs, and dark grey bulletproof bar. As expected, the flow of conversation stops as dozens of eyes turn to take us in.

They look wary rather than threatening. No doubt Jefferson's already told them who has stopped by today. That two of the New York Dusters are in their sleepy little town. Slowly they continue on with what they were doing.

"PJ." Another blonde-haired biker I recognize approaches us, this one wearing a beaming smile. It's Ace's former VP.

"How's things, Clay?"

My eyes drift to his cut. Prez. A promotion he probably didn't want as it saw him losing one of his closest friends.

"We're doing good."

Jaine gets captured in another hug. Then, he stares down at her with his hands on her upper arms. "What you did…"

"Was nothing, Clay. You would have done exactly the same given the opportunity, and you know it." It's clear she doesn't want to talk about it, let alone take any praise for it, especially when, with Luciano on the run, it's not over yet.

She turns to look at me and Eoin. "It's been a while, Clay, but you've met Padraig before when we were dealing with the Bratva situation. I think you may have met Eoin too when we handled the fallout in Nevada after Reaper."

"It's good to see you, fellas, again." Still wearing a beaming smile, he shakes both our hands before turning his attention back to Jaine. "Now, are you sure you want to do this today because you can take as long as you need, PJ? There's no rush."

"It's time, Clay." She exhales sadly. "There are some things I wanted to pick up for JJ, so I may as well get it over with at the same time."

He nods.

"Jaine." We all turn our heads toward the deep Irish voice and take in Liam O'Brien. He's a big man. He's not overweight. It's all muscle. He's not what you would define as handsome. He has a unique something that makes him stand out from the crowd with his angular features, long, greying blonde hair, pale blue eyes, and well-kept beard.

He smiles warmly at her, but she only half smiles back. For some reason, Jaine's unsure of herself around him. Their interaction is awkward. She walks hesitantly over to him, and he wraps his arms around her. She can't wait for the hug to end. He's reluctant to let her go.

There's something going on there. Is she going to tell us what it is?

She looks between us all.

"You've met Eoin before in Nevada, but I don't think you've ever met Padraig." She stares at me, and I look at her questioningly. I can read her like a book. She knows I know something's up, and my brother's no fool. He won't miss it either.

"It's good to see you again, Lucifer." Eoin hugs him and slaps him on the back.

"It's good to meet you at long last, Mr. O'Brien." I smile widely as I greet him in the same way.

"You've been raised well, son. Your manners are impeccable, which is rare in this day and age. Your parents must be proud."

I smile distractedly, only part listening. Jaine nods in Clay's direction, and he nods back. She motions her head for Lucifer, Eoin, and me to follow her. We end up in their council meeting room—a space dominated by a huge walnut table engraved with a skull head with flaming angel wings.

Jaine waits while we all take a seat, but she remains standing. She fidgets as she starts to pace the floor before stopping and looking at me and Eoin.

"As you know, Lucifer is the prez of both the Undertakers and the Sons of Satan." She pauses. "He's also my biological daddy."

And there it is.

CHAPTER SIXTY-SEVEN

JAINE

The Angels of Hellfire Clubhouse, Rising, California

SILENCE. IT'S WHAT I EXPECTED.

"How long have you known?" I turn to look at Eoin. His face doesn't give anything away. Is he as shocked as I was?

"I discovered that my pop wasn't my biological daddy just after Cillian and Sarah's visit to the west coast. I was heavily pregnant at the time. The knowledge wasn't something I felt equipped to handle. Not on top of the ongoing Finian situation." I glance at Irish before turning back to Eoin. "I didn't want to know who my real daddy was. My pop raised me, so to me, it didn't matter if he was blood or not. Ace knew who he was, as did Duke."

"And when did you find out it was Lucifer?" Eoin again.

"On the anniversary of Ace's death. When I came back to Rising several months ago."

He stares at me, guilt crossing his face. He's realized now why I went AWOL. Because what I had to do was personal. My time with Ace. My discussion with Lucifer.

"I know it won't have felt like a year, but it was. I came for an overnight stay and arranged to meet Lucifer at the same time. I knew I had to speak to him. My thanking him for taking a bullet for Ace was long overdue. It turns out Ace assisted with the Nevada situation because he was helping family."

I can feel the tears running down my cheeks, but I ignore them. I will always cry for Ace. If I can't do that in front of these three men, then none of them deserve to be in my life.

"So, Jessie."

"Jessie is my full sister, and Tadgh is my full brother. Bailey and Conor are my half-siblings."

"What… how?"

I turn to Irish. "I haven't asked any questions of Lucifer yet. When I saw him last, there just wasn't time. I was under pressure to return to New York due to the blatant security risks. I knew things would turn messy if I stayed away too long." I pause. "It also didn't seem right somehow. To discuss it in minute detail when Jessie and the others didn't know. Then, with everything going on, it's just never been the right time. Since Lucifer's here today, I've chosen to tell you because I want to tell Jessie. As well as being my sister, she's also my business partner. She has a right to know. I know if I tell her, she'll immediately want to tell Dylan, which is understandable."

"So, Dylan was your brother-in-law twice over." Irish chuckles.

I laugh. "I guess so."

Eoin visibly tenses at the *was* part. He doesn't like to be reminded of the fact that we had to have our own marriage annulled.

"Anyway, I need to go pack up Ace's room, so if you have any questions you want answers to, then please go ahead and ask

Lucifer. All I ask is that you don't tell me. Not until the situation with Luciano is resolved. Anything else on my plate right now would just be too much."

"And Dylan and Jessie?"

"I'll speak to Jessie now. It doesn't seem right you knowing when they don't." I turn to Lucifer. "I'm happy for you to tell Tadgh, Conor, and Bailey. They deserve to know. Once this issue is resolved, maybe we can meet up. Jessie and Bailey are already a big part of my children's lives. I'd like the rest of you to be part of them too."

Lucifer reaches out and squeezes my hand as tears fill his eyes. I squeeze his back, then leave the room, stopping outside to listen momentarily.

"So, you're my little boy's granda."

Lucifer chuckles. "It would seem that way."

I GLANCE AROUND THE ROOM.

At the familiar, blue-painted walls and the double bed with the US flag still hanging above. Nothing's changed in here. It's like time stood still. I wish it had because Ace would still be alive.

I inhale. Tears prick my eyes. I can still smell it. I'm sure I can. His aromatic cologne. It's faint. Then again, maybe it's just a memory.

So many memories. Not enough memories.

I lie on his bed, on the side, Ace would have laid on, and I stare around the room he lived in for almost thirty years.

The shelves are still filled with bike parts, but long gone are the porn magazines, condoms, and all the other essential things that almost nineteen-year-old Jason Steele needed because, like the rest of us, he got older. His needs changed as he grew up into the most beautiful of men, inside and out.

Until all he needed was me and the kids.

I miss him. I will always miss him. Who would he tell me to choose between Eoin and Irish, I wonder?

I dial Jessie's number from where I'm lying on the bed. I haven't spoken to her in a while. I've been too busy using up most of my nine lives.

"Jessie."

"Well, I'll be damned, partner. Is it really you?"

"Yup."

"How are you? In fact, where are you?"

"I'm okay. I'm at the Angels' clubhouse. I'm about to start packing up Ace's room. Eoin and Irish are here. There in the meeting room, talking to Lucifer."

"What's my daddy doing there?" Typical accountant. Straight away, her curiosity is piqued.

"He just stopped by."

She snorts. "He lives in Colton. Why would he just stop by Rising?"

"I think he knew I would be here today, so he stopped by to see me."

"And why would he stop on someone who doesn't think that highly of him? What's going on, Jaine?"

"Jessie…"

"It's *soon,* isn't it?" Her voice is quiet.

"It is."

"Tell me."

"Lucifer is my daddy too."

Silence. It's a lot to take in.

"But… how?"

"You're a bit old for the birds and the bees talk, Jessie." I chuckle as I try to lighten the mood, but it's met with more silence. "I only found out myself when I returned to Rising on the anniversary of Ace's death. That's what Lucifer wanted to speak to me about. I haven't been able to talk to you about it because ever since then, I've either been trying not to die or wishing I was dead."

"And my momma?" she whispers.

"Was my momma too. My pop was her second husband."

"So, she left my daddy to be with your pop?"

"Yes, although I don't know too much about it. She passed when I was seven, and my pop never mentioned anything about him not being my daddy."

"I don't understand."

"Me neither, but I told Lucifer I didn't want to know. It didn't seem right him telling me in detail and not telling all of you too."

"You have four siblings."

"I do."

"You're my sister."

"I am."

"So, does that mean you still think I'm the genius in the O'Brien family, or do you think that it's you now?"

I laugh. "Well, naturally, it's me."

"That means you're going to have to call Lucifer Daddy."

"Or I can just call him Lucifer."

"My daddy would be upset if you didn't call him Daddy. He may not say so, but I know he would be."

"We'll see. One step at a time."

"You know, I always did wonder why you and Bailey looked so similar. You both look like Daddy. I look like my momma. You have her eyes, you know. Our momma had green eyes."

"I didn't know that."

"We can share those memories like proper sisters now."

"I guess we can."

"Oh, dear Lordy Lou, Jaine!"

"What now?"

"You've had four years' worth of sex with your soon-to-be brother-in-law!"

"Thanks for reminding me that I used to fuck my sister's fiancé."

"Razr definitely has a type. Sisters."

We both chuckle.

"Can I tell, Dylan?"

"Of course. Eoin and Irish already know. That's the reason I called. I didn't want them to know without you both knowing too. I've told Lucifer he can tell Tadgh, Conor, and Bailey, but let's leave it there for now, at least until we conclude this matter with Luciano."

"Sure thing, partner. Do you think I should replace partner with sister now?"

I roll my eyes with a smile on my face. "Partner is just fine."

I'M JUST FINISHING PACKING THE LAST OF ACE'S STUFF AWAY WHEN my burner vibrates.

"Dylan," I answer with a smile, thinking it will be to do with my recent announcement to Jessie.

"I've just had Nate on the phone, Jaine. He's got him. Luciano. He wants to know where we want him to be taken."

I frown. "Why isn't Nate insisting that he go back into custody?"

"That's why I called. I was wondering if you knew the answer to that."

"I don't." But I'm sure as hell going to make it my business to find out. “If he wants it to be handled mobster to mobster, then go ahead and make the necessary arrangements.”

“You trust him?”

“I trust him.” And for some reason, I really do. “Where did they pick him up?”

“Trying to board a flight for LAX.”

“So, he was coming for me.”

“He was, but now he can’t. You know what this means, Jaine.”

“What?” But I already know.

“It’s over. You can come home.”

CHAPTER SIXTY-EIGHT

JAINE

The Docks, Hudson Yards

I haven't heard from Eoin or Irish since we returned two days ago.

Why bother coming all the way to the west coast to check up on me to then blank me as soon as we return to New York? Maybe their silence has something to do with their talk with Lucifer. A conversation that, through choice, I wasn't party to.

I stare up at the containers and inhale the familiar oppressive air into my lungs.

Today is Luciano day.

Stepping off the hog, I glance around. There are several Duster vehicles here. Maybe the entire family wants to pay their last disrespects to the Sicilian. Who can blame them? He tried to kill all of them, after all. Each has an axe to grind.

I make my way on foot but hesitate when I get there. Which

container? I follow my gut, approaching the rusty door of the house of horrors that witnessed the demise of big Malky McGrath within its freezer-like confines, then I push it open.

Good guess.

I take in all of the adult O'Connells. I then make eye contact with Jessie, watching as tears immediately fill her eyes. I walk slowly over and stand in front of her. I know she'll want me to acknowledge what we are.

I refuse to let her become another keeper of secrets. I know that her over-confidence is bravado in the main. She's way too sensitive a soul to carry that heavy burden.

"Just so you know, there are no refunds or exchanges allowed, so it looks like you're stuck with me as your sister." My voice pierces the silence.

She wraps her arms around me to the sound of hushed whispers and shuffled feet, hugging me so close I'm struggling to breathe for the second time in recent weeks. This time, it's in a good way. I smile at her when she eventually lets me go.

I'm aware those present will now be comparing us and looking for physical similarities. While there are several, I know that my doppelganger is my other sister, Bailey, who also now knows about our blood relationship, as do Tadgh and Conor and Delaney.

Everyone present will also now know that my biological father is one of the most feared MC presidents on the west coast. That I live the life I lead not through choice but because I was born with MC blood running through my veins.

Because I *am* a biker.

Turning around, I nod at Duke, and he smiles gently in response. We still haven't spoken about Ace. About the fact that a comment I made three years ago resulted in the death of his only son. We need to do that. We need to find our own closure.

I then take in Luciano Ruocco. He's chained to the ceiling and hanging down like some sort of fucked-up Sicilian pinata. His mouth has been taped shut, which I'm grateful for. I've heard more than enough from him in this lifetime.

"There's one more thing I need to say while everyone is here. It may not be the best timing in the world, but then again, maybe it is given our present company. I shared it with his sister before she met her maker at the hands of her husband, so it's only right that her brother takes the same secret to the grave."

I stand before Luciano and stare up at him, the hatred in his eyes is almost tangible.

I then turn to look at Fergal, my guts churning as I ready myself to deliver my last reveal, this time to the patriarch of the O'Connell family himself. I make eye contact with those who already know—Irish, Duke, Dylan, Roisin, and finally, Eoin.

"This secret goes no further than this room. If it ever travels beyond, I will know that it's been spilled by someone present because the only person outside these walls who knows is Paul Delaney. He would never betray me. I trust him with my life." My eyes connect with Sarah's, and she nods. "If it goes any further, family or not, I will hunt you down and I will kill you."

I raise my gaze to the ceiling, suddenly flooded with second thoughts. I push them aside. These people are my family. They're Fin and JJ's family.

I walk across to Fergal and stand in front of him. I can tell from his marred brow that he doesn't know what I'm about to say. That Roisin has held on to my secret as I have hers.

I put my hand in my pocket. My fingers tighten around the engraved bullet. I motion for him to hold out his hand, which he does. Holding mine over his, I unclench my fist, letting the bullet drop. As soon as I move my hand away, it immediately becomes visible.

Everyone stares at it. Everyone knows exactly what it is.

Disbelief. Realization. Gratitude. There's a plethora of emotions that cross Fergal O'Connell's face all at once.

"All this time, it's been you." It's not a question, it's a statement of fact.

We stare at each other. More hushed whispers. I know it will take time for everyone to digest this breaking news. We both turn our heads simultaneously as an agitated Luciano starts swinging around on the chain that's keeping him suspended. I can feel his fury as he stares at the individual responsible for thwarting his plans.

Irish walks across and passes me a dagger.

"He may not be Julius Caesar, darlin', and it may not be the Ides of March, but we've agreed between us that everyone deserves to have a hand in this fucker's demise."

I look around. We're all holding identical weapons. I glance at Jessie once more. I know she's not a natural-born killer. Not like the rest of us.

"Are you sure?" I ask her.

She nods. "I'm sure. He tried to kill my sister, and for that, he has to pay."

Jones & Associates Legal, Upper East Side, New York

Perhaps you need to have a heart-to-heart with both of them.

Tim's advice echoes around my head as I half-listen to Jessie on the other end of the line. It's been two days since Luciano met his abrupt end, and I've still had no direct contact with Eoin or Padraig.

"Are you even listening to a word I'm saying, partner?"

"Of course I am. You said something about the IRS."

"What did I say exactly?"

"Truthfully? I switched off as soon as you mentioned them. Sorry, Jessie. My head's all over the place these days."

"Being in love with one of those O'Connell boys will do that to you. I can only imagine what it must be like being in love with two of them." She sighs sympathetically. "Can I suggest something, Jaine?"

"I'm all ears."

"Can I suggest, now that the danger's passed, that you spend some time with each of them and do something normal? I know that *normal* isn't really in your vocabulary, but can you at least try to be a mere mortal like the rest of us for just one day?"

I chuckle.

"I know you did normal when you were younger with Paddy, but that was twelve years ago. You've both changed since then. And with Eoin? Well, you and he have never done anything remotely normal. Everything was mind games, and since then, all you've ever done is bicker and, well, you know."

"Fuck."

"That's it."

"Is this exercise in normalcy meant to help me decide?"

"Unless you've got any better ideas."

"The choice has already been made for me, Jessie," I say quietly.

"What do you mean?"

"Irish doesn't love me."

She snorts. "I'm sorry, but I must be hearing things. I thought you just said that Padraig O'Connell doesn't love you."

"He doesn't. Or at least he's never said as much."

"He had to pretend to be in love with Sophia, Jaine."

"What about since?" I hate that I sound so needy and pathetic.

"She's only recently been turned into soup."

"I guess." I'm still not convinced.

"I reckon you need to spend some one-on-one time with both those boys. Talk. Do whatever you need to do to make sure you really are compatible with each of them because, whichever one you choose, they'll be living your life with you and vice versa, and both brothers are completely different."

She's right. Eoin's the future Da Duster. As part of his remit, he has no option but to run a business empire and rub shoulders with like-minded individuals, whereas Irish's business commitments are strictly office-based.

"Have you and Paddy ever… you know?"

"If you're asking if we've fucked since he's returned from Sicily, then the answer is no."

"Then maybe you should switch things around a little. Fuck Paddy. Don't fuck Eoin. Because you really do need to be sure, partner. You know as well as I do that next time around, there will be no annulment. You need to choose wisely."

"What if I can't choose?"

"Unfortunately, you're going to have to. Anyway, I need to go sort out this IRS situation. You know, the one you still know nothing about because you weren't even listening to a word I said."

"Sorry, Jessie."

"It's just as well I'm good at my job."

"You're not just good. You're the best." I tell her what she loves to hear.

"I know, and have I told you lately that I'm worth every dime?"

"Not today."

"Well, consider yourself told. I'll remind you again tomorrow."

I chuckle as I disconnect the call.

CHAPTER SIXTY-NINE

EOIN

The Hudson Dusters' HQ, Manhattan, New York

I STARE OUT MY OFFICE WINDOW, BUT I'M TOO DISTRACTED TO TAKE in the view.

It's been two days since we ended Luciano Ruocco's life. As a family, we all wear his blood on our hands. Duke delivered the fatal blow. It seemed only fair. Luc was responsible for the death of his son, after all. Since then, there's been nothing from Jaine.

I retake my seat before placing my feet on the desk.

"Jessie suggested to Jaine that you need to spend some one-on-one time together now that the danger's passed. You know… go on a proper date or something." I frown at Dylan who's sitting in the chair across from me. He shrugs. "You know as well as I do that your relationship with Jaine never recovered from what it went through. It was nothing short of a miracle that you managed to fall in love with each other in the first place. But all you've done since is bicker, fall out, and then have make-up sex."

He's right. Jaine and I seldom did anything together as a couple. We did used to speak at length. At least until Paddy returned, and I then deliberately extracted myself from her life so she could make an informed decision.

"It won't have been helped that for the duration of our time together, Jaine was on lockdown as she had a gun pointed at her head," I argue.

It's weak. We both know it. Even if she hadn't been firmly in the Ruocco's sights, there's every likelihood we still wouldn't have done anything *normal*.

"I agree, it wasn't, but that's no longer the case, Eoin. She has a future now. A future she can share with someone."

"So, where would you suggest I take her?"

"Where would you normally take a woman on a date?"

"Out to dinner, then back to her place? I'm not sure going out to dinner is Jaine's thing, though."

"How do you know what her thing is?"

"I don't."

"That's exactly my point. I would suggest, in the absence of knowing what her *thing* is, do yours. If you enjoy going out for a meal, then do that. It has to be a two-way street for it to work anyway. Who knows, maybe you'll find things you both like doing or discover that you already have things in common. If you and Jaine do get married a second time, it will be for life. There won't be any back-peddling allowed this time. You have to be completely sure that she's your person and vice versa."

"I've never been surer of anything in my life."

He raises an eyebrow. "That goes for outside the bedroom as well as inside. A marriage can't be sustained on sex alone. It goes way beyond the physical. In fact, I know abstinence isn't really your thing, but I suggest you keep sex off-limits for now. You two need to connect on a different level."

"Like how Jaine and Paddy connect, you mean?"

"I never said that."

"But you were thinking it."

He shrugs. "Well, look at them. They love each other, yet they've probably only been intimate a handful of times, the last time over three years ago when Fin was conceived. Their connection is on an emotional level. Your connection with Jaine is on a physical level. It needs to be both."

"What if we don't share the same connection on an emotional level?"

"Then maybe she's not the right girl for you."

"Of course, she's the right girl for me. I love her!" I hiss.

"Love isn't enough, Eoin. Marriage is for life. It needs more than love and intimacy. It needs communication, honesty, understanding, selflessness, and the list goes on."

"What if I'm too set in my ways and she hers?"

"I guess there's only one way to find out."

"Have you had this same conversation with Paddy?" He frowns. I may have just put him in an awkward position. "You don't have to answer that if you don't want to. I understand you have a closer relationship with him."

"You've fallen for the same woman as your brother. So, tell me, how will you explain all of this to him? That you've effectively stolen his life?"

I'm well aware that Dylan is just another part of the life I stole.

"That's not true, Eoin, or at least not now. It's just that you don't tend to let people in, whereas Paddy's a bit more of an open book."

He's right, of course. I'm notoriously private. I always have been. I look at him. He knows I'm still waiting for a response.

"Yes, I will be having a similar conversation with him, but only because I want to relay what Jessie said to Jaine. It's only fair. I'm not taking sides. I wish everyone could come out of this a winner, but I know that's not possible."

I nod, then watch as he leaves the room.

Will Jaine be receptive if I ask her on a date? I'm not so sure she will be. Our relationship had already deteriorated to the point of being non-existent before we split up.

My thoughts drift to her and my brother. I know she and Paddy have kissed. The recent bruising on both their necks was clear evidence of this. There's been no indication of them having gone beyond that. If they haven't, I realize it's out of respect for me, even though Jaine and I aren't together.

We're all single.

Not that I've been with anyone else. I won't pretend otherwise. Not like I did with Candice.

My thoughts then drift to her recent reveal. Jaine is The Exterminator.

She was upset by my reaction, but then I was pissed that she never shared that part of herself with me, even though I had no right to be. It's not like I shared all of myself with her.

"I thought you'd treat me differently. That you'd wrap me up in even more cotton wool because you'd see me as some sort of trophy."

She held that one thing back because she didn't trust me with it. Because she thought it would make me even more possessive and even more protective.

She's right. I know everything there is to know about her. In turn, I've been holding parts of myself back. I know precisely why.

Aside from wanting to allow her freedom of choice.

Guilt.

Over what I put Paddy through. Over what I put them both through. Sleep became a distant memory when remorse became my new bed partner. Night after night, I lay awake as my selfish wrongdoings slowly slide showed through my brain.

I had also convinced myself that our relationship was destined to be short-lived. That when my brother returned from Sicily, her forced affection for me would wane, her true love for him far outweighing any short-term feelings she'd ever held for me.

I was wrong.

She loves me still. Even though I've continually pushed her away, she's stubbornly refused to let go.

She's saved my life twice. I know now why she rejected my protection. As The Exterminator, she felt she didn't need it.

She did.

Because in return, I've saved her life four times.

Maybe we both need protection. Maybe we need to compromise and find a balance that works for us. That's if she chooses me, of course. Which I suspect she won't.

While she may love me, she and Paddy are meant. I can't compete with that, no matter how much I love her or how many dates I take her on.

Public Dining Room, Palace Hotel, Manhattan

I halt my conversation as Jaine enters the room. I'm seldom rendered speechless, but the sight of her MMA-honed body wrapped in a short cream silk dress has achieved just that.

She's simply stunning.

My eyes drift over her slim shape. No doubt, the eyes of every male in the room are doing exactly the same thing. Jealousy sweeps through me.

She's mine. Or at least, she was.

Confidence oozes out of her as she approaches. In this environment, she's not the girl from Rising, California. Neither is she her sniper alter-ego. She's Jaine Jones, the legal professional.

I've asked her here tonight because this is my domain. I have a business empire to run. In order to do that successfully, I build alliances, and I end them.

Many Duster deals are closed behind the four walls of this very establishment. As my wife, Jaine would be expected to interact with high rankers on both sides of the law. It's something that would pose no problem for her as it's something she already does, and exceptionally well.

There's no one better equipped to stand by my side.

A lawyer and a serial killer. She's the most perfect woman in the world for me.

Whether she wants to is a different matter, however. We'll find out soon enough. Things are coming to a head. Now the immediate danger has passed, the current situation is no longer sustainable. All three of us cannot continue to live lives of limbo.

"Eoin."

As is the perfunctory method of greeting in places such as this, she places her hands on my shoulders and air kisses me politely on both cheeks. The smell of wildflowers instantly envelops me. Paddy's right. She smells of Rising.

I watch as she turns her attention to the person I was conversing with, a genuine smile crossing her face.

"Well, if it isn't Detective Gabriel Prescott. It's good to see you, Gabe."

She greets him in the same fashion. I watch as his hands drop to almost indecent levels. My jealousy flares further. I make eye contact with Jaine, and she gives a subtle shake of her head.

As a female in an extremely male-dominated environment, I expect she has to deal with such borderline manhandling regularly. I also suspect she knows when to react and when to let it slide.

"It's good to see you too, Jaine. How long has it been?"

"Three years."

I frown inwardly at that response, my jealousy immediately replaced by even more guilt. It's a stock answer from her. Three years. Back when she was expected to pack up everything she knew and leave town even though her life was full and her responsibilities many.

Gabe lets out a low whistle. "I can't believe it's been that long. Time flies."

"When you're not having fun." She smirks at him. "I hear Sabrina's been giving you a hard time."

He laughs heartily. "Let's just say she loves to bust my balls. She's not to your level of bitch, but she runs a close second." He glances over her shoulder. "Well, it looks like my dinner date has arrived. Don't be a stranger, Jaine or I may take offense to the fact that you dumped me and made the DA your new best friend." He smiles, using the opportunity to air kiss her a second time. Jaine ignores his wandering hands once more and smiles politely. We both then watch as he walks off to greet his female guest.

I turn to look at her, raising an eyebrow. "Do you have to tolerate that sort of behavior frequently?"

"Only from a handful of individuals, one of whom is no longer with us."

I nod. She's referring to Luciano. If I'd known that, I'd have hacked off his fingers and shoved them down his throat before we ended his miserable life.

She glances around. I'm sure several of the other guests are as known to her as they are to me. I agreed to meet her here as she was tied up in a meeting. Now that she's no longer mine, I couldn't insist on having her collected.

My reality is that she may never be mine again. We both know this evening is a make-or-break for us. I have to be the right fit for her and vice versa. Dylan's right. A marriage can't be sustained on love and intimacy alone. Not when you undertake the roles in life we do.

"You look breathtaking, Jaine." My eyes sweep over her once more, and her cheeks pinken. Another inward frown. Have I never complimented her before? I realize if I had, it would have been infrequently. I gifted every other female with such words without a second thought, but seldom the one who mattered most and the words truly meant.

"Thank you."

I help her into her seat before taking my own.

"And Sabrina is?"

"Sabrina Hawthorn. She's a senior attorney at JAL. Has been for several years. When Cherry went off on her sabbatical, I had no choice but to redistribute some of my workload. Sabrina inherited my having to deal with Detective Prescott. Do you know her?"

"Not that I can recall, although her name does sound vaguely familiar. And how are the children?"

"Both are still a handful." Her face softens.

I haven't seen either of them since we returned from California. It didn't seem appropriate somehow, given everything that's happened between Jaine and me in the very recent past. I'm not sure whether I'd have been welcomed or not.

"JJ misses you," she adds quietly.

Reaching across the table, I cover her hand with mine. Our physical connection instantly flares into life. I want her. The feeling's mutual. I'm not sure how we'll ever be able to deny its insatiable hunger if we do have to permanently draw a line under what we have.

"I miss him too." I squeeze her hand.

We talk about many things as we eat. All are safe subjects, which concerns me. If we're to try to make things work between us, we need to discuss more than the mundane. We need to discuss our future path.

Perhaps she's avoiding the topic as she's already decided we don't share the same one.

She excuses herself to the restroom. When she does, I motion my head to one of the waiters, requesting that we be moved to one of the private booths in the bar area.

Standing, I wait for her to return. When she does, I take her hand in mine. I'm conscious she's staring down at our connection as we walk. We've never held hands in public. I'm flooded with more regrets. There are so many everyday things that we never did.

I only hope I'm allowed the opportunity to rectify all of my mistakes.

Deep down, I know it's unlikely.

She faces me across the small booth table, the high-back black leather seating easily shielding our private conversation. Now that we're no longer in the public eye, I watch as Jaine Jones, the biker, surfaces.

"Thank you for the hog. Sorry… I should have said something sooner rather than just take the keys and ride off into the sunset."

"You're welcome, Jaine. I can't even begin to imagine what it must have been like for you when I opened…."

"It felt like another death," she interrupts quietly. She clearly doesn't wish to be reminded of the moment.

"They tried to destroy the things that you loved most."

"And they succeeded. With Ace. With my hog. But they didn't destroy you, or Irish, or my boys."

She loves me. We both know she does. She's not attempting to hide it.

She stares at me across the table then looks at the shiny, black surface as she considers what she's about to say.

"I'm sorry I never told you... about my alter-ego. Being a serial-killing sniper isn't something you just casually announce."

I'm quiet for a moment. I can't hide the fact that I'm disappointed. I don't want to hide it. We were husband and wife. We should have had no secrets. Instead, our relationship was built on the same house of cards we both used to gameplay.

"How did everyone else find out?"

She takes a sip of her sparkling water. "Ace, Duke, and Irish found out during the Bratva situation. It turns out it was me they were after. My sniping secret was given away by the then VP of the Scorpions. The Russians decided they wanted to marry me off to one of their benefactors and have me carry out my services on their behalf. Irish and Ace were abducted with me as they wanted us to perform for the camera."

"Perform?" My hand tightens around my whiskey glass. I'm sure she notices, but she says nothing.

"Porn. The benefactors wanted to ensure they were getting enough bang for their buck, pun intended, before placing bids on me. Rather than use strangers, the Russians decided to use Ace and Irish."

"And that's when you fell pregnant with Fin."

She nods. "Dylan found out about my secret when I needed intel on Lebedev."

"And Ma?"

"The weapon I used to take out the two snipers on Irish's wedding day was still at the church. Roisin spotted the engraved bullet in the puddle of Molly's brains."

"Thank you for saving my life in Nevada and at the church, Jaine."

She stares at me. "And thank you for saving mine. In hindsight, maybe I needed your protection more than I realized."

And maybe I needed hers too. Just like I need her.

"Speaking of churches, I haven't been able to face going back to St. Peter's." Her lips turn downward. She's emotional, I suspect, because she knows how much that place means to Padraig.

"It's not as bad as we first feared. Most of the damage was confined to the roof. The walls are still intact. I'm told plans are already underway to reinstate the building while retaining as many of the original features as possible. Paddy's dealing directly with Father O'Reilly on the matter."

"But all of the ancient furniture and fittings will have been destroyed." The guilt is evident in her voice. She thinks it's her fault. That the comment she made all those years ago was the cause.

It wasn't.

Paddy would still have been married off to Sophia. He would still have detested her and asked for an annulment. The Ruoccos would still have retaliated.

What Jaine isn't seeing is that, on the contrary, if The Exterminator hadn't played their part, the Ruoccos may well have achieved their goal.

"We'll salvage what we can, Jaine, but they're only things at the end of the day."

"Things that Irish loved."

I can't help but feel disappointed that our make-or-break evening has so quickly turned into a conversation about my brother. He's clearly seldom out of her thoughts for very long, even when she's alone with me.

"He loves you more, Jaine."

She stares at me. "That's where I think you're wrong. He doesn't love me, or at least he hasn't said as much."

I search her face for signs that she's joking, but she's deadly serious. She really thinks Paddy doesn't love her.

Is that the only reason she's here with me now? Because I'm her second choice?

"He was in the church at Cillian and Sarah's wedding. In the safe space."

I nod reluctantly. I know exactly where this conversation is now headed. "I know he was."

"He didn't even come out."

"Because I stopped him from doing so."

"So, even back then."

"Yes, Jaine." I throw the whiskey I've been nursing back in one. "Even back then, I wanted you for myself. I'm fully aware that I destroyed my brother that day. Trust me. I will never get the sights or sounds of his devastation out of my head. Yours either, for that matter."

"You saw me?" She frowns.

"I witnessed it all. I was standing right beside him."

I saw her at the precise moment she reached rock bottom. When their hands would have touched had it not been for the glass.

I can feel her eyes boring into me. I've already admitted what I did. I didn't expect to have to dissect my wrongdoings in minute detail during an evening that was meant to be about us.

I place the empty glass back on the table and run my hand through my hair.

"Guilt is the other reason I pushed you away. I knew you and he were meant, but I still stood in your way."

"You did it because you loved me."

I'm not sure if it's a question or a statement.

"There's no past tense, Jaine. I will never stop loving you."

"What if I don't choose you?" she whispers.

"Then I'll have to accept someone else."

"You would do that?"

"I would have no choice! You know the role I need to fill!" I rest my head back against the leather seating, annoyed with myself for raising my voice. "Jaine, I want to be completely honest with you."

"Go on."

"Possessiveness. Protectiveness. You bring out both in me. If we were to remarry, you would need to accept them. I can try to rein them in, but I'm not sure I would ever be able to where you're concerned. At least not to the level that you desire."

I don't want to deceive her anymore. If she agrees to be mine, then that's what she'll be. Mine. I will, of course, try to compromise, but I don't want anything to happen to her. I don't want anyone else touching her either.

"If you were mine and Gabe were to manhandle you the way he did earlier, I'd kill him." She knows I mean every word.

"Thank you for being so honest with me." She frowns again. "I'm sorry, Eoin… I think I should go."

More disappointment radiates through me. She clearly doesn't wish to talk further, even though most of our discussion this evening has been about my brother.

"Jaine."

She looks at me once more. Her forehead is marred. Clearly, her mind is already made up. I've already lost her.

How can you lose what was never yours in the first place?

"Padraig loves you more than anything in the world. Never doubt that."

I tell her what she needs to hear. I may be digging my own grave further by doing so, but I won't stand in their way a second time.

She stands, then leans over and kisses me softly on the lips. It's a chaste kiss, nothing more.

Does it signify the end?

If it does, then it's no more than I deserve for falling in love with the girl who was destined to be my brother's future, not mine.

I rest my head back against the seating once more, watching her leave and taking my heart with her.

CHAPTER SEVENTY

PADRAIG

Padraig's Apartment, Hudson Yards, New York

I'M LYING ON THE SECTIONAL AND STARING UP AT THE CEILING, having just been on the phone with our Dylan.

He's not sure how things went, but apparently, Jaine and Eoin went out for dinner last night.

A proper date.

I suspect they're trying for real this time. No more under duress or false pretenses. Not when they're planning on starting a family. Why wouldn't they try again? They may drive each other up the wall, but they have so much in common.

I'm not sure how I feel. Have they been in contact the entire time? Aside from when we were ending Luciano's life, I've not heard a word from Jaine since we returned from Rising.

I put it down to her needing time. Apparently not. Or maybe she just needed time away from me.

I stare at my blank phone screen. Removing the handset from the case, I study the image of me and Jaine. Back when the future was still ours for the taking. Back before it all went wrong. Back when the innocence of youth had me believing that love really could conquer all.

It can't.

Dylan suggested that I also take her on a date. Should I? Will she even respond? I type a message, trying to appear cocky and confident, even though I've never felt more unsure of myself in my entire life.

Padraig: *I'll get Liam to pick you up at two p.m.*

I wait for her to reply. I can tell she's typing. Is she deleting and re-writing the words, or is she too busy messaging my brother and moving on with her life? Is she going to turn me down?

Jaine: *I'll ask Duke to look after the kids. Should I wear anything in particular?*

I can't contain the smile as I message back.

Padraig: *Dress like you would have done back when we were nineteen.*

Yale University, Connecticut

I sit on the bench we shared on our third date twelve years ago.

Back when we had so much to look forward to. Back before what we shared was slowly eroded by lies, deceit, assumptions, and betrayal, most of it at the hands of my family or supposed friends.

Jaine still has a future to look forward to with my big brother.

Taking the vows, having kids, and growing old together. All the things I wanted. The only things I wanted. And all of them with her.

I'm not sure how I'll cope.

I guess with all my wishful thinking, foolish hopes, and pipe dreams. I expected our fantasy ending to be different. Welcome to your reality, Paddy.

Moving forward, Eoin will become her sounding board, her confidant, and her life raft. I'll just be left to drift farther and farther away on a bottomless sea of memories and what-ifs.

I close my eyes as I'm sucker-punched by a barrel of emotions.

Love. Desperation. Resignation.

How the fuck will I ever be able to move on from her? I won't. She's my everything. Why the fuck couldn't I have been her everything too? I close my eyes to try to stop the tears from running down my face.

She's it for me. Doesn't she fucking realize that?

I wipe my face. She'll be here soon. I don't want her to feel guilty on my account. I don't want her to feel like she has to choose me. She's been through enough. She deserves happiness.

I want her happy, whether or not it's with me.

Raising my face to the sun, I close my eyes, appreciating the warmth as I inhale the smell of freshly cut grass.

She's here.

As I did years before, I lower my face, then open my eyes, so I can blatantly admire her. A smile crosses my face when her cheeks flush pink as they did back then. My gaze drifts over her.

My straight up and down Jaine Jones. A few more battle scars and a little bit older and wiser, but still the same girl I gave my heart to twelve years ago.

A heart that she never gave back.

She's wearing white jean shorts and a tank top, her beat-up

high-tops finishing off the same look she wore back when she was nineteen.

I close my eyes and lift my face back up to the sun. I'm sure this time around, she won't bother blatantly admiring me in return. Why would she?

I swallow the lump in my throat just as the seat shifts, and she sits down.

"Penny for them."

I smirk at the same opening line. "Would you go back and change things if you could, darlin'?"

We sit in amicable silence listening to birdsong as she considers her response.

"What I think is that Fate meant for us to be on this very bench at this very time, Irish. I think this is all part of the great masterplan he had in store for us all along."

"Do you think he'd let us change his plans?"

"Probably not. I think all we can do is hope that our plans align."

I turn to face her. Reaching out my hand, I gently cup the side of her face, my gaze dropping to her lips. She knows I'm going to do what I did twelve years ago. I lean toward her until she's breathing me in, and I'm breathing her in.

She may not be my end game in this lifetime, but I pray to God she is in the next.

I slowly press my lips to hers. It's a chaste kiss, nothing more. Resting my forehead against hers, I stare into her eyes. "In the absence of a bed or a sectional, I brought a blanket."

And that's what we do. We lie side by side on a blanket on the grass, and with her head resting on my chest, we put the world to rights, talking until we eventually drift off to sleep. It's the drop in temperature that wakes me in the end.

I lie with my Jaine Jones in my arms, comforted by her heart beating against mine and her steady breathing as she soundly sleeps. "I love you so fucking much, darlin'." I sob the words against her hair.

I then watch as day turns to night until we're blanketed under a million stars, and when one shoots across the sky, I pray that tomorrow never comes and for this day never to end because right here, right now?

It's perfect.

CHAPTER SEVENTY-ONE

JAINE

Jaine's Apartment, Upper East Side, New York

"How does it feel being back in your own apartment, Jainie?"

I motion my head for Duke to step inside, then, closing the door, I glance around the familiar monochrome space in its shades of black, white, anthracite, and silver.

"While I'm grateful to Roisin and Fergal for letting us stay with them, it's good to finally be home."

He turns around, and we stare at each other. This is the first time we've been alone without the kids present since the news broke. That my comment was the reason Ace was targeted. That my comment is the reason he's dead.

Tears run down my face, and I wipe them off with the back of my hand.

"It's all my fault, Duke," I sob.

He takes me by the hand, then leads me to the sofa. We both sit down, and he pulls me tightly against his chest.

"Now, you listen here, Jainie. What happened to Ace wasn't your fault. What you said wasn't what infuriated Sophia. What made her mad was knowing that you and Padraig loved each other. No one had control over that. We love who we love."

"But…"

"There are no buts, Jainie. The outcome would have been the same whether you said the words or not. As far as Sophia was concerned, if she was never going to be happy, then you weren't allowed to be either. She held you responsible for the failure of her marriage when I'm told it was her personality that ruined things for her. All of us have to move on now. Sophia's dead. Luciano's dead. That toxic Ruocco bloodline has been ended, and the Steele one will continue through JJ. That's what's important. There's no point dwelling on things we can't change. There isn't anything that will bring Ace back."

I cry, and I'm sure I can hear Duke shed a tear too. I don't acknowledge it, as I know he wouldn't want me to. Like me, he'll just be relieved that it's over and that Ace can finally be laid to rest.

"I miss him so damn much, Jainie."

"I know you do."

And then we cry some more. Me for my best friend. Duke for his son.

Time passes.

"So, what's next on the cards?"

I shrug. "Well, we left the apartment in such a rush, so I need to get it child-friendly again, then bring the kids home, and…."

"Between you and Padraig and you and Eoin, I mean."

I exhale. "Well, I've finally thanked Eoin for the hog."

"So, you've decided to keep it."

"I'll never be able to part with it now, or at least not willingly."

That ride and I have been through so much together in such a short time. It will never replace the Softail Pop gifted me on my eighteenth birthday. Nothing can ever replace something or someone you loved with your whole heart. Just like my loving Irish and Eoin will never lessen my love for Ace. My remarrying, if that's what I decide to do, won't detract from the vows I took with him either.

I stare down at the barely-there band on my finger. Ace was buried with his still in place because I disagree. Death does not do us part. I will always be Jason Steele's old lady, his wife, his best friend, and the mother of his son. Fact. Death can't change that.

"And what's happening with you and Eoin these days?"

I exhale in frustration. "We went out for dinner, and he admitted that he's been pushing me away in part because of the guilt he's been feeling. He feels responsible for me and Padraig not ending up together. He isn't. If you removed Eoin from the equation, Irish and I would still be exactly where we are right now. The catalyst was the arranged marriage itself, not what subsequently happened. But he refuses to see that."

"He will do eventually, but it will have to be in his own time, Jainie. So everything's been aired between you and him? There are no more secrets?"

"As far as I'm aware, everything's out in the open."

"And are you thinking of marrying him a second time?"

I move Ace's wedding band up and down my finger on a place where, not so long ago, two rested. The ring Eoin gave me also signified something binding.

Something sincere. Something honest.

Even though there was no love behind it when he placed it on my finger, his having them commissioned showed his commitment to our marriage. Because in the beginning, he *was* committed to trying to make things work between us, whereas I was only ever committed to destroying him.

I hurt him intentionally. I damaged him deliberately.

I promised him everything, then gave him nothing. When all he ever wanted was to be a husband and a father and to be loved in return.

Our relationship was broken beyond repair before I finally reciprocated his love. I realize that now. I changed him for the worse when I repeatedly threw his love for me back in his face.

I do love him.

Totally. Completely. Unconditionally.

For the first time in a long time, I can think ahead. I can actually see a future. I have an opportunity to make more memories. The only way I can do that is by living life.

Can I do that with Eoin when he's openly admitted he doesn't think he'll be able to change?

"While all the cards have been laid on the table and all the truths have been revealed, he's been quite vocal about the fact that he won't be able to change his possessive, protective ways. What concerns me most is how can we expect it to work the second time around if what we had didn't work the first time. The situation with the Ruoccos won't be the last time we have guns pointed at our heads."

"It's not just about him changing, Jainie. Marriage is a two-way street. You know that. Ace wasn't perfect. Eoin isn't perfect either, but then neither are you. You have to compromise. Make allowances. Find a middle ground. You have to be prepared to adapt for him too. If you want to, that is."

Duke's right. I know he is. Have I been putting all the responsibility for change on Eoin simply because I refused to?

Yes.

"And Padraig?"

"We revisited the place we went on our third date."

"And how did that make you feel?"

"Spending that time with him reminded me of all the reasons I fell in love with him in the first place."

"But?"

"I don't think he loves me."

Duke chuckles, and I look up at him. "I've spent a lot of time with Padraig these past weeks. If you don't mind me saying, I don't think I've ever seen a boy so in love with a girl, Jainie."

"But he's never said the words, well, at least not recently."

"Do you need to hear them when you can feel them? Surely, you know in your heart that he loves you, just like you know in your heart that Ace is always with you."

We sit in silence.

"What's on your mind, Jainie?"

"They want me to choose between them, and I don't think I can, Duke."

"Can I give you my advice?"

"Please."

"In our life, we need to grab love and happiness where we can, so follow your heart and don't try to second guess what it's telling you. Sometimes, when facing two paths, a third miraculously appears."

Or one gets removed.

The O'Connell Home, Darling, New York

"It's good to see you, Jaine. How have you been?" Roisin motions her head for me to step inside the house before politely kissing me on the cheek and giving me a hug.

Given that my visit is unannounced, I imagine it's not as good to see me as she's making out.

I walk past, taking in the familiar gold-flocked wallpaper and the ever-expanding shrine of photos filled with so many images of my own two boys. It feels like a lifetime since I've lived here, but it's only been two days. I miss it, and I don't.

She's dressed formally in black pants, a cream twin set, and black kitten-heeled shoes, a sign that she's either just had a visitor or she's expecting one. Now that we're no longer on lockdown, a much-needed sense of normalcy has returned for all of us.

Does she know why I'm here? Like with Duke, I haven't had the opportunity to speak to her one-on-one without the kids or another O'Connell being present, and what I have to say requires privacy. For anyone else, it would have required an engraved bullet.

We stare at each other.

She knows.

I've got to give it to her. That Ma Duster intuition of hers never lets her down. It always seems to know exactly when to kick in, more so when it comes to safeguarding Roisin O'Connell when she's about to be confronted by her own wrongdoings.

"Come through, Jaine."

I follow her into the living space. She takes a seat on the sectional while I remain standing.

"How are the boys? I've…"

"Why?"

She frowns.

"I don't know what…."

"You know exactly what I'm asking." I interrupt her once more. I then wait for her to find her words.

"You loved each other. It was the only way."

I run my hand down my face. "Have you learned nothing, Roisin? The lies? The deceit? What it leads to?"

"Eoin loved you, Jaine."

"And I loved him, but that didn't give us an automatic pass, and it definitely didn't give you permission to interfere." I start pacing the floor. "That you could sink so low and send a message from Irish's phone."

You and Eoin have my blessing to move on with your lives together, darlin'. I wish you all the best.

I stop and stare at her. "Those twenty generic words made me feel like everything Irish, and I had gone through meant nothing to him. I felt cheated by those words. I expected more. I needed more. I fucking deserved more. Letting him go was a big deal for me. I couldn't understand why it wasn't the same for him. But he never did let me go, did he? He didn't actually give me that all-important permission to be with his own brother. You did!" I stare at her, my cheeks wet. "I had no choice but to reveal my alter-ego to Eoin. Ask me why."

"Why?" Her voice is quiet. She doesn't really want the answer, but she's going to goddamn get it.

"Because Irish challenged Eoin to a duel." I laugh dryly as her expression changes to one of shock. "And you know what would have happened had I not intervened, don't you?"

She doesn't reply.

"Don't you, Roisin!"

Still nothing, and her lack of response makes me even angrier.

"Eoin would be dead because with the amount of guilt he was carrying over the part he played in all the betrayal, he would never have pulled the trigger."

I walk to the window, staring at the exact spot where Eoin took down the third sniper.

"I'm sorry, Jaine."

"Save your apology for Irish because, once again, it was him you let down. In fact, you let both of your sons down, and do you know why?"

"I'm sure you're going to tell me!" She lashes out as her guilt gets the better of her.

"Because now I've been asked to choose between them."

She stares at me, the enormity of what she's done now clear on her face. She knows I would never have moved forward with Eoin without Padraig's blessing in the same way I would never move forward with Irish without Eoin's blessing.

"So tell me, Ma Duster. Are you going to take an impossible decision out of my hands for a second time? Are you going to tell me which of your sons I should choose and which I should break the heart of?" I walk over so I'm standing right in front of her. "Because do you know what you didn't stop to consider when you were sending that message? The deceitful one sent to convince me to enter into a relationship with Eoin to fit in with your grand Duster plans?" I lean over until my mouth is right beside her ear. "The fact that Irish was always going to come back, and then the truth would come out."

I stand upright and walk toward the door before stopping and looking over my shoulder. "No more lies. No more secrets. And might I suggest that you spill your own? Your sons have a right to know they have a big brother. And don't pretend you don't know exactly who he is because I've done my digging, and I know you've had access to the same files."

I slam the front door on my way out.

CHAPTER SEVENTY-TWO

PADRAIG

Padraig's Apartment, Hudson Yards, New York

"So, you know now about the message Ma sent from your phone."

Dylan sounds sheepish, which means he'd already worked out who sent it.

"Jaine mentioned it moments after she stopped me from shooting our big brother in the head. She said that I'd given my blessing to their union. I would never have willingly given my approval to the love of my life being with my brother."

"I'm sorry, Paddy. I suspected it was Ma as soon as Jaine showed me the message. The fact that it was sent from your old number was a dead giveaway, given that the handset was still in New York. I never mentioned anything because they had fallen in love with each other, and I thought you were happy with Sophia." His guilty voice fades away.

"It doesn't matter now. Even if Jaine hadn't entered into a relationship with Eoin, she was still in love with him by that point, so it changes nothing. The damage was already done."

"True. I think Ma's well and truly learned her lesson. Apparently, Jaine went around and had a right go at her."

"She had every right, Dyl. Our family's been trying to manipulate her life to suit their own purposes for over three years. Ma should consider herself lucky Jaine never pointed a gun at her skull and pulled the trigger."

"I think she realizes that. Anyway, what's next?"

"Who knows? Jaine and I had a nice time on our date. I'm guessing she also had a pleasant enough time with Eoin." He'll know full well that I'm digging. It's not like I can ask Eoin direct.

"I'm not so sure their date was such a resounding success. He told her in no uncertain terms that he would never be able to change his ways and that she'd have to accept him for what he is. Possessive and protective."

"At least he was honest."

"I guess. Jessie was asking what Lucifer spoke to you and him about. She's tried to prize the information out of her da, but he's not prepared to discuss it."

"Let's just say he mentioned something that I'm receptive to. Whether the same can be said for Eoin is a different matter. Whether we're willing or not, the final decision would rest with Jaine, although I'm starting to think she may just hightail it back to Rising so she can get as far away from our fucked-up family as possible."

"And who can blame her?"

"Did Ma mention anything else?"

"Just that Jaine told her about the duel and the fact that it left her with no option but to reveal her alter-ego to Eoin as much as she was reluctant to."

"And still, he won't turn the protection down a notch?"

"Can you blame him, Paddy? He loves her, and he's had to save her life four times recently. She'll be running out soon."

"I'm sure they could find a workable solution if they tried."

"I'm sure they could if each were prepared to compromise. But everything's black and white with those two. They go out of their way to be deliberately obtuse with each other."

"I think they just enjoy winding each other up."

"I think you're right. Neither will back down, and it's not because they can't. It's because they don't want to. I reckon they both get off on the angry sex."

"Too much information, brother."

"Sorry. Speaking of sex, have you and Jaine… you know."

"No, we haven't. I suspect Jaine would slap me down if I even hinted at taking things further. She only agreed to sleep with Eoin because she thought she had my blessing. I reckon for us to move our relationship to the next level, she'd need the same from him."

"And have you heard anything back from the Ruoccos' lawyer? As the last family member standing, that leaves you the sole beneficiary of all their assets."

"And also the person responsible for all their debts, of which I'm sure there's plenty. I've just sent an email to their family lawyer. I've mentioned that two skulls believed to belong to Sophia and Luciano have been found. If he accepts these findings, I suspect he'll want to carry out due diligence to ensure there are no other claims against the estate before signing things over."

"Whatever happened to Sophia's mother?"

"She died in childbirth, so it must have been when she had Sophia. I'm told she was actually a decent human being. It was the father who was the louse."

"Good riddance to them all. Anyway, keep me posted. Later, brother."

"Later, Dyl."

I disconnect the call, my mind going back over the conversation with Lucifer.

I reckon I need to have a heart-to-heart with my eldest brother, as depending on how things progress with Jaine, we may have no option but to revert to Plan B.

That's if he's willing.

CHAPTER SEVENTY-THREE

JAINE

The Hudson Dusters' HQ, Manhattan, New York

LOVE HURTS.

It can open you up to so much pain and wound you way more than any bullet or blade ever can. It's a hurt that can't be measured on any known scale, and the moment you reach love's dizzy heights, the person you love is automatically in control. That person can destroy you with just one look, word, or action.

Love makes you weak. Love can leave you second-guessing. Love can make you doubt yourself, even when you're certain.

I've loved, and I've been loved. I know better than most what love can do to you when it's not reciprocated or when it's ripped away like it was with Ace.

Love drowns you in so many feelings and emotions that, at times, you feel like you can't breathe, and if you hurt the person you love, you hurt yourself even more. There's no winning. Love is a loser's game. It's like poker but without the chips. You have to play with something way more valuable—your heart.

Eoin and Padraig.

If I choose one, I hurt the other. If I choose neither, I hurt both.

There's no right answer. There's no wrong answer. The solution is indeterminate because there is none. On this particular flowchart, no arrow points to the happily ever after.

My stiletto heels click on the marble flooring as I pass the reception quartet. Number one immediately picks up her phone. She's stopped trying to be discrete about it. I watch as her mauve-tipped talons clutch the handset for dear life.

I wonder which Duster she's pre-warning. The eldest or the youngest. I checked in advance. I'm well aware that both are in the building today. Two O'Connells. One stone. There's no point in delaying the inevitable.

I press the call button for the elevator. Stepping inside, I stare at my reflection in the mirrored surface, taking in the female biker hiding beneath the guise of a legal professional. She's no longer living on borrowed time, but her life might as well be over, given what she's about to do.

I smooth down my grey pantsuit just as the elevator door opens. I make my way straight to Eoin's office. As usual, Candice is sitting guard outside his door. I wonder if Mr. I-need-to-have-sex-at-least-six-times-a-day has taken to fucking his PA at lunchtimes again. Jealousy floods my veins, but I ignore it.

Who Eoin O'Connell fucks is no longer any of my business.

"Jaine."

"Candice."

She doesn't attempt to stop me from walking straight into his office. She knows better after the last deceitful stunt she pulled.

The first thing that hits me is that spicy cologne of his, which lingers in the air, and almost stops me in my tracks. He's talking on the phone, leaning back on his chair, with his perfect Italian leather-clad feet resting on top of the desk.

I just want to get this over with. I want to interrupt, but the professional businesswoman in me won't allow it. So I wait. Impatiently. As I do, my eyes are drawn to his forearms which are on display thanks to his rolled-up crisp-white shirt sleeves.

Veiny. Strong. Deadly.

My eyes then scan his torso, pecs, abs, and biceps. All are perfectly displayed by the snug tailor-made fabric of his shirt. They then drift past that powerful throat, that full bottom lip, before resting on those aquamarine eyes.

Smug eyes. With one eyebrow raised as he catches me blatantly admiring him.

I turn to look at the images on the walls—the lineup of past mobsters. I can see my son's eyes in every single one of their evil gazes. This is his future. There isn't anything I can do to alter that. There isn't anything Fin can do to change it, either.

I'm unaware that Eoin's finished his phone conversation until he says my name.

"Jaine, to what do I owe the pleasure?"

I turn around. He motions his head to the seat facing him, but I remain standing. He knows exactly why I'm here. I just need to say what needs saying, then leave.

Simple. Or at least it should be.

I take in the eldest Duster, my eyes greedily drinking him in. His hair has gotten too long again, and it's curling on his collar. My fingers itch to yank on it, but I know I can't.

I walk forward until I'm standing in front of his desk. I stare at him. Does he realize how much I fucking love him?

Our physical bond flares up in such close proximity, but today, it won't be sated.

"I just wanted to say that I'm sorry for everything that happened before. I know I said it then, but I'd like to reiterate it. What I did was cruel and damaging. We both know our relationship never recovered." I pause. "Maybe I wasn't meant to love you, Eoin, but I do all the same, and loving you means I want the best for you. That's not me."

He stares at me but says nothing. Standing, he walks until he's on my side of the desk. His hand fists my hair and yanks my head back until my neck feels like it's going to snap. And he could snap it. Quite easily. I swallow as his eyes worship my face before his gaze drops to my mouth.

"Thank you for the *it's not you, it's me* speech. The delivery was exceptional, I have to say, but your actions betrayed your words."

"What do you mean?" But I know exactly what he means. I can feel the heat of his breath against my lips, and it's making me feel light-headed. What am I doing, allowing myself to be alone with him? I'm playing with fire, that's what—foolish idiot.

"You were eye-fucking me the entire time, Jaine."

I shake my head in weak denial. "I…"

My response is cut off as his mouth claims mine. Hard. Brutal. Demanding. I keep my lips firmly closed. He yanks my hips forward so our groins collide. I gasp at the connection, allowing his tongue to immediately take possession of my mouth.

He spins me so my ass is pressed against the desk. So, there's no escape.

I don't want to escape.

I bite his lip. Hard. He curses me as he devours my mouth, the copper taste invading both our senses. He eats me alive until I can't breathe. Until I can't think.

Until there is only him.

I groan before kissing him back in desperation.

Want. Need. Crave.

My core feels empty, clenching at nothing.

The hand fisting my hair drops to grace my throat. I want it there. Need it there. Crave it there. I groan against his mouth, faint with desire. He knows what he's doing. The reactions he's evoking. His arm immediately snakes around my waist to stop me from collapsing in a pathetic heap on the floor. He stops kissing me. His lips hover over mine, our breaths mingling. I don't want him to stop. I want him to keep on kissing me.

Want. Can't have.

"I'm sorry," I whisper the words I came here to say. The words to end everything we've ever shared. He stares down at me, his face impassive, then he releases me and walks back to the other side of the desk before retaking his seat.

"Close the door on your way out, Miss Jones."

I lean against the door briefly after I've closed it, immediately flooded with regret.

I never did get a photo.

I STARE AT THE DOOR, MY HEART STILL POUNDING IN MY CHEST.

Am I about to make another mistake? Should I do this in a more public place after what just happened with Eoin? I don't want a repeat performance.

Liar.

I don't knock. I push the door open and step inside, scanning the space to take in my surroundings. It's the first time I've been in Irish's office. Everything is either polished silver, white, or black. The desk grabs my attention. It's metal, the top finished in leather.

My eyes are then drawn to the walls, each crammed floor-to-ceiling with legal tomes and what I suspect is contract paraphernalia, all of which are organized and displayed alphabetically for ease of reference on tall metal shelving units.

I never knew Padraig was so structured. His persona is obviously nothing more than a smokescreen suggesting that he never takes things too seriously. He does. It would appear he takes his Duster duties extremely seriously.

If we worked side by side, I'm sure I could help him rein in his bloodthirsty ways so he could represent his family organization in the outside world. But we won't work together. We will never work together.

My gaze drifts to him, taking in his toned form as he leans back in his chair with every inch of defined muscle straining deliciously against the white fabric of his shirt. If he was wearing a tie today, it's been discarded. The top two buttons of his shirt are undone. My eyes drift to the exposed skin, and my mouth waters.

Lick. Suck. Bite. I want to do all three.

Get a grip, Jaine.

My gaze rises to full lips and perfect features before landing on laughing eyes of ice blue.

"Are you done blatantly admiring me, darlin'?"

No. I'm not done. I will never be goddamn done.

He closes his laptop. He's letting me know that he is now my captive audience. I now have his undivided attention, and I don't know what to do with it. I watch as he slowly rolls up his sleeves—another O'Connell who means business. I lick my lips. I want to be on the receiving end of whatever that business is.

I stare at his muscular forearms as he leans them on the desk, his expression switching from joking to intense. I think I like the intense Padraig O'Connell just as much.

I try to find the words, but nothing seems fitting, so instead of trying to put them eloquently, I decide just to say it how it is.

"I've loved you since I was nineteen years old." Tears of self-pity immediately prick my eyes as I suddenly feel overcome with emotion. "I don't know why Fate chose to keep us apart, but he did.

He then decided to put me on a different path and, in doing so, made it impossible for me to ever rejoin yours." He knows exactly what I'm saying. How could I ever be with him now? How could I ever choose between him and his brother? "We were meant, Irish. We both know that. You're right. Our souls *have* always been intertwined. I guess all we can hope is that we're allowed to be together in our next life. I love you. I will always love you. I want you to know that."

My heart skips a beat as he stands, my gaze drifting slowly over him.

"Are we really to be star-crossed lovers, Jaine?"

I smile sadly. "Unlike Romeo and Juliet, at least we get to live to tell the tale." We survived, but for what? To face a lifetime of regrets and what-ifs?

I swallow thickly as he walks slowly toward me. I know exactly what he's going to do.

Do it.

He doesn't stop until he has me pressed right up against the door.

One hand grips my waist, and the other fists my hair, causing me to whimper. He smirks. He clearly likes that sound. He stares down at me. Duke's right. I don't need to hear what I can already feel.

Love.

He tilts my head back, his lips grazing my neck before dropping to my throat. My nails dig into his powerful shoulders as he sucks and then bites. Tugging my hair, he arches my neck further to expose more of my flesh for his hot, wet mouth to feast on.

Soft. Warm. Coaxing.

I'm immediately lost in him. His smell. His touch.

His tongue trails the length of my throat before his mouth finally covers mine. I groan against his lips as my arms snake around his neck, and his hands drop to my hips to pull my front firmly against his. I gasp when my clit collides with his erection, his tongue seizing the opportunity to push past my lips to tangle with my own.

He's drugging me. His mouth is intoxicating. He's intoxicating.

Pressing me harder against the door, he deepens the kiss further. I don't ever want him to fucking stop.

My hands fist his hair as he lifts me off the floor, my legs instinctively anchoring around his slim hips. I mewl my pleasure against his mouth when he thrusts his hard dick against me over and over again.

Slow. Steady. Seductive. Until I'm losing control of my sanity.

"Irish."

I didn't come here to fuck him against the door of his office, but if I don't put a stop to this, that's exactly what's going to happen.

His lips hover over mine as he lowers me to the floor, then he stares down at me.

"I'm sorry," I whisper.

"As you wish, Jaine."

He stares at me but makes no attempt to stop me from leaving.

Am I disappointed? Yes. No.

CHAPTER SEVENTY-FOUR

JAINE

Jaine's Apartment, Upper East Side, New York

"Hey, little big guy. Please don't do that." I take the sponge from Fin's hands to stop him from filling it with bath water and squeezing it out over JJ's head for the third time. "I think you should apologize, don't you?"

"Sorry, JJ."

I watch as he hugs his baby brother. Fin has the same emotional soul that his daddy has, and he's starting to realize his words and actions can be hurtful to those around him. JJ immediately forgives him because he has the same beautiful soul that Ace had.

I watch as he clings to his big brother with tear-filled eyes. The sight of Fin then comforting him causes tears to spring to mine. They love each other so much.

Just like brothers should.

It's why I could never have come between Eoin and Irish.

I love both of them so fucking much, and to walk away was one of the hardest things I've ever had to do, but it was also the right thing. I refuse to destroy a bond as precious as the one that exists between brothers.

It's been six days. I miss them more than I ever thought possible, but I guess it's magnified by the finality of our situation. That this is it. That there's no coming back.

I ignore the empty feeling inside my chest. The hollow echo is just a stark reminder that there's no one left who can piece my heart back together again. I'm not going to wallow in a bottomless sea of self-pity. I've been given another chance. I've got to live my life for Ace and my boys, even if it's something I must do alone.

I know Eoin and Padraig have been spending time with the kids. I work from home in the mornings that Duke's got commitments with the Scorpions, and every weekday, Sarah collects both boys and takes them to Roisin's for the afternoon. She's mentioned she's bumped into Irish and Eoin during most drop-offs.

They'd never come here. Maybe in time. When things aren't so awkward, or they've both moved on with other people. That's not something I'm looking forward to. I don't know how I'll cope.

But I will.

I suspect Irish will take his time. He's already done his Duster duty and provided an heir. He won't be in any rush to get involved with someone.

But Eoin?

He has an imminent role to fulfill. He'll be under pressure to move on now that what we shared has ended once and for all.

Having put the boys to bed, I sit on the sofa and stare across the room. While it's great being back in my apartment, I find myself missing the safe space. I had gotten used to the hustle and bustle of living in the O'Connell home.

But I'm not family. I will never be an O'Connell. There was no point continuing to pretend otherwise.

I stare at my vibrating phone before answering.

"How are you doing, partner?"

"I'm doing okay, Jessie."

"You don't sound okay."

"I guess I'm missing the revolving doors of the O'Connell home."

"And you miss them." She doesn't have to mention any names. We both know who she's referring to.

"And I miss them."

"Have you given any more thought to this charity function tomorrow? It's for a good cause."

"I'll think about it?"

"You've been saying that for days."

"I've got a busy calendar." More lies.

"Yeah. Moping around the house and feeling sorry for yourself is taking up all your free time."

"Stop lecturing me, Jessie."

"I'm your big sister. It goes with the territory of being born first. It's my God-given right to lecture you."

I chuckle. "I haven't got anything to wear."

"So, I'm guessing out of the Disney princesses, you must be Cinderella."

"She had ugly sisters."

"I take that back. Bailey and I aren't ugly. Treat yourself, Jaine. You can't show up in a tank top and combats."

"Can't I just make a generous donation?" I huff.

"Jaine, you've just admitted you miss the hustle and bustle of the family home. You're going to go stir-crazy if you're not careful. You need to get out. Meet new people. Meet new m…."

"I'm not interested in meeting new men, Jessie."

"You know what they say. You have to get straight back in the saddle."

"I'm not a cowboy, even if you do call me partner."

She snorts. "You know what I mean."

"If you're going to introduce me to who you think are eligible men, then I'm definitely not going."

"I won't. Cross my heart and hope to die. Anyway, you need to go. Dylan will be there, and you haven't spoken to him in ages."

"With good reason. He knew about the message, Jessie. He knew the whole goddamn time that it was sent by Roisin and not Irish."

"He didn't want to get involved, Jaine. He'd been dragged into so many things that he was losing track of the number of secrets he had to keep."

Most of which were mine. She doesn't add it, but we're both thinking it.

"That's not the point."

"Jaine, everyone's been keeping secrets from everyone else, not just Dyl. You can't just single him out."

"I guess." I grudgingly agree with her because she's right.

"We'll pick you up at six p.m."

The Meeting Rooms, New York

"You really didn't have to come and get ready with me, Jessie." We're sitting side by side in the back of Liam's SUV. Dylan's making his own way there, apparently. He's obviously gone from being a recluse to being quite the social mobster butterfly.

"Oh, I did. I knew if I didn't, you'd wait until I was already there before messaging me with a list of excuses."

We both know she's right.

"Plus, what's the point in having a sister if you can't get ready together every once in a while? Anyway, I was shopping, and I knew that dress would be perfect for you. Just think of me as your Fairy Godmother. The Disney princess shall go to the ball, after all. You're welcome, by the way."

"Thank you, Jessie." I roll my eyes exaggeratedly at her just as the SUV pulls up at the destination. I stare at the building. I'm sorely tempted to ask Liam to take me back home. Nothing good has ever happened to me in this place. I doubt tonight will be any different.

It was here that I delivered the line to Sophia that resulted in Ace's death. It was here that the Colombians abducted Sarah and me. It was here that Brittany admitted that she'd lied about Irish cheating on me.

It was here that Eoin cornered me in the restroom.

Maybe not everything was bad.

My mind immediately drifts to the kiss he and I shared and then to the one I shared with Irish. Each so different.

Eoin so dominating and demanding. Irish so sensual and giving.

I'm not sure which I prefer. *Both. I prefer both.*

"Are you ready, partner?"

Jessie interrupts my thoughts. I stare at my sister as we stand on the familiar steps. She looks beautiful in a floor-length pale pink silk dress that clings to her tall, slim frame. I smooth down the material of my black one. Mine is a racerback style, and it's tighter than I would normally choose for myself.

I didn't have the heart to tell Jessie that it isn't really me.

We make our way inside. My guts are already telling me that I should turn and run. Adrenaline spikes through me. I know why. He's here. I can feel him.

Irish.

"Jessie." I grab her hand before we've even entered the function room.

"What is it?" She frowns at me. I'm tempted to ask if this is a set-up, but I don't. I ended things. If either Padraig or Eoin is here, it's not because they want to collide with me. It's because it's an important charity social event in our outlaw calendar.

I'm immediately spotted by several of my clients when we enter the venue. Each nod in my direction, and I smile in acknowledgment. "Jessie, I'm going to have to do the rounds," I whisper.

"Me too, partner. I'll meet you back at Dylan." She squeezes my hand as she watches me fidget. "Quit pulling at your dress. You have a fabulous figure. Flaunt it."

"Flaunting's not really my thing, Jessie," I mutter.

I make my way around the room, stopping to make polite small talk with those I need to. An hour has passed before I'm finally able to excuse myself.

I approach Jessie and Dylan from behind, watching as he whispers in her ear with his arm wrapped around her waist. She giggles in response.

I can't help but smile at their interaction. I'm glad they found each other. It's good to see them happy after everything they went through.

"Jaine." Jessie turns just as I approach. "You remember, Dylan, don't you?"

I roll my eyes at her, my lips curving upward.

"Jaine." I stare at him. His expression is laced with regret.

"What's done is done, Dyl. We can't change it now," I say quietly.

He nods slowly, then glances at Jessie, who's now staring across the room. We both look to see what's caught her attention, and my gaze immediately connects with the aquamarine eyes of Eoin.

My eyes graze over him as he stands, looking his ever-perfect self in a tuxedo. My gaze then connects with Padraig's, who's right beside him and also dressed to impress. Neither gives anything away, their masks held firmly in place.

My eyes then fall to the person standing between them, her red-sequin dress skimming her hourglass curves, her long blonde hair cascading down her back in thick waves.

Sabrina Hawthorn.

It's quite common for women to get up close and personal with Eoin.

It would seem so. That comment would also appear to apply to his youngest brother.

I watch as my employee makes a play for both brothers, running her red-tipped fingernails seductively down the front of both their jackets as she whispers in Eoin's ear. He whispers something in return, and she giggles exaggeratedly. She then whispers something in Irish's ear. He responds by snaking his arm around her waist.

Both are clearly receptive to her blatant admiration.

Why wouldn't they be? She's a beautiful woman. I stare across the room, not sure how I feel. Angry. Disappointed.

Jealous.

I realize I have no right to feel any of those emotions. I ended things. They have every right to move on.

"It looks like Sabrina didn't even wait for the dust to settle," Jessie comments.

"In her defense, she won't be aware of what's gone on, and she does know them both pretty well," Dylan responds.

"What do you mean?" Jessie frowns at him. I don't reply. I already know where this is headed.

"She's fucked them both."

"And how do you know that?"

"Paddy used to share his escapades with me before...." He stops. Again, I know what he was going to say. Before Irish and I reconnected.

"If I recall, he met her at some legal conference a while back."

"Well, right now, it looks like she can't decide which O'Connell brother she wants to sample first."

"She won't have to choose, Jessie."

"You've lost me."

"I'm sure a woman of your higher intelligence can work it out."

There's a pause. Then she places her hand on his arm. "Dear Lordy Lou. Do you mean both of them? At the same time?"

Dylan's silence speaks volumes.

I'm not sure how I feel as I watch Eoin whisper in Sabrina's ear once more.

Not that I can recall, although her name does sound vaguely familiar.

Yeah, right. I'm guessing his vague memories of Sabrina have now been refreshed, and she's reminded him of all the other forgotten parts of her too.

I glance around the room.

Then again, how many women in this place have he and Irish slept with? Given their sexual conquests reach four figures, I suspect most of them.

I look at Padraig as he stands there with his hand resting just above Sabrina's ass. He shoots me the smile that gets him anything he wants. I don't acknowledge it. I realize I'm being petty and immature.

Sabrina then makes eye contact with me. She smiles, looking like the cat who got the cream. Does she realize she's the meat in my ex-boyfriend-ex-husband sandwich? I'm not so sure that she does. I don't tend to discuss my personal life in the office.

"Jaine."

I spin around. "Nate."

Could this evening get any worse? I'm now confronted by the person who witnessed firsthand the moment I lost the will to live.

I've avoided him ever since. Does he know that I know about his secret?

He looks across the room and takes in the scene unfolding between my employee and my two exes. Then, snaking an arm around my waist, he smiles down at me.

"I think we need to talk."

I never thought I'd see the day when Nathan Hawke would prove to be the better option.

CHAPTER SEVENTY-FIVE

JAINE

Nate's Apartment, Upper East Side, New York

WE DIDN'T SPEAK ON THE CAB JOURNEY HERE, BOTH OF US NO doubt thinking about what to say given the content of our last morbid one-sided conversation.

Nate unlocks his apartment door and motions his head for me to step inside. I walk past him taking in the immaculate monochrome space once more.

"Drink?" He raises an eyebrow at me as he stands with the crystal decanter in his hand.

"I don't drink, Nate." I watch as he pours one for himself.

"Prefer to keep your wits about you?" He nods at the sofa, and I take a seat.

"From my experience, it's usually the best way." I pause.

Time passes.

"What you did, Jaine."

We both know he's referring to the night I was buried alive. When he was given no choice but to listen to my final words. "Anyone in my position would have done the same thing."

"You mean someone else who had nothing left to live for?"

"I can confirm that rock bottom actually exists."

He removes his tux jacket and throws the whiskey back in one, grimacing at the burn. "Most of us have been there at some point, Jaine. I'm not sure paying it a visit means you have to come away with a death wish." He pours himself another before removing his tie.

"The Ruoccos killed my husband. They tried to kill my son. They almost killed Eoin. Need I go on? They would never have stopped until they themselves were stopped. We both know that's the case. Given my regrettable comment to Sophia about Padraig is what inspired them to go on their rampage in the first place, I figured the responsibility for stopping them in their tracks lay with me."

"So, you used to date Padraig."

"You know I did."

"And your eldest boy is his son."

"Don't play coy. You know everything there is to know about me."

"Everything?"

"Everything." Because call it a sixth sense, but I know he knows about my sniping secret. What I don't know is how.

"How did you find out?" I don't feel panicked for some reason. Maybe it's a combination of things. That I've had to reveal it to so many people recently. It's just becoming second nature, combined with the fact that I trust him.

"The fire alarm incident at Padraig's apartment. I like to keep a close eye on what those O'Connell boys are getting up to. I looked at the footage. The person who set the alarm off wore the same biker jacket you wore when you came here. Then I noticed some other similarities, say if I removed the leather jacket and replaced it with a puffer style. It was then that I had the *eureka* moment."

He smirks, his auburn hair perfectly styled as usual, his eyes striking blue against a way too good-looking face.

"Don't worry. I've deleted the footage, Jaine. It can be our little secret."

"And why would you do that?"

"I like to think that you and I are both vigilantes in our own way. We both take out the trash. One legally, the other not."

"Any other reason?"

"I know that you know my own secret."

"How?"

"As soon as anyone accesses those personal files, I know about it. I then decide if they can read them in depth or not."

"And you let me."

"A secret for a secret."

"Do any of the others know?"

"Two of them."

We sit in silence. I know who one of them is. I don't bother asking who the second one is because he won't tell me.

"Is this cozy heart-to-heart the only reason you pulled me out of the function?"

"No."

"What was the other reason?"

"You looked troubled. I thought I'd rescue you."

"I was fine."

"I was the recipient of your final words, remember, Jaine. You willingly became a dead person walking in part because you thought they were both gone. I then had to listen as you took your last breath and died. I only wish I could experience a love that deep and meaningful."

"You mean you didn't marry for love?" I smirk. We both know Nate married his ex-wife for political gain, nothing more. "Trust me. It's not all it's cracked up to be."

"Obviously not, as the moment you found out they weren't dead, you let both of them go."

"I couldn't choose."

"Who said you had to?"

"What are you saying?"

"You know what I'm saying. It's clear they've shared women in the past, given the way Sabrina Hawthorn was pawing at them both. It's common knowledge in our legal world that she's quite partial to a menage-a-trois."

"You sound like you've had firsthand experience."

"I don't. It's not really my thing, but each to their own."

"Maybe I don't want to be shared."

"You're a lawyer. At least try to make it sound convincing."

"Maybe they don't want to share." I snap.

"I'm sure you could convince them. Surely, it's got to be better than witnessing them be with other women."

I stand. "I think that's my cue to leave."

He laughs dryly. "Jaine, you're meant to be one of the top legal brains in Manhattan, yet here you are, running away because you don't like what you're being told. Debating is what our kind do, or is it because you don't have a valid argument?"

"No, Nate. I'm leaving because this is about me. It's not about a client. My personal life isn't up for debate. My personal life has got nothing to do with you."

"Where the O'Connells are concerned, I beg to differ."

I stare at him. I get it now. "That's the other reason you're keeping my secret, right? Because I'm one of them."

He smiles, saluting me with his glass before throwing his drink back in one.

"Do yourself a favor, Jaine. Stop playing the martyr because one of these days, you really will run out of lives, and it'll be too late. Given the number of times you've almost died, you should know better than most that when we're faced with death, it's not the things we've done that we regret, it's the things we didn't."

Jaine's Apartment, Upper East Side, New York

"Did anything go down between you and the very tasty and extremely single Nathan Hawke last week?"

"Jessie, what did I say last time we had this conversation?" I roll my eyes.

"That if you fucked the DA, I'd be the first to know."

"Exactly, and given that I haven't said, 'Hey, Jessie. Guess what? I fucked the DA' then it means it never happened."

"A girl can dream."

"Married girls can't dream about having sex with divorced, single men who cheat on their wives."

"Sabrina didn't go home with Eoin or Padraig that night, even though she was throwing herself at both."

"They don't take women home. They hook up at their willing victim's apartment. Maybe they all met up later for their menage-a-trois."

"They didn't. Dylan was on the phone with both his brothers the moment we got back. Can you believe Sabrina fucked them at the same time? I know how demanding one O'Connell male can be. I can't imagine how hard it must be trying to satisfy…."

"Jessie," I warn.

"I mean, Eoin on his own must be exhaust…."

"Jessie!"

"Did you ever think about it?"

"About what?" I play dumb.

"Being with them both intimately at the same time."

"No."

"Would you consider it?"

"No."

"Liar." She snickers.

"Why ask the questions if you already know all the goddamn answers?"

"So you *have* been thinking about it."

"Once or twice. It's nothing more than curiosity."

"Do you think you could handle both?"

"I'm not even going to dignify that question with an answer."

"I'm your sister. Sharing's caring. If the option was on the table, would you be in a relationship with them both?"

"What is this, twenty questions?"

"I'm curious too. Maybe it's an O'Brien family trait."

"Great. I hope I haven't inherited any of the others."

"Well, would you?"

"Jesus Christ. No, Jessie. I wouldn't!" She knows I'm lying, but she drops it at the sound of my exasperated tone.

"So, what did you and the dishy DA talk about?"

"Work." Among other things. "Anyway, I need to go. I'll talk to you later." Another lie leaves my mouth as I disconnect the call.

Resting my head back against the sofa, I stare at the ceiling.

I'm relieved they didn't go home with Sabrina. As much as I now know both Eoin and Irish have fucked her in the past, I'd rather never have to consider comparing notes with one of my employees.

Given some of the stories Irish regaled me with about his brothers when we were at Yale, I knew they occasionally shared. I just never expected to see them with one of their joint conquests as she blatantly demanded a repeat performance.

Is fucking my ex-boyfriend and ex-husband a sackable offense?

I know how childish that sounds, but I'm not sure I'll be able to look at Sabrina now and not think of her with them. I can taste the jealousy in my mouth.

Her with them. Me with them.

I haven't been able to think about much else aside from the latter ever since.

What would it be like?

I think back over my conversations with Nate and Jessie. Would I ever consider being with both Eoin and Irish?

No, I wouldn't.

It's got nothing to do with the sex. I mean, I fucked Ace and Irish at the same time. It's more to do with the fact that it wouldn't change anything. In the end, I'd still be made to choose if I wanted to have a relationship with either of them. And therein lies the problem.

I will never be able to.

I'm not sure I've ever read a fairytale where the happily ever after sees the princess end up with the prince *and* the future king.

Maybe it's time for a retelling.

My phone vibrates once more. I roll my eyes with a smile, thinking it'll be Jessie.

Eoin: *Can you meet me at the local park at noon?*

I stare at the message, my guts immediately telling me this isn't a good sign.

Say no, Jaine.

Jaine: *I'll be there.*

Fool. I haven't spoken to either of them since my unscheduled visit to Duster HQ. What else was there to say? They asked me to choose. I couldn't. How do you choose between the man you love and the man you love?

You can't.

CHAPTER SEVENTY-SIX

PADRAIG

Weeks Earlier

The Angels of Hellfire Clubhouse, Rising, California

WE KEEP THINGS LIGHT-HEARTED UNTIL WE'RE SURE JAINE'S OUT OF earshot. We have to respect the fact that she doesn't want to be party to this conversation. At least not yet.

The small talk eventually evaporates. We then sit in silence, staring at Lucifer across the walnut table. Was it Jaine he came here to see today or Eoin and me? I reckon we're just about to find out.

"Jessie's told me what's been going on."

"You'll have to be more specific, Lucifer." Eoin makes a fair point.

"That Jaine's in love with you both."

"I'm not sure what business that is of…."

"She's my daughter. That's what business it is of mine!" He

slams his hand down on the tabletop before closing his eyes and muttering, no doubt annoyed with himself at his over-reaction.

"I want to know what your intentions are. She's been through enough with Ace. I don't want to see her suffer any more."

"She's been asked to choose between us," I answer this time.

"I thought so," he grumbles.

"What does that mean?" Eoin frowns.

"I came here today because I wanted the chance to explain what happened between me and Jaine's mom."

So it was Eoin and me that he came here to see. Jessie or Dylan must have let him know we'd be paying a visit. Neither of us replies. We wait for him to continue. I watch as he runs a hand down his beard. He looks exhausted.

Who can blame him?

He must be worried sick about her, given she's currently on the run from my brother-in-law.

"Jaine's mom, Paula… was the love of my life."

"What happened?" He looks at me, no doubt thinking on how best to respond.

Minutes pass.

"We were happily married. We had two young babies, Tadgh and Jessie. I was already prez of my own club, so we had a good life. I knew Duke even back then. He used to drop by sometimes when he had business to attend to in Vegas. Occasionally, Jeremiah would tag along. He was a quiet man, but he came alive whenever Paula was around. I should have seen the signs, but I didn't. I thought she loved me. She did. But it turns out she had also fallen in love with Jeremiah."

I know immediately where this is going. I suspect Eoin does too.

"Jaine's mom also had the ability to love more than one man."

And there it is.

We wait for him to continue. I can tell this is hard for him, the memories difficult to revisit. He runs his hand down his beard once more. "In the end, she admitted to me that she loved us both." He pauses, his expression riddled with guilt and pain. "When they were old enough to ask questions, I told Jessie and Tadgh that their mom left through choice. I lied. I threw her out. I felt betrayed, even though I knew nothing had ever happened between her and Jeremiah. I didn't even allow her to say goodbye to the children. She only had time to grab a handful of things before I locked her out of the house. It was the middle of the night, and she had nowhere to go. I didn't realize she was pregnant with Jaine at the time."

"How did you work out Jaine was yours?" I ask.

"I knew the moment I saw her on the screen in Nevada. It was the day after Reaper's demise. It was like looking at Bailey. And when I heard the surname. Well, it was too much of a coincidence. Ace confirmed that she was Jeremiah's daughter, but I knew she couldn't be."

"And why is that?" Eoin questions.

"It came up during a conversation between him and Paula. It was one that she just happened to share with me. The fact that he was unmarried with no little ones. Jeremiah was infertile. He couldn't have children of his own."

"I don't understand why he never told Jaine." I frown, disappointed on her behalf. She spent so much of her life alone when she had a ready-made family. She's lost out on so much. The pain of missing out on Jaine's life is permanently etched on Lucifer's face. Thirty-one years that neither of them will ever get back.

"It won't have been malicious. Maybe he was waiting for her to return home. I'm pretty sure he never expected to die when he did and in the way he did."

I nod. Now it all adds up.

"I kept asking myself if I could go back in time, would I change things? I like to think I would be more understanding than I was back then. But I still wouldn't have understood how one woman could love two men at the same time. I thought Paula had just been pacifying me. I thought she had been telling me what I needed to hear because she didn't want to admit that she'd fallen out of love with me. Until I heard about Jaine going through the same thing with you two boys."

"I'm pretty sure your wife would have chosen you and her children over Jeremiah."

He looks at me defeatedly as he nods. "Maybe so, Padraig, but knowing she loved another man would still have ended things for me and her."

"What point are you trying to make, Lucifer?" Eoin is starting to get agitated.

"You've asked Jaine to choose." He looks at him, then turns to me. "She's loved you longest, I'm told. I'm also told that everything she's done these past three-plus years has been for you. With that in mind, you would think her choosing you would be the most likely outcome, but how would you feel if she didn't? How would you feel if she chose your brother to spend the rest of her life with?" He then turns his attention to Eoin. "And you, Eoin? How would it feel watching from the sidelines as the love of your life spends the rest of hers with your brother? As the future Da Duster, you'd have no choice but to marry someone else."

"Lucifer, what…."

"Don't make her choose, Eoin."

"What do you mean?" Eoin frowns and shakes his head. Now he's worked out exactly what Lucifer's suggesting. That we share Jaine.

My brother stands and starts pacing the floor. "Our parents would never condone that sort of relationship."

Lucifer stands, slamming his hand on the table once more. "I'm told part of the reason you're all in this mess is because your parents meddled! Your da manipulated a marriage of convenience between you and Jaine to suit his own purposes, and then your ma sent Jaine a message she had no business sending! They can hardly hold my daughter responsible for the mess she's in!"

I watch as my brother's face falls. He's already riddled with guilt over the deceitful part he played in the past.

Lucifer's right. We both know it.

They both retake their seats.

"She won't be able to choose." Lucifer's tone is quiet. "I'm worried you'll destroy what's left of her if you try to make her."

Two Days Earlier
Eoin's Apartment, Hudson Yards, New York

I glance around Eoin's apartment as he pours himself a drink. You'd expect his place to be cool, clinical, and immaculate.

It's not.

It's a calming space with its dark brown furniture and accents contrasting against a warm cream backdrop. He motions his head toward the crystal decanter. I shake mine in response. Whiskey is not my friend. After what happened in the past, it's permanently off-limits for me.

"Have you given any thought to our conversation with Lucifer?" I just come right out with it.

"I have." He throws back his drink in one, then pours another.

"And?"

"I'm too possessive to ever consider it, Paddy."

"We've shared women before now."

"That wasn't my wife!" he snaps.

"We don't actually have to be intimate with her at the same time, Eoin."

"I realize that!"

The silence stretches. I wait for him to speak. There's no point winding him up any further than he already is.

"And have you given it any thought?"

I shrug. "I have no issue sharing her with you. I would have shared her with Ace had I been given the opportunity. I did, in fact, share her with Ace. Once."

Eoin throws back the second whiskey before walking across to stand directly in front of where I'm sitting on the sectional.

He frowns at me. "You both fucked her at the same time?"

I nod my head slowly, and he immediately starts pacing the floor once more.

"Our parents…" he begins.

"Would be accepting of the arrangement, and you know it. They want Jaine to be an O'Connell. And Lucifer's right. If anyone's responsible for this mess, it's them. You reap what you sow."

More silence as he digests what I've said. "I would like to have children of my own."

I shrug. "You'd have to cross that bridge with Jaine whether we were sharing her or not. I would never stand in the way of that."

"She can only marry one of us."

"I know."

"How would we decide?"

"We could do a simple coin toss."

"I'm not sure, Paddy." I watch as he pours himself a third drink.

"Would you rather be in the same situation I was in, where you have to consider a future with someone you'd much rather not while watching Jaine move on in a life without you in it?"

"There's no guarantee she would be accepting of any of this."

"No, but if we're both in agreement, at least it's a starting point," I argue.

The trouble is, I'm not so sure that we are.

CHAPTER SEVENTY-SEVEN

JAINE

Local Park, Upper East Side, New York

MEMORIES.

Of pushing the kids on the swings. Of having a picnic on the grass. Of enjoying a family day out.

I glance around the familiar space as I inhale the smell of freshly cut grass. The kids and I used to come here most days before we went into lockdown, yet I only ever invited Eoin along that one time.

Why?

Because I deliberately excluded him. I intentionally left him standing all alone on the sidelines of my life because I wanted him to pay for something he didn't do.

Creating memories is what I should have been focused on. Not the bickering or the fighting or the countless confrontations. On the things that truly mattered, not the ones that didn't.

I realize now that our relationship didn't end recently. It ended when I spat out the ugly word *karma*.

We never recovered from that.

What we had before then wasn't a lie. In many ways, it was the only real time we ever spent together. I was just too stupid and too blind to realize it.

Back then, Eoin didn't ask for much from me. He asked for my love. For me to spend time with him. For me to let him in. He wanted to be part of my life. He wanted to be part of my family. I dangled it all in front of him, then deliberately pulled it away.

He'd given me his love. He made himself weak. He made himself vulnerable. He trusted me to do the right thing with his heart. I didn't. Instead, I crushed it beneath my unsubstantiated personal vendetta.

Did I then think handing him the story of my life was enough? It wasn't. He didn't want the novel that contained my past. He wanted the unwritten part.

My future.

I walk forward reluctantly, watching as my shaky breath collides with the cool air. It's a bleak, depressing kind of day. It's like all the color has been sucked out of the world, and it's then been injected by a fusion of morbid greys. It's one of those days that can instantly sour your positive mood, turning it melancholy in the blink of an eye.

It's then that I see him. Tears fill my eyes at the sight.

Eoin O'Connell is a powerful man. Feared. Respected. Envied. But right now, when he thinks no one's watching, he looks defeated as he sits on a bench, staring across the little pond.

The pond where he taught Fin how to skim stones.

For a man who has it all, he actually wants very little. He wants a wife. He wants children. He wants a family. Because this man was born to be a husband. Born to be a father. Born to head a family.

I didn't give him any of that. In hindsight, all I did was hand him the rule book according to Jaine Jones, then expected him to comply with the content and follow it religiously.

No arguments. No deviations. No compromises.

I wanted him to change for me when I wasn't prepared to change for him. I was selfish in many ways. I realize that now. I may have told him the story of my life, but what good are words without actions to back them up?

And now it's too late.

Because I know exactly what today is.

I approach the bench. He stands to greet me, dressed casually in black jeans and a black leather bomber jacket.

My eyes drift to his face, taking in the dark circles around his eyes. He looks tired. He looks worn out with life. I did this to him.

Me. No one else.

He makes no move to hug or kiss me. Instead, he stands there staring, his gaze slowly drifting over me as he imprints me to memory while I do the same.

"Thank you for agreeing to meet with me, Jaine."

I want to turn and run. I don't want to hear what he has to say, but I have no choice. I nod. I don't sit. Instead, I turn and walk toward the pond's edge to stand in the same spot he did with Fin.

"Is this our place?" My voice remains calm. The question itself sounds childlike. Pathetic almost. But I don't care. I want the answer even though I already know what it is.

I feel him approach me from behind. I squeeze my eyes shut, my nose tingling as tears prick my eyes. *Don't cry, Jaine.* All my senses are immediately overwhelmed by him.

Craving him. Wanting him. Loving him.

He doesn't touch me. We both know why.

"We've never had a place, Jaine."

The guilt tastes bitter as it floods my mouth. Because he's right.

We never had a place. We never had a photograph. We never had anything apart from a song, and even then, I only gifted him that because I thought he was going to die.

"We never even tried, did we?" I whisper as I blink back tears of regret.

"We tried several times. In the end, we didn't work."

His words hold no conviction. He's lying. We didn't try. Not really. He knows it as well as I do. Time passes as we both stare across the water.

"Jaine." How many emotions can you pack into one word? Pain. Anguish. Sorrow. So many, and all of them laced with endless regret. I don't want to hear what comes next. My heart is in pieces as it is. Seconds feel like hours.

"I'm leaving New York."

I swallow the lump that's now threatening to choke me. *Please don't fucking go.*

"Why?"

"To make things easier."

Easier for who?

"But you're needed here. Your family needs you. The business needs you."

I need you.

"The family will survive without me for the duration, and I can work remotely."

"Where will you go?"

"We recently acquired several properties in Chicago. As you know, we've had plans to extend our reach for quite some time. I've decided to bring them forward."

Is this because I refused to make a choice?

Because our incompatibilities were never insurmountable, we both know that. This decision hasn't been reached because he's too protective or possessive. Neither is it about me refusing to meet him halfway or vice versa.

He pulled back. He stopped trying. And there was a reason for that.

Guilt. Remorse. Regret.

Is that why he's distancing himself?

I thought that if he finally laid bare his truth, that if his brother forgave him, then the slate would be wiped clean. Obviously not. Admitting to the wrongdoings clearly hasn't undone any of their lasting, negative effects.

Is this his way of removing himself from an equation that, in his mind, he should never have been part of in the first place?

He knows I can't make a choice. That I never will. Is he leaving, so I don't have one? In his mind, he stole me from Padraig. Is he now trying to right his wrong?

Is he now giving me back?

I can't argue with his reasoning. I understand. I get it. He has to come to terms with what's gone on before. The same as I had to. The same as Irish had to. It's something he has to address on his own. I can't do that for him. No one can.

But then what?

Nothing.

There's no future for us because Irish and I are meant. *But maybe Eoin and I are meant too?*

Realization.

That this is it. That this is goodbye.

I love every side of Eoin O'Connell. I don't want a future where he's not in it.

He's making another decision on my behalf. I should be angry. But I'm not.

Because by letting him go, I'm giving him what *he* wants. What *he* needs. And it will be the first unselfish thing I've ever done for him.

"I love you," I utter the three words that will never change.

Words they refer to as little when they're, in fact, quite the opposite. They're the biggest words you will ever say out loud to another person.

The most important. The most exposing. The most damaging. And right now, I am the latter. I am damaged. Even though I don't show it outwardly.

Won't. Can't.

I found one brother and lost another. Does that balance the scales of love? What do I do with all the love I have for Eoin O'Connell when he leaves?

"I know you do, Jaine, but it's no longer enough. I'm sorry, but I've made my decision. You and I don't have a future together. I'm no longer an option."

I fight to hold back the tears that are threatening to overwhelm me. He has enough guilt. I don't need to add to it. I slowly turn to face him.

My nemesis. My enemy. The antagonist in the story of my life.

Until he wasn't. Until he became my savior.

Because when I returned to New York, our constant back and forth and push and pull is what saved me from drowning in a sea of grief. He became the buoy that kept me afloat.

I hated him. Until I didn't.

"When do you leave?"

"Today."

I feel sick. I want to scream at the unfairness of it all, but I won't because that would be selfish. This isn't about me. It's about him. He needs to be allowed to bury the past before he can move on to his future.

A future that I now know doesn't include me.

"Jaine. I want you to be with Paddy. I know you won't consider it without my blessing, so I'm giving it to you. He's been through enough. He deserves his happiness. You both do."

We stare at each other. I'm not sure how long passes. And then, with a nod, he turns and leaves.

I watch until he's out of sight. He never looks back once.

CHAPTER SEVENTY-EIGHT

EOIN

Local Park, Upper East Side, New York

I WALK AWAY.

I don't look back. Not because I don't want to, but because I can't. I'm a mobster. I fear nothing.

Apart from the depth of love I have for her.

I already miss her. Want her. Need her. Crave her.

My drug. My addiction. My equal.

My person.

She's infected my blood. Jaine Jones is my kryptonite—the thing I want most and the only one that could ever destroy me.

"She won't be able to choose. I'm worried you'll destroy what's left of her if you try to make her."

My strides are long as I cross the park. My chest feels constricted, each step I take away from her causing it to tighten further.

Heartache.

I need to put as much distance between us as possible before I regret my decision and turn back.

I made the choice for all of our sakes. I will not destroy her. I will not destroy him. They have suffered enough at my hands.

I'm far from being a martyr. I'm merely accepting my well-deserved penance for the part I played in the pain I caused when I stole something that was never truly mine.

I was never destined to love you, Eoin. You made me love you.

Padraig didn't have to force her feelings. Loving him was as natural to her as breathing because they were meant.

I was nothing more than the villain who hijacked their fairytale. A villain who then selfishly and continually thwarted their happily-ever-after ending.

No more.

Prince Charming will have the Disney Princess he has loved since once upon a time. She's not mine. She was never mine. She will never be mine.

I'm not sure I will ever love anyone as much as I love her, but it wasn't my love she wanted or needed all this time.

It was his.

Did she see through my deceit? Does she realize it was guilt over the part I played in their past that saw me walk away? That I now need to self-flagellate in private?

That I need to get away. Away from her. Away from him. Away from everything I've ever known.

Is that the reason she let me go so easily?

Or was her choice already made? That her forced affection for me paled when compared to the depth of feeling she held for my youngest brother?

I try to compose myself before answering my phone. For the second time since I was a little boy my cheeks are wet.

"Dylan."

"Eoin, where are you? Da's been trying to get hold of you."

"I've just been to see Jaine." I make my way out of the park toward the parked-up SUV.

"Why?" He sounds confused.

"To let her know that I'm leaving town."

There's a pause.

"What do you mean you're leaving town?"

"I'm going to oversee the office refurbishment in Chicago."

"We have people for that."

"I want to do it personally." He's not a fool. He knows exactly what I'm doing.

"Eoin, don't do this."

"Don't do what?"

"Don't run away."

"I'm not running anywhere."

"Jaine loves you."

"I know she does. That's why my staying will only see her hurt further. She won't move on if I remain. You know it as well as I do. And I'm no longer a viable option for her. She and I have tried and failed too many times. There's no other way. With time and distance, she'll soon forget about me and move on with Paddy. It's how it was always meant to be."

"So this is about your compatibility issues?"

"Yes." Liar.

"I'm sure you could easily work through them now you're no longer living with a timebomb ticking under you?"

I think the same, but I can't tell him that. In the end, I don't even bother to reply. There's no point.

"Paddy mentioned sharing."

"Sharing is not the way forward! This is Jaine Jones we're talking about! She would never agree to such a thing, and nor should she! Regardless, they shouldn't have to compromise what they have together. Not for me."

"Did you stop to ask Jaine what she wants?"

"There's no point. And there would still be no guarantees. Adding another person to the mix may well just exacerbate the situation. Jaine and I can't keep going around in the same circle."

"And have you told the family that you're leaving?"

"I'll call da mid-flight. I'm on my way to the airport now."

"So, what happens next?"

I swallow the lump in my throat. I'm struggling to find the words, but maybe that's more to do with their content.

"I want her and Paddy to be together. They deserve their happiness. Whether he needs it or not, he has my blessing to be with her."

"Are you sure, Eoin?"

"I'm sure." It's the bitterest lie I've ever had to swallow.

I disconnect the call and stare up at the overcast sky.

I'll now need to learn how to survive each new day without my person. I'll need to move on. As the future Da Duster, I'll be given no choice.

This is the only way. I refuse to let their ending be a tragedy.

CHAPTER SEVENTY-NINE

JAINE

Jaine's Apartment, Upper East Side, New York

It's been a week since Eoin left for Chicago.

The kids and I went to the park this morning before I dropped them off at Roisin's for a sleepover. We played on the swings and had a picnic. I found my gaze constantly drifting toward the empty bench. Each time I looked over, I hoped Eoin would be sitting there.

He wasn't.

I love him. I know better than most that you can't switch that emotion off. Or at least, I can't. My love for him is unconditional. I will always love him, even when the day arrives that he no longer loves me. Because one day soon, he will move on. I need to prepare myself for that.

But I'm not sure how to.

We were on and off so many times. I should be used to his absence by now. But I'm not.

It's deafening.

I miss Mr. Smug. Selfish. Pompous and Mr. Dominating. Dangerous. Deadly. I miss all three hundred and sixty fucking degrees of Eoin O'Connell.

He gave me his blessing to be with Irish. Did he give Padraig the same? I suspect he will have done. In his mind, he fucked up Padraig's life. To absolve himself of the associated guilt, he left town to allow Irish and me to be together as we were always meant to be. Or at least that's what I'm reading between the lines.

There should have been another way. This way feels like a death. I've been mourning what we had and didn't have ever since. What we will never have again.

I can't help but feel responsible for this outcome, but then I guess we're all of us guilty.

Apart from Irish.

In exchange for doing nothing wrong, first he lost me and then he lost his eldest brother. He's also been silent for a week. My phone vibrates.

Wiping the tears from my cheeks, I stare at the message.

Speak of the devil.

Padraig: *Can I see you, Jaine?*

Is it wrong that when I think of moving forward with him, I feel a pang of guilt? That some part of me still thinks I belong to his eldest brother? That I would be betraying Eoin or cheating on him in some way? Irish and I have kissed, but we've never gone beyond that in over three years.

Jaine: *Where shall we meet?*

Padraig: *In half an hour. At St. Peter's.*

St. Peter's Church, Upper East Side, New York

I park my hog on the same grass verge I always do before removing my helmet and staring at the church. It's the first time I've witnessed the utter devastation caused by the fire.

Closing my eyes, I take a deep breath, inhaling the smell of burning that still hangs in the air, its acrid and unpleasant scent an unwelcome reminder of everything that happened before.

I know everyone says that it's not my fault, but it is. I did this.

A container has been placed to the side of the building. I'm guessing it's to house the workers. Their short-term contract now extended to the *foreseeable future*.

There's no one to be seen.

I look once more at the church. The ancient grey stone walls are still standing, and the spire still stretches into the sky, but the imposing doors have gone, as has the roof. Does that mean the bats have too? A wave of sadness washes over me at the thought of them losing their home. I hope they survived.

I walk toward the only thing that hasn't changed. The small graveyard with its uneven headstones. I use the time to walk around, reading as many visible inscriptions as I can. The final words spoken between the living and the dead. Some of the departed are old. Some were like Ace. Way too young to die.

I feel Irish approach even before I see him, our connection vibrant and strong.

Our gazes connect. His hair has grown, its inky blackness so long it's falling into his eyes. My eyes drift over the snug-fitting black jeans. He's wearing a leather jacket, just like Eoin did on that last day. They're so similar on the outside, yet so very different underneath.

Do they realize how much I love them both? I fight back the sob of self-pity that's threatening to escape.

"I'm sorry." I motion my head toward the church as I stare at him. "I know how much it meant to you."

"It's only a building, darlin'."

But it was way more than that. It was his building.

It was our building.

He stands in front of me and gently pushes my hair behind my ear before placing a kiss against the tattoo for him and Fin. Taking my hand, he leads me to the rear of the property, where there's a rickety old bench that I've never noticed before. We both sit down.

"How have you been, Jaine?"

"Coping." Just.

He pauses briefly. "Eoin had his reasons for doing what he did."

"I know." Were they reasons or excuses? Neither makes the hurt any less.

"He'll still be traveling back and forth for our Reservoir Dogs-style meetings, as you used to call them."

I chuckle sadly. "I'm not sure if that's a good or bad thing. Out of sight and mind might make things easier." Although I'm almost certain Eoin will make sure we never attend the same one.

"Jaine."

"It's fine, Irish." I smile sadly at him. "I know I need to get over it. Get over him. That life moves on because it has to."

I wouldn't have a life if it weren't for Eoin.

"Am I enough, darlin'?" The words are quietly spoken.

I frown at him. "What do you mean?"

"I'm not Eoin. I will never be Eoin. The future Da Duster is a pretty tough act to follow."

Does he feel insecure? I've been so busy wallowing in my own grief that I never stopped to consider how my outward display would affect him.

"How can you follow when you came first?"

"The original and the best. Is that what you're trying to say?" He forces a weak smile.

"Now you're just being vain." I snort.

He chuckles as he takes my hand in his.

"All joking aside, Jaine, I know you miss him. We all do. But he's made his decision, and we all have to respect it. Who knows what the future holds? You and I both know things have a way of working themselves out in the end, if they're meant to. An hour, a day, a week. Sometimes it even takes twelve years."

Tears prick my eyes because he's right. We sit in amicable silence, each of us lost in our own thoughts before he finally speaks again.

"You said something a while ago. You said, 'What I think is that Fate meant for us to be on this very bench at this very time. I think this is all part of the great masterplan he had in store for us all along.' Well, it may not be the same bench, but I reckon it's still part of the same plan. What do you think?"

I turn to look into eyes of ice blue and nod.

"Because our souls have always been intertwined. You feel that too, darlin'?"

I try to swallow the lump that's appeared in my throat as he says what he first did over three years ago now, but it escapes as a painful sob. Seconds pass before I can speak.

"I feel it, Irish." My voice is barely a whisper.

"You see, every day since I met you in that old admin office that stunk of lavender, I prayed to God that he would let you be mine."

He takes my hand in his and squeezes it gently.

"I love you so fucking much, Jaine. Right from that very first moment, I knew you were it for me. I've refused to let you go because I truly believe that we were meant in every life that's ever been and in every life that's yet to be. You have always been my end game."

I nod with a watery smile, then look straight ahead. "I reckon you're right. I reckon I was born to be yours, Irish."

In our life, we need to grab love and happiness where we can, so follow your heart and don't try to second guess what it's telling you.

That moment right there, where I'm staring across the little graveyard with the uneven stones, is where everything suddenly makes sense. All of my past, all of my present, and all of my future were built around three men who made me who I am, and I am so grateful for all of them.

Ace. Eoin. Irish.

Irish tilts my chin and places a soft kiss against my lips. It's not heated. It's full of promise and anticipation. I stare at the boy that I've loved since I was nineteen, his face filled with hope.

Is love really all that matters? I reckon it is.

Maybe it's not something you need for balance, but someone.

I smile then at the realization. Duke was right. I stare at Padraig O'Connell, knowing I finally have my missing balance.

CHAPTER EIGHTY

PADRAIG

St. Peter's Church, Upper East Side, New York

WITH HER HEAD ON MY SHOULDER AND MY ARM WRAPPED AROUND her, we sit and talk until the sun starts to set.

I'm hoping this can be our place moving forward. The cheating allegation tarnished our time at Yale. The boating lake will always be known as where she lost the will to live. As much as it's a ruin for now, this little church will forever hold me in its grasp, the same as she always will.

I love it. I love her.

I'm well aware my next suggestion could go either way, but it's my opinion that we have to fully move on if we're to be together. I love my big brother, but she has to let him go just as he's let her go.

I stand, then offer her my hand, smiling when she places hers in mine. I pull her to her feet and wrap my arm around her slim waist.

"Jessie's going to ride your hog back to your apartment, Jaine. You're staying with me tonight."

"Why?" She frowns as she looks up at me.

"Because I'm going to make sweet love to you with no cameras around and in a proper bed instead of on the front seat of an SUV."

I can immediately sense her inner turmoil. She feels like she's cheating on Eoin, I know she does, but she isn't. With a feeble excuse about lack of compatibility, he walked away and left her standing in the middle of a park with nothing to hold on to but her grief.

I open the passenger door of the SUV, and she gets in. The atmosphere changes as we set off. I can't help but smile.

"Are you nervous, darlin'?"

"No." We both know she's lying.

"Aroused then?" I wink at her.

"Why are you even asking that?"

"You've started fidgeting in your seat, so I was just curious."

"You know what it did to the cat."

I chuckle. "You forgot how blunt I am, didn't you, Jaine? There's no hiding from me. You know that."

"This will take some getting used to, Irish," she whispers.

She's right. It will. "I know that, darlin', but we have the rest of our lives together to figure it all out."

Padraig's Apartment, Hudson Yards, New York

Jaine's silent the rest of the way.

She's nervous as much as she tried to deny it. I mentioned that we'd be having sex. I don't think Jaine's much of a pre-planner when it comes to fucking. It happens spontaneously.

It's been a while, and neither of us was at our best back then. It's difficult to be natural when you have a camera trained on your arse the entire time. Getting out of the SUV, I walk around to her side, open her door, then take her hand to help her down. I don't let it go. I'm a tactile fella. She knows that. If she's forgotten, then she needs to get used to it all over again.

We make our way up in the elevator. It lets us know we've arrived on my floor at the same time as her phone vibrates.

"Who is it?"

"Roisin. She's just letting me know that the kids are in bed and that everything's fine."

I take my phone out of my pocket.

"What are you doing?"

"I'm letting everyone know not to contact us unless it's to do with the kids or an emergency. We'll be otherwise engaged."

She stares at me and swallows thickly. Jaine's not used to someone taking control. I'm sure Eoin tried, but she enjoyed bickering with him way too much to do his bidding. That was part of their problem. It's a different story with me and her. We've never bickered. She doesn't quite know how to react.

We exit the elevator, and I unlock the apartment door. Once inside, I pull her straight into my arms before staring down at all of her perfection.

"Do you want to take a shower, Jaine?"

"I haven't brought anything to wear."

I kiss her gently on the lips. "I'll get you a t-shirt and some shorts."

I let her use the shower attached to my bedroom while I use the one in the guest room. Even though I got in at least ten minutes after she did, she's still not finished when I'm done. I'm enjoying seeing this other side of her. The side that's just a little bit unsure of herself.

Half an hour passes before she finally comes out of the bedroom.

I take her in from where I'm standing in the kitchen. My t-shirt reaches to mid-thigh on her, and I can't stop my eyes from drifting up her slim legs. My dick twitches at the sight. I try to calm him down as I'm only wearing a pair of grey sweats.

"Do you want anything to eat or drink?"

She shakes her head.

I walk slowly toward her, her eyes drifting over me to take me in. She won't be able to miss it since I'm now shirtless. Her eyes widen as they take in her name, which has been tattooed across my heart.

"When did you get that?"

I stand in front of her, and she traces the letters slowly with her finger. Jesus Christ, her hands feel so good on my skin.

"When we were in Rising. Your friend Gusto did it for me." It seemed the right thing to do and the right person to do it, given he's done all of hers. I haven't got the heart to tell her that Eoin got exactly the same one.

"What if I'd said no?"

"It wouldn't have made any difference. It wouldn't have changed how I feel about you."

She leaves her hand on my chest and stares up at me.

"Are you nervous, darlin'?"

"Is it stupid that I am?" She bites her bottom lip, and I nearly give in and push her back against the wall. It would be so easy just to let her anchor her legs around my hips and sink into her.

"It's not stupid. It shows that you care. That it means a lot. Will you dance with me, Jaine?"

"There's no music."

I reach into my pocket and pull out my phone. She smiles when the song comes on.

"Ed Sheeran."

"It is. It's called *Thinking Out Loud*." I toss the phone on the sectional. "Put your arms around my neck, darlin'."

CHAPTER EIGHTY-ONE

JAINE

Padraig's Apartment, Hudson Yards, New York

I DO AS HE ASKS, CONSCIOUS THAT MY BORROWED T-SHIRT IS NOW skimming my ass. In the end, I decided not to wear the shorts but only because I couldn't get them to stay up.

He snakes his arms around my waist as he pulls me tight against him, and then we sway together. Pressing my nose against his neck, I inhale the scent of his cologne, my heart thudding in my chest, making me feel breathless.

I gasp when his hips grind slowly against mine, my gaze raising to connect with his as my hands tangle in the back of his hair.

"Do you like the song choice, Jaine?" I can't reply. His hot breath against my ear is making me feel too dizzy.

My fingers move to grip his shoulders and keep me steady. He gives a low growl of approval as he circles his hips against mine again, his hands dropping down to my ass to pull me tighter against him. I groan when I feel his erection press against me.

I don't think I've ever felt so aroused with so little contact.

His mouth drops to my neck, his tongue sliding over my skin. My nails dig into his flesh when he bites down, my own hips now pressing against his.

Asking. Needing. Begging.

His hand moves to my already pebbled nipple, the touch making me instinctively part my legs so he can push his thigh between them.

He looks down at me, his blue eyes dark with hunger. "You decided not to wear the shorts, then?" I shake my head and lick my dry lips.

His eyes never leave mine as his hand skims the bottom of the t-shirt. Lifting the hem, he runs his fingers through my slickness. The groan that escapes me sounds feral. I can't help it. I want his fingers inside me, but he deliberately doesn't let them sink in. He studies my reactions intently.

Every move. Expression. Breath. He doesn't want to miss a thing. I feel exposed for some reason. Like I'm suddenly transparent.

There's no hiding from me. You know that.

He's right. His soul has known mine since the beginning of time.

"Irish." I sound needy.

"I'd like to kiss you, darlin', if that's okay." Ice-blue eyes bore into mine.

I nod, and he slowly tilts my chin. His mouth then covers mine, and his tongue thrusts deep. I part my lips to welcome the taste of his unique flavor as my hands yank on his hair. I groan, and he responds by kissing me harder until all I can taste is intensity and desire.

Until all I can taste is him.

I drag my nails down his torso, and he emits a low growl of approval, his abs clenching beneath my fingertips. The sound is like an aphrodisiac.

My nails drag lower until they're toying with the waistband of his sweatpants. He lifts me so I can anchor my legs around his waist, and then he walks. I bite down on his neck, and he curses. I immediately press my lips to his.

I want to taste his growls and his curses because they're mine.

He's mine.

We fall onto his bed, my legs still wrapped around his hips, then we kiss until kissing is no longer enough. He parts our mouths to yank the t-shirt over my head, leaving me naked.

I watch as he lowers his gaze to take me in, gasping when he rubs my pebbled nipple with his calloused thumb before sucking it into his mouth. I press against him, needing more of his hot, wet mouth on my skin. I groan my approval as he kisses down my stomach before pushing my thighs apart.

"Fuck, you're even more beautiful than I remember. I'm going to lick your sweet little pussy before I fuck it. You want that?"

I nod.

He grips my chin in his hand. "Always use your words with me, Jaine, because I won't always be this gentle." His tone holds a threat of something much darker.

I look at him, my hands fisting his black hair. "I want that."

My hips jerk off the bed when he thrusts his tongue inside me. I grip his hair and press my pussy against his face when he moves his mouth to my clit while thrusting two fingers inside. Closing my eyes, I throw my head back, mewling my appreciation as I grind against his hand, each expert stroke of his fingers lifting me higher.

"Irish, please," I whine.

He increases his pace before adding a third. The combination of pleasure and pain pushes me over the edge. I cry out as my hips buck and my thighs clench tightly around his hand. I'm still coming down from my high when he lifts my leg around his waist.

"Eyes on me, darlin'."

I open my eyes to look at him, letting out a small cry as he fills me with his cock in one hard movement.

We stare at each other as he remains motionless. He's letting me take what I need from this moment. I know he's doing the same. His taste. His smell. His heart thudding against mine. The feel of his dick buried deep inside me. We're exactly where we were meant to be. Right here. Right now.

Me and him. Him and me.

"You feel right, Jaine. You're the only one that ever has."

He sucks on my neck, and his teeth graze my skin when he finally pulls back and then pushes in deeper than before. His movements are slow and precise as he spreads and stretches me with each powerful thrust.

His mouth finds mine, tongues tangling and colliding through heated, whispered breaths as we moan and swallow each other's guttural sounds of appreciation.

My nails dig into his strong shoulders as he pounds into me until there is nothing but him. I can feel blood under my nails as he lifts me higher with each thrust, his mouth and teeth marking my skin.

My hands skim down the hard muscles of his back to press against his ass, letting him know I need more. He curses at my greedy demands before giving me exactly that as he pistons into me until our bodies are glistening and slippery with sweat. My mouth connects with his skin, my tongue flicking out to lick the salt from its surface.

Just when I can't take any more, he tilts my hips upward, and I whine my appreciation as I shatter around him, my walls clenching tight to claim his dick as mine. He watches me as I welcome my release.

Emotions. Feelings. Pleasure.

He wants to witness it all because it's all his.

"Breathe, darlin'." He rubs his nose down mine and pushes my hair behind my ear. "Because I'm not done with you yet."

He grinds his hips against mine once more, and then with his dick still inside me, he lifts me onto his lap. I wrap my legs around his waist.

So close. So intimate. So fucking deep.

I snake my arms around his neck, our bodies fused so tightly together that I can feel his heart beating in time with mine. I rest my forehead against his as I breathe in the intoxicating scent of his cologne mixed with clean male sweat.

Dropping his hands to my ass, he starts to lift me up and down on his cock, his hips thrusting upward with each movement to deepen the connection. I throw my head back, and he sucks on my neck as his hands bruise my flesh. My fingers tangle in his damp hair as our bodies slide against each other, our whispered words of encouragement the only sound.

Gripping his shoulders, I start to ride him hard and fast, the sound now of flesh slapping against flesh. I grind against him until there's no part of his cock that isn't sheathed by me, and he answers with a punishing thrust of his own.

He holds my chin, so I can't look anywhere but at him. He wants to share the moment of his own release with me. With a low groan, his face contorts as he finds his own pleasure, the sensation of his dick jerking inside me, taking me with him.

Hearts thudding. Breaths panting. I breathe him in. He breathes me in.

I rest my forehead against his and stare into ice-blue eyes as he wraps his arms tightly around me until there is no space between us.

I press kisses against his lips. Softly. Gently. Tenderly.

"Our love is soul-deep, Jaine. You feel that?" he whispers.

"I do."

And then we lie side by side like we always have and always will. I gaze up at him, my heart full that the boy I fell in love with when I was nineteen is now mine.

My sounding board. My life raft. My confidant.

My Irish.

"Are you blatantly admiring my handsomeness again?" He smirks.

"Well, someone's got to find you good-looking, so it may as well be me."

"Ouch."

I snicker as my fingers trace the tattoo of my name on his chest. "What did you say to Ace at his graveside?"

He places a kiss on my forehead. "I thanked him for thinking of me with his dying words, and I thanked him for loving and caring for my son."

Tears prick my eyes. "Anything else?"

He looks down, and our gazes connect. "I told him that if I were lucky enough to get a second chance, I would do everything in my power to make you the happiest woman in the world. And I will, Jaine. Every day."

I smile and roll my eyes exaggeratedly. "You mean I'm stuck with you?"

"You're stuck with me in this life and all the others we've yet to live, darlin'. Forever. For always."

"Promise?"

He holds up his pinkie, and I hook mine around it.

"Pinkie promise."

CHAPTER EIGHTY-TWO

DYLAN

The O'Connell Home, Darling, New York

OUR LIVES ARE NEVER STRAIGHTFORWARD.

Each day is like opening a new storybook. Some days have a happy ending. Some have a cliffhanger ending. Some have a sad ending.

Two things are guaranteed. No two days are ever the same, and not everyone will appreciate the content.

Ma decided to lay bare the final skeleton in the O'Connell family closet. The fact that she gave birth to an illegitimate child when she was a mere twenty-one years old. A little one she gave up for adoption because the biker daddy she'd had a dalliance with refused to make an honest woman of her and instead married one of his own kind.

Now we know why she hates bikers so much.

I'm sure our outlaw peers would have a field day if they knew that the District Attorney, Nathan Hawke, was actually our big brother. To say the rest of the family was shocked was an understatement.

I suspect, given their lack of reaction to the breaking news, that both Jaine and Padraig were already aware.

Everything now adds up.

He saved his sister-in-law's life. He also handed Luciano across to us on a plate because he didn't trust the Sicilian not to escape Rikers a second time.

Nate's fully aware of who his ma is. He always has been. Apparently, his adoptive parents never kept anything hidden from him.

He's on the right side of the law. We're on the wrong side. One can only hope that we can work covertly together to help rid New York of two-faced scum legally. A win-win for both parties. He gets his smug face in the press, and the Dusters can reduce the number of concrete shoes they have to fit.

As for Eoin and Padraig?

They fell in love with the same woman. Wars have been started over less. Lives have been lost over less. One was lucky in love. The other not so much.

Paddy hit the Jaine jackpot, but only after our eldest brother threw in the towel. He cited compatibility issues. Is that the case, or is there more to it than that?

I think only he and Jaine know the answer to that question. My big brother is an extremely private individual, so it's unlikely he'll ever spill the beans. It's my guess Jaine won't either.

They may not be together, but the love they share hasn't been lessened by time or distance.

I speak to him several times a day. He asks after her. She asks after him.

Once more, I'm in the middle, this time between Jaine and another brother. The only positive is that everyone is aware of it.

Paddy knows Eoin loves Jaine and vice versa. He's accepting of it. He knows what it's like to love her and then lose her. There is no web of lies and deceit being spun this time around, at least as far as I know.

My folks are over the moon for Paddy. Anyone with half a brain can see that he and Jaine were meant. I know Ma struggles over Eoin's situation. If she hadn't sent that message from Paddy's phone, things between him and Jaine would never have progressed after the initial personal vendetta malarkey.

She holds herself responsible for Eoin's pain, and she is mostly. While he was already in love with Jaine prior to the message being sent, it may still have been easier for him had Jaine then not reciprocated.

He found his pot of gold at the end of the rainbow, but in the end, it turned out to be fool's gold. How long will he reside in Chicago? That's anyone's guess.

It's early days. My worry is over what happens next. At some point, he'll have to start courting someone else. How will he feel about that? How will Jaine feel about that?

Would my folks be accepting of the three-way relationship that had previously been suggested? Who knows. It's certainly not the norm.

But then, who are we to judge? Who are we to measure love, quantify love, or decide what love looks like?

Padraig has loved Jaine since he was nineteen years old. A love so pure. A love so simple. A love that always has and always will stand the test of time.

Jaine and Eoin? Does it really matter now?

My brothers are obsessed with her. They're besotted with her.

They adore her. Their person is one in the same. Who knows? Maybe in the end, all three of them were meant.

Time will tell. It always does.

Jaine loves Eoin, she loves Padraig, and even though he's gone, she will always love Ace because true love?

It never dies.

EPILOGUE

JAINE

Two Months Later
Play Gentlemen's Club, Manhattan, New York

I GRIND AGAINST HIS HAND AS SOON AS HE CUPS MY PUSSY. Coating his fingers with my slickness, he thrusts two inside.

"Irish," I whine.

"Look at us." His other hand fists my hair to yank my head to the side as his fingers slide slowly in and then out. We've just showered, and we're both naked. I look at our reflection in the full-length mirror of the restroom.

His dark against my blonde. His pale against my tanned.

The blood from his finger is a stark contrast to where he's marked it across my skin, its unique metallic flavor still lacing my mouth.

I stare in the mirror as he removes his fingers from inside me before sucking them into his mouth. He then lifts me so I'm sitting on the counter before parting my thighs and lining up his hard cock.

"Now look at me."

Gripping my chin with one hand so I can't look anywhere but at him, with one thrust, he seats his thick cock deep inside me. I gasp as my pussy welcomes his return, clenching tightly around him.

Missing him. Loving him. Never wanting to let him go.

"Fuck. Would you listen to the sound of your body sucking me in?" His voice is low and guttural, his grip on my hip painful.

He slowly pulls out and then pushes straight back in, a pleasure frown crossing his face. And then he pistons into me with powerful strokes.

Hot. Hard. Sweaty.

"Watch me fuck you." He fists my hair once more, turning my head to the side, giving me no choice but to watch as he takes what he needs from my body. Ice-blue eyes meet mine in our reflection as my gaze then drifts over every inch of his perfection. Taut muscles, ink, and skin sheened with sweat.

Resting the backs of my legs against his torso, he begins to fuck me slow and deep. Each stroke is precise and unhurried. Each connects expertly with my sweet spot, lifting me higher and higher until there's nowhere else to climb.

I can feel him swell inside me as he nears his end. His movements become quicker and more erratic as he struggles to hold back.

And then, with one final thrust, I shatter. My walls tighten around him, and with a deep groan, he allows himself to be pulled over the edge with me.

We stay there. Wrapped around each other. As we were always meant to be.

He steps back, watching as his cum drips from my pussy to the floor. Has he changed in the last two months and since we've started living together?

No.

The only thing I've noticed is that when he fucks me in this unhinged state of his, he wears the same possessive look his eldest brother used to wear.

His lips find mine, and he devours my mouth once more. He wants to taste his blood on my tongue.

Do I tell him now, or do I wait?

His mouth moves to suck on my neck, and I groan when he bites down. He's not done with me yet.

I guess what I have to say can wait.

Jaine and Padraig's Home, Darling, New York

I look around our new home.

We're still decorating, so there are a lot of unpainted walls, bare floors, and unpacked boxes. Irish and I have agreed that we'll spend a couple of hours each day doing house stuff, but that's it. After everything we've been through, we've agreed that life's too short to worry about an unfinished bedroom or a missing carpet.

Life's all about living and spending quality time with the kids and each other.

It's all about making new memories.

The house is almost identical to the O'Connell family home, which is only a five-minute drive away, but it has even more outdoor space.

The kids love it. They also love the fact that Irish lives with us. Fin loves having his daddy around.

JJ loves having Irish around too, but I can't help noticing his wistful look whenever the front door opens. Each time, he's hoping that it's Eoin. I know he is. He's too young to understand why he's no longer around. All he sees is his absence. Having already lost Ace, it's heartbreaking to witness my little boy's soulful eyes fill with tears as he pines for the man who became the father figure in his life.

I have so much to be grateful for. I also have so many regrets.

Our lives have changed. We no longer have to look over our shoulder twenty-four-seven. Yes, we will always have enemies, but it's no longer such a constant threat. I never realized how much living day by day affected me. How much it changed me as a person.

I was angry. I was scared.

It made me volatile.

Eoin bore the brunt, and for that, I will always be truly sorry.

I want to apologize, but I know my words would offer no salve against the deep wounds I inflicted on him. And to apologize, I'd need to be in contact with him.

I'm not.

I know he speaks to Dylan several times a day. I ask after him. I'm told he asks after me too. But we never talk to each other directly.

No calls. No messages. No emails.

He's alive. He's well. He's no doubt fucking his way across Chicago.

I keep asking why my life deviated.

Ace and I were meant. Irish and I were meant. Why did my path decide to take a detour? Why did my thread get tangled with Eoin's when we were clearly never meant? When all it left was a bitter taste and a forever heartache?

I guess we'll never know.

I love him. I will always love him. And like little JJ, I miss him.

My thoughts are disturbed by my vibrating phone.

Delaney: *Extra-curricular just in. Call me.*

I lean my head back against the sectional. The Exterminator's been in the news a few times recently. In the end, Nate didn't manage to send all of the trafficking scumbags down. The few high rankers he didn't thought themselves off the legal hook until they found themselves on the receiving end of one of my engraved bullets.

These days, the press is no longer so adverse when it comes to the surreptitious sniper. The public is finally seeing him for what he is. An outlaw vigilante trying to rid the world of scum one diseased skull at a time.

I'm about to call Delaney when I hear the front door open.

A smile covers my face as Irish throws himself onto the sectional before dragging me down until we lie side by side.

"Tell me about your day, darlin'."

I laugh as I press my nose against his neck so I can inhale the smell of Old Spice. "Well, I watched you kill someone, and then you fucked me twice in quick succession."

He laughs heartily. "Hopefully, not too quick."

I snort-laugh.

"And the kids?"

"At your ma's. They're having a cousin day with Sarah and Cill's kids."

He presses his smiling lips against the side of my head. "They say third time's a charm, Jaine. What do you say?"

I snort again. "I say you're insatiable."

He shrugs with a smirk. "Well, I've got twelve years to make up for, along with the first three months where you kept me hanging. Did I tell you that my doc said…."

"You had the worst case of blue balls he'd ever seen. I know, I know. Anyway, I have something to show you. Wait there."

I extract myself from his arms, suddenly feeling nervous.

I make my way to the restroom, then quickly make my way back, my heart pounding in my chest.

He's on his side, resting his head on his elbow when I return. His gaze drops to what I'm holding, and he immediately sits upright.

"Jaine." His eyes raise to connect with mine, shock registered on his face. "Are you?"

I offer him the piece of plastic with the two blue lines clearly displayed.

"I'm pregnant."

He stares at me, tears filling his eyes. He looks melancholy for a moment before his face breaks into a broad grin. I know he was just revisiting the past. That the old regrets had briefly resurfaced.

While he appreciated the box of Fin's memories I gave him, it's not quite the same as living through them. This time, he'll get to experience all the firsts.

He pulls me down to sit beside him, then wraps his arm around me like I'm the most fragile thing in the world.

"I didn't even know you'd stopped taking birth control."

I shrug. "I haven't been taking it regularly in months. It's difficult to do when you're being held hostage or buried alive. I've always missed periods and been irregular, but I'd been feeling off-color for quite a while now, so I thought it best to rule it out."

"Do you know how far along you are?"

I shake my head. "I have an appointment with the ob-gyn first thing in the morning."

"Can we have more after this one?"

I raise both eyebrows at him in mock horror.

"We can have one more."

He looks at me, a broad grin taking over his face. "You'd do that for me, darlin'?"

I roll my eyes at him. "Have you not been paying attention all this time, Irish?"

I smile as I wipe away the happy tears from his face before wrapping my arms around his neck. I can feel his love for me radiating out of him—my emotional Padraig O'Connell.

"Everything I've ever done has been for you."

WANT TO KNOW
WHAT'S COMING UP NEXT IN DUSTERLAND?
FOLLOW ME FOR UPDATES OR JOIN MY FACEBOOK GROUP!

Facebook Group: Harley's Hangout

Author's Note

I hope you enjoyed Padraig's story.

DIRTY PADRAIG is NOT standalone.
DIRTY PADRAIG is BOOK 6 of a SERIES, which contains an INTERCONNECTED STORYLINE.

These books contain MULTIPLE POVs from characters across the entire series.

Due to the nature of the CONTINUING STORYLINE, these books MUST be
READ IN ORDER.

The Outlaw Chess Reading Order

ACE

DIRTY CILLIAN

RAZR

DIRTY DYLAN

DIRTY EOIN

DIRTY PADRAIG

These books are NOT standalone.

Due to the nature of the CONTINUING STORYLINE

PLEASE READ IN ORDER.

Acknowledgments

For Anshul
Thank you for being you.

For Cat
Thank you for going above and beyond.

For Ashton
A million acknowledgments would still never be enough.

About the Author

Harley Diamond is a writer of romance novels with plot twists that will leave you begging for more. In every dirty story, an angsty bad boy and a badass queen lead the cast.

When Harley's not reading, she's writing. When not doing either, she's plotting to unleash her next novel on you from her non-working farm in West Yorkshire, England, surrounded by her faithful but very needy companions. Her seven rescue dogs.

Facebook Group: Harley's Hangout
Facebook Group: Harley's Spoilers

Printed in Great Britain
by Amazon

60990781R00342